THE HOUSE OF I

Novels

The Great Fire of London
The Last Testament of Oscar Wilde
Hawksmoor
Chatterton
First Light
English Music

Non-fiction

Notes for a New Culture
Dressing Up
Ezra Pound and His World
T. S. Eliot
Dickens

PETER ACKROYD

THE HOUSE
OF
DOCTOR DEE

HAMISH HAMILTON · LONDON

HAMISH HAMILTON LTD

Published by the Penguin Group
Penguin Books Ltd, 27 Wrights Lane, London w8 5tz, England
Penguin Books USA Inc., 375 Hudson Street, New York, New York 10014, USA
Penguin Books Australia Ltd, Ringwood, Victoria, Australia
Penguin Books Canada Ltd, 10 Alcorn Avenue, Toronto, Ontario, Canada m4v 3b2
Penguin Books (NZ) Ltd, 182–190 Wairau Road, Auckland 10, New Zealand

Penguin Books Ltd, Registered Offices: Harmondsworth, Middlesex, England

First published 1993
1 3 5 7 9 10 8 6 4 2

Typeset by Datix International Limited, Bungay, Suffolk
Filmset in Monophoto Garamond
Printed in England by Clays Ltd, St Ives plc

A CIP catalogue record for this book is available from the British Library
ISBN 0–241–12500–6

ONE

I INHERITED THE house from my father. That was how it all began. I had heard nothing about it until after his death, and it was not until the summer of this year that I visited it for the first time. The house was in Clerkenwell, an area I scarcely knew, and I took the tube from Ealing Broadway to Farringdon. I hardly needed to save the expense of a taxi now, but since childhood I have always enjoyed riding under the ground. I am so accustomed to travelling into the City or West End, in fact, that I recognized nothing out of the ordinary in the course of this particular journey – except, perhaps, for a more powerful sense of the change. It begins to happen when I leave the Central Line at Notting Hill Gate, and ride the escalator to the Circle Line platforms on a higher level. The stations along this route have always been less familiar to me; a slight adjustment is necessary, therefore, and I adopt another layer of anonymity as the train moves on from Edgware Road and Great Portland Street to the old centres of the city. Each time the automatic doors close I experience a deeper sense of oblivion – or is it forgetfulness? Even the passengers seem to be transformed, and the general atmosphere of the carriage becomes more subdued and, on occasion, more fearful.

Just before the train arrived at Farringdon it emerged from the tunnel and, for a moment, I noticed the pale sky; it reminded me of the mild, depressing Ealing light, but as soon as I stepped out of the underground station into Cowcross Street that illusion was dispelled. For the light of the city changes – pearly in the west, sombre in the south, misty in the north, sharp in the east – and here, close to the centre, it had a particularly smoky quality. I could almost taste the scent of burning.

No doubt this accounted for my nervousness as I made my way towards the house which my father had left to me – the house about which I knew nothing except its address. I had looked up Cloak Lane in a London atlas, and in my imagination I had already placed it among other streets packed with shops and offices; but as I made my way down Turnmill Street towards Clerkenwell Green, I realized that this was like no other part of central London. It seemed both more open and more desolate, as if at some point the area had been laid waste. Cloak Lane itself was difficult to find. I estimated that it was some thirty yards north-west of the Green, but when I walked in that direction I found myself circling around Clerkenwell Close and the church of St James. It was a late Friday afternoon, and the grounds of the church were deserted; three cats sat along a portion of ruined wall on the south side, and pigeons murmured among the gravestones, but of human life there was no sign.

And then I saw it. It was at the end of what looked like an alley, sprawled across a patch of waste ground, and for a moment I closed my eyes; as I opened the gate and prepared to approach it, I found myself concentrating upon the pale bindweed, the dock and nettle, growing up among the broken stones of the path. I have always disliked weeds, because they remind me of my childhood; I still remember my father telling me that they spring from the bodies of the dead and, as I walked down the path, I crushed them under my shoe. It was only then, when I stopped and looked up from the mangled remains of the ragwort, that I noticed the strangeness of this house. I had assumed at first glance that it belonged to the nineteenth century, but I could see now that it was not of any one period. The door and fanlight seemed to be of the mid eighteenth century, but the yellow brickwork and robust mouldings on the third storey were definitely Victorian; the house became younger as it grew higher, in fact, and must have been rebuilt or restored in several different periods. But its most peculiar aspect was its ground floor: it ranged beyond the area of the other storeys and, as I walked closer, I realized that the basement covered the same more extensive ground. These parts of the house were not faced with brick; the walls seemed to be fashioned out of massive stone, and suggested a date even earlier than the eighteenth-century door. A much larger house must once have existed here, of which the ground floor and the basement were the only visible remnants; later additions were on a more modest scale, so that now the central section rose up like some broad tower from its rambling origins. No. It resembled the torso of a man rearing up, while his arms still lay spread upon the ground on either side. When I walked towards the steps, it was as if I were about to enter a human body.

I took the keys which my father had bequeathed to me, and opened the door. A draught of air enveloped me for a moment, and I thought I detected a sweet or perfumed aroma within it; it was as if the dust of this old house had somehow been overlaid with syrup or marzipan. Then I walked into the hall and, crouching down just beyond the threshold, listened intently. The truth is that I have a particular horror of rats – of anything, really, which invades and lives within an empty house – and if there had been the slightest sound or shadow of movement, I would have shut the door behind me and never returned. I would have sold this place and secretly been grateful for the excuse to do so. But there were no sounds. The house was only a few yards from the Farringdon Road, and was overlooked by a small estate of Peabody Trust flats; yet it was entirely quiet. I might just as well have entered a sealed room.

I stood upright and walked down the wide hallway. There was a staircase to my left and, on the right, a dark-brown door which appeared to lead to some other room. It was locked. I shook the handle impatiently, and there was something like a dead echo from the other side which suggested to me that this door opened upon some basement stairs. So I left it, and made my way towards the room at the end of the passage. It was much larger than I had expected, and covered almost the whole of the ground floor; but it had a low ceiling, so that it seemed unnaturally restricted. I could see that the interior walls were fashioned out of the stone I had glimpsed from the path, and there were several elongated windows cut into it which seemed almost as old as the fabric itself. The room was also of an unusual shape, since it linked both wings of the house and formed a kind of enclosed courtyard around the hall. There were one or two items of furniture – a chair, a sofa, a wooden chest – but they only served to emphasize the bareness and silence of this place. I was baffled and, I suppose, rather depressed: I knew that all this was now mine, but I did not feel I could claim any possible connection with it. But if I did not own it, then who did?

I went back into the hallway, and climbed the stairs. There were two rooms on both of the other floors; they were all light, with high ceilings, and had an altogether freer atmosphere than the room I had just left. From the windows here I could see the small housing estate and, just beyond it, the spire of St James; Clerkenwell Green was also visible, although the 'Green' itself was merely a space in the middle of the shops, offices and houses which had been fashioned out of the grand eighteenth- and nineteenth-century dwellings of the area. From the back windows on these upper floors I could see the viaduct covering the underground railway, and beyond it the old steep streets leading to Saffron Hill and Leather Lane. I was still a stranger here, and now I experienced a distinct though related sensation – that somehow this house, and myself within it, had no connection with the world which surrounded us. What had my father done here? All the rooms were simply furnished and, although they showed no sign of being recently inhabited, they were not in a state of neglect or disrepair; the electric lights worked and the little kitchen, in an alcove off the ground-floor room, seemed to function. It looked as if the real owner had embarked upon a long journey, with everything left in readiness for his return. Yet my father had never mentioned any house in Clerkenwell. He had so many other properties that perhaps this should not have surprised me – except that the others, as far as I knew, were all commercial sites. And this was also the only house he had explicitly mentioned in the course of his bequests to me. Why was it of such importance to him?

I had not seen as much of him in his last years – perhaps because

4

he was always busy with his 'empire', as my mother sarcastically called it. I suppose he was disappointed to discover that his only child was a failure, really, but I don't know. He never mentioned the subject, and my mother seemed too concerned with her own affairs to worry about mine.

I had not been with him when he died. I had been working in the British Library throughout that day, and by the time I reached the hospital my mother was, as she said, 'winding things up'. I did not even see the body: it was as if he had simply disappeared. Of course I had visited him in the final stages of his illness, but the cancer had engorged so much of his flesh that he was scarcely recognizable. My mother was with me on the last occasion I saw him alive, and she greeted me in the ward with a brief kiss on my cheek.

'Hi there.' I tried to be as cheerful as I could, but in her presence something always held me back. We both knew, in any case, that she was waiting impatiently for him to die. 'How's the old man?'

'I wish you wouldn't call him that. He's sinking.' We went into his room, and sat on either side of the bed. He was staring up at the ceiling, his eyes very wide under the influence of morphine, but my mother began to talk across his body as if we were grouped around the kitchen table. 'I suppose you were at the library today, Matty?'

I was twenty-nine years old but, from her general tone and manner, I might as well have been a child again. I hated discussing my work with her, and so I found myself talking to my father while taking care not to touch him. 'I've been asked to do some research on Elizabethan costume. A theatrical company.' I think he was sighing. 'Did you know that young men in the sixteenth century often wore leather caps? I suppose things never change.'

He parted his lips, and then moved his tongue across them. 'Sit here beside me.'

The idea horrified me. 'I can't, father. I'll upset all this stuff.' Plastic tubes had been inserted into his nostrils, and a drip had been attached to his arm.

'Sit here.'

So I obeyed him, as usual, while my mother looked away with what appeared to be an expression of disgust. I did not want to come too close, so I perched on the edge of the bed and started talking even more rapidly than before. 'It never really occurred to me,' I said, 'but some human gestures must remain the same.' I had always discussed general or theoretical matters with him; we pursued them with an analytic passion that was the closest we ever came to companionship. I was quite different with my mother: I stayed on the most banal level of everyday incident, where she seemed quite happy to leave me. 'Take Elizabethan sewing-women, for example. They always sat on the floor with their legs crossed. People have sewn that way for thousands of years.'

'Haven't you ever heard of the Singer machine, Matty?'

My father had understood nothing of this, but now he leaned over and touched me. 'Something is coming through the veil,' he said into my ear. I could smell the cancer on his breath, and quietly returned to my seat beside his bed. He lay back, and began to talk to someone I could not see. 'Let me brush your coat, good doctor. Do you know this music? It is the music of the spheres.' He gazed around the room, and both of us flinched as his eyes passed over us. 'Do you know these shining lanes and alleys, the river of pearl, and the lighted towers rising into the blue mist?' He was looking at the plastic tubes around him. 'It is as old as the universe, and the city from which you first came.'

'Don't listen to anything he says.' My mother whispered intently to me across the bed. 'Don't believe him.' She got up abruptly and left the room. I glanced at my father and, when he seemed to smile at me, I followed her. We walked down the corridor of the ward; it was painted lime green, and the rooms on each side were decorated in a similar shade. I knew that there was someone lying in each bed but I tried not to look: only once did I glimpse some movement beneath a blanket. No doubt all of these patients were lost in a morphine dream, like my father, and death here was no more than the last stage of a process that was monitored and contained. This was not like death at all. 'It's nice and peaceful here,' she said. 'Everything is well under control.'

6

I had been so shaken by my father's outburst that I spoke quite freely to her. 'I suppose you'd like piped music, too. They could all be wearing pink pyjamas, and holding balloons.' I was silent for a moment as a nurse passed. 'There is such a thing as holy dying, you know.'

She looked up at me in distaste. 'You sounded just like your father then.'

'And why not?'

'I suppose you'd prefer to be sitting in an old churchyard, like he used to do. Talking about ghosts and all the other nonsense.' I was surprised by this description of him, but I preferred to say nothing. 'Do you love him, Matty?'

'No. I don't know. Everyone uses that word, but I don't think it means anything.'

She seemed curiously relieved by this. 'That's my opinion, too.'

Together we went back into his room, where he was still talking animatedly to someone I could not see. 'Do you smell my decay? It means that my change is coming, and I will be restored. This is your work, good doctor. This is all your work.'

'I wish there was a real doctor here,' my mother said. 'Why don't you call someone?'

My father had taken my hand, and seemed to be gazing earnestly at me. 'Do you feel the light coming through the stone of this wonderful city? Can you feel the warmth of the true fire that dwells in all things?' I could not bear to hear any more of his delusions and, without saying another word to my mother, I took my hand away and left the room. I never saw him again.

But then I inherited everything. More pertinently, perhaps, he bequeathed nothing to my mother; even the Ealing house, in which we had all lived, was given to me. How he must have hated her. Of course I told her at once that she should consider it her home, but this did nothing to allay her anger and bitterness against me. In fact it served only to increase them, since she believed she was being offered something which was already properly hers. She tried to conceal her feelings beneath a loud and vulgar manner, as she had always done, but I could sense her suspicion, her

7

resentment, and her rage. She put me to the test soon after the funeral by inviting her boyfriend – 'the lover', as she called him – to live in the house with us. I said nothing. What could I say? But it was then I decided to visit my father's house in Clerkenwell.

'My darling,' she said to me a few days ago. 'The lover and I were thinking of a new car.' She always adopted what she supposed to be a sophisticated tone, but managed only to sound false and inappropriate.

'What kind of car?' I knew what she expected me to say, but I enjoyed leaving her in suspense.

'Oh, I don't know. The lover fancies a Jag.' That's how she always betrayed herself, with 'fancies' and with 'Jag'; her common vocabulary and genteel manner were perpetually at odds.

And still I did not say it. 'A new model, mother?'

'Oh, darling, I don't know anything about transport. Shall I bring the lover in to explain?'

'No,' I said quickly. I could bear it no longer. 'Of course you must let me pay for it.'

'You musn't do that, darling . . .'

'Father would have expected it, wouldn't he?'

'I suppose so. If you put it like that. I suppose, in principle, it is my money too.'

That had become her story; my father had left her nothing, but 'in principle' it was all hers. I understood now why he had disliked her so much, while as a superstitious Catholic he had refused to leave her. Geoffrey, 'the lover', had come in. I suspected that he had been waiting outside until the financing of the new car had been satisfactorily resolved, but he was not about to bring up the subject now. He was a very ordinary man, with one saving characteristic – he knew that he was ordinary, and was always implicitly apologizing for the fact. He was a surveyor who worked for one of the London boroughs; he had an awkward, diffident manner and seemed to fade still further in the company of my brightly clad mother. The strange thing was that both of them seemed to enjoy the situation.

But why was I thinking about these people, as I sat in the house at Clerkenwell? They were no more than phantoms conjured up out of my weakness, their voices less real to me than the shape of this ground-floor room and the texture of its thick stone walls. Here, at last, there was a chance of freedom. I could leave that terrible house in Ealing which had hampered me and injured me for the last twenty-nine years – for the whole of my life – and come to a place which had, for me at least, no past at all. I heard myself talking into the air in my sudden exaltation: 'Let the dead bury their dead.' But even as I said it, I did not know what I meant by it.

Then I noticed something. The shadows within the room seemed to fall at a curious angle, as though they were not properly aligned with any of the objects that created them. And there came upon me a curious fear – that there were, somehow, shadows where no shadows should have been. No, they were not shadows. They were patterns in the dust, caught suddenly in the changing light of that summer's evening. So had my father come here secretly, and entered this room? Had he sat, like me, with his head bowed? And hadn't he once told me that dust was simply the residue of dead skin?

I might have stayed there all evening, gradually enshrouded in darkness and shadow, but I shook myself out of my trance. I had left my suitcase in the hallway and, in the gathering dusk, I collected it and slowly climbed the stairs: there was a bedroom on the first floor, with a bathroom beside it, and I began to unpack my clothes as neatly as if I were in the house of a stranger. But I was so tired that I was hardly able to complete even this minor task. I lay down upon the bed and, closing my eyes, found myself walking along Cloak Lane. I had imagined everything; I had not yet entered the house which my father had left for me. It had four doors, the first of which was black, the second as white and as transparent as crystal, the third was green, and the fourth red. I opened the first door, and the house was full of black dust like gunpowder. I opened the white door, and the rooms within were pale and empty. I opened the third door, and there appeared a cloud of water as if the house were a fountain. Then I opened the fourth door, and I saw a furnace. Before I could move or do anything, I heard a voice close by me distinctly saying, 'You are utterly undone, my little man.'

I sat up, for a moment convinced that the voice had come from somewhere within the room, until I realized that I must have slept and dreamed. But the brief rest had left me unsettled; the room was not cold on that summer's evening, but somehow coldness had entered it while I lay asleep. I got up from the narrow bed and switched on the electric light, hoping that it might dispel the ghost of my unease, but it spread too much brightness; the room must have been built in the early nineteenth century, and this was the wrong kind of light.

★

I woke up the next morning, feeling more hungry than I had ever been in my life before. But even though I had brought no food with me, I was still reluctant to leave the house: for some reason I was afraid that I would never be able to find it again. I lay upon the bed and waited. But who, or what, could I be waiting for? I was not going to wall myself up here like some sixteenth-century monk, however strong the temptation, and I roused myself at last. I had woken upon the bed fully dressed, and conceived a horror for the clothes I had slept in: so I took them off and laid them carefully in a corner. Then I washed and dressed again, before hazarding the outer air. I retraced my steps down Cloak Lane, but I could not resist looking back at the old house. It was mine now, I knew that, but I turned because I had the strangest fear that it might already have disappeared.

I approached Clerkenwell Green, carefully skirting the grounds of the church, and looked about me. Once more the area seemed empty, somehow bereft, and as I walked down Jerusalem Passage towards the Clerkenwell Road I could see only boarded-up build-ings, closed offices and tattered advertisement hoardings that no doubt concealed patches of waste ground. There was no evidence of a supermarket, or even a grocery, and it was as if the whole district had been separated from the rest of the city. I paused for breath beneath the remains of St John's Priory, but it was not until I had gone through Charterhouse Square and the congerie of narrow streets around Smithfield that eventually I came to a shopping precinct. What did I need? Bread. Soup. Cheese. Milk. Butter. Fruit. What people have always needed.

But I enjoyed walking among the shelves of this Smithfield supermarket: the sandwiches in their sealed wrappers, the salads packed in cellophane, the plastic containers of milk and orange juice, all seemed to glow in the artificial light. I lingered among the chilled foods, and took particular delight in the cabinets of frozen goods where slices of plaice and breasts of chicken lay beneath a white covering of frost. Then there were the shelves of pickled vegetables and fruits, the rows of tinned peas and tomatoes, the piles of packaged bread and crumpets. I was at peace with a world which afforded so much bounty, and began to enjoy living at the very end of time. Just as I left with my carrier-bags, a wind started up among the green litter-bins and the black plastic sacks filled with rubbish; scraps of newspaper and discarded wrappers flew around the gaudily painted precinct, and I looked for my way home.

I managed to find a taxi but, since the driver could not enter the one-way streets near Cloak Lane, I left the cab on the south side of the Green near a small printing works. I was beginning to understand the geography of this area now, and had no difficulty finding my way back to the old house. I had opened the gate and was about to walk down the stone path when I stepped back in alarm: there was a man in a dark coat bending over by the side of the path among the weeds and thistles. He had his back to me, and seemed to be tying his shoelace, when suddenly without looking around he hurled himself sideways as if he were trying to knock me violently to the ground. But nothing happened. He had melted away, or somehow melted into my own body.

Of course I realized at once that this was my own foolishness – I had seen a shadow which moved, no doubt the shape of a large bird which had suddenly flown upward. But I was still shaken, even by my own delusion, and hurried towards the door. When I came inside the hall, I realized that the right leg of my trousers was torn; there was a wide gash there, just as if it had been made with a knife, and I must have ripped it when I stepped out of the taxi. Suddenly and unaccountably I became very angry – angry at myself, angry at my own fear, angry at the house for so unnerving me. After a few minutes I went into the kitchen, and arranged the groceries neatly upon their shelves. There was something about this house which demanded order. But I had no appetite now, and sat looking at the brightly coloured packets and bottles as if I did not know what they were.

★

Now all is done; bring home the child again. There was a steady knocking, which seemed to be coming from inside the room. I arched awake, with a confused noise something like a cry, and found myself still sitting in the kitchen; but I was in a different chair, and the noise was growing louder. I was so bewildered that I looked around to make sure no one was in the room with me, knocking against the wall with a clenched fist and grimacing at me; but then, as the sound echoed around the silent and sparsely furnished house, I realized that there was someone at the front door. I hesitated still. I went over to the sink and dashed some cold water against my face; then, very slowly and cautiously, I walked down the hall. Daniel Moore was standing on the path outside, looking up at my bedroom window as if he had known where to find me.

'You're wet,' he said.

'I know. I was asleep.'

He looked at me curiously for a moment. 'I couldn't reach you on the phone.'

'That's because it's not connected.'

How can I explain Daniel? He was a professional researcher, like me, and we had seen each other so many times in the British Library, the National Archive Centre, the newspaper collection at Colindale, and elsewhere, that we began to talk. There is a camaraderie that grows up among those who work with old books and old papers, largely, I suspect, because we understand that we are at odds with the rest of the world: we are travelling backwards, while all those around us are still moving forward. I must admit that I enjoy the sensation. One client might want me to investigate some eighteenth-century deeds, while another might need information on a nineteenth-century toolmaker, but for me the pleasure is the same; it is as if I were entering a place I had once known and then forgotten, and in the sudden light of recognition had remembered something of myself. On certain occasions this had a curious but no less pleasurable sequel: I would look up from the books or documents I was reading, and find that the immediate world around me had become both more distant and more distinct. It had become part of the continuing historical process, as mysterious and unapproachable as any other period, and I gazed around me with the same delighted attention that I would give if I suddenly found myself within a sixteenth-century scene. If my work meant that I often viewed the past as my present, so in turn the present moment became part of the past. I have always tended to keep my real feelings to myself, so I had never discussed any of this with Daniel Moore. He would have listened to me with his usual dry attention, his bright eyes resting upon my face, before moving on to some other topic. In any case he saw his work in a different light; it was for him, I suspect, simply an inconspicuous job which he could pursue in solitude. 'I presume,' he said, 'that, as usual, I'm too early?'

I had quite forgotten that I had invited him to explore the house. 'Of course you are. Welcome to Nightmare Abbey.'

'Thank you, Matthew. You do look a little Gothic, after all.' He was staring at my leg, and I realized with horror that I was still wearing the trousers which had been so unexpectedly torn.

'A domestic accident.' I tried to laugh. 'Just give me a minute.'

I left him in the hallway while I rushed upstairs to change, and when I returned he was examining the ground-floor room with his usual sharp, almost scornful, attention. He was a small man, with pale neat features, and he was on tiptoe as he put his hand against one of the walls. 'How old is this house?'

'You tell me. You always give the impression of knowing about such things.'

'At first I would have said eighteenth-century, but I would have been wrong. This room is older. Much older.'

'That's what I felt.'

'Sixteenth-century?'

'*Possibile.*' I sounded like my mother then, and instantly regretted my tone.

'Of course it's very unusual to find a house of this age in London. Rather a surprise, in fact.' He walked past me into the hallway, and went up to the basement door.

'You can't,' I said. 'It's locked.' But as I spoke, he turned the handle and the door opened. He seemed to have no fear of the darkness below, but I followed him down the stairs more hesitantly. 'Do you think,' I whispered, 'there might be rats?'

'Of course. Enormous ones.' It did not seem peculiar at the time, but there was no smell, no odour of dampness, no suspicion of rotting things. Then something moved softly across my face, and I stumbled backwards with a cry; Daniel laughed, and pulled what was the cord of an electric light.

'Quite a little screamer, aren't we?' The basement room could be clearly seen now, with its stone floor, its whitewashed walls and its shallow alcoves, all seeming to ebb and flow in the sudden light; it covered the whole area of the house, and yet it was completely empty. Daniel had walked over to one of the walls. 'There was a door here, Matthew. Do you see how it has been sealed up?' He turned around, delighted to be in this ancient enclosed space. 'It looks westward, so it must have opened out near the Fleet River.'

'O gliding down with smooth and subtle course.'

'What?' He looked at me in surprise for a moment, but I just shrugged my shoulders. 'Now do you see this?' He pointed to some marks above the door, where the lintel must once have been, and his pale, carefully manicured hands seemed almost transparent against the white wall.

'Aren't they just scratches?'

He examined them more closely, although in fact very little could now be traced. 'No. They look like symbols.'

'Builders' marks.' I put my hand up to my sweating face.

'Do you know what I think? This wasn't a basement at all. This was the ground floor, and it has slowly sunk through the London clay. This old house is descending into the ground.'

★

We were sitting upstairs again, although my sense of what was above or below the ground was now subtly confused, and I was apologizing for having fainted away. I blamed it upon my hunger.

'You didn't faint,' he said. 'You just closed your eyes and leaned against the wall. It was all very restrained.' He was looking at me intently but it was impossible to gauge what, if any, feeling lay behind that steady gaze. 'I do think, Matthew, that we ought to find out who owned this house. It's almost a professional duty.'

'I'm not sure that I want to know.' I was very restless and, rising from my chair, I went over to a side-table which had been pushed beneath one of the narrow windows in this ancient room; it opened on to the west, in the same position as the door in the basement, and through the dusty pane I examined the area of the Fleet River where the Farringdon Road now flowed. My hands were upon the polished wooden table, and I could feel the handle of a drawer; I looked down, opened the drawer, and saw a glass tube lying there. It resembled a test tube from a laboratory, but it was about two feet in length and seemed curiously distorted at the end. I was disgusted by it, and closed the drawer quickly. 'It's very close in here,' I said to Daniel. 'Shall we go for a meal?'

He did not answer, so I turned to face him. He was no longer there. He had vanished, and in a sudden panic I rushed out of the room; only to see him coming down the staircase with a smile of triumph. 'I just had to look around,' he said. 'I did ask permission, but you were miles away.'

'I don't . . .'

'You were lost somewhere. Looking out of the window. So I

took matters into my own hands. Did I hear you say something about going out?'

I looked back at the house as we left, and noticed for the first time that the eighteenth-century façade of the ground floor had been designed as a casing or shell for the sixteenth-century interior. I understood then that it had truly become my responsibility: it was as if some lost creature had come up to me, had attached itself to me, and pleaded silently with me to take care of its quiet life. That, at least, was what I thought at the time.

★

'Ah. Here's the well in Clerkenwell.' We had come out of Cloak Lane, on our way towards the Green, and Daniel had found a clue to the area which I had not seen at all. There was a flight of metal steps, leading down to a circular opening in the ground; there was even a wooden bucket, and a small model of the well as it would have looked five hundred years ago. I had not recognized any of this because it was protected by a thick glass window, and was now part of an office development in the street beside St James's Church. There was a small handwritten notice pinned to the bucket, and I crouched down in order to read it: 'There has been a well on this site since the twelfth century, when it was known as the Clerks' Well. Religious plays were performed on this ground during Advent, since wells were often considered to be emblems of spiritual blessing.' The water of life. And I had a vision of Clerkenwell as a holy place, a land of hills and running streams, where now the water underground was piped into my house.

'This might be interesting. But no. It doesn't solve the mystery.' I stood up and went over to Daniel, who was looking at a small map framed just behind the plate glass. 'In the sixteenth century, this whole area was covered by a nunnery.' He looked at me for a moment, with the most peculiar smile upon his face. 'I see that nothing much has changed.' Then he went back to the map. 'Your house isn't marked as a separate dwelling.'

'So I'm living in the nuns' house?'

'Something connected with them, anyway. But don't worry.

They didn't brick themselves up in the sixteenth century.' Yet I had an image of them already, silently moving against those thick stone walls and treading softly upon what was now my basement floor. 'In any case someone must have lived there after the Reformation. Your house survived.'

And what else survived? I could imagine the sacred hills and fields of Clerkenwell but, just as clearly, I recalled every detail of my walk that morning through the streets which now overlaid them. There were so many watchmakers and watch-repairers in the Clerkenwell Road, so many small printers in the lanes leading down to Smithfield and Little Britain: had they chosen this place, or had the place somehow chosen them? Were they like the pilgrims who had once come to this well?

'Now here is something unusual, Matthew. Do you see where a medieval brothel has been marked, just beyond the nunnery? Does it say Turnmill Lane?' He spun around, his bright eyes taking in the line of streets and buildings around us, before marching off in the direction of Farringdon.

'I know it,' I said, trying to keep up with him. 'There's nothing there now except offices.'

We walked beside the Green, and then crossed down into what is now Turnmill Street before coming to a sudden halt. There was a police van outside one of the nondescript office entrances there and, as we watched, three women were being led away. One of them was screaming abuse at a policeman, and Daniel seemed for a moment very shaken; it was as if some kind of violence were spreading out into the air. 'I do hate scenes,' he murmured. 'Do you mind if we go back the way we came?'

I was silent until we had turned the corner. 'If you promise not to laugh,' I said, 'I'll tell you a very curious thing.'

'I'll try.'

'About a year ago I was walking by the Thames. Do you know, near Southwark? When suddenly I thought I saw a bridge of houses. A shimmering bridge, lying across the river.'

'London Bridge is falling down, falling down, falling down.'

'No, seriously. It was like a bridge of light. It only lasted for a moment, and then it was gone. But there was, for that moment, a bridge connecting two shores.'

'It could have been anything, Matthew.' He scarcely paid any attention to me, and looked back as the police van was driven away.

'And there was something else, too. Are you listening, Daniel? When I saw the bridge shimmering above the water, I thought I saw people crossing it along a line of light. They rose and fell together, just as if they were walking across waves. But I don't expect you to believe any of this.'

He was silent for a few moments. 'Can we eat dinner now, please? I'm extremely hungry.'

There was an Italian restaurant on the opposite side of the Green, about twenty yards from the site of the holy well, and he raced towards it as if he were being pursued. By the time I caught up with him, he was already seated at one of the tables. 'I've been thinking,' he said. 'Next week I'll find out more about the house.'

I changed the subject and, as we ate, I tried to discuss my plans for the future – how I had decided to move to Clerkenwell permanently, how I intended to decorate and furnish the rooms, how I would hire a garden firm to clear and plant the waste ground around it. I was concerned only with restoration and renovation; by implication, its past did not matter.

'Now that you're rich,' he said suddenly, as if we had been discussing nothing else, 'you won't have any interest in our old pursuits –'

'I'm not giving up work, Daniel, just because of an inheritance.'

'That's probably very silly of you. But let me finish my sentence. If you're busy with other things, I'm quite prepared to do a little digging.'

The phrase alarmed me. 'No. Don't. It's my house. I want to do my own research.'

He seemed disappointed. 'And how far do you intend to go?'

'Right back. Back to the beginning, if that's necessary.'

We left soon after. He told me that he had an appointment on the other side of London, but I decided to linger in the summer night. I sat in the churchyard of St James, and looked out across the rooftops in the vicinity of the old house. And then there was some kind of movement: it must have been a bat, but for a moment I seemed to see the dark shape of a man soaring upward above Cloak Lane.

THE SPECTACLE

'WHAT BECAME OF the flying man?' one of the concourse beholding this scene asked of his neighbour. 'Where was the wire?'

'I saw no wire. This is somewhat like the old fashion of magic.'

'It is a deceit of the eye,' said another. He was a pert little man, in green jerkin and leather doublet. 'All these things are but toys.'

I could have whipped him at the cart's arse for such empty words. Here was no deceit, no, nor even any magic; here was thaumaturgy, or the science of wonders. It is the mathematical art which gives order to appearances, and makes strange work of the senses of men. So I, Doctor Dee, am come to dazzle your imagination with *mirabilia*: these are my shows and apparitions which draw the eye cunningly – and what knave, gazing about like a fool with an apple or piece of spice-cake in his mouth, can unriddle their mystery? In all affairs of the world which we command, there is somewhat that is true and somewhat that is false: so who here can tell me what is real and what is unreal?

By sundry means these wonder-works are made: some by pneumatics, some by strained ropes, some by springs that imitate lively motion. Painting is more powerful upon ragged walls than upon fine marble, and so my artificial house shows itself best in a flickering light. My candles are lit behind bottles of painted colour, with a bright basin to reflect their varied rays upon the scene, and every eye can invent for itself a deeper shadowing. But all have their source, or root, in optical perspective, which along beams and natural lines does recreate the world. Light is thus the origin of wonders, and through its emanations it controls all action and passion in this lower world. So let this spectacle abound with light, as the house revolves and the grave ancient man flies above the city. The beholders are removed from their own corporeal shapes in the surprise of this action, and in imagination fly upward with him to their first cause. These words are plain and easy English, but the reach of their meaning is further than you think.

I have performed many wonders before this time. Once I created a flying wooden dove, much like the statue of Diomedes which plays a trumpet, and in my green days my Aristophanes scarab mounted up to the top of Trinity Hall. I already knew the history of mechanic marvels by that time, and out of old books had read their secret: in Agellius, how there was a wooden fly which the mathematician Archytas made to hover in the air; in Plato, how Daedalus fashioned strange images; in Homer, how the engine of Vulcan moved itself by concealed wheels. And then again there was in Nuremberg of late days a beetle of iron which, being let out of the artificer's hand, flew about by the guests at table and at length, as though it were sore weary, returned to its master's hand again. Moreover an artificial eagle was ordered to fly out of the same town a mighty way towards the emperor coming thither and, all aloft in the air, to follow him until he came to the gate. So do we cause the material residue of the earth to quicken and stir itself beyond the confines of its proper sphere.

Yet there are greater wonders still which I alone have performed. I have a mirror that reveals an image hanging in the air between you and the glass, and by perspective I can devise many strange things: you may come into my chamber and there see the lively shows of gold, silver or precious stones but, going to take them in your hand, you will find them nothing but air. By wind, smoke, water, weight or springs I can move you with all manner of display. And now, on this day, I have made a man fly upward through the air.

I came to this place a month ago, in order to construct the machine of the spectacle. Nathaniel Cadman, gentleman, warmly entreated me and asked me to prepare a disguising to mark his coming into his inheritance; and since part of his land lay beyond the Spital where there was a great wooden barn only recently erected, it was here considered best for the show to be staged. It is on the right hand beyond Shoreditch Church, on the other side of the highway from Bishopsgate and Houndsditch, a little past Hog Lane where there is now a continual building of small cottages. Each morning I have come here by horse from Clerkenwell, riding very speedily at break of day when the misty air is as thick as ancient butter and the dew lies on the fields outside the city like frog-spawn. I pass along the Clerkenwell Road and cross St John Street among the carts and drays coming in from the farms around Hockley – there is no garden, no arbour, no weathercock, no yew tree that I do not know in this parish which harbours my own sad rambling house. The quickest path is by way of Pardon Churchyard and Old Street, which thoroughfare is now pestered with cobblers' benches and cooks' stalls and stocking-menders who put out their worm-eaten signs as if they were within the city itself; here too I ride speedily by the white cross down into Chiswell Street, for fear of the cutpurses who haunt the lanes hereabouts. My satchel of dogskin is tightly bound to my side for I know these to be the scum of people who, like the worm in the straw, see but are not seen. Then I pass on my way by the windmills of Finsbury Fields, where the bogs and quagmires of the marshy land send up their foul stench, until I come to Hog Lane and the Curtain Road. In earlier years the fox was hunted here, and over Mallow Field and Bunhill Field the horns and the cries of the riders could be heard at the death; but now all that is clean gone, and where there was level grass there are now many buildings being erected. So I turn me down Shoreditch and enter into Cold Lane, lately a filthy passage into the fields but now both sides builded with small tenements. Then I ride over the grass where, a week or two since, Nathaniel Cadman came forward to greet me. He is a young blade, a square-set fellow brightly apparelled in a black taffeta doublet and spruce leather jerkin with crystal buttons; because his doublet was new, the sleeves hung down very properly and he wore round breeches of white with two guards about the pocket-hole. What a piece of work is man, I said to myself as I came down from my horse, when he attends more to his doublet than his destiny.

'Why now,' he said, approaching me, 'you smoky persecutor of nature, what have you in your satchel there? What new budget of papers to order our spectacle?'

'This is no show for Houndsditch pump or Cheapside,' I replied. 'I bring with me here new fashions in geometry and opticks, with all the mechanical arts of weight and measure.'

I knew this was the honey to catch the fly, and at the mere utterance of 'fashion' he pricked up his ears. 'Man may do many wonderful things, Doctor Dee,' he said. 'May I?' He took my papers and seemed to survey them. 'You have been a busy fellow with your pen, but it is all one to me. I am not of your order of the Inspirati. Is that how you call it?' He had a quick way of speaking, so I had room only to nod and say nothing. 'I do not understand any of your meaning herein.'

I fart at you, was my thought; but with a show of patience I explained to him how those who had most diligently examined the conditions of space occupied by matter, and observed that the surfaces of neighbouring elements are joined together by the law and force of nature, may thereby display wonderful things. Air, fire and water go in all directions according to their natural tendencies, and it is for the mechanic to harness them accordingly. 'So the craft of hydraulics,' I continued, 'can lead us to the executing of such things as no man would easily believe.'

'You are a dark man, Doctor Dee —'

'I come from a dark house.'

'— and your doings are still quite hidden from me.'

I smiled in my sleeve to think how I had puzzled him. 'There is no secret,' I replied, 'unless it is the secret of the whole world in which the elements are intermingled.'

'But these are hard and indigestible matters. Hydraulics. Elements. There are few indeed who care a nutshell for them.' At that he smiled, bowed, and returned to me my papers. 'But all eyes will be dazzled by your display.'

'All things tend towards the same end, Nathaniel Cadman. I am content.' At which point he wrapped his blue velvet cloak around himself, and walked with me towards the wooden barn where the scene was being constructed. You are very like the peacock, I thought, who is wrapped in the pride of his beauteous feathers but is known to be a dunghill bird by reason of his foul feet.

The carpenters, joiners and painters were all busily at work when we entered in, though no doubt they had gone on but ploddingly before our arrival. Theirs is no light or fanciful work, since sundry slaughters and mayhemmings of the people have happened by ruin of scaffold, frames and stages, or by the engines, weapons and powder employed in the spectacles. It is true that blood is the humour wherewith we are all nourished, but I do not wish any infant of my own devising to see it sadly spilled. Yet it is not enough to have good intentions in such a work and, before ever I began this scene, I made for myself a small model of wood and paper wherein I set down piece by piece and joint by joint until I could judge perfectly how the spectacle was to be revealed. Now, as I entered, I could see how everything had been resolved according to that judgement: one scaffold was at the level of men's eyes with a second scaffold above it, while a third was set at an incline so that the scene could more easily be viewed. Meanwhile the craftsmen were working in wood and copper, in tin and lead, setting up so great a din that I could scarce hear myself thinking. Piled up around the scaffolding were the pulleys for the clouds, the hoops and blue linen cloths for the sky, together with the bodies of men cut out of pasteboard and daubed in pink and white. The painter, Robin Mekes, had been desperately at work and now before me I could see the house and the streets about it, the frames of doors and windows, the counterfeit moss and the flowers made out of glue and paper. Already in the centre of the scaffold were double doors which, according to their machinery, revolved with decorated faces; there was a false wall fair painted and adorned with stately pillars, while beyond it were the cranes and engines which would lift my apparitions into the air.

Mr Mekes approached me, and gave a low bow. 'My good doctor,' said he, '*beso los manos*. How do you?' He was a little fellow in a taffeta suit cut to the skin, and he carried a nosegay to ward off the stink of the workmen.

'Well, I thank God.'

'Say nothing of God here, my good doctor. The very noise of this place puts me in mind of hell. I love an interlude or a show as much as any man but, lord, the preparation!'

I was about to complain about the state of the painted cloths, which lay unfinished on the ground, but I stopped myself and offered him a smile. 'All great work takes time,' I replied. 'We are corrupted nature.'

'I thought you would say so, Doctor Dee.' I could have struck him for his malipert sauciness. 'But I wish that we might have only a *dumb* show before the tragical act.'

He laughed at his own wit, so I cut him short. 'Now that you speak of acts, Mr Mekes . . .' Whereupon I began to remind him of the order of representations; how in the tragic scenes it was necessary to have columns, pediments and statues, while the comic would require mere balconies and windows. 'And for the satyric,' I continued, 'we need your trees and herbs and hills.'

'Silk,' said he. 'Silk for the flowers. It is much more commendable than the natural things themselves.' He gave a little turn, as if it were a figure in a dance. 'Oh good lord, what magnificence there might be with sundry trees and fruits, herbs and flowers, all made with fine silk of diverse colours. And shall you want watercourses with banks of coral and mother of pearl? And shells of ivory laid between the stones? Oh good lord!'

'There will be a greater marvel still, Mr Mekes, when your trees and flowers descend.'

'Descend?' He was in a little effeminate pang of perplexity.

'There will be an engine underneath the stage, which will cause all your display gently to sink.'

'And what will come in its place?'

'Oh a miracle, Mr Mekes, a miracle.'

★

And so it was, as the various parts of the scene began to yield.

The notes of the viol and the lute moved strangely so that the music became, in a mysterious manner, the emblem of the whole spectacle: there were such harmonies within these changing chords that they echoed the very harmony of heaven. On my stage, numerology, geometry and astrology were all combined in one. As the music played, a roof of stars appeared, many shining spheres wrought within a background of the deepest blue; and upon the same ground of artifice it seemed as if the eleven circles of the eleven heavens revolved wonderfully with the planets and the stars. Nothing perishes, but stands in eternity: which is to say the moon, Mercury, Venus, the sun, Mars, Jupiter, Saturn, the fixed stars of the firmament, the crystalline heavens, the primum mobile, and then the imperial heaven which is the godhead and the source of all our life and light.

Whereupon the roof of the stars opened and suddenly there came down circles of light and glass, one within another, all within a sphere and all as it were turning perpetually; which light and motion so occupied the eyes of the concourse that they hardly saw above this glistening sphere an infinite number of lights which blazed down upon the scene. These were the fixed stars which ever stand at like distance one from another, and neither come nearer together nor go further asunder. At which moment came a louder and fuller music, *harmonia mundi*, like the primum mobile itself which ravishes all the spheres; and then, as this great image was set before them, a sweet odour crept forth among the beholders. Image – no, not image, but emblem. O thou picture of the celestial world drawn in little compass! O thou perspective glass, in which we may behold upon earth all the frame and wonders of the heavens! So then it was that three figures came down from the painted vault of the universe and seemed to hover in the air (held up by iron chains which could not be seen), and in their majestic attire of robes coloured white, black and red they were the tokens of astrology, of natural philosophy and of opticks, through which the cabala of nature may be known. Then all vanished away behind a curtain of mist and darkness, and the spectacle ended.

Whereupon there was a hum of conversation, as if flies in

swarms were buzzing about the hall. There were some who sat in silence, scarcely able to take the measure of what they had recently observed, while others discoursed as loud as ever they could upon the merits of the engines, the painted scenes and such like.

'There is nothing new here,' said one. 'It is all old stuff dressed up. Wherefore does he dwell upon past topics when there is so much in the present world to concern us?'

'Newfangleness,' said another, 'and without meaning. Some new new nothing.'

'Like the frozen zone,' said a third. 'Without humane actions or passions to move us.'

Others again merely stretched, and sighed, and gaped at the fellows beside them. I stood at the back, my head bowed, like some aged reverend gentleman in my black velvet coat and black cloth gown. I said not a word but watched everything, as my heart sank rapidly beneath me: for what end had my spectacle been prepared, now that the larger part of the hall merely yawned and scratched their heads as if they had seen nothing at all? I had displayed to them certain secrets of the known world, but the glistening spheres were to them no more than children's toys or a trickery and a deceit which signified nothing. Was this always the path by which true knowledge would be received? I, who had taken much great care to produce this artificial spectacle, was of no more account than some old forsworn mathematician whose diagrams are viewed hastily once and then forgotten. I had created wonders but, truly, there is no wonder greater than the folly and forgetfulness of the world.

Nathaniel Cadman came up to me smiling aimlessly, like some vagabond boy. 'Here is my hand,' said he. 'Take it. By God, sir, I love you. I could not love you so well as I do if you were the heir of a kingdom.' I bowed to him. 'I could scarce make an end to my words, sir, in a thousand years —'

But then he stopped abruptly when an idle fellow clapped him on the back. 'Is this he?' he asked. 'Is this the cunning man? The doctor?'

Nathaniel Cadman flapped his hand like a Frenchman. 'The right worshipful master, John Dee,' he said.

'At your service, sir,' I replied and bowed again, while all the time locking my fingers together beneath my cloak.

'When he was in *my* service,' the fool Cadman added, 'he cost me more angels than are in heaven.'

At that I crossed myself. The newly arrived gentleman (though in truth little more than a squab) was dressed in dainty gear, with a great monstrous ruff of cambric, and boots that might have come up to his very eyes if the ruff were not there as a barricade. 'I think,' he said, introducing himself to me as Bartholomew Bodele, 'that I have known you before?'

'If you knew me before, sir, you may the easier know me now.'

'Oh you are a Platonist, sir. I cry you mercy. I took you to be a maker of engines.'

'The world is filled with errors and vain reports, and if I were to answer them all I could not find enough words.'

At this retort he held his peace, but we were joined now by others of his kind who, being also known to Nathaniel Cadman, set up a clamour that we should eat and drink together. I do not care for companions, whether they be gallants or car-men, since they leave me bereft of that intercourse with my own self which aids my work: to spend too much time in company leads me into so great a storm of doubting and misliking that I scarcely know myself. But there was no help for it at this present juncture: they saluted me with fair words and pressed me to ride with them into the city. 'But the engines,' I said, 'and the scenes of the spectacle must all be carefully preserved.'

'No rats or spiders will injure them in the space of one night,' Nathaniel Cadman replied, 'and I doubt that any jarkman or cross-biter will remove the spheres or stars. You concern yourself too much, Doctor Dee. Pass the time with us, your followers. Come and eat.'

I thought I heard one whisper 'Doctor Dog' and laugh as I assented to his earnestly expressed wish; I did not turn, but walked a little ahead of them and let my eyes burn away their anger into the fields. It was a very fair calm evening, and so it was agreed that we should leave our horses munching upon the grass (in the care of some hired men to ward off the priggers of prancers) and make our way by foot through the gates. They had decided upon the Seven Stars in New Fish Street, a tavern or ordinary where the meat was fresh, and so we entered the city by way of Artillery Yard and Fisher's Folly. By the time we had arrived at Bishopsgate Street, these idle fellows were skipping and leaping like the jacks on a pair of virginals; with their lace sleeves, and their silk stockings, and their ruffs, and their jewels, they might have been a troupe of Italian mountebanks, but for the excess of English oaths which they used wildly among themselves.

It was not easy even for these monkeys to keep from the wall as we crossed over Bishopsgate Street, and entered lanes and crooked windings much like those that lead to the top of Paul's steeple; they pushed their way past the narrow houses of the citizens, shouting out 'By your leave! By your leave!' as they buffeted the porters and merchants who still walked here in the remaining hour of light. One knave among them had a carved wooden stick which he knocked against the signs of the shops and the houses, where-upon I held back as the images of the sun and moon, and various sundry beasts or planets, shook violently in the evening air. Such confusion as there was, with barrels and carts and ladders being moved aside, with the flanks of the horses and cattle being whipped, was now worse compounded by the cries of drapers and grocers, ironmongers and goldsmiths, whose hot shouts of rage mingled with the general noise of car-men and tradesmen. So goes the general tumult of this wonderful city.

We had come down into Thames Street, my idle rakehells making merry all the while by leaping over the upright wooden posts there, when we chanced upon a troupe of jugglers in their pied coats and pied caps doing such tricks as an apprentice would spit upon – viz. taking out coloured balls from drinking-cups and hoops from table-cloths. They were cavorting about a fire in the manner of Turks when one of Nathaniel Cadman's acquaintance, a popinjay wearing a hat without a band and his hose pinned up, leapt among them and with his rapier lifted off two hoops and tossed them into the air. At this the leader of the jugglers, a thin-visaged man with a nose the size of an Amsterdam cheese, threatened him with a dagger. 'Ah, you beggar,' he screamed. 'You beggar!' But my lord coxcomb laughed at that and walked on his way, whereupon the juggler took up a stone and threw it after him, as after a dog, before resuming his tricks in a most furious rage. So, thought I, we must all take up our shifts and counterfeit shows in the teeth of those who condemn and mock at us; and what am I to the world but a street juggler, with all my knowledge no more than a cozening art? I might have been brought to despair in the company of these turbulent strangers, but piece by piece I recovered as I walked through the loud and noisome streets. The great sun was declining over the rooftops, which then shone red as blood, and the old stones of the city were all on fire. Let my masters of light take up their garments, let them open the windows of their secret chambers, and all shall be saved!

We had come up to the ordinary in New Fish Street, next door to a pewter-seller; it was a low, lewd, loud place, where even the timbers seemed worm-eaten to the last degree, and I shook as if I were about to enter my tomb. They threw off their cloaks as soon as they entered, and the tapster came forward with his 'Welcome! Welcome! A cloth for the gentlemen!' We were placed upon joint-stools against a long trestle table, so scarred and pitted with age that it seemed to boast cabbalistical scribblings. Then the boy approached us with 'What do you lack?' and 'What is it that you would have brought?' Truly these are the words of the age, far beyond the poets' lines of tin, and yet they will all crumble away into the night of dust. 'What lack you?' he asked again, and at once they called for meat and drink – not your poor pots of ale, known as 'mad dog' or 'lift leg' or 'stride wide', but rich wine mingled with sugar in the new fashion. Nathaniel Cadman called for stewed mutton, and goose, and woodcocks, while all around him these coxcombs took out their tobacco-boxes and spat upon the rushes. What a smoke-filled cave this was; but then, as Paracelsus tells us, what is the material world but solidified smoke?

Then they began to converse, laugh, talk, anything, and with so much loud waggishness and frowardness that it made my head ache; they were already drinking their fill of wine, and now a popinjay opposite to me began to speak.

'You look upon us with owl's eyes, good doctor. I cry you mercy. Have we offended your remote wisdom with our laughter?'

'I am waiting for my meat,' I replied.

'Perhaps this place displeases you? Or its company?'

I could not abide his sauciness. 'No, sir, it is all one. As they say, there is no difference of bloods in a basin.'

'Is that what they say? I will tell you something else they say, good doctor. They say that you constellate and planet, cast nativities and generally prognosticate. That you employ charms and exorcisms and amulets.'

'You grow high in your words,' I replied, trying to keep my good humour. 'Well, the lowest trees have their tops.'

The others had grown silent but now they laughed at this, and the popinjay became angry. 'I thought in the old days,' he said, 'that sorcerers and suchlike were accounted vagabonds.'

The meat was brought smoking to the board, and so I checked my words, which would have been none other than 'May you lead apes in hell!' But then he vomited out his thoughts even as the others fell to their dishes. 'I am not one of your credulous disciples,' he said, 'and you cannot seduce me with any of your spells or characters or anagrams. Would you have me piss through my wedding ring to get my wife with child? I would as soon use a twig cut from an elm as your sixpenny Jacob's staff! Your toys and gambles mean nothing to me.'

I laughed at his absurdity but, as he continued to stare at me, I put down my knife and bread. 'I could easily answer your fond comparisons, no doubt taken from some flibber-jibber knave that feigns tales. But I am not disposed to argue of the matter. Not now. Not in this place.'

But he stayed on the hunt. 'What, do you fear eavesdroppers who stand under a wall or window to hear the secrets of a man's soul? That horse has long bolted, sir, and there are many in this city who condemn your doings –'

'Scornful and malicious people.'

'– and say that you are a renegade who raises the dead, and creates new life.'

I put out my hand, which, as I saw, trembled. What could I answer to such things without great grief of mind, since he had hit upon a truth which he could not understand? Yet I kept my countenance, and smiled upon him. 'You told me you were not credulous, and now you speak of raising the dead. Come, this is child's stuff.'

'This is what the world says, good doctor. Not what I believe. Report has it that you are a bankrupt alchemist, a conjuror who cannot complete his dealings without the secret assistance of you know who.'

I could put him off no longer. 'Foul and slanderous words,' I said, 'which should never have been spoken of me.' He merely laughed at this, and my anger grew higher. 'Shall the folly of idiots, and the malice of the scornful, become the new gospel among all of you here? Shall I be robbed of my honest name and fame by those so far beneath me that I can scarcely see them?'

'They are to be seen.'

'Heard, but not seen. You eagerly listen to their reports, and so I am in hugger-mugger condemned as a companion of the hell-hound and a caller of damned spirits.' They were all now so drunken that they scarcely heeded me, except for the coxcomb opposite. 'All my life,' I continued more quietly, 'I have spent in learning. If I seem to you another Faustus, why, so be it.' Then I called for more wine, and asked the knave his name.

'Bartholomew Gray,' he replied, not at all abashed, though he had witnessed the full extent of my wrath and had, as it were, been burnt by my heat.

'Well, Mr Gray, perhaps you have had enough of fables. Would you like now to hold on to wisdom, and to judge truly of things?'

'Go on, good doctor. But eat no more salt, I pray you, for fear of sharpening your anger.'

'Fear not the anger, Mr Gray, if you fear not the truth.'

'In truth I fear nothing, so proceed.'

'For the past thirty years continually,' I began, 'in diverse manners, and in various countries, with great pain, care and cost, I have sought to come by the best knowledge that anyone might attain in this world. I found at length that no man living was able to teach me those truths I desired and longed for, and so I concluded with myself that it was only in books and histories I might find the light for which I searched. I do not cast figures and conjure, as you so fondly imagine, but rather build upon the wisdom I have gained in all these years –' I broke off for the moment, and drank more wine. 'But if this is to be a true chronicle, I must begin at the beginning.'

'That is the white to aim at,' he said. 'The *tabula rasa.*'

'My parents were honest and of no little esteem among their neighbours, my father being agent to the estate of my lord Gravenar. I was the last of my mother's children and, since the others were much more advanced in years, I stayed pretty close to myself (as they say) and played in the fields next to our ancient house in east Acton. There is no telling the wonderful diversity of children's natures, the spirit itself being combined from so many contrary influences, but I myself was of a shy disposition and haughty mind: I played alone always, shunning fellows as I would shun flies, and when my father began to teach me I fell naturally into the company of old books. I learned my Latin and my Greek even before my tenth year, and had no little delight in reciting from memory the verses of Ovid or the sentences of Tully as I roamed among the lanes and hedges of our parish. I would preach *Eliot's Dictionary* to the sheep and *Lily's Grammar* to the cows, and then run back to study Erasmus and Virgil at my own little table. Of course I shared my bed and my chamber with my two brothers (now both under the earth), but my parents understood my solitary disposition and gave me a chest, with lock and key, where I kept not only my apparel but also my texts. I had also a box of papers in my own writing, for my father had instructed me in the secretary hand, and there I concealed many verses and lessons of my own composition.

'I rose at five in the morning, my father calling out to me "Surgite! Surgite!" while I washed my face and hands very quickly.

All of the household prayed together, and then he took me into his own chamber where I practised upon the lute: my father's care was always to increase my skill in music, and by daily exercise I grew more bold in singing and in playing upon instruments. At seven we came into the hall, where the table was already laden with meat and bread and ale (in those days called the angel's food) for our breakfast; after the meal was concluded I began my lessons in grammar, verse extempore, construction, translation and suchlike. Horace and Terence were my playfellows, though even then I had a true interest in the history of my own country, and from these early years I was the scholar and never the gamester.

'But soon enough it was time to rise into another sphere, and I was in November *anno* 1542 sent by my father to the university of Cambridge, there to begin with logic and so to proceed in the learning of good arts and sciences. I was then somewhat above fifteen years old, as being born *anno* 1527 July 13 —'

'Your birth,' Bartholomew Gray said very suddenly, 'is out of its place, and should have come at the beginning of your discourse. Ordering, as well as inventing, is true argument of a fine wit. Surely so premature a scholar should know that?'

I ignored the coxcomb, and continued with my theme. 'For the most part of these years I was so vehemently bent to studies that I inviolably kept this order — only to sleep four hours every night, to allow for meat and drink two hours every day, and of the other eighteen hours all (except the time of divine service) to be spent in my studies and learning. I had begun there with logic, and so I read Aristotle his *De sophisticis elenchis* and his *Topic* as well as his *Analytica Prioria* and *Analytica Posteriora*; but my thirst for knowledge was so great that I soon found myself bent towards other learning as towards a glorious light that could never be extinguished, no, nor even dimmed. I cared nothing at all for the lewd pastimes of my college fellows and found no comfort in banqueting and whoring, in dicing and in carding, in dancing and in bear-baiting, in bowling and in shooting, and other suchlike trifles of the town. Yet though I had nothing to do with dice or with primero, I did have a chess-board with a little bag of leather

for my men: these I would advance from square to square, remind-
ing myself of my own history up to that time. I knew then, as I
picked up my ivory pieces and stroked them a little with my
forefinger, that monarchs and bishops would be as nothing to one
who could predict their movements.

'After seven years I had attained my Master of Arts and, presently
leaving the university, I went to London in order to follow my
studies philosophical and mathematical. I had heard by report of a
poor studious gentleman, by name Ferdinand Griffen, who had for
many years past been buried deep in his rare studies and who (it
was said by those knowing my own course of learning) would
teach me the use of the astrolabe and the astronomer's staff as a
proper continuance of my exploits in geometry and arithmetic. He
lived in a rambling tenement in the Bishop of London's rents, in a
court near the waterside just by St Andrew's Hill –'

'I know it,' he said. 'By the glassworks on Addle Hill.'

'A little westward from there.' I refreshed myself by taking some
more wine.

'I came to him on midsummer's day in the year 1549, and found
him working among his globes and vessels with the nimbleness of
an apprentice. He greeted me with bright words, having expected
my coming after several learned letters had passed between us, and
pretty soon he displayed to me certain rare and exquisitely made
instruments upon which (as he told me) he had bestowed all his life
and fortune – among which was one strong quadrant of five-foot
diameter, an excellent *radius astronomicus* which had its staff and
cross very curiously divided in equal parts, a fair astrolabe and a
great globe of metal. So it was that Ferdinand Griffen became my
good master and with him I began my astronomical observations
in earnest, all the time working with those very fine and very apt
instruments which he taught me how to use carefully and
circumspectly. We began observations, many to the hour and
minute, of the heavenly influences and operations actual in this
elemental portion of the world –'

At which point I broke off, fearing to say too much to one who
was not practised in these arts, and in my confusion drank my fill

of wine before continuing along another path. 'We were so close to the waterside that we would take our quadrant from his rambling lodgings down Water Lane to Blackfriars Stairs where, among the barges and the herring buses, we called out "Westward! Westward!" until one of the passing watermen noticed us. The wherry took us by the open fields beside Lambeth Marsh where, with the quadrant established upon firm earth, we would make various observations of the sun's progress. Sometimes, coming or going, we were close to falling into the Thames over head and ears with the cumbersomeness of the quadrant, but we always escaped on to dry ground. What instrument of the sun could be deluged with water? No, it could not be. There were sly citizens who were accustomed to call us sorcerers or magicians for all this measuring but it was all one to Ferdinand Griffen, and since that time I have taken my lesson from him in despising and condemning the ignorant multitude. On many other matters he also proved my good master, or should I say magus, with books, pamphlets, discourses, inventions and conclusions upon grave arts. You asked me if I raised the dead; no, I raise new life . . .' Again I broke off, fearing that I had fallen into too deep a vein, but Bartholomew Gray did nothing but pick at his teeth and call for more wine. 'Then,' I added, 'I went beyond the seas to speak and confer with some learned men.'

'Magicians,' he replied, now quite lost and wandering in his drink. 'Sorcerers.'

'They had nothing to do with what is vulgarly called magic.' I took more wine to consume the fire within me. 'Mine are wonderful sciences, greatly aiding our dim sight for the better view of God's power and goodness. I am by profession a scholar, sir, and not some magician or mountebank. Whose opinion was it but my own that the court sought for, relating to the great comet of 1577, after the judgement of certain so-called astronomers had unduly bred great fear and doubt? And who was it that prepared for our trades and voyages to Cathay and Muscovy with true charts and tables for our navigators? And who was it again that gave Euclid's propositions to the mechanics of this realm, from which they have derived inestimable benefit? I alone have achieved all these things. Is it the work of a mountebank?'

'Lord,' he said, drunken to the highest degree. 'I understand not one word of this.'

'But I understand. I have spent these last fifty years for good learning's sake – what a race have I run, so much done and so much suffered, for the attaining of wisdom! Do you recall that time when a certain image of wax, with a great pin stuck in the breast of it, was found in Lincoln's Inn field?' He seemed to shake his head, but I was now launched upon a tide of words. 'It was said then by malicious backbiters to be an image of my own making, and that I endeavoured by enchantment to destroy Queen Mary. All spiteful falsehoods, all brain-sick perjuries, and yet for many weeks I remained prisoner in the Tower while all the doors of my lodgings in London were sealed up and I was close to being overwhelmed by the circumstances of my grief, loss and discredit. Well well, I said to myself then, my unkind countrymen, my unnatural countrymen, my unthankful country-men, I know you now and I know what I must do. In recent years they have said that I impoverish the earth, that I rob the man in the moon, and any such stuff as can be hurled upon me. But do you know what is worse still? That I must take a purse from one such as Nathaniel Cadman here, and provide mere shows and gewgaws.' I paused for a moment, but no one else had heard my complaint. 'So, Mr Gray. Now you know of the very great injuries, damages and indignities I have sustained. I ask you not to increase them.'

He seemed a little abashed, yet he drank some more wine and then with a high-pitched but not unpleasing voice began to sing out a verse from 'Fortune My Foe':

> 'The moon's my constant mistress,
> And the lowly owl my morrow,
> The flaming drake and night-crow make
> Me music to my sorrow.'

'It is a fitting tune,' I said, 'to accompany me on my way. For now I must rise and leave you gentlemen –' I looked across the board, where they lolled in various stages of drunkenness. 'I am tired now after my spectacle.'

'I sat amazed,' one of their number said, looking down into his cup, 'when the spheres came down amidst the brightness. And all revolved. It was well done. It was very well done.'

'I wish you good night,' I said again. 'I must return to my own proper sphere.' I bowed to Nathaniel Cadman, who could not raise his head from the table and sat like some poor shrunken thing. 'I wish all of you good night.'

I came out into New Fish Street, when a boy walked forward with a lantern. But I waved him away. It was a clear night, and the fixed stars were all I needed to light my path to Clerkenwell.

TWO

I DECIDED TO walk through the night. I had already left the churchyard and started in the direction of the old house, but I hesitated and stopped. I did not want to go back to Cloak Lane, not yet, and, as so often before, I turned towards the winding streets of London. I prefer the city in darkness; it reveals its true nature to me then, by which I suppose I mean its true history. During the day it is taken over by its temporary inhabitants, and at those times I feel as if I might be dispersed and lost among them. So I keep my distance. I imagine them in the clothes of another century, for example, although I realize that this is very fanciful. But there are occasions when a certain look, or gesture, plunges me back into another time; it is as if there had been some genetic surplus, because I know that I am observing a medieval or a sixteenth-century face. When the body of a neolithic traveller was recovered from an Alpine glacier, sprawled face down in the posture of death, it was considered to be an extraordinary act of historical retrieval. But the past is restored around us all the time, in the bodies we inhabit or the words we speak. And there are certain scenes or situations which, once glimpsed, seem to continue for eternity.

No, that's not the way to describe it. They are already part of a continuing history even as they occur and, as I said once before, there are times when I walk through the contemporary city and recognize it for what it is: another historical period, with all its mysterious constraints and docilities. There was a sentence which my father taught me – 'To see eternity as part of time, and time as part of eternity'. I once saw a photograph of Whitehall, taken in 1839, and it imparted to me something of that; there was a small boy in a stove-pipe hat sprawled beneath a lamp-post, while across the road a line of hansom cabs waited. Everything was in the eye of eternity, and even the dirt of the streets seemed to glow. But that is also the sensation I experience now, as I walk away from the churchyard and watch that woman opening her street door while at the same time I hear the sound of a car backfiring in a nearby street. These things fade, and yet somehow they exist for ever.

I crossed Clerkenwell Green into Jerusalem Passage. It was almost midnight, as I could tell from the neon clock which hung from the building beside me; I watched it for a few moments as it swayed in the wind, and the digits glowed upon its face. In the fourteenth century there was one stone which was very highly prized – it was called sadastra. In its outward appearance it was black or dark brown but, when it was broken open, for a few moments it glistened like the sun. I imagine it had the same kind of brightness as this neon clock which I now passed. There were two or three people nearby; their pale faces gleamed in the orange street-light, and they seemed to be walking silently over the pavements. I came out of Jerusalem Passage, crossed the Clerkenwell Road, and made my way beneath the arch of the Priory of St John of Jerusalem. There was a foundation stone here, marking the site of the twelfth-century abbey of the Knights Templar, which had been destroyed at the time of the Reformation. No doubt its stones had been used to construct some of the grander houses of the neighbourhood (perhaps some of them were still lodged within the walls of my own house), but they were the sad remnants of a great wreck. This was one of Daniel Moore's beliefs, at any rate, and I had come to accept it – that the destruction of the great monastic libraries, with all their manuscripts and treasures, meant that a great part of the history of this island had also been lost. Not only had an entire Catholic culture been erased, but, just as damagingly, the old monastic records of early British history had been destroyed. A large structure of the past had effectively been buried.

But what was this noise by Holborn Viaduct? A furious shout seemed to be coming from some place beneath the earth; it was stifled, enclosed, echoing in some small space. Then I turned the corner of Giltspur Street and saw an old woman bowed within a telephone booth; she held the receiver up to her ear, and was screaming into the mouthpiece. I carried on walking towards her, until I could see an 'Out Of Order' notice pasted on the window. So what kind of connection had she made? I remember the time I had picked up one of the telephones at Chancery Lane station, and heard a multitude of voices murmuring like the sound of wind about a house. Perhaps there is always someone at the other end of the line. No, all this is nonsense. Do you see how a journey through the night can provoke strange fears? There was a small satellite dish on the roof of the flats at the corner of Snow Hill, and as I watched it absorbing its patterns from the sky I saw again my vision of the man rising upwards into the air above Cloak Lane.

'What? Is it you? Are you here, after all?' The old woman had come out of the telephone booth, and was shouting after me. I walked away as quickly as I could. 'You know about all the shit on the streets, don't you? It's not the dogs. It's the old-age pensioners.' She started laughing as I made my way towards Fetter Lane and High Holborn. There is a video shop by the entrance of Dyer's Rents and, as I hurried towards it, I could see a dozen screens glowing with the same picture; there was so much light and energy here that the shop window itself might have burst open or exploded. When I came closer still, having looked back to make sure that she was not following me, I could see many stars and planets hurtling past the screens. It must have been one of those science fiction epics of the seventies or early eighties, and there was a young man watching the cosmic adventure with a look of absolute concentration. He had put his arms out against the plate glass window, and it looked as if he were being crucified by all that brightness. I wanted to tell him that it was all delusion, a trick of the cinematographer, but for him it was probably a true vision of the universe. I said nothing and walked on.

I can tell you when I first began to understand London. I must have been fifteen or sixteen, and I was travelling on the bus which goes from Shepherd's Bush to Dulwich; the sky above Notting

Hill Gate and Queensway was covered by cloud, but suddenly those clouds broke and a shaft of sunlight shone down upon the metal rail in front of me. I could not turn my eyes from that intense brightness and, as I gazed into the depths of the light and the shining metal, I was filled with a sense of exhilaration so profound that I left my seat and jumped off the bus as it came to a halt by Marble Arch. I felt that some secret had been divulged to me – that I had glimpsed some interior life and reality which glowed within all things. I thought of it as the fire-world, and as I turned into Tyburn Way I believed that I would be able to find traces of it everywhere. But that fire was also within me, and I found myself running through the streets as if I possessed them. Somehow I had been present at their beginning; or, rather, there was some presence within me which had always existed in this soil, this stone, and this air. That original fire has left me now, which is perhaps why I seem such a stranger to myself; slowly, over the years, the city has darkened within me.

But there were certain places to which I still returned. Sometimes I found myself walking down Kingsland Road and stopping at the old Hoxton asylum by Wharf Lane; it was here that Charles Lamb used to take his sister, at her own request, and once I tried to track their footsteps through the fields which are now concealed beneath the stone pavements of the area. She always carried her strait-jacket with her, and they wept when they came up to the gate of the asylum. I stopped where they had stopped, just before the archway, and whispered my own name. I often revisited Borough High Street, and followed its route from Southwark Bridge to the site of King's Bench Prison and the Marshalsea; this journey always weighed heavily upon me, and yet I continued to make it. There were times when I walked around the area until I was lost and tired and unable to think. I wanted the Borough to bury me, to hold me down, to suffocate me. Surely among all the dark shapes of its past, there was one in which I could be concealed? But not all my haunts were so oppressive. There was one place in particular where I knew I could find rest: again and again I returned to Fountain Court within the Temple where, beside a small circular pond, a wooden bench had been placed beneath an elm tree. The sense of peace, even in the middle of the city, was so strong that I presume it came from some powerful event in the past. Or perhaps it was simply that people like myself had always chosen this place, and over the years it had accepted the stillness of its visitors. I often think about death as if it were a state such as this – as if I were waiting beside an elm tree and a pond. My father had approached his own death peacefully enough, almost happily. I remember him whistling in the bathroom, even when he knew that he had only a few months of life ahead of him. He never complained, and showed no signs of self-pity or anxiety. It was as if he possessed some information about the next stage of his journey; he was a Roman Catholic, as I said, but he seemed to harbour some more private belief which reassured him. And once again, as I came out into Red Lion Square from High Holborn, I considered the old house which he had bequeathed to me. Why was it that, during all my walks through the city, I had never seen Cloak Lane or its vicinity? Why had I shunned, or forgotten, Clerkenwell?

I had come up to the fragment of the old stone pillar which marks the site of the Red Lion Fields massacre of June 1780; at the time of the Gordon Riots a group of children were killed by troops here, and three months later John Wilkes started a subscription for this memorial. The stone was now so cracked and worn that it might have been a piece of nature in decay but, on an impulse, I knelt down and touched it. I had another connection with the place, after all. Only a few yards away, on a stall by Red Lion Passage, I had first come across the work of Piranesi. It was a book with many of his etchings reproduced; its title was *Imaginary Prisons*, but as far as I was concerned there was nothing imaginary about them at all. I recognized this world at once; I knew that it was my city.

I took the book home with me – it must have been six or seven years ago now, but I still remember the excitement with which I turned its pages. In the first etching two small figures were standing in front of a vast stone staircase; there was nothing but stone all around them, spiralling upwards into galleries, arches and

43

domes. Piranesi's world was one of endlessly ruined masonry, of labyrinthine passages and barred windows; here were blocks of stone, massive, dark, their textures swamped in shadow; here were giant recesses of brick, huge banners of tattered cloth, ropes, pulleys, and wooden cranes that towered up to broken balconies of stone. The artist often used the framing device of a ruined arch or gateway, so that I was drawn into the scene and knew myself to be part of it; I was in prison, too.

Everything looked as if it had been abandoned – the bridge hanging precariously between two decayed towers, the rotten beams, the cracked windows, the massive porticoes with inscriptions too faded to read. A giant race of builders had declined and died, leaving these monuments behind them. But no, that could not be true. There was a sense of continuing power, of living force, here. It was beyond death; it was the condition of the world. I was looking at the last etching, which showed an indeterminate small figure mounting a stone staircase only to be confronted by another steep bulwark of stone. In this tiny figure I thought I could see something of my own self, when my father tapped me on the shoulder. He must have been watching me for a few moments because he said, softly, 'It needn't be like that, you know.' That was all he said, and then he put his hand upon the back of my neck. I shook him off and looked down at the etching again, only to see another flight of steps that seemed to lead down into an abyss of stone. It occurred to me then that this was really a city under the ground. It was the eternal city for those who are trapped in time. I was still kneeling beside the memorial in Red Lion Square, but now I seemed to be entering the stone wall of the basement in Cloak Lane. I was becoming part of the old house.

I got up quickly, brushed the dirt from my clothes, and walked out towards New Oxford Street and Tottenham Court Road. There is a patch of cobbles just by Bloomsbury Square, where a row of new Mercury telephones had been placed, and in the dark I stumbled over them. 'London stone is different from this,' Daniel Moore had told me when I showed him *Imaginary Prisons*. 'You have to learn Italian just to look at Piranesi.' I had been trying to share my enthusiasm with him, but he simply peered at the reproductions with something like distaste. 'He's a sentimentalist,' he said, 'not a visionary.'

'But don't you see the wilderness of it?'

'No. Not really. You may see the stone, but I see the people. Why do you think I'm writing my book?' This book, upon which he had been working ever since I had known him, was to be a history of London radicalism. He had explained it to me once, in his usual embarrassed dismissive way, but all the Muggletonians, and Ranters, and Behmenists, and members of the London Corresponding Society, confused me and seemed to become members of one vast sect or community. But this was his great theme – this fastidious, delicate man was obsessed by the aspirations of some disturbed, even dangerous, Londoners. Once he took me on a tour of the taverns and meeting-houses which they had used; only a few survived, mainly in the east of London by Limehouse and Shadwell, and they looked so insignificant, so grubby, that it was hard to imagine the visions and dreams that had been conjured up within them. The Behmenists believed, as far as Daniel could explain it to me, that men and women carried the heavens within them and that the universe itself was in the shape of a single person; he was known as Adam Kadmon, or the Universal Man. They did not necessarily believe that the entire cosmos was in fact a human form – although there were some radical Swedenborgians who proclaimed that there was just such a correspondence – but rather that the world, and the entire universe of being, was infused with the qualities of humanity. We had come up to the Seven Stars in Arrow Lane, where some Moravians used to meet in the early eighteenth century, and Daniel told me the story of the mystic who was continually asked by a small girl to show her angels. At last he agreed to do so and, taking her into his house, led her over towards a curtained recess. 'Do you really wish to see an angel?' he asked her. She was still very eager, so he pulled back the curtain and, on the wall behind it, was a mirror. 'Look there,' he said. 'There is an angel.'

'It's a charming story, Matthew, don't you think?'

45

'Oh, yes.'

'But do you understand how radical it is? The humblest person can be filled with grace. Divinity is within us, and there is no sin. There is no heaven, no hell.'

Why should such strange doctrines emerge in this city? This was the question he posed to me as we walked down Shadwell Reach. The answer seemed obvious enough: this was the area where artisans and small tradesmen were to be found in the largest numbers, and they were the ones most prone to this form of madness. And yet Daniel seemed to believe that it had something to do with the spirit of the place itself. But I had seen enough. Limehouse was filled with the fumes of traffic, with smoke, with the debris of unfinished buildings; I found it hard to get my breath, but I managed to drag him away to the upper level of the Docklands Light Railway. That was the end of our journey in search of what he called the 'everlasting gospel'.

There was also the time he drove me to the south-west of England, and to the old radical centre of Glastonbury. A fourteenth-century London sect, God's Brothers, as they called themselves, had fled from persecution in the city and established a community in that area. We must have chosen the worst day of the year for such a journey – from London to Andover we were buffeted by rainstorms, and then on the way from Hampshire we were caught in a thick fog which hovered along the motorway. We crept towards Glastonbury, since the road was hardly visible; the posts along the route looked like sentinels huddled in their clothes, while the pylons seemed to be the spires of churches rising out of the mist. There were clumps of trees in one field that we passed, and they might have been the members of some small congregation struggling onward. No doubt these are the materials out of which local legends and 'sightings' are manufactured, but all I could think of was the warmth and safety of London. There were no remnants of the old community when eventually we arrived in Glastonbury itself, and the area which they had colonized was an industrial estate – we should have guessed as much, but Daniel was oddly silent during the return journey. The fog had lifted by the time we came home; it was late in the evening, and I knew that we were approaching London from the diffused red light in the sky which blotted out all the stars. It was as if we were returning to a furnace, and I was at peace.

I came out from New Oxford Street into Tottenham Court Road just as the clock of St Giles-in-the-Fields struck the hour; I walked more quickly here, since in the porches and doorways along the street lay the army of the night. I was afraid of them, these men and women huddled in filthy blankets, but it is not simply the vagrant or the homeless who disturb me. I know very well that I turn away from any kind of human extremity. I turn away from suffering. Now as I crossed the street and glanced towards two piles of clothes stirring uneasily in the night air, I was afraid of dirt, and of disease, but I suppose that I was most afraid of being attacked. What had they got to lose? If I were like them, I would scream against the world and burn the city. I would want to destroy everything, and everyone, that had conspired against me. I would pillage the shops which denied me entrance, and break up the restaurants which denied me food. I would even rage against the street-lamps which displayed me to the enemy. Yet, as I walked by, none of them asked me for anything, or spoke, or looked at me; I might have been part of some other world. Were they truly resigned, patient, uncomplaining – or were they waiting for something, like the Moravians who met in the Seven Stars?

No, there was this difference. The city had grown immeasurably larger and, as it expanded in every direction, its inhabitants had become more passive and docile; these people who slept upon its streets were true and faithful citizens, but vast London had by some alchemy drained away their spirit. I looked down Tottenham Court Road and, not for the first time, noticed the silence and over-brightness of the city at night. Two centuries ago these streets would have been darker, more malodorous, more treacherous, and they would have been filled with cries, and screams, and laughter. But now as I stood with the homeless around me, all I could hear was the vague hum of the neon street-lamps and the gusting of the wind around Centre Point. Why was it that, in a place such as this, all the natural sounds seemed fabricated and unreal, while the artificial noise seemed most natural? This city was too bright because it was celebrating its own triumph. It had grown steadily larger by encroaching upon, and subduing, the energy of its inhabitants. They hardly moved as I made my way towards Charlotte Street.

I turned the corner, and saw at once that there was a globe shining at one end of the thoroughfare. Of course there was another reason for this constant and ubiquitous brightness: these signs and emblems, shining out into the darkness, were also ways of evading death and the knowledge of death. They celebrated a kind of artificial life, in which the spiritual world was obliterated. It was peculiar – it was something my father might have said. But these were my own night thoughts.

The globe brightened the surrounding air, and Charlotte Street was very still. It was a vision of the world and truly of the world since, as I walked closer, I could see that it was a neon representation of the earth with the continents picked out in variously coloured lights. There was a sign beneath it, 'The World Turned Upside Down'; it was a bar, or night-club, and a row of metal stairs led precipitously from the street to a small basement area and a closed door. There was a light shining behind it and, as I looked down, the area was suddenly illuminated when the door swung open. A woman came out and stood upon the threshold, but there was so much light behind her that I could only see her shape and the outline of her hair; still, I was interested. I stepped back into the shadows of the street as she climbed the stairs; her heels rang out on the metal, creating an echo which stopped abruptly when she stepped on to the pavement. She looked around uncertainly, as if she were waiting for a taxi; then she turned her face towards me, and I put up my hand in surprise and horror. It was Daniel Moore. I saw him plainly. I knew his face, beneath the make-up. He had placed a large blonde wig on his thinning hair, and he was wearing a red dress. I could even smell the perfume of violets. But it was Daniel. He had not noticed me, because now he turned his head and began walking slowly towards Fitzroy Square. It was a casual

48

walk, nothing like his usual nervous pace, and he seemed quite content to enjoy the sensations of the London night. I stood there, in the doorway of a shop, bewildered. I could think of nothing. I just stared and stared at the bright globe of the world turned upside down.

THE LIBRARY

THE GREAT WORLD is unrolled before me, and on my desk ride the blue dolphins that love young children and the sound of musical instruments; here are the serpents, coloured in green and grey, that live six hundred years and whose heads are changed into the shape of dogs or men at will; here are sea-dragons also, marked in red, that breathe fire into the water and so cause the oceans to boil; among them glide the gryphons, the whales, and all the tribes of lesser fish that sport upon the surface of the deep. Neptune with his trident rides high upon the horses of the sea, while by quicksands and whirlpools sit the mermaids with mirrors in their hands. Everything on earth has its fellow within the sea, yet upon the face of this other world I also view the galleons, the cross-sailed merchant ships, the square-rigged barques, and the fishing-vessels. Who could observe such things and not wish to travel with them? For this is a map of the entire world I have before me, *theatrum orbis terrarum*, upon which have been placed the cities, the mountains, the woods, the rivers and a vast number even of the towns which make up this lower world.

At the northern gate there stands Terra Septemtronalis Incognita where, it is said, dwell a tribe which hold the fire-stones in their mouths; in the southern extremity is conjectured to be another land of desolation. Yet not all is unknown: much has been discovered by means of good geometry and the voyages of recent years, so that the world is now marked out far beyond the confines of Bohemia or Tartary. Our navigators and cosmographers have traced the outlines of Atlantis, or the New World, where have been found the crocodile that lives for a thousand years and the quail that has the falling sickness: certain provinces or domains there we have named Norumbega, Nova Francia and Mocosa, in which latter part of the world has been found the horse that weeps and sighs like a man. There also is the agopithecus, the ape-like goat whose voice is very like a man's but not articulate, sounding as if one did speak hastily with indignation or sorrow.

Africa is underneath my hand, and within it Barbarie where live the lions that couple backwards and the panthers that have the odour of the sweetest spices. In Numidia, not so far distant, live men with the tails and heads of dogs, as well as the infamous yena that inhabit the tombs of the dead and eat only corpses. In Libya dwells the monoceros that feasts upon poison, and can make itself into male or female as it wishes; there are people here called Astomii, who live very long and neither eat nor drink but feed upon air and the smell of fruits. In Selenetide there are women who lay eggs and hatch them, from which come children fifty times greater than those which are generally born, and the far-off Land of the Negroes is inhabited by the basilisk that kills at a look, the hydrus of two heads, and the salamander of perfect coldness: I have not the reports close to hand, otherwise I would give them to you in this place. O bright theatre of the world, in which I might lose myself! Here I stand by a table in my library room while I fly in the air like the great artificer, Icarus, and find myself suddenly aloft in the yellow land of Samotra and on a wonderful path to Monacabo, Capasiasa, Taprobana, Bacornara and Birae. Then can I see the men whose bodies shine at night, and the phoenix tree which blooms for an hundred years and imparts an odour more perfumed than musk or civet or ambergris. On this far-off shore I view the wonders of the world beneath the stars, and see before me the creature that is born twice, crying out upon the top of a mountain and saying, 'I am the white of the black, and the red of the white, and the yellow of the sun, I tell truth and lie not' . . . at which I started and awakened, for I was in a dream of my own devising.

Yet in truth I care not if I sleep a little more, and there are times such as this when all my learning seems to be a dream in which my wits are only half awakened. Last night I drank too much wine with those flibber-jibber knaves, so this morning I am dumpish and drowsy and dazed. See, I am even entranced away from my proper studies and talk idly over this *mappa mundi* here before me – but yet, as I look down upon the banks and rocks, the countertides and whirlpools, all marked by the delicate engraver, I am reminded of another journey. It was one I made through all manner of weather, and through all the variety of ways and passages upon the earth.

It was after my time with Ferdinand Griffen that I set out upon this pilgrimage. Having understood all that he could teach me, and growing tired for the moment of scales and hour-glasses, I decided to visit the true scholars and practitioners of learning beyond our shores. I had one great mark at which to aim in the course of my travels, since I had a desire to see the birthplace of that master of wisdom, Philippus Aureolus Theophrastus Bombast, known by the name of Paracelsus. He was born *anno* 1493 in the little town of Maria-Einsiedeln, not above two hours on foot from Zurich, and to reach that high country situated within the Alps I was forced to toil in dangerous damps and cold, in fear of violence by men or destruction by wild beasts, in lodgings of small ease and less comfort, almost bereaving life in order to come upon one of the fountains or sources of my life. But though it was a very painful and dangerous winter journey, it was made when I was young enough to scorn danger: I was drawn towards the lodestone of my art, Master Paracelsus, and no storm or hurricane (as I thought) would have the power to delay me.

I set forth in the dead of night and by wherry went to Greenwich, where I waited until there came a great tilt-boat to take me on to Gravesend. I took ship there, some miles distant from London, and carried aboard with me my own provisions for the journey, including biscuit, bread, beer, oil and vinegar; in my wallet I also had a good store of parchment, quill and ink (together with black powder to make more), so that I might keep a record of my travels into foreign lands. From there we sailed into the main, but on the third day of our sailing the merchant fleet of twelve vessels – our ship being one among them – was dispersed by a fog and tempest.

I had with me my own pocket dial and compass of variation, willingly bequeathed to me by Mr Griffen, and I feared nothing. So I spoke readily enough with the captain of my vessel about the sea compass and the meridian compass, the astrolabe and the cross-staff, but when I discoursed with him upon eccentricity and parallax, he told me in a few words that he was master of ebbs or floods and not of instruments. This perplexed and dismayed me, thinking that only knowledge would lead us out of the tempest, but he clapped me upon the back and laughed.

'All is well, my star-shooter,' he said. 'I know my courses and my soundings, my landings and my marks, better than I know the lines upon my own hand.'

'But, good captain, surely you and your pilot know the elements of hydrography and astronomy?'

'In my head I have marked all the rocks and races. What more is there to say? Look, let me draw our path for you –'

With his finger upon an old deal table he mapped out our course, and I looked at him amazed. 'But what of the steadying and the midnighting of the stars? We are lost in this tempest, and only by expert conjecture will you find your way.'

He laughed again at my eagerness. 'Will the fixed stars or the planets lead me out from the countertides and whirlpools? I think not. Can you gaze at the sun and predict for me tempests or spouts? No, no, John Dee, you may lead a merry dance among the points of your arithmetic and geometry; but let me steer by my own light.'

I left him soon after, just as the tempest eased and the fog lifted, and I believe he still laughed after me. But who has the last laugh? You may plot a course by experience, but only knowledge brings you to a true and fitting destination. The eye may take you, sweet captain, across this little stretch of sea; but the astrolabe you condemn will impart to you the motions of the celestial orbs. It is not enough to move easily through the world: it is necessary to view it in the sun of understanding. Tell me. Is that not so?

On the fourth day at sea we came upon an island called the Holy-land (vulgarly Heiligland) and, not daring to enter the River

Elve before the next morning, we struck our sails and suffered the ship to be tossed to and fro by the waves all that night – which mariners call lying at hull but which I call lying in foulness. Then on the next day we entered the river and landed at Stode, from which place we departed in a wagon, crossed the river, and travelled through many thick woods of oak to Hamburg. So began my entire winter's journey over land: by coach across marsh and sandy plains, by wagon through mountains and woods, on foot in hail and fog, by horse past lakes and groves, all the while taking my path by way of Hamburg and Leipzig, Witterburg and Dresden. I had made my way to Witterburg, quite contrary to all rules of progress and good travel, because it had been reported to me that some very curious and rare maps of the hitherto unknown world were lodged in the muniment room of the great cathedral church there. How could I not change my course, and reach out for the lands lost in the mist and darkness of our own ignorance?

Witterburg is a town filled with scholars, but I had with me a letter of introduction to the great astronomer Hegelius, a native of that place, and after we had dined together on fish and flesh he consented to accompany me to the cathedral, where his name was a key to unlock all the treasures contained therein. I might view the maps of the unknown world with ease enough, he continued, but did I not know that there was another mysterious region closer to hand? (We conversed in Latin, which I choose to translate here even though it may reach the eyes and ears of the vulgar.) He went on to tell me that the famous conjuror, Dr Faustus, lived in Witterburg about the year 1500; at my earnest entreaty, he very readily agreed to show me the house in which he had dwelt. We rose from the table after grace and, after some talk on the principles of magic, went on our way through the stinking streets of the town: yet it was a poor errand, since the old house of Faustus was no more than a fusty tenement with no relics of his art.

Hegelius, observing my downcast looks, then asked me if I would like to enter a wood adjoining the town, where it was said that Dr Faustus practised his magic art and where he died – or was rather fetched by the Devil as the sum of all his labours. Yes, I replied, yes. I had a sickness upon me from the conditions of the winter, but I was still so young that no circumstance could check me. We walked out beyond the gate of the town, where there were various heads carved out of stone, much like the bloody heads of malefactors on London Bridge, and pretty soon we came upon the boundary of the wood. I was well wrapped inside a fur coat, and with a cap upon my head lined with cats' skins after the Muscovy fashion, yet it was so cold within the domain of Faustus that I could not bring myself to speak. It was three of the clock in the afternoon, but already so dark beneath the canopy of trees that I could scarcely find the path. All the while Hegelius walked before me until he came up to the withered and blackened base of a tree, some six feet in diameter. 'Here it was,' he said, 'that Faustus stood and was taken away.' I jumped upon the remnant of this very ancient tree, and all at once the raw cold left my bones. At that same moment, also, the sickness departed from me. I do not know if the Devil had preserved some relic of his fire here, but I was exceedingly healthy and joyful when I followed Hegelius back through the gate of the town. There seemed to be some force beyond the world directing my steps, and now I wished to know everything. I wished to understand everything. Hegelius took me on to the cathedral where we looked with wonder upon certain ancient maps, but it seemed to me that I had already found a greater world within that ancient ruined tree. I say no more in this place.

And so, much enlivened and refreshed by my cure in the wood of Faustus, I travelled onwards. Following Witterburg and Dresden I came to the wooden pillar that divides the territory of the Saxon elector from the kingdom of Bohemia, and then, across sandy and stony hills, through valleys filled with snow and many stark woods, I came by coach into Prague; from Prague I travelled on to Nuremberg, being six days' journey, partly through plain, partly through rocky mountains, until we reached that city, which was seated in a barren sandy ground overcovered by frost and ice and falling snow. It was marvellous hard weather yet I was still one of the nomads, every day changing my dwelling in town and village, and living upon stinking beer, brown bread and no clean straw. I had little money upon me at this time, for Englishmen give to their younger sons less than in foreign parts they give to their bastards – but this is by the by.

From Nuremberg I travelled on to Augsburg and, having hired a horse from the city carrier there, I went into the west parts of Germany and so into the Low Countries. Passing through Lindow by the lake called Acronius, I crossed by boat to Costnetz upon the confines of Germany and Switzerland and then on to Schaffhausen. The swiftness of the Rhine made the miles seem short, but lord, what a journey was that! It almost marked the end of my quest. I hold water in no fear, knowing it to be so necessary an element in this sublunary world, but in our setting forth upon the boat it inclined so much on the other side that it was half full of the river; we sat wet to the knees, and the water still came beating in more and more. But there was worse. There was a great fall of the waters over a rock some fifty cubits downwards, passing with huge noise and ending all in foam, and I had a panic fear that we would be drawn that way and lost within the mighty turbulence. Yet I remembered Faustus, and prayed out loud to my own good genius or daemon; at that instant the boatman took off his ragged apparel and, with the rope of the vessel in his hands, swam towards the landing stairs while dragging the boat behind him. I took up the oar and, with the assistance of another traveller, we helped steer our vessel towards the land while ever being in danger of sinking: I believed myself close to dying then, but the knowledge of it seemed only to increase my strength. But at last we came upon the shore, and were tumbled out upon the dry land. What a restoration that was; I felt like a giant who had somehow survived the Flood. I put up my hands to pray, but all the time I had a vision of myself in the wood with a light shining about me; I tried to murmur the words of thanksgiving after danger, but I was as dumb as if I was lost in some great amazing. Then a dog barked and I recovered myself. It was time to move on, for I could not abide loitering: my true destination was only a little way before me.

For a while I was compelled to take my journey on foot, with more sighs than paces, and came in five hours with much pain to the little city of Eglisaw. I did nothing there but cry out for my bed, and dined in the old fashion with the cloth spread upon it. Next morning by twilight I began my journey once more, having the gates opened early for a little reward to the guardian, and in six hours' space (for the miles of Switzerland are so long that they reckon the journey on horse or foot by the hours and not by the miles) I traversed woods and hills and enclosed pastures before I caught sight at last of Maria-Einsiedeln within a long valley. A sudden short and vehement storm of rain delayed my progress for a little, but I wrapped my cloak around me and pressed my wallet against my chest to withstand the wind until I slowly descended to the very walls of the town where the great master, Paracelsus, first heard the harmonies of the heavens.

It lay on the northern side of Lake Tigerinus, being a clean-swept town where the buildings for the most part were of timber and clay; the streets were narrow enough, but within the walls there was a castle very strong and new ruinated. I soon found myself lodgings at the Sign of the Hand and enquired of the servant there, a pert young woman well tucked up in a red kirtle and a white garment like an Irish mantle, where I might find that house of Paracelsus which I so earnestly sought. She answered me easily enough in her native tongue, and at once I went out again into the freezing air. Since this was no mighty city I turned down two lanes and then came suddenly upon a little bridge crossing a stream which she had mentioned to me; and there, just beyond it, I saw a house-wall with the painted head of the magus. It was skilfully done, and showed him as ever without any beard. Above his image were daubed some of his words in Latin, which I translate thus: 'That which is above is also that which is below, and hence proceed wonders.' I looked up then at the ancient carved windows of this house, in the firm knowledge that one of them illuminated the infant figure of Paracelsus when first he looked upon the beauty of the sun and stood gazing at the dancing of the stars.

A door opened and a very ancient man came forward across the threshold, beckoning me to come in, come in. He spoke to me brokenly in the French tongue, thinking me a traveller from that country, and I replied in the same. 'Do you wish to see his clothes?' he asked me. 'We keep them here.' I assented to this and he led me through a passage, all the while wiping the rheum from his eyes and nose; then we ascended a worm-eaten stairway while he spoke his French into the air above me. 'The townsmen yearly keep a festival in his memory,' he went on, 'and on that day we show this apparel he was accustomed to wear.' I could not tell how they came by it, since Paracelsus left his native land at the age of ten in order to dispute with the German scholars, but I kept my peace. He led me into a chamber where there was placed a very large chest or casket. 'Our relics,' he said, opening it with much ceremony. 'It is reported that they have cured the sick with their very touch.' He held out towards me a hat and gown, which with due reverence I took in my hand for a moment. Then, much pleased at my modest demeanour, he conducted me around the chamber and showed to me an ink-pot, quill and pen-knife; furthermore he showed me some books, which were not so ancient neither, and a ring which (he said) was taken from the hand of Paracelsus after his death. He was about to show me more, but I had seen enough, and though straitened in means I found a silver coin for him. 'You should know,' he murmured as he led me once more towards the door, 'that we still have our spirits in Einsiedeln.'

'Spirits, sir?'

'Like those which the good master saw. We have many vaults and caves around us, and the men that work there with burning lamps are troubled by these – these –'

'But do you not recall what Paracelsus has taught us? That the spirits are all within us? That what exists in heaven and earth exists also within the human frame?'

He did not understand what I meant by this, so I wished him good day and came out into the narrow street. I was returning by way of the little bridge when a desperate cry made me look down at the bank of the stream: and there, sitting upon a boulder in an expanse of mud, was a young woman dressed in all the colours of the maypole, while her face and hands were as white as milk.

'What ails you,' I shouted in what I took to be her own tongue, 'to cry so?'

'I care not,' she replied. 'I am content. Have with you.' At that she cried and laughed in turn, but in so strange a manner that my own limbs began to shake. Then all at once her whole body seemed to be pulled to and fro with convulsive motions, so that she slid from the boulder on to the bank of the stream; her belly was lifted up and then depressed, while there was a great distortion of her hands and arms. All the time, too, she made many strange faces and mouths, sometimes holding her mouth open or awry with her eyes staring up at me. I was about to hurry on when she called out 'Du! Du!', which I knew to be an angelic name. Her voice at this time was loud and fearful, proceeding from the throat like a hoarse dog that barks, and when I looked down upon her I saw that she cast forth from her opened mouth an abundance of froth or foam. The noise and sound of her voice was expressed by the word 'chek, chek' or 'kek, kek' and then again by 'twish, twish' like the hissing of a violent squib. After a moment came forth another sound comparable to the loathsome noise that a cat makes when trying to cast her gorge, and indeed this young woman now vehemently strained to vomit.

'In nomine Deo –' I began, wonderfully alarmed in case some devil possessed her.

'What? Is it you? Are you here?' She sent out these loud cries, as her body sank down upon the mud. Then her mouth being shut, and her lips closed, there came a voice through her nostrils that sounded very like 'Burn him. Burn him.' At that I moved as if to walk away when she cried out to me, 'Some news this day will make you very merry.' Then there was a silence and, when I turned, I observed her sitting upon the bank, weeping bitterly and in her extremity wringing her hands.

So I returned to my lodgings, weary and sad, having obtained nothing of what I sought and having found that which I did not seek. It was now about midday, and the sunbeams were glancing across my face as I lay upon my bed; but then I seemed to see a shadow passing by, and I sat up in a sudden sweat. At that moment I heard the words that my mother was dead. I rose and wrote the day and hour, with all the circumstances, upon a piece of paper which I kept about me all through my hard and perilous journey back to England. And yes, as it was written so would it be: on my return I heard the news of my mother's death, which had occurred on the same hour and day as I had witnessed the vision. She had expired after daily shaking with continual fever (thus in strange sort imitating the movements of the demoniac by the house of Paracelsus), but I was so elevated by my travels and by my increased thirst for learning that I cared not a fig for her. Had not Paracelsus himself left his own family to find wisdom elsewhere, and who was I to be bound down by such ties? I had a world of my own to conquer, and had no room at all for those who traced their inheritance only by blood.

So I gathered my books about me once more and took up lodgings in Carpenter's Yard, not far from Christopher Alley and to the south of Little Britain, near the covered sewer. Here the booksellers and printers kept their shops, and though there were stalls with such common stuff for mad-headed knaves as *Sir Guy of Warwick* or *The Budget of Demands*, I found many other books, printed pamphlets and discourses in diverse arts which furnished me with strange and profitable matter. I could have stayed and read here for ever, but within a few months I had hot words with the keeper of my lodgings. She was no more than an ale-wife but she dressed as if she were in the very eye of fashion, and such was her sauciness that once she came rashly upon me in my chamber without so much as knocking at my door. I was intent upon my studies, and since she could not perceive perfectly what I was doing she broke in with a speech concerning some trifle, while all the time glancing upon my papers.

'What is this,' she asked me, 'that you are drawing with your pen? It looks like some witchcraft.'

'I know nothing of such things, Mistress Agglintino.'

'Oh? Is that so? Well, in my opinion –'

'What do I care for your rash opinions?'

'Not a fart?' She laughed too loudly.

'Less than a fart. Less than nothing.' Even as I spoke my anger grew higher than before. 'And how dare you burst in upon me?'

'I am not afraid of you,' she replied, fingering the lace upon her russet petticoat as I rose from my desk. 'I am afraid of no man. No man whatsoever.'

'There is little enough to be afraid of, mistress. But I will not have my papers overlooked, or my work become a mockery. I will not.'

'Work?' she said. 'Now that I have looked closer, I see that these are nothing but student scribblings.'

At that I flew into a desperate rage, and all at once gave notice to quit. On the following day I moved into a tenement at the corner of Billiter Lane and Fenchurch Street; it had been lately rebuilt and was known as the New Rents, but there were old damps and agues steaming from it which sent me away soon enough.

So now you find me once again in my own world, far removed from the blue expanse of Tartary and the red domains of Germania or Italia. *Theatrum orbis terrarum* has been taken away, bound up within its press and locked in a chest, and now before you I have unrolled another, with its own ebbs and floods, its marks and dangers – the great globe of London, that is, which I have circumnavigated through all these years. From Billiter Lane I moved once more back to the west and found lodgings for myself in Sea-cole Lane near the glass-house on Saffron Hill, which was very serviceable to my exercises in perspective. Yet I need no glass or compass to remember my way through that lane where I once lived! It runs down into Fleet Lane but not before it turns into another called Wind-again Lane, which is so named because it stops at the Fleet Brook and there is no way over. So back again and, in imagination, join me as we tread a few paces northward to Holborn Bridge and Snow Hill where there stands the conduit. Then, stepping southward, retrace the ditches of Fleet Lane by the very wall of the prison and then go on to Fleet Bridge and the City

Wall. Go on, go on! All is now as it was then, and will always be, for the city is so compacted of virtues and humours that it can neither decay nor die. Look, it is all around you.

For the past twenty years or more I have walked among the draymen and the car-men, the merchants and the idle people, the rakehells and the porters; I know the cassocks and the ruffs, the caps and the periwigs; I know the hospitals for the poor and the fair churches for the rich. I know the wards of Portsoken and Downegate, where there are many murders; of Langborne and Billingsgate, where those commonly known as jarkmen and courtesy-men are to be found; of Candlewick Street and Walbroke, which are notorious for suicides; of Vintry and Cordwainer, where there are crimes not to be mentioned. I know Ratcliffe, Limehouse, Whitechapel, St Katherine, Stretford, Hogston, Sordycke and all those sad regions beyond the walls. It was in Thames Street I met a female, in Tower Street that I courted her, and in St Dunstan that I married her. In Crutched Friars I buried my still-born children, two male and one female, and beyond the postern gate in the Minories I laid my brothers in the earth.

Yet within this city of death I hear again the cries for *Cherries ripe, apples fine*, for *Fine Seville oranges* and *Ripe hartychokes*, for scarves and rushes and kindling wood. I know where to find a pair of gloves or a pair of spectacles, a painter's easel or a barber's comb, a trumpet or a close-stool. I know such places of common assembly as the ordinaries and the gaming-houses, the cockpits and the bowling alleys. I know the haberdashers of London Bridge and the goldsmiths of West Cheap, the grocers of Bucklersbury and the drapers of Watling Street, the hosiers of Cordwainer Street and the shoemakers of London Wall, the skinners of Walbroke and the ironmongers of Old Jewry. Wherewithall there rises such a noise of tumbrils and carts, such a thundering of coaches and chariots, with hammers beating in one place and tubs being hooped in another, with men and women and children in such shoals, that I might be in the belly of the monster Leviathan. Yet it was here, even here, that I conducted my studies philosophical and experimental; among the clamour, and almost in the very midst of the stinking crowd, I searched within the bright glass of nature and found the exhalations of the *spiritus mundi*.

I am now removed to a house in Clerkenwell with my wife and household, and have been these last fifteen years (my father, being feeble and frail to the last degree, is lodged within a charity). It is in a place of healthfulness, close by Clerkenwell Green and to the side of Turnmill Street where the clerks' well is still to be found; my garden at the back slopes downward to the Fleet and to the north are the fields of Hockley where the archers shoot at their targets. But it is an ancient, rambling pile, and would require another Minos to trace its regions, with its bedchambers and by-rooms and passages and parlours and other rooms severally partitioned. Here I sit in my library, on the upper storey, with my papers scattered around me. For this is the room in which all my labours and pains have been bestowed to win glory for my native country, and where I have pored over diverse manuscripts and pamphlets and other printed matter. Close beside this chamber, across the upper landing, is my laboratory with all the necessary vessels, some of earth, some of metal, some of glass, and some of mixed stuff; here are my retorts and receivers for the purposes of pyrotechnia, so that the walls and ceiling are now heavily smoked by my fiery studies. I have a little partition wall here also, beyond which is my storehouse replenished with chemical stuff and such curiosities as may advance my art, viz. one great bladder with about four pounds' weight of a very sweet substance like a brown-ish gum. Here, too, are bags containing certain powders together with leaden caskets holding glasses of liquid for the greater service and profit of my studies. There is also a transparent tube here, to be mightily covered by earth and dung. Of which nothing more may be revealed at this time.

Yet there are few things in this house, few things in this kingdom, that can compare with my library. Here are my globes of Gerardus Mercator's best making – though with my own hand I have set down upon them certain reformations both geographical and celestial, such as the places and motions of several comets that I have observed. Here also is my hour-glass to measure the time of my studies justly, and the universal astrolabe new minted by Thomas Hill in Cheapside. But my true glory lies within my books: printed or anciently written, bound or unbound, there are near four thousand of them. Some are in Greek, some in Latin, some in our native tongue, and yet all found by me, yes, found and gathered even when I was ready to die by false accusation of magic in Queen Mary's reign. Some of these hardly gotten monuments were taken in a manner out of the dunghill, since they were found by me in the corner of despoiled churches or monasteries where they were close to ruin from rotting away. Some came from a great case or frame of boxes which I took up from the decayed library of an ancient house (still lying desolate and waste at this very hour, beyond Pinner): each had their peculiar titles noted on the forepart of the boxes with chalk only, yet at the sight of them my heart leapt up. I knew them to contain hundreds of very rare evidences, which now I keep here in stalls and presses or locked within great barred chests. For their exact copying, and for my own writings, I need a plentiful supply of pens and inks; so here, at my left hand, are quills of all sorts. When the ink runs down the hollow trunk of my pen, then on this writing-table, with all my notes scattered about me, I begin to chronicle marvels.

But I need not tell you that there are also marvels within my books – among them wonderful and rare works by Zoroaster, Orpheus, and Hermes Trismegistus, as well as the sheets of old ephemerides. This room has become a very university or academy for scholars of diverse sorts, and there are such writings here as are above price, viz. Reuchlin his *De verbo mirifico* and *De arte cabalistica*, Brunschwick's *Book of Distillation*, *The New Pearl of Great Worth* set forth by Petrus Bonus of Pola but newly edited by Janus Lacinius, Cornelius Agrippa his renowned *De occultia philosophia*, *De incantationibus* by Pomponazzi, the *Corpus Hermeticum* collected by Turnebus as well as *Clavicula Solomonis* and *The Sun of Perfection*, which are both very useful and pleasant to read. Nor can I forget that most precious jewel of other men's labours which I have yet recovered, Trithemius his *Steganographia*. Neither will I omit the wonderful and divine sciences which are published forth by

Paracelsus himself, or the connections therewithal to be traced through *De harmonia mundi* of Francesco Giorgi, *De institutione musicae* of Boethius, and Paciolus his *De divina proportione*. These are not to be found for money at any market or in any stationer's shop, since in truth they are works for secret study.

Among these bound volumes lie fair copies of my own writings which, for the everlasting memory of men, are marked with my London seal of Hermes. I have not spent these many years in composing riddles or merry tales, but have rather thought continually of the generations yet to come. And just as the levels of the cosmos are to be known as elemental, intellectual and celestial, so have I placed my own works in varying degrees of art: from those which are suited to the best understanding of mechanics, such as *The Elements of Geometry* and *Mathematical Preface* (here I include *General and Rare Memorials Pertaining to the Perfect Art of Navigation*, together with sundry volumes in horology, perspective, geometry and other arts), to those which are framed for the comprehension of the wise, such as my *Propodeumata Aphoristica*, leading ever upwards to those most excellent and valuable studies which I keep here beside me and are known only as *Liber Mysteriorum*. The scope of my enterprise is so great that, as to this time, it has never to my knowledge by any been achieved; that is why I must keep my papers in closed chests within my study, away from the eyes or tongues of vulgar sophisters. It is hard in these our dreary days to win any due or common credit for work in rare arts: so, since I can in no way rely upon the testimony of my countrymen, I join myself here with my ancestors and place my own work beside theirs. When I consider the rash, lewd, fond and most untrue fables conceived of me and my philosophical studies, I find my refuge from bleating tongues here in my library where all the ages lie silently before me. It is my *quietus est*, my pass-port (as they say) to freedom. Where is liberty to be found but in the memory and the contemplation of the past?

Of course not all is known or can be known, and even of our own kingdom much is lost, yet I have by me here *Historia Regum Britanniae*, together with various manuscripts concerning the past of Britain collected by Nennius and Geoffrey of Monmouth. I once had a book – I do not know what has become of it because it was taken from me when I was clapped up in the Tower as a conjuror, but I can see it now before me. It was a short, thick old volume with two clasps, printed *anno* 1517, and it gave some account of the ancient places long buried within this island and now so many lost cities under ground. That wonderful book was stolen, as I say, but the loss is as nothing compared with the general destruction and burning and spoiling of so many notable libraries in the reign of King Henry; the whole stock and store of our past was close to utter extinction, and our antique learning was used to serve the jakes, or scour candlesticks, or rub boots. What I have kept and preserved here are the notable jewels which I have found scattered across the land, so that in this library lies something of the treasure of Britain's antiquity, the everlasting seeds of its continual excellence, the remnants of a once incredible store of the passing excellent work of our forefathers. To Britain's shore once came the giants and, afterwards, those who escaped from the deluge of Atlantis. Their great truths must never be forsaken.

That is why, in order to become a very excellent scholar and a learned man, it is necessary to find the path towards learning through books; otherwise it were as well to be a sophister, a quack or an empiric rather than a philosopher. There are those who say that learning effeminates a man, dims his sight, weakens his brain and engenders a thousand diseases; Aristotle himself tells us, '*Nulla est magna scientia absque mixtura dementiae*', which is as much as to say, 'There is no excellent knowledge without mixture of madness'. But I deny even Aristotle in this, since he who has learning holds the flower of the sun, the perfect ruby, the elixir, the magisterium. It is the true stone, the home of the glorified spirit, the virtue of the soul of the world.

Books do not perish like humankind. Of course we commonly see them broken in the haberdasher's shop when only a few months before they lay bound on the stationer's stall; these are not true works, but mere trash and newfangleness for the vulgar. There are thousands of such gewgaws and toys which people have in

66

their chambers, or which they keep upon their shelves, believing that they are precious things, when they are the mere passing follies of the passing time and of no more value than papers gathered up from some dunghill or raked by chance out of the kennel. True books are filled with the power of the understanding which is the inheritance of the ages: you may take up a book in time, but you read it in eternity. Look upon this text here, *Ars Notoria*, perfected from the Greek by Master Matthew – note how every word signifies the quiddity of the substance, and how every sentence signifies its form. What learning this is (even in a latter and doting age of the world) when every line may reveal how the secret and unknown forms of things are knit up in their originals! Yet this is not for those with mere cabbalistical brains, who see nothing but mysteries and read nothing except to fall upon some revelation; out of one root comes the wild olive as well as the sweet, and these men do nothing more than gape and whisper 'Micma' or 'Fisis' or 'Gohulim' without understanding the meaning of the sacred names.

But I have found the source of all that wisdom. I drink at the true fountain because here I have around me the inheritance of our island. Just as I may contemplate the portrait of Paracelsus upon my wall, and send his image through these pages so that it may be seen as a glimmering light by those who turn their eyes this way – so can I distil the very essence of the books around me and impart it to the world. These volumes will be a continual silent presence not only for me, but for the posterity of many ages. It is vulgarly said and believed that there are spirits who live in private houses and who inhabit old walls or stairs of wood; yet if there is a spirit in this library, it is the spirit of past ages. There are some who mock and condemn me for living within the past, but they are far off the mark; like the navigator who charts his course by the aid of the glistening fixed stars, those who understand past ages do then master the present. Like changeable silk which turned to the sun has many colours, and turned back from the light has none, so does the present day contain all the hues and shades of times long gone which are visible only to one who looks upon them correctly.

So I sit here at the great table in the middle of my library room, retired from the multitude and haunts of the world; with my books I am preserved in safety from all follies and assaults, and thus I become more truly myself. I am at peace.

Yet I am not so foolish as to ignore the teaching of the great masters, Pico della Mirandola and Hermes Trismegistus among them, when they assert the following: that to be myself is to be the world, to look into myself is to look into the world, to know myself is to know the world. The human form is more powerful than the sun because it contains the sun, more beautiful than the heavens because it contains the heavens, and he who sees it truly is richer than any king, for he has the entire art and understanding of the earth. No, not my poor mortal body, not this poor shambling thing of fifty years' growth, but the true spiritual body with which I am endowed: it is this which thirsts for learning and rises into glory when I sit among my books.

★

I went into my garden to take some air after the sweet mustiness of my library, and had just walked down towards the edge of the Fleet where herbs grow when I heard noises much like those of a man talking in his sleep. They came from a little enclosure of baked brick framed like the walls of a house, and when I stepped in front of the open side of it I leapt back at the sight of a man in a threadbare black coat unbuttoned and open before his breast. He wore a filthy foul cloth on his head, being cut for the purpose with a narrow place to put out his face. He raised his head and for a moment looked at me, without his eyes blinking.

'Oh master,' he cried, 'I was resting myself by the riverside here. You seem a gentleman of good worship, so pity me.' I said nothing, but with my foot touched the felt hat that he had left upon the ground, moving it towards him. 'I have the grievous and painful disease called the falling sickness,' he continued. 'I fell down on my backside, and here I have lain all the night.'

'You have no disease,' I replied, 'that could not be cured at the whipping pillar.'

'Oh dear God, sir, I feel as if I were born there since I am used so badly by all. My name is Philip Jennings, and I have had the falling sickness eight years. I can get no remedy for the same, since I have it by kind. My father had it before me.' He interested me a little more now; I had once read a very learned work upon the nature of diseases which we inherit. 'Give me a penny for God's sake, sir, to keep me a true man.'

'Surely you are not brought to so low a sail,' I replied, stepping back at the stench of him, 'that you cannot steer your way to a charitable church door?'

'Oh, I know all the churches. I know St Stephen in Coleman Street, St Martin's at Ludgate, St Leonard's in Foster Lane, but all turn me away with no more than a flea in my ear.'

'And no doubt they made threats to burn you through the ear also? Is that not their way?'

'Well you know, sir, these priests have heads higher than their hats. The greatest clerks are not the wisest men.'

I did not assent to this. 'You are not a foolish man,' I said, 'despite your apparel. How have you lived in this sad world?'

'I go solitary walking, with no man to comfort me, but only a dog.' There was indeed a bundle of skin and bones nestling close up to him, which stirred now that he touched it. 'We eat what we can. It is forbidden to kill kites and ravens in this city because they devour the filthiness of the streets, so they are our companions.'

I felt a little pity for him then. 'I can give you some rye brown bread –'

'Better porridge than no repast, as they say. Better an old bone than an empty plate.'

'You give great words,' I replied, laughing. 'There may also be a hot pie for you and your dog.'

'Then I will leave you afterwards. I will bing Romeville.'

'What was that?'

'It is the canting speech, sir. I said that I will leave London.'

These strange words interested me. 'Cant me some more, good canter.'

'I couched a hogshead in a skipper this darkmans.'

'Which signifies?'

'I lay me down to sleep in this shed last night. Now big me a waste to the highpad, the ruffmans is by.'

'And that?' These words were like some ancient tongue of the country, unknown to me.

'It is as much as to say, well, let me go past to the highway. The woods are at hand.'

'I do not understand these words, or the reasoning for them. Tell me something of their age, and of their origin.'

'I cannot say how old they are, or from where they came, but my father taught them to me, and his father did likewise, stretching far back. I give you a demonstration. Look upon this.' He pointed to his nose. 'A smelling cheat.' And then to his mouth. 'A gan.' And then to his eyes. 'Glaziers.' Then he lifted up his hands. 'Fambles.'

'Wait,' I said, 'wait till I fetch food for you.' I hurried back into the kitchen, where the servant-girl was already preparing the meal, and demanded from her plentiful bread and meat. I piled this upon a plate, but I also brought into the garden a piece of chalk and slate so that I might write down the words he spoke.

'Peck,' he said, holding up a lump of the meat I gave him. 'Pannam,' thus signifying the bread. 'Bene for my bufe. Good for my dog.' They both fell upon their food now, but when they had eaten heartily he wiped his mouth upon his filthy sleeve and continued. 'The lightmans is the day and darkmans is the night. Solomon is an altar and patrico a priest, while autem is canting for church.' All these I wrote down as he spoke. 'Glimmer is fire. It was bitter cold last night, sir, and I wished to put my prat in ken or libbege with new duds.'

'Which is to say?'

'I wished to put my buttocks in a house or bed with new clothes upon me.' He raised himself now a little, and patted his dog. 'I will not filch your bung,' said he, 'because you have fed us both. But do you have some lour? Can you translate this for me?'

'Money?'

'Which is so! Money! I need money!'

I went back into the house, and found some pennies left in the chimney corner; on returning to him I gave them with a right good will, for had he not opened to me a new language and thus a new world? 'There's for you,' I said. 'And what is the name of your dog?'

'Dickins, sir. He is very much like the Devil.'

He left me soon after, but not before I walked with him to the bank of the Fleet. 'There is a theory,' I said, 'that parallels, because they maintain diverse lines, can never join. Do you think it is true?'

'I understand none of that, sir. But I do know that you should not place a patch of fustian in a damask coat. I am not of your kind, and I must leave you.' At that he paused; taking some papers of close writing from the pocket of his ancient coat, he presented them to me with a smile. 'I have been wonderful troublesome to you, sir, and am without doubt much misliked –'

'No, no. It is not so.'

'But read these words I leave with you.' He said no more but went on his way with his dog, going by the side of the river and singing the old hanging tune, 'Fortune my foe, why dost thou frown on me?' I watched him until he was quite out of sight, and then with a sigh turned back to the house and went up again into my library.

★

Shall I tell you of my dreams? In my first dream I had a vision and show of many books, newly printed and of very strange argument; among them was one great volume, thick and in large quarto, which had on its first page my house as its title in great letters. In my second dream I was walking between Aldgate and the posterns on Tower Hill when a great tempest of mighty wind followed me, at which I said out loud to several great personages around me, 'I must ride to Clerkenwell; someone is writing upon a theme concerning me and my books.' In my third dream I knew that I was dead, and after my bowels were taken out I talked with diverse people of a future time. In my fourth dream I dreamed that my wife, Mistress Katherine Dee, had an abortion; I helped to find the dead birth within, one hour after I had caused her to be given myrrh in warmed wine, and the dead thing was a volume with a black cover which stuck to my fingers. In my fifth dream I found myself within an excellent little library room, which seemed in times past to have been the chamber of some student skilful in the holy stone; a name was in various places noted in letters of gold and silver, 'Petrus Baccalaureus Londoniensis', and among other manifold things written very fairly in this study were hieroglyphical notes on the houses, streets and churches of our city. Certain verses were inscribed over the door, viz.

Immortale Decus par gloriaque illi debentur
Cujus ab ingenio est discolor hic paries.

I look down at myself, and find myself with letters and words all upon me, and I know that I have been turned into a book . . .

There was a cry somewhere and I awoke. I must have poured out my eyes in this place, for I had closed them in a state between slumbering and waking without thinking to steal a nap. But I returned to myself in a moment. It was eleven before noon, and I had been called to dinner by Mrs Dee. I was hungry for my meat and was brisk in coming down the stairs into the hall where, to my delight, the table was already covered. I had long since dismissed any sullen drabs out of the kitchen, and now I have only good and clean servants to aid my wife. She sat opposite to me at the long table, and bowed her head meekly enough as I prayed for grace. Then I began to carve the veal and with great silence and gravity we began to eat our boiled meats, our conies, our pies and our tarts. There are but two courses with us for, as I have told Katherine Dee, too much bread and meat induce melancholy; hares are thought particularly to cause it, so they are banished from our table. Melancholy is cold and dry, and so melancholy men must refrain from fried meat or meat which has too much salt; they must also eat boiled meat rather than roasted. For the same reasons I abstain from the drinking of hot wines and, to preserve myself from distempered heaviness, I abjure cow milk, almond milk and the yolks of eggs. Katherine Dee knows the disposition of her husband and has full keeping of the foodstuffs: I give her money for the month and, having been trained by me in the secret virtues and seeds of all foods, she goes to the market with her maid and buys only good butter, cheese, capons, hogs and bacon.

'Did you see the maypole set up in Cow Lane?' she asked me as I drank my white wine opposite to her.

'I came back another way.' I had already determined to keep silent concerning the canting outcast in the garden, because I knew that it would disturb her.

'It is for the wedding. Did you know? The daughter of Grosseteste, the merchant, is to be married today.'

'So what of it?'

My wife was well tucked up in a russet petticoat, with a bare hem and no fringe, as I like her to be dressed with plainness; yet she had a red lace apron upon her, and she plucked at it with her hand as she spoke to me. 'Nothing, sir. Nothing at all. Some say she is fair, but I have always found her ill dressed. Who would have guessed it with the money in that quarter? No doubt many a man will envy her husband.' She continued plucking at her apron. 'And the maypole is very sumptuous, Doctor Dee. I have seen nothing like. Shall we go to see it? If you will?'

'Wife, can we go to the dinner which is set before us? Will you always be chattering and never quiet?'

'As it will please you, sir.' She was silent for a while as we set upon our meat. 'Husband,' she said soon afterwards, 'I pray you pull a piece of that capon. You eat nothing. You have not yet even tasted of these cabbages.'

I put my finger into the bowl and licked it. 'I cannot taste of them. They are so much peppered and salted.' I saw that I had put her in an ill humour, and it pleased me to provoke her a little. 'And what meat is this? It is the cut I love best, but it is marred. As Londoners say, God sends us the meat and the Devil cooks it.' I had scored a notable hit. 'It is stuffed with garlic to hide the rottenness: if I touch it now, I will smell for three days after. You learn nothing. It is a great shame.'

'If it pleases you to speak so, Doctor Dee, then I can say nothing. But I have tried to do everything to the best.'

'Well, well, there has been talk enough. Now eat. You may talk after dinner.'

It is an excellent room to sit in for meat, having great oaken chests and chairs curiously carved in the old style; the walls are hung with painted cloths where several histories, as well as herbs and beasts, are stained. Here are the sorrows of Job, the opening of the seventh seal, and the building of Jerusalem, all of these a perpetual allegory by which we train our souls even as we eat upon our joint-stools. There is a fine chair in one corner, trimmed with crimson velvet and embroidered with gold, yet it is seldom used except for high company. When I was a boy we lay upon straw pallets with a log beneath as a bolster but now we lay our heads upon pillows, and we dine off pewter where once clay was fine enough. We have Turkey work, brass, soft linen, cupboards garnished with plate, and the chambers of our houses are so decorated with inlaid tables and carefully worked glass that they dazzle the eye on first entering. Well, well, the world turns; but there must also be a light within us to reflect the meaning of such changes.

I had been eating and thinking all the while, when my wife suddenly checked me with a laugh. 'What, sir, you love mustard so? It will make you a red nose and crimson face, without the help of any wine. But lord, how you drink it!'

I stared at her for a moment, yet I could not break her look of defiance. 'If the wine is bad, mistress, then naturally it inflames the passion.'

'The fault is not in the wine but in him who drinks it.' I said nothing, and I believe she repented. 'I will bring you cake-bread then, sir, which will draw the liquor like a sponge.'

When dinner was almost at an end, and these last dishes had been removed from the table, I washed my fingers in the bowl and then called for my book.

'What book?' said Katherine Dee pertly enough.

'Where I read yesterday after dinner. Did you not see it? Are you purblind?'

'Oh, do you mean your book of old fables which you enjoy by the fireside?'

'Not fables, madam. The acts of the ancient kings of England.'

74

'I put it away,' she replied. 'Away from the fumes of the meat you find so bad.'

She had a sharp tongue upon her still. 'Go to, gossip. Fetch me the book.' She did not budge from her seat. 'Have I not power to command in my own house?'

'As you will.'

'Well said. Then bring me my book.'

With a laugh she rose and went over to a chest, whereupon she opened it and with a flourish presented me with *Gesta Regum Britanniae*; then she sat down beside me on a close-stool to watch me read. But I was not to be granted peace. 'Oh,' she said after a few moments. 'A message came. Your father is still ill with fits of the ague.'

'It is an evil sickness,' I replied as I continued with my reading.

A few more moments passed. 'So tell me, husband. Shall we visit the maypole? It is good to walk after meat.'

'Enough!' I put down my book and, going into the passage, called for a chamber-pot to relieve myself. I retired into the little room next to the hall and, having pissed mightily, I intended to throw it forth at the window (for it had begun to rain) when I caught the savour of my urine in my nostrils; it had a high odour to it, like that of fresh cinnamon, and put me in mind at once of the wine I had taken the night before. But there was more virtue in it now, having been dissolved within me and then congealed again; it had become a humid exhalation from which the volatile substance had been removed and, if all moisture were finally to leave it, then at last it would become a stone. If it were to become a dry or powdery substance, in form a mineral, could it be used to fructify the land – as the urine of man is said to do – and in its sublime state generate a thousandfold? There was something here worthy of closer study, and so I took my pot up to my laboratory where I determined upon some further experiments of sublimation and fixation.

I am not some poor alchemist, new set up, with scarcely enough money to buy beechen coals for my furnace; over these years I have found or purchased all my instruments and substances, so that

I have no need to rake some dunghill for a few dirty specimens. But neither have I anything to do with the cthonic magic of the past which secreted itself in caves and woods: those were times of witches and hags, dwarfs and satyrs, conjurors and changelings, invoking the incubus, the spoor, the hell-wain, Boneless and other such bugs of the night and the mist. Into what blind and gross errors in old time we were led, thinking every merry word a very witchcraft and every old wife's tale a truth, viz. that the touch of an ashen bough causes giddiness in a viper's head, and that a bat lightly struck with the leaf of an elm tree loses his remembrance. But these are trifling matters of which I do not complain. Indeed there was a certain truth to them if they had, as they say, been viewed in the light – light being the bright path of life, by which the virtues of the sun and stars are generated within the world.

But if I am no moth-eaten alchemist, neither am I some newfangled astronomer who feigns eccentrics and epicycles and suchlike in order to save the phenomena, when he knows full well that there are no such engines within the orbs. Each of them follows the newest way, which is not ever the nearest way: some going over the stile when the gate is open, and others keeping the beaten path when they may cross better by the fields. They are like eager wolves that bark at the moon when they cannot reach it – even though, if they did but know it, the very same moon, and stars, and all the firmament, lie within their own selves.

Shall we then look upon the heavens as a wolf, or an ox, or an ass does? No, it cannot be. Yet to find or receive some inkling, glimpse or beam of what are the radical truths, it is necessary to unite astronomy with astrology, yes, even with alchemy which is known as *astronomia inferior*; by so doing we may in the method of Pythagoras restore the ternary of these arts to unity or One. Such is the infinite desire of knowledge and, as I have proved for myself, such is the incredible power of man's search and capacity: it is the learning of that which lives for ever and not of that which passes through time. No doubt these studies are dispraised by those who understand them not, but there must come an age when all true lovers of wisdom turn their hands and bend their minds to these doctrines.

Here is the eternal connection. In our astronomy we view the seven planets in their eternal order, Jupiter, Saturn, Mars, Sol, Venus, Mercury and the moon, while in our experiments we proceed through the seven alchemical doors, calcination, fixation, solution, distillation, sublimation, separation and projection. Then in astrology we compound the two, by scrutinizing the secret influences of the planets and the stars while at the same time loosening the chains of each element in this elemental world. The stars do live and, through the *spiritus mundi*, influence us; there is sympathy or disharmony between all living things, and to gain mastery over this point is to exercise control over the entire world. There is nothing done in the lower world which is not controlled by the powers above, nothing moved or changed in the sublunary sphere except with the aid of the incorruptible heavens whose emblems and messengers are the planets and stars. Thus when the moon lies between the twenty-eighth degree of Taurus and the eleventh of Gemini, then is the time to search for the hidden seeds of life. I have demonstrated before this time that when Saturn and the moon are three score degrees of the zodiac apart, then it is good to gather those seeds and bury them deep within the warm earth. The natural beams of the lighted stars are to be found at work equally in both spheres, in things visible and invisible, at all times and in every horizon assigned. So may these beams be distilled and, like the morning dew, refresh and excite new life.

What is above also lies below; what is below is also above. And here we approach upon our knees another great secret: the sun, gold, and the heart of man are analogous. If I control the light and the heart's passions, then I can begin to discover or refine the material substance of gold. If I wish to make that metal, therefore, I must make my own self pure and become (as it were) an agent of the light which dwells in all things. Yet if I can create the most precious and sacred substance from the mere dross of the world, then in similar manner I must proclaim how within the mortal world of decay and within our own selves there is that which is constant, unchangeable and incorruptible.

I have done so many rare and precious experiments upon this

truth that I cannot reckon up all of them now. So many strange speculations and incredible practices have been made manifest to me that to speak of the objects created from smoke or vapour, of the secret balances of sulphur and mercury, of the consummation of the chrysolite and beryl, would be a task fit only for the great Hermes Trismegistus himself. I will say only this. While mortal sense rules within us, so gross is our comprehension and dull our sight that it is necessary to curb our outward faculties and look towards the inward world; therewithall you will see yourself as a being made of light. The true man is astral man, containing within him not the star-demon (as some commentators say) but the material of divinity itself. If in the event you do not therefore make yourself equal to God, you cannot know God – like is intelligible only to like. Man was once, and will again, be God. And so I say once more: at death material and corruptible things will become invisible and, just as the dross of the world can in the chemical wedding be turned to gold, so can we return to light. Yet there is a greater mystery than all; for what if it were possible, before death ever came, to assume that light and mingle with the godhead? Why, then I might arise, climb, ascend and mount up to behold in the glass of Creation the form of forms, the exemplar number of all things numerable. Then I might foresee great particular events long before their coming, or view the passages of antiquity as if standing there in bodily shape from everlasting to everlasting. But more than this is there, and still more: why, I might use that light to quicken life itself within my own hands. I have beside me a glass vessel prepared and waiting for my little man, but of this no more can be said or written. Oh comfortable allurement, oh ravishing persuasion, to deal with a science whose subject is so ancient, so pure, so excellent, so surmounting all creatures in their distinct parts, properties, natures and virtues, so implicate with order and absolute number!

Enough. I will use no tedious discourses or colour of rhetoric which, though they are deemed courtly by the lowly sort, are by no means necessary. The purest emerald shines brightest when it has no oil. It has grown twilight gloomy, and a few moments ago there was a clap of thunder with some lightning. I take up the pages which the canting beggar gave to me in the garden, but can see only a certain kind of curious writing in the English tongue. There are the words 'house' and 'father', all closely inscribed, but in the gathering darkness I can read nothing more. So I light my candle and watch its fire. As the darkness is lifted the wax is consumed: the substance does not die, but is transformed into flame. This is the final lesson. By means of that fire the material form of the candle before me rises into its spiritual being. It has become a light and a shining within this poor shambling room, my library.

THREE

I REMEMBER VERY little about my childhood. Sometimes it is hard to believe that I had one at all. Even if I was lying on my deathbed, I doubt that I would recall anything more distinctly; it would be as if I had come into being, and passed away, within one night. Yet often, when I close my eyes, I see certain streets or buildings which I must have visited once. Then again, in my dreams, I recognize the faces of people who are talking to me. Oh yes, I do remember something. I remember a violet colour. I remember the dust in the air, when a ray of sun came through the glass. 'I suppose,' I said, 'it must have been a window.' I had never talked about myself in this way before; it was as if the silence of the old house disturbed me, or provoked me, and I listened to my voice as it fell back into the darkness and was covered by it.

'I wonder why it is that you remember so little.' Daniel Moore and I were sitting in the ground-floor room, a few days after I had seen him in Charlotte Street; it was a fine summer evening, and the white walls seemed to be trembling in the light.

'I was probably a very dull child.'

'No. It's something more than that. You have such little curiosity about yourself. Or about your life. It's as if you were trying to ignore it.'

'You never mention such things, either.'

'Ah, but that's different. I am intensely curious about myself.' He looked away for a moment. 'I have almost an obsession about it, which is why I say nothing.'

Even as he spoke, I was thinking of that night when I saw him dressed in women's clothes. I could think of very little else as we talked together: it was as if someone were sitting with him, waiting for the opportunity to break into our conversation. There is a theory that the first human being was androgynous; so when I looked at Daniel, was I looking at some quest for the original state of the world? 'Let me get you a drink,' was all I said. I went out into the kitchen, and looked with something like pleasure at the pile of shining plates, the gleaming knives, and the shelves neatly stacked with food. In fact I could not quite remember placing everything so carefully, or polishing the crockery so brightly. But where were the wine and the whisky? The bottles had been moved, and it took me a moment to locate them in a cupboard beneath the sink. I was becoming absent-minded, and I pinched myself very hard before returning to Daniel. 'I wish I had your passion,' I said as I poured him his usual whisky.

'But you do. You have a passion for some more general past. You have a passion for your work.'

'And now you're going to tell me that I'm escaping from myself. Or that I'm avoiding the present.' He said nothing, but began examining his finely cut fingernails. 'Well, you would be right. I can't bear to look at myself. Or look *into* myself. I really don't believe that there's anything there, just a space out of which a few words emerge from time to time. And perhaps that's why I never see people properly. I have never really seen myself.'

'I think it's more interesting than that.' He got up from his chair and went over to the wall, tracing a narrow crack in it with his forefinger. 'I suspect that, without realizing it, you are reinventing yourself. It's as if you were trying to create some new family. Some new inheritance. And so you have forgotten your own past.'

I replied more angrily than I expected. 'But what about you? What do you remember?'

'Oh, I remember everything. I remember sitting up in my pram. I remember walking for the first time. I remember hiding under the dining-room table.' He noticed my look of surprise. 'It's not that unusual, you know.' He paused, and once again I could feel the presence of the woman he had become by putting on the red dress and the blonde wig. 'I suppose that nothing has been quite the same since.'

'So you miss being a child?'

'Doesn't everyone? Everyone except you?' He was drinking his whisky too quickly. 'Do you remember that bridge you saw across the Thames?'

'Of course.'

'I have a theory about that. I don't suppose you'd like to hear it?' His usual sceptical, even supercilious, manner had for the moment disappeared.

'Has it something to do with your Moravians, or whatever they were called?'

He pretended to ignore me. 'I think time may be a substance as real as fire or water. It can change shape. It can move to a different position. Do you see what I'm getting at?'

'I'm not sure.'

'That was your bridge. It was a part of time that had stopped.' He helped himself to another drink. 'Have you ever wondered why this area is so peculiar?'

'So you've noticed it, too.'

'It's because all the time has flowed here, into this house, and there is none left outside. You hold all the time in this place.' I was too surprised to say anything at all. 'And there is another theory, as well. That there are some dimensions in which time can travel backwards.'

'So I'm over before I've begun?'

'Isn't that the title of a song?'

'I don't remember.' We looked at each other expectantly, and I knew that I had to speak. 'I saw you the other night, Daniel.'

'I don't know what you mean.'

'I saw you in Charlotte Street.'

For a moment he held on to the edge of the chair very tightly. 'I could give you a very good theoretical explanation,' he said. 'There was a group of radicals who used to dress up as a protest against Old Corruption. It's a very ancient tradition.' I looked at him in astonishment, and then I began to laugh. 'I'm glad you can see the funny side,' he said. But he would not meet my gaze, and stared into his drink. 'Identity is a very strange thing, Matthew, and I can't begin to explain it. I told you I was intensely curious about myself, but I still haven't really found the clue to the mystery. In that respect, at least, we resemble each other. In earlier times no one gave such matters any thought, perhaps because they were part of an orderly universe –'

'Oh no. People have always wondered.'

'– but we are so puzzled. Wouldn't it be nice to return to some of the old theories? Soul and body? The four humours?'

'Oh, they never worked.'

'Of course they did. Everything works in its own period. Don't you think that people were cured by medieval doctors, soaking up black melancholy bile with white saltpetre? We could no more use their remedies than they could use ours, but they did work once. That's what you have to remember. Of course some people say that they might work again.' He was paying very little attention to me now, and seemed to be looking at something in the corner of the room. 'I suppose that's why so many are interested in magic. Sexual magic.'

'What?'

He seemed embarrassed, almost furtive, for a moment. 'Nothing. I was really thinking about my interest in – what you saw. I have never understood it properly. Sometimes I feel as if I'm excavating some lost city within myself. Do you know what I mean?' He got up from his chair, and started pacing around me. 'Why does everything have to be so secret, so deeply buried? It's like the sealed window upstairs.' He stopped. 'I'm sure there must be a sealed window here, aren't you?' He began walking around the room again, even more agitated than before. 'We think that there must be some secret part of us which is made of gold. Which does not rust, and which is not corrupted. Do you know the quotation? And yet, if we found it, it would probably be fool's gold.' He went over to one of the old walls, and ran his delicate hand across its mottled stone texture. 'When I dress up, I must look a fool. And yet it is part of me. It gives me the strangest pleasure. It is like sex, without having sex. I don't understand it at all.'

I did not want to hear any more about his concealed life, and I tried to divert him. 'Is it true what you said about the radicals?'

He turned round and faced me. 'Oh yes. London breeds strange habits. In the eighteenth century a group of Marjories, as they called themselves, started fires at Tyburn and burned down the gallows. That's why the executions were switched to Newgate.' He smiled now, and went back to his chair. 'I'm afraid I'm much more docile.'

I sensed that he was still holding something back but, as I said, I did not want to get too close to the source of his obsession; it would have been too painful, too extreme. He sensed my nervousness, and waved his hand in the air as if he were dismissing the subject. 'Now,' he said, 'in real ghost stories they always explore the attic of the old house.'

'But there is no attic.'

'Oh. What about the basement?'

'We've done the basement already.'

'That's true. A room under the stairs?'

'Non-existent.'

'I think you will find at least a cupboard.'

We went into the hallway and there, as he predicted, was some hollow panelling just beneath the staircase; I had not noticed a small catch on the side, but Daniel knelt down and unfastened it at once. It was almost as if he had not needed to look for it. 'How did you know it was there?' I asked him.

'There is always a cupboard under the stairs. Haven't you read Lady Cynthia Asquith?' But at that moment I realized he knew this house very well. 'Ah,' he said, more quickly now. 'Pipes. I wonder if you get your water from the old Fleet River. That would account for your behaviour.'

'What behaviour?'

'Hello, what's this?' He pulled out, with some difficulty, a wooden box with a black cloth laid across it. I turned away as he uncovered it. 'Toys,' he said. 'A child's toys.' I closed my eyes for a moment. When I turned round again, he was taking out a small cardboard fish with a tin hook attached to it; there was a glove puppet beside it, and a spinning-top. I picked up a small book, the pages of which were made from some kind of shiny cloth. 'I

84

remember this,' I said, looking at the letter 'D' which had a child climbing upon it.

'What?'

'I do remember something about my childhood now. These are my toys. But what are they doing in this house?'

At that moment there was a loud knock upon the front door, and both of us were so startled that for an instant we clutched each other. 'Matthew! Matthew Palmer! Where's my little sprout?' It was my mother, calling through the letterbox, and in my dismay I quickly brushed the toys back into the cupboard and closed it: I did not want her to see them in my hands. Daniel stood up, and seemed unaccountably nervous as I went over to the door; my mother offered me her cheek to kiss, and I could smell the Chanel upon her skin. It was the same perfume she had used when I was a child. 'The lover is parking,' she said. 'He'll probably never get here.' I introduced her to Daniel, and she looked at him with the strangest mixture of curiosity and distaste. 'Haven't I seen you before?' she asked him.

'Not as far as I know.'

'But there's something familiar about you.' She seemed puzzled. 'It will come to me in a minute.'

Geoffrey suddenly arrived in the hallway, and Daniel took advantage of the temporary confusion to leave. Once again he seemed embarrassed, and my mother watched him go with a somewhat grim expression. I noticed then how old she had become; she had lost weight, and her right hand shook slightly. 'Now,' she said. 'Do show me and the lover around.'

I went to the door and watched Daniel as he opened the gate and, without looking back, hurried down Cloak Lane. It suddenly occurred to me to walk around the side of the house: I looked up and there, on the top storey, was a window sealed with brick. He had known about it, just as he had known about the cupboard under the stairs. It was clear to me now that he was acquainted with this house, and might even have been deliberately leading me towards my old toys. But how was such a thing possible? How could he have known?

'Your father was such a dark horse,' my mother said as I came back into the hall. 'Fancy keeping this to himself.' She walked into the ground-floor room as nonchalantly as if she owned the place herself. 'I suppose he used it for a bit on the side.'

'I don't think, mother, it's that sort of house.'

'How would you know?' At moments like this I recognized the depth of her animosity towards my father and even myself; it was as if we had been involved in some act of vengeance or violence against her. 'Well, never mind. Where's the lover gone?' I turned round, but Geoffrey had disappeared. Nothing in this house seemed to stay in the same place.

'Just poking around,' he said. He had gone up the stairs without us, and I resented his familiarity in my father's house. 'You'll probably get a good price for it.'

'I'm not putting it on the market. I'm going to live here.'

I enjoyed announcing my intention so flatly, and I was delighted to see the expression of fear upon my mother's face. 'But you're not going to sell up in Ealing?' she asked me very quickly.

I hesitated for a few seconds, unwilling to reassure her. 'Of course not. It's yours.'

'That's a good boy.' She seemed to breathe more easily, and took a pocket mirror out of her handbag; she peered into it, and brushed some powder from her face. I saw it falling on to the old stone floor. 'Well, my darling, you're a better man than your father. I'll give you that.' I wanted to ask her about the toys I had just found, but I could not bear to mention my childhood to her. 'Now will you show me the house, please?'

The trouble did not begin until we reached the top floor. 'There's a lot of dust up here,' she said. 'Typical of your father.' She waved a hand in front of her, as if she were scaring away a fly or wasp; but I could see nothing. We went downstairs to the next floor and, to my surprise, I realized that there was no dust at all in my own bedroom; it looked as if it had been swept clean in preparation for my arrival. Geoffrey had adopted his professional role as a surveyor, for want of anything better to do, and was busily tapping the walls and scrutinizing the ceiling. My mother seemed to enjoy the process: it was as if the house, and therefore my father, was being subjected to some long-overdue judgement.

'What was that?' she said.

'What?'

'I thought I saw something over there.' She pointed, strangely enough, towards the wall beneath my window.

'It must have been a fly,' I said. 'A summer fly.'

But then, when we descended the stairs to the ground floor, she started back again in horror. 'Something just moved again.' She was looking at that part of the hallway in front of the basement door. 'Did you see it? It was like some creature. Some little thing.'

Geoffrey was laughing at her. 'It's the old girl's eyes. All sorts of bits and pieces floating in them at her age.'

She was looking at me accusingly, as if I were responsible for these distortions in her vision. 'Come on,' she said. 'Let's finish the grand tour.'

I approached the basement with some caution, with the momentary fear that my mother had glimpsed a mouse or even a rat. I shook the handle as loudly as I could, and then opened the door. 'Come down here,' I told her. 'This also has been one of the dark places of the earth.'

I don't know why I said this: she managed to laugh, but I suppose I was pleased by the horror that passed over her face. She followed me down the stairs, but when she reached the last of them and stood within the basement itself, she looked around in fear. 'There *is* something here,' she said. 'It's just as if it were in the corner of my eye, but it's not in my eye. It's here.' Then, roughly pushing past Geoffrey, she retreated back up the stairs.

He turned to look at her in astonishment. 'It's not like your old mum,' he said. I conducted him around the basement, while explaining Daniel's theory that this was once the ground floor of a house which had gradually sunk into the earth. He was particularly intrigued by this, and went over to look at the marks above the sealed door. 'They're not made by a surveyor,' he said. 'They don't mean anything at all.'

I suddenly felt very tired, and turned to leave. Reluctantly he followed me up into the hall, where we found my mother sitting on the stairs. 'What has the lover been telling you?' She tried to sound light-hearted, but quite failed to do so. There was an expression upon her face, at once preoccupied and vindictive, that I had never seen before.

'I was giving him a surveyor's judgement.'

'I wouldn't talk to him about judgement, if I were you.' She was brushing something off her sleeve, with a look of disgust. 'It might frighten the little sprout.' Now she stared down at me, with the same look. 'They say that beetles thrive on dirt. Is that why you've got so many of them? This is a filthy house. Something happened here, didn't it? Something smelling of filth and shit. I can smell your father here.' I was climbing the stairs, in order to help her, but she put her arms out to ward me off. 'You smell of him too,' she said. 'You always did.' Now she got up, and gazed at me with such ferocity that I expected her to hit me. I put my hand up to shield my face, and she laughed. 'Don't worry,' she said. 'Your father is still looking after you, isn't he?' She went down to Geoffrey, who took her arm and led her gently out of the house without saying anything.

I was so shaken that I went up to my room and lay on the bed, looking at nothing in particular. What had suddenly aroused all this anger and madness? I went over to the window; they were standing at the bottom of Cloak Lane. Geoffrey had his arm round her; they were talking quietly together and looking back at the house with something like fear.

I took a bath at once, and scrubbed myself clean with an old-fashioned brush I found there. Then I lay in the water as I would lie upon a bed, but there was so much mist and steam around me that I seemed to be lying in some tube of opaque glass as the water poured over my face and limbs. And, yes, it was a dream, since I put out my arm and touched the glass with my barely formed fingers. I struggled to get up, and a more terrible sensation overwhelmed me: what if it had been that creature she had seen here? What if something in the basement had goaded her to fury? I stepped carefully out of the bath, and wrapped a towel about me as gently as if I had entered some other kind of dream.

★

88

On the following morning I left for the National Archive Centre in Chancery Lane. I had often worked in that dark building just opposite Carnac Rents, and I had often been comforted by it; its familiar echoing presence, its subdued lighting, its muffled sounds, its scarred wooden desks, seemed to protect me and lead me towards my true self. Most of the old parish registers and rate-books were now on microfiche, but I still preferred to consult the bound volumes which had been placed in the Blair Room. The staff knew me well enough to let me wander there at will, and a quiet protracted search guided me to three leather-bound volumes which contained the records of the parish of St James, Clerkenwell, in the sixteenth century. I could hardly lift them from the shelves, and when I held them in my arms I savoured the stink of dust and age. It was as if I were lifting down corpses wrapped in their shrouds. And of course this was precisely what they contained – names, signatures, the long-dead set down in lists, lying one upon another just as they might have been buried under the ground. I am accustomed now to the peculiarities of sixteenth-century script, but even so it was hard to decipher some of the words scratched in an ink which had faded to the lightest brown.

A door opened behind me, and I could hear the footsteps of one who was coming closer to me. I did not turn round, but waited. 'Let me tell you an interesting story, Mr Palmer.' I knew the voice of Margaret Lucas very well; she was the archivist in charge of the Blair Room, a thin, almost skeletal woman who dressed in the most vivid colours. She also had a habit of saying the most extraordinary things – largely, I suspect, because she had no confidence in herself. She concealed herself from ordinary attention by always being surprising. 'Have you read Swedenborg, by any chance?'

I turned round, and tried to smile. 'I don't believe I have. No.' All the time my hands were lying across a deed written on parchment; I could feel the texture of the paper beneath my fingers, and it was like earth baking in the heat of this modern city.

'Oh, have you not? I happen to be something of an admirer. Dip into *Heaven and Hell*, and everything will be explained. But this is the point I'm getting to, Mr Palmer.' She had come round to the side of my desk, and I saw that she was wearing a purple two-piece outfit, with a scarf of bright blue loosely wrapped about her meagre neck. 'Swedenborg tells us that, after death, the human being is taken to the society where his love is.' I did not know what she meant and so great was my eagerness to carry on with my work that, without thinking, I had looked down again at the names in the old parish records. She did not seem to notice. 'He says that each of us goes to a house and to a family – not the same ones we possessed on earth, not them at all, but to the house and the family that correspond to our ruling passions. Whatever we wished for on earth we shall find after death.'

She was silent for a moment, and I was not sure how to reply. 'That's quite a coincidence,' I said. 'I'm looking for a house and family too.'

She examined the volume for a moment. 'In that case, Mr Palmer, I suggest you try the churchwarden's accounts first. You'll find them at the back.' The pages were heavy enough and as I turned them, year by year, it was as if I were uncovering the dead; in the sudden revelation of each page, I brought their names blinking into the light. 'There is a curious story attached to this, you see.' Margaret Lucas was still standing over me. 'There was a young man who used to come to the Blair Room a great deal. Did you ever see him? Short, and rather fat. Very shabbily dressed. His name was Dan Berry.' I shook my head. 'He used to do what you're doing now. Going through the registers and accounts. At first I thought he was a researcher, but it turned out to be something more private. He had a small notebook, and I could see that he had written down certain names. He told me that they were his ancestors. But not in the sense that you and I would mean it.' I stopped turning the pages, and looked up at her. 'He told me that the names came to him in dreams.'

'That is a mistake,' I said, 'a researcher would never make.'

'I'm not someone who believes in madness, Mr Palmer. I believe people can lose their normal identity for a while, but that is all. They simply regress. Now our friend Dan Berry was convinced that they were the names of his true family.'

I still had my hand upon the ancient register, with the corner of a page curled up between my fingers. 'How did he know?'

'Somehow these were people who had been like himself. Who had felt the same things. Thought in the same way. Perhaps they even looked alike, although I can't remember if Dan told me that.' I was surprised that she had allowed this young man to wander unimpeded through the archives, yet I began to sense what she must have sensed – that there was something wonderful about such a quest. 'He had a list of ten or twelve. He wasn't sure from what period they came, but I was able to help him in that department. Where are you going to find Raffe Kyteley except in the sixteenth century?'

'But what did he hope to discover? Even if he found some of the names . . .'

'That was the interesting part, you see. He was sure that they had all lived in the same area of London. He came here believing that they had at various times inhabited the same street, or even perhaps the same house.'

'And then?'

'Well, then he disappeared.'

'I see.'

'But I didn't see. That's the point. It was a Friday afternoon, about three months ago, when he arrived in a state of great excitement. He had found one of the names a week before, in a parish register of 1708. And he thought he was close to finding another. He wanted to make the connection.' She pulled up a chair and, although there was no one else in the room, began whispering to me. 'On that particular morning I happened to be consulting Key's *Guide to Early Parish Registers*, a very disappointing work, when I heard Dan cry out. I thought for a moment he was ill, but then he came rushing up to me. "I've found it," he shouted. "I'll be back later!" Now you know very well that I'm a discreet person.' I nodded. 'I didn't even take a peek at his desk until it was time to close. In fact there wasn't much to see, just a nineteenth-century rate-book from Stoke Newington. But in his excitement he had left behind his satchel, so of course I expected him to return.

He never did. He never came back.' She had been twisting her scarf round and round in her fingers, so that now it was danger-ously tight around her neck. 'Would you like to see his bag?'

I could hardly refuse, so I followed her to the back of the Blair Room where she had a small office; it was littered with volumes, ancient and modern, but I noticed a copy of *Vogue* slipped beneath Young's *Eighteenth-Century Estates Compendium*. 'I keep it here,' she said. She opened a drawer in her desk, and took out a nondescript canvas backpack with 'Dan Berry' daubed on it in red ink. 'I can't prove it,' she went on, 'but I think something happened to him. I wrote to the address he gave on his research application, but it was returned unopened. He had lived in a hostel. I visited it. Hold on a second.'

She was about to jump out of her window. She had opened it very wide, and was now leaning out at a perilous angle above Chancery Lane; I was poised for some kind of rescue, when I saw a puff of white smoke rising above her right shoulder. She was having a cigarette in a building where smoking was forbidden, although the sight of a woman hanging from a window some five storeys high might itself have caused comment. I picked up Dan Berry's satchel for a moment, and it was as if I had touched some dead creature. And yet there was something so poignant about his story that I could understand why Margaret Lucas had been moved by it. To attach yourself to those who came before you, to dream of a home, and then to vanish . . . She backed into the room so quickly that she startled me. 'I don't know why I keep it.' She took the canvas satchel from me. 'He doesn't need it now.'

There seemed little else to say, and so I returned to my desk and to the ancient volume. The churchwarden's registers, as I ought to have known, provided the most immediate evidence; here were the church rates for the parish of St James, Clerkenwell, formerly known as the nunnery of St Mary, and I chose the period between 1560 and 1570 for the beginning of my search. They were easy enough to decipher, primarily because there seem to have been very few private houses in the vicinity of the old nunnery; and then I saw it. There was a reference to 'Cloack House, beyond the nuns' priest's chapel'. I had opened upon 1563 and, in a ruled column alongside the reference to the house, someone had written 'Acc't of John Dee, his customary tithes'.

I gave out an involuntary shout of triumph (I wonder now if it was the same cry Dan Berry had made, at the moment of his discovery): Cloack House beyond the chapel was obviously my sixteenth-century house in Cloak Lane. The name of its owner was also familiar to me although, in the surprise and excitement of my discovery, I could not quite remember how I knew it. Margaret Lucas had come up beside me. 'When I heard that shout,' she said, 'I presumed you had found something.'

'I've found the house, and I've found its owner.'

She scrutinized the page with her usual ferocity. 'Now that is a name I do recognize. John Dee.'

'I know it too, but . . .'

'I hate to tell you this, Mr Palmer.' She was smiling in the most peculiar way. 'The previous owner of your house was a black magician.'

THE HOSPITAL

THERE IS AN old ruinated monastery by the way to Uxbridge, near St Giles-in-the-Fields, which has of recent years been employed as an alms-house and hospital for the aged: I rode there on the Saturday forenoon by way of Holborn and Broad St Giles, having received word that my father was sick unto death. It was a short journey but a pleasant one, across the Red Lion fields and along the path which leads past Southampton House; on this winter's morning the breath of the animals rose as vapour into the air, and the water-cans, piled high by the conduit at Drury, seemed about to burst their wooden bands. Everything in the world was filled to overflowing with life, and in the cold I could feel more keenly the beating of my own blood. It is of all liquors the most spiritous, and so it was with a good and fiery spirit that I sang out the ditty, 'An Old Man Is a Bag Full of Bones'.

The hospital of St Martin, once the monastery of that name (so called because it looks upon St Martin's field), is a very ancient pile, which I have no doubt was established at the time of the first Henrys. There is still a gatehouse tottering in face of the road and, as I passed beneath its arch, I smelt the odour of old stone and sensed a chill which was not like that of the winter air. A serving-man came running out to greet me. He had a buff leather jerkin, all greasy with the droppings of meat that must have fallen from his beard. 'What, sir,' says he, 'God give you good day. Are you cold enough? It looks to snow and freeze together, so come into the kitchen. Come in, sir, and warm yourself while I call my master to you.' He led me across a decayed cloister into a vaulted room where there were two hearths merrily blazing, yet I could not help

94

but think of the roofless church a few yards distant – now so forlorn and fallen that only the Devil might say a mass there.

Soon enough the master of the alms-house, a pretty fellow by the name of Roland Holleyband, came within to greet me. 'God save you, Doctor Dee,' he said, 'you are welcome here.' He knew me well enough, since it was by courtesy of my lord Gravenar that I had despatched my father to this place; my father had been the good lord's agent for his estates by Acton, and to my great comfort and liking he had consented to provide for him in his extremity. I wished to lead my days in some quiet and comfort and, lord, to meet him at every twist and turn of my house in Clerkenwell was not to be thought of. So, the rest of my family being gone into the earth, I thought it best to procure him a chamber where he could disturb no one on his way towards death. 'Your father is very bad,' Mr Holleyband vouchsafed to me. 'He is ill at ease, and shakes like a leaf upon the tree.'

'Well, well,' I replied. 'If he goes before, then we will follow him hereafter.'

'It is a noble philosophy. But I am sorry I am not able to bring you better cheer.'

'For one pleasure, a thousand sorrows.'

'Well said again, well said. Shall I bring you to him now?' He took me back across the cloister, which still showed signs of destruction and disturbance from the recent purges, and led me up some rough stone stairs into a long room with so many thick pillars that it looked like nothing so much as a crypt. There were beds or pallets along both sides, with distressed objects lying upon them, but Mr Holleyband moved between them merrily enough with a 'God give you good morrow' and 'How do you this morning?' and 'How is it with you since yesterday's supper?'. The air within was so close and stifling that I put my handkerchief up to my face, which he observed with a smile. 'Your father is apart from the others,' he said, 'as my lord Gravenar wished.' I followed him closely until he came to a little apartment or chamber, separated from the rest by a wooden screen intricately carved; within there were plain walls of stone, and it was no doubt some form of chapel in earlier days.

My father lay upon a bed, his hands clasped upon his breast, and at once I observed spots of black or red upon him – some big and some little, as if they had been sprinkled on him with a pen. He looked up at me curiously as I stepped over to his bed.

'How does your health since I saw you last, father?'

'So so.'

'You seem to look better always.'

'How know you that?'

'By your face, which is so ruddy.'

'No, sir, no. I have had five or six fits of the ague which have much weakened me, and taken away all my stomach. I feel some fit of it yet, sir, because I have not broken my fast.'

'Well, you are a hardy man. God will give you a good and long life yet.'

He still looked upon me curiously, and now spoke in a more halting voice. 'I think to have seen you some time, sir, but I do not well remember where. Was it in London?'

'Yes, truly, I am of London though I was born elsewhere.'

'Shall I be so bold as to ask your name?'

For a moment it seemed that he played with me, but there was such a look of perplexity on his face that I refrained from biting back at him. 'I believe it is known to you.'

'Truly? How do men call you?'

'They call me many things, but my name is Doctor Dee.' I walked away from his bedside, and saw Mr Holleyband still attending our discourse with much interest and pleasure; but at my look he bowed and departed. Then, oh God, what was it dimly shadowed upon the wall behind him that I suddenly took notice of? In my bewilderment it seemed to me the face of some monstrous thing rearing up from the floor. But then at a second glance I knew it to be a tree of life, painted long since (no doubt by the monks of this place) and now as much part of the stone as the stone itself, with ancient crumbling leaves and animals all striated with the dust and decay of time.

My father was whispering something even as my back was turned. 'I have gold, sir –' He broke off, making a noise with his

96

mouth as of the clinking and counting of coins. At this my ears pricked up, for I remembered that my lord Gravenar had presented him with twenty angels of gold at the end of his service; what had become of them, truly I did not know. 'I have white money, sir, as well as gold.' He beckoned me over to him, and then whispered in my ear. 'I placed them in a bag. I tied the strings with a strong double knot, for fear they might untie themselves. I put the bag at the bottom of a wall, an old crumbling wall amidst the roots of thorns. Look how they have torn my fingers.'

'Your sentence is confused, in respect of the place. Where might I find this wall of which you speak?'

'It has a name –' He motioned with his hand, plucking at the coverlet on his bed. Upon which I asked him if he needed pen, ink and paper; but at that he shook his head. Then I asked him if I should write such words as he was to speak, but he gave no certain answer. 'Make haste, sir,' he said a moment after. 'Bring me some water to wash my hands. I will have no river water because it is troubled. Give me well or fountain water. Make haste.' I went behind the wooden screen, and in a corner was a basin and ewer which I caught up without any ceremony: I was in mortal fear that he would lose the thread of his discourse, and leave me in the dark. I poured the water upon his trembling hands, although in truth it was brackish enough; the drops ran down his meagre wrists as he held them up to the light, and then he put out his palms to me as he spoke again. 'Shall I wash my mouth also, sir?'

'So be it.'

But he only licked the water from his wrists, and spat it into the basin before whispering once more to me. 'Walk on till you come to a high elm tree, then make twenty paces forward and turn at the left hand for fifteen paces before you take another five to the right. It is very bright there, sir, the brightness puts out my eyes. Take this taffeta to hold before your face, and it will keep you from the sun.'

He was close to rambling again, and so I cut him short. 'I am afraid that I am out of your way. I do not know this place.'

'It is very damp there, sir, but gold cannot rust.'

'So it is taught. Is there more to be known?'

'They call it the De La Pry wall, yet I understand not why.' And then I saw it very clearly, as it were in my mind's eye: it was the remains of some old hermitage, long since decayed among the Acton fields. As a boy I had rambled upon the ruins, dreaming of time long gone and contemplating the very wrack of mortality. My father was looking at me curiously all this while, and now at once his countenance changed. 'Away with you, Doctor Dee! Away with you! Cease your praying, and your prying. I am nothing near the earth, not yet. And would you have all my inheritance even before I am laid in the tomb?' He sat bolt upright in his bed, with so fierce a look that I turned away in wonder at his alteration and gazed upon the tree of life.

'I came here to comfort you, sir,' I replied.

'You came to cheat me. You are no better than the cutpurse who hides among the lanes, or the mountebank who makes riddles at Bartholomew Fair.'

'I came out of reverence, father.'

'What? What reverence is this? From a son who came close to ruining my household with his demands for money, but who then avoided and neglected us in the hour of our keen distress?' I said nothing. 'Did you come when your brothers caught sick of the falling evil, and died? Did you comfort me on the death of your mother, my dear wife? Did you assist me in my old age? No, you went your own way. With the Devil leading you.'

'I have my work, father —'

'Your work! No more than tricks and japes: if it be something else, then it is the work of hell itself. I placed you above my other sons and did what I could to teach you, endeavouring every day to assist you with your learning. But I am rewarded with pride and greed such as have never before been seen.'

'I have done nothing. I have done no harm.'

'Deny what you have done. Deny that you used me and abandoned me, forgetting all the laws of nature in your pursuit of wealth and fame. If you cannot deny it, John Dee, then confess all and cry that you have done great wrong.'

If he was aiming to cut my heart-strings, then he was using left-handed shears; nevertheless I humoured him with a stale device of the sinner. 'If I have offended, I beg pardon.' Then I went on with more matter. 'But I acquired knowledge not for my own sake, but for the sake of truth itself. My life is not held in my own hands.'

He laughed at that. 'How poor is the power you boast of! You have forgotten your own knowledge, and are become of vanity and ambition blind. Such a beginning, such an end. You have become a deceit, comprehending the image of falsehood. Well, well, be it unto you according to your disposition.' He tried to rise from his bed but he was too enfeebled, and sank down again upon the bolster. 'Now be packing hence. Go.'

I was content to take my leave of him with a few murmured words. 'At least, grave and reverend sire, I shall not be made contemptible and in my last days become a laughing-stock.' I put my hand upon his mouth, and spat upon it. 'How do you?'

And at that a change came over him, as once more he shrank back into his bed. 'Leonard,' says he, 'are the chestnuts roasted? I pray you cut that cheese.' He rambled I know not whither, until he looked up at me again. 'Pray do not listen to him, sir. He will deceive you.' Then with his hand earnestly smiting his breast he continued with, 'I think that two speak, or else this voice gives an echo. What was it you said, sir?' He had become once more an infirm, piteous old man, and I could scarcely bear to look upon him: what was I now to do with him, this thing upon the bed, or he with me? What does death signify, if it is not my own death? By what necessity was I here, contemplating the agony of this old man? He was muttering something again, and I put my ear up to his lips. 'I feel a thing about my head, sir, as if it clawed with hawk's claws.' He tried to take up my hand for comfort, but I pulled it from him and walked further away. 'Look not near me now,' he said, 'for he seems to be telling money behind my bed.'

I kept my back turned. 'Who may that be, father?'

'Does his music make you merry, sir? Sir, what is your name?'

I laughed at this and left him, walking down the avenue of sickness while the rest of them groaned upon their pallets. Mr

Holleyband was waiting for me at the foot of the stairs, and smiled as I came down towards him. 'How did you find him, my good doctor?'

'He is a man of sharp wit.'

'Yes, a very merry and ingenious gentleman.' He was still smiling as we walked together into the cloister. 'But, as all of us, inclined to stray.'

'I would talk further with you on this matter, Mr Holleyband, but now I utterly lack the leisure . . .' Indeed I was in haste to be gone, having conceived a sudden fear that he had overheard my father's whisperings about hidden gold. 'I have a journey to make before the sun goes down.'

'Have you so great haste, Doctor Dee? Let us warm us first, and then perhaps we may ride out together. You are returning to your house, I suppose, and to your necessary labours?'

I understood him to mean, like the dog do you fall to your old vomit? So I cut him short. 'No. I am riding on a little, and I am afraid that I will not return by daylight.' I walked quickly towards the gatehouse, as he followed me. 'Soon I shall recompense you for your courtesy,' I continued. 'But now, where is my horse?'

It was saddled by the greasy servant, and then I rode away, sniffing up the cold air to remove the noisome stink of that place from my nostrils. I took my path to Acton without forethought, as it was along the lanes I had known since my childhood – across the gravel pits of Kensington, through Notting Wood, and then past the new enclosed fields of Shepperds Bush. I did not know what I would find concealed beneath the De La Pry wall, yet now in imagination I saw myself bending down over the cloth bag, untying its strings, and pouring over my hands some Edward shillings, some Harry sovereigns and some Elizabeth angels. I could be heir to nothing besides, for there never came a penny to me from my father (even when want and discredit grew more and more upon me) and it was certain that no revenue or inheritance would fall into my pocket after his death. So why should I not take now what rightfully belonged to me? In his rambling humour he accused me of stealing and embezzling from him, yet in my early years I never asked one farthing off him even though there were times when I feared the extreme pinch of all manner of want.

I do still fear the damage of the world, and so pricked my horse to journey swiftly towards my father's hidden gold. I have watched often enough the blinded lady, Fortune, and know full well that no high estate can ever be secured; at the very peak of my prosperity (which was not so great), I had a panic fear that I might even at the very next instant be brought to stepping out of doors and becoming no more than a wanderer like the vagabond I had found in my garden. Even now I contemplate the means to save myself from starving, and keep remembrance of all my monies by score, tally and notebook. I have the fear, also, that I might fall under the thralldom of the usurer's gripes. And what if my house were robbed, and all my silver stolen, what then?

It was close to midday when I went down into the fields where I had once played, and I could see some little distance to my family's old weatherbeaten dwelling. Yet this was not a time for memory. Ahead of me was the De La Pry wall, which was no more than clumps of stone and a ragged trace of masonry that made an outline in the freezing grass. I got from my horse and refreshed him by a stream there, which ran but sluggishly in winter; I let him drink well and gave him some dates from my satchel, before leading him to a ruined barn over against the wall to find shelter from the cold. Then I toiled back upward to the bare elm which stood by the side of the field. The sun was low in the sky, and the ancient tree cast a long shadow over the ruined wall: I had my father's directions by heart, and stood against the bark. I took twenty paces forward, and then fifteen to the left, which brought me to the very edge of the wall; then I took five to the right hand, which led me to a section about eleven inches in height and so covered with moss and lichen that the ancient stone was scarcely visible; here, concealed, must lie my bag of gold!

I fell to work at once, my heart beating high, and with my little pocket-knife I began to cut at the cold earth; it came away in roundish lumps, not so big as a penny loaf but thick enough to make progress still. There was earth, and nothing but earth, but I dug down to the very foundation of the wall; here the soil and stone fell all in pieces, as small as ashes, and there was no gold yet. How long I toiled there I cannot say, but I laboured to the going down of the sun; I dug a pit on both sides and, even while I did so, I cursed myself for all hoping or dreaming upon anything that was not! I cursed my father, too, stinking within the alms-house, for crossing me in this matter: had I the back of an ass to bear all his foolish prattling, and the snout of a swine to say nothing? No, it could not be. I was not to be turned upon the wheel with Ixion, and he who is bitten may soon bite back.

So I laboured and drudged in the Acton fields, lathing myself in a sweat despite the bitter coldness of the air, and for all my labouring and drudging I had found nothing at all. There was no concealed gold, no bag of coins, no, no nothing. True it is that we are never long at ease but some cross or other afflicts us, and now at the waning of the day I had quite forgotten my good health and spirits of the morning. With heavy heart I led my shivering horse from the barn, and slowly in the darkness made my journey back to London.

It was good that I could find my way even being blind, because it was a wonderful dark evening in which my horse had to feel for the path homeward. And yet I feared for myself all the while, not knowing if a band of robbers or cutpurses might not make a rush at me; but even though I was grievously molested by such terrors, it was my own failure that almost brought me to despair. I, who had wanted a tower of gold around me, had been reduced to stooping before an old ruined wall where there was nothing but dirt and rubbish to be found. And what if I had caught a fever in the dampness? I felt a strange pang in my joints even as I rode, and suddenly my right shoulder and elbow joint were so extremely in pain that I could have cried aloud – even in my fear of calling forth robbers and other desperate men.

Yet perhaps these grievous pangs and pains were signs of some more general corruption; I remembered that, two or three weeks before, a humour had so suddenly fallen into my leg that it was as if a stone had hit me, and I had pain so intolerable that the veins and arteries seemed broken by some extreme stretching. In the autumn of last year, also, I had a show of grief in my kidney which I had thought to have cured. These present pains were no doubt part of the same very dangerous sickness, which now terrified me in my thoughts; then a humming in my ears began, as I stared into the darkness around me. And what if I were to die too soon? What if I should die, like him, alone and rambling? I conceived for myself every frame of agony upon which I might be stretched, picturing all the innumerable ills of the flesh and all the distractions of the brain till there was scarce any life left in me. Great pain I could perhaps bear, but to lose my wits in some fit or fever, to have the memory utterly dissolved and then to die in the corner of some hovel or upon the streets ... Yet why is it that I am surrounded by so much great anxiety and grief of mind that I can scarcely stay upon my horse, and am as frightened by the darkness within my own mind as by the night around me? I am still within the net of the demons who govern time: matter is in a perpetual flux, never at a stay, and I am so tossed upon its waves that I have become sick unto death. All my life I have tried to proceed *gradatim*, from things visible to consider of things invisible, from things bodily to things spiritual, from things transitory and momentary to things permanent. Yet why can I not change my own self? I am very much like glass, than which there is nothing more bright and nothing more brittle. How is it that I have any place in the world? How do I survive? Fear and wretchedness all at once crowded around me, at which point I leaned over toward the path and vomited up my terrors. Oh God within me, I must be strong. *Gloria laus et honor Dei in excelsis.* And now that I had fetched up a great vomit, I began to sing out loud from the old song,

'One and One is all alone, and ever more shall be so.'

Yes, ever more first and pre-eminent. By my art I shall be sublimed and exalted, brought to the third region and then returned in such a high state of grace that I need not heed the revolving world. Then, fear, I would bid you good day. No longer would I be held down by some man's first tripping of my feet, and by others afterwards overlying me with worldly policy and subtle practices. I would have no terror of mutability because I would know all, and the pygmies who now surround me would be spiteblasted away. I would fear no one. I would envy no one. So I must be like the iron drawn to the adamant: I must come closer every day to the great secret. Was I not already on the way to making new life without the help of any womb? And if I can create an everlasting creature, then will I have found the divinity within, that soul, that spark, that fire which drives the spheres. See. I spit upon the world. And in so doing I cleanse the last traces of vomit from my mouth, as London comes before me once again.

★

I was hard at my work on the following morning, considering the moist element in which the homunculus must breathe, when my wife's servant came to me. She called out, 'Are you up, sir?' and then knocked hard upon the door of my chamber.

'I have been up these past several hours, Audrey Godwin. What is it o'clock?'

'It is not so late as you think. It is but half an hour past seven. But come quickly, sir. It is your father.'

I turned pale for an instant. 'My father here?'

'No. A messenger has come from the alms-house, saying that he is ready to give up the ghost.'

'So. It is time.'

'Make haste, sir, or it may be too late.'

Yet I dressed myself with care, before I rode out with the messenger to my father's latest and last lodgings upon this earth. It was a day more bleak and bitter than the one before, so I wound a cloth around my mouth and nose to keep off the cold as we came out on to the Uxbridge way. Mr Holleyband was not within sight as we rode past the gatehouse, but I knew my path: I crossed the cloister and, having mounted the stairs which led to that dormitory of the dying, I advanced towards the wooden partition behind which my father was closeted. But he was not upon his bed, and for an instant I had a vision of him lying already within his grave; then I saw him. He was standing against the opposite wall, next to the tree of life, as pale as a corpse and naked unto his paps and privities; his hands were folded across his breast, and then he stepped across the floor towards me. I flinched away, but he passed me without sign or mark of recognition and, having crossed the room, lay down upon his bed in silence. Then he gave me a look, and burst out in laughter. 'What that black scarf signifies,' he said, 'I know not. But I suspect.' His eyes were set or sunken into his head, and there was not enough flesh upon him to hide his bones. I said not a word and presently he lifted his eyes from me towards the ceiling, and he began to utter a great deal of speech as to himself which I did not hear. Upon a sudden he asked me, what did you say? I answered, that I spoke nothing: whereupon he wondered what creature did use that voice. Then he said that he felt something crawling, as one writing on his back and at length ascending into his head. 'See it now before you,' he cried, rising bolt upright in his bed. 'There is a very little creature there on the cushion beside the window, making to play with you. Do you not hear it? Listen, it is saying *Put out your candle for you shall have nothing more to do today*. Do you not hear and see it, sir?'

'I see nothing. Nothing at all.'

'No, no, you are right. It is gone now. I see not a sign of it any more. And I fear, sir, that you are growing foggy and misty also.' I knew it to be the mist of death descending upon him and, though he beckoned to me, I did not wish to come too close. 'Boy,' he said to me then, 'bring some light. Make some fire that we may rest.'

I smiled at his foolishness. 'Cry once more aloud to that naughty boy. He does not hear you.'

'Give me my hose. Where is my doublet? Bring my garters and my shoes. And a clean shirt, for this one is foul.' He had lapsed now into his rambling speech, and many times plucked at his face as if there were already cobwebs upon it. 'Where is my girdle and my inkhorn, my jerkin of Spanish leather? Where are my socks, my cap, my cloak, my gloves, my pumps?' His voice rose higher as if it would become a scream of woe. 'I have nothing here. I have nothing beside me.' He began to sob then, but I thought nothing of it: when I had so much fear of the darkness within me, how could I pay any heed to the darkness now covering my father? I looked upon him as no more than a forerunner in the race, and not one to be especially pitied for it. I began even to condemn out loud his screechings and whisperings, for why should I listen to one who had but lately reviled me and cursed me and led me quite out of my way? Yet he heard nothing.

'Love me.' He uttered this so clearly that I looked at him astonished. 'And love my dog. Where is my dog? Have you seen him, sir?' At that he loosed such a volley of general lamenting that it made me fart. I recollected then that there had once been a dog who had followed him everywhere and who had kept house with him (so to speak) when he had lived alone in east Acton. What had become of it, I did not know. 'Good dog,' he said. 'Good god. Good dog.' Then he set up another keen wailing, so I went over to him and clapped my hand across his mouth.

'Do you love dog or god?' I asked him. He nodded in his delirium. 'Then shall you presently go to your reward. But keep your peace now, I pray you. Truly you are tedious.'

At that he quietened a little, as I knew he would: there is a force within me which could still a tempest if I so required it. After a few moments he began to count one to ten, over and over, and grasped at invisible objects upon his bed-sheet. Then he put up his hand as if to offer me something. 'Fill the glass,' he said. 'Fill not so full, that I may drink more easily.' I could see now that he was ready to expire, since he lay with his eyes closed as if already dead. Let him be gone, was my thought, I have seen enough. I have seen all. Let him no longer encumber my life, which is the more precious to me now that I have seen his dissolution. Go, sir, go and lead apes in hell! I had not spoken aloud, or so I thought, but at this moment he opened his eyes very wide and seemed to look upon me.

No, no, there was nothing to fear. At a glance I knew that there was no power of seeing and no light left within him. He had departed from life. Yet I could not withstand his dead gaze and might have stared at him for ever, were it not for a sudden noise coming out of the floor: it was a whistling, very base or low, like a *whu, whu, whu.* It was the wind, no doubt, or some screech-owl perched upon the roof, and I walked away from the corpse to look out of the window. There was no breeze stirring, and no sign of any bird. Then I felt something touch my shoulder softly, and with a great groan I turned as quickly as a leaf in a hurricane. 'Be not so sad.' Mr Holleyband stood behind me, smiling. 'He was a man of a good wit, and I exhort you to take his death very patiently.'

I glanced towards the corpse; the breath was scarcely out of him, and the body was still panting with heat, yet in truth I felt nothing but thankfulness. And I alive! 'You will bury him, Mr Holleyband, will you not?'

'If it please you, Doctor Dee.'

'Yes. It pleases me.' With a bow I left him, and went laughing on my way; he would be carried to the graveyard now without so much as a piss from me. I had saved four shillings on the charge for the winding-sheet, and six shillings on the charge of the burial. The cat loves fish but loves not to wet her foot: I had consigned him to decay and darkness, but at no earthly expense.

I called for my horse and was soon riding down Broad St Giles as the wind whipped about me; all the while I thought to have heard a horse and rider close behind, but when I turned at the crossroads there was nothing upon the path except an old wooden stall upon wheels. In the bitter cold the hooves of my own horse must have rung out on the hard earth, and so caused an echo all around. Yet it was not so cold that I could not be merry, and I resolved to make my way across the river to Paris Garden. The stage had lately been erected there, just on the spot of the old archery ground near the bear-ring, and who can resist a play when he is merry? Whether it be a work tragical or historical, it enlivens the passions and excites the spirit of emulation in those who wish to make their own progress across the stage of the world. I cannot look upon a great personage portrayed without wishing that I was standing in his place – yes, even before the stinking multitude. Then would I be able to master them all, without recourse to any other art except that of my own presence.

I rode down into Thames Street, where all manner of small fires were lit for the sake of the warmth; their smoke stung in my eyes as I rode forward, but then, when I came up to the great clock, I saw through my tears a barber's shop down the side alley known as Paltock. In my gay mood I thought it right to trim and perfume myself, so without any delay I gave my horse in charge and entered the sweet-smelling shop. There was one already in the chair, presenting himself in all the colours of the rainbow; he had a pair of moustaches like a black horse-tail tied up in a knot, with two tufts sticking out on each side, and the barber continually dipped into a little basin filled with soapy water. The morning is the idlest time of day, when men that are their own masters – as gentlemen of the Inns or captains out of service – do wholly bestow themselves upon such pleasures as these; I would rather be burned in hell-fire than waste the time so, but on this day of great joy and departing I conceived a strange passion to sit and stare at all the world.

The little barber had half-a-dozen silver rings on his fingers, worth no more than threepence a piece as I should guess, and it was an art for him to keep them from tangling with the hair. But it was all one to the roaring boy sitting before him, who continually enquired about periwigs of the new curl and ruffles of the new set. Then he asked the barber the price of tooth-picks and of comb-cases, of head-brushes and of beard-brushes, as if he were about to set up in trade for himself. But truly he was one who took his continual diet in a tavern, the only rendezvous for company such as his, and now he began to speak of his games and devices. 'Do you know Tick-Tack?' he asked. The barber shook his head. 'Or Lurch?'

'No, sir. If I am at leisure I will sometimes sit close to the cards with Ruff or Colchester Trump, but these are all I know.'

'But come now, Mr Hadley, you should be a fresh gamester and find those who will bear you company with Novem Quinque or Faring. Surely you know Doublets? It is the French game for as many who will.'

So he talked on, all the time examining his moustaches from side to side, and at every angle conceivable, within an oval mirror which hung on a nail against the wall. I was longing for him to be gone and the barber, seeing my impatience, finished him with a few curls and then bid him good day. He then came back to me and led me to the chair, smiling as he took up his scissors and his comb. 'It is a pleasure,' he said, 'to serve a grave and reverend gentleman such as yourself. These young bloods, well, they hardly understand our practice. They come and ask for their hair to be cut after the Italian manner, short and round, or like a Spaniard long at the ears. This fellow here asked to be Frenchified with a lovelock down to his shoulders, but with hair such as his I could not oblige him. Now, sir. What will it be?'

'I desire to be trimmed,' I said, 'in the old English fashion.'

'Yes, it is the best, sir. You cannot beat the English style.' So then he set about me with a very good will, as he prattled on like a newly married wife. 'Did you see the pageant at Fenchurch Street, sir?' he asked me as he cut into my beard. 'It was a goodly show, truly, and the street was hung with cloth of gold. There was the sweetest playing with all manner of musicians and lord! there was one trumpet that seemed to be blowing all day long.'

'No, I did not see it.'

'The new French ambassador had come to witness it and, sir, you have never seen such a ruff on a man. It was wrapped about his neck like a wicker cage, and on his head he had a little hat with brims like the wings of a doublet.' He laughed at his memory. 'He wore a murry cloth gown, do you know the sort, laid thick on the sleeves with lace? He bore it up very quaintly so that we might all see his white taffeta hose and his black silk stockings. Well, if the Mayor had not been beside him, he would have been stoned.'

At that I laughed out loud. 'I would have rather seen his head smitten off, and his body burned by the Tower.'

'It may come to that, sir, in these days.' He stopped and sighed, before jogging off once more along his own path. 'Ah, sir, the inconstancy of fashion. I see it all before me here, you know. There is nothing in England more constant than the inconstancy of dress. Now they use the French fashion, and now the Spanish, and then the Morisco gown is in favour. It is all one thing, and then another.'

'It is the way of the world.' I revolved my own thoughts for a moment. 'Well, I for one am not afraid of their disdain.'

'Of course not.'

'You know what they say of envy, do you?'

'Tell me, sir. I always seek knowledge from gentlemen such as yourself.'

'Envy is a crocodile that weeps when he kills and sighs with none but he feeds on.'

He was silent at that but, since it was nothing to do with his own theme, he continued after a moment. 'And lord, sir, the country-people who flock here. In the dog-days of summer they pass by this shop, and come in without any need of my services to ask me for directions to the tombs at Westminster or the lions in the Tower. Can you believe it, sir?'

This put me in mind once more of my own expedition, and I asked him to finish his trimming with all speed. He consented willingly enough, and a few minutes after he was washing my face with sweet water. 'Now, sir,' he said. 'You look like an artist.'

'Yes,' I replied, 'and one who would remake the world.' I left him, and when I turned at the corner of Paltock I saw him looking after me.

It was a short ride now into New Fish Street, which led me over against the bridge. There are those who cry up this bridge as a great glory of London, standing upon its twenty arches of squared free-stone, but it is a narrow thoroughfare across the river and one so hemmed in with shops and houses that there is scarcely room to pass; I led my horse slowly through the busy press of people and there was so great a crowd of porters, street-sellers, merchants and travellers that many times I came to a halt, surrounded by cries of 'Make way there!' and 'By your leave!', until I found my path to the south end and came out by the bankside. I rode on a little to Winchester Stairs, and left my horse with the keeper of the stables there, and then advanced on foot to the patch of waste ground by Dead Man's Place where the bears are baited. It is no more than a penny to ascend the wooden scaffold to watch the spectacle, but I came in as one of the last and had to peep over heads and shoulders as the bear was brought forth into the court and the dog set to him. It pleases the crowd to see blood shed, and what a noise they set up when the dog plucked the bear by the throat and the bear clawed him off by the scalp! There was such a fending and tugging, such scratching and biting, that the court seemed no more than a puddle of blood – and to see the bear with his pink nose leering after his enemy's approach, to see the nimbleness and the wait of the dog to take his advantage, was as good as a play. If he were bitten in one place the bear struggled to get free in another and, when he was loose, he shook his ears two or three times with the blood and slaver about his face; what shifts, what biting, what clawing, what roaring, what tossing and tumbling until the whole action seemed like some emblem of this madcap city. Truly these people love suffering and death.

I left the scaffold in high good humour and walked towards Paris Garden and the stage lately erected there. I had just come out by Molestrand Dock, when suddenly I heard a voice close by me. 'Jesus,' he said, 'who would have thought that I should have met you here?' I turned, and knew him at once from his dirty white satin jerkin: it was my old assistant, John Overbury, who had quit my service a year ago for (as he said) a better master. I knew him also to be a morose and suspicious fellow, much given to back-biting. 'What reason have you to be here?' he continued, stepping up and walking alongside me.

'No reason in the world, John.' We had just come to Falcon Stairs, near the stews bordering on Pike Lane, and he eyed me curiously. 'Except,' I added, 'to see a play.'

'And nothing more, sir?' I kept my mouth closed and was eager to shake him off, but still he followed me. 'Did you see the bears in the yard?' he asked me now.

'I stayed for a moment.'

'You chose your day with skill then, as always. Did you hear how the scaffold there fell down all at once no more than a month ago, being full of people? Many were killed and hurt, sir. Did you hear?' I nodded. 'There were some who say that it was pulled down by enchantment.'

'Many will say anything, John, simply to amaze those with no wits left in them.'

'That is so, Doctor Dee. But you and I know the truth of such matters, do we not?'

I did not reprove his sauciness, yet I knew him well enough. After he left my service I found by chance in a box some papers in his own handwriting, and there was brought to my knowledge evidence of his knavery in writing down my experiments. I had no doubt that he would have sold them to anyone who wished for gold or power, but it was sad stuff hastily construed. He had altogether missed his mark, for there are no true secrets except those that lie buried in the shadow of men's souls.

I had come up now within sight of the scaffolding, and already a great concourse of people were flocking for the play, but the fool was still waiting on me. 'What is your pleasure, sir,' he said. 'To go in with the rest, or pay for a chair?' He meant the wooden forms arranged to each side of the scaffold, away from the press, and I knew then that he designed to stick closer to me than the sole does to the shoe.

'But where shall we sit?' I replied. 'All is full. All the forms are occupied.'

'We will find place enough, sir. Care not for that, but follow me. I will enter first, thrust hard, and cause a way to be made.' At which he went in crying, 'Make way! Make way for the venerable Doctor Dee!' There was laughter at this, born out of the scum of vile minds, and then the hypocrite turned smiling to me. 'Are you still following, good doctor? I never saw such a multitude!' I said nothing and was about to turn aside in order to lose myself among the stinking crowd, when he took me by the sleeve and led me over to the wooden forms. 'Sit here against the scaffold,' he said, 'and you will miss nothing.' Then he tapped upon the shoulder of a man wrapped in a velvet coat. 'I pray you, sir,' he said, 'sit aside a little and make us some room here by you.'

'With a very good will,' the man replied – yet I am sure he could not help but overhear John Overbury muttering to me behind his hand, 'Do you see what a pair of buttocks he has? He occupies more room than any of these others.' How he came by his bold sauciness I do not know, but I would have soon sent him home by weeping-cross if I did not suspect that, by some fraud or guile, he had not come upon me unawares. So I kept my peace.

'It is well known that you study too much,' he whispered to me as the procession began. 'So it is good to see you pass some time at the play.'

There were many noble personages, attired in rich robes of crimson and blue and yellow, who now came out upon the scaffold in stately guise. By the signs of their garments and their demeanour I knew them to be actors in an historical tragedy, and so I looked for a prologue upon the theme of mutability. There were seven upon the stage, like the spheres above us, and they were of their humours all compact: so can the essential world be depicted in such masques and pageants and performances. One principal in the robe of a king stepped forward to address us, when John Overbury leaned against me and pointed towards the crowd. 'Do you see Marion?' he asked me. 'Do you know her? There, holding up her gown almost to the middle that the world may see what a fine leg and dainty foot she has.' I turned my eyes that way, and saw a pert girl standing amidst the people. 'She lodges under the sign of Venus,' he continued. 'And look, there is one ogling her. Do you see that old whoremonger beside her?'

> O spheres, tell me, where is thy wonted motion
> To make this stage resound thy lamentation?
> My spouse is dead, and dead is my devotion,
> Now base and sour is love's most high vocation
> Which throws my life and fate into confusion!
> O doleful hour! O sad destiny of passion
> That leaves me now the sport of base oppression!

'The whoremonger knows how to choose his mate, as the custom is here. Do you see the gold rings upon his fingers with which he catches at the light, the more to ensnare her?'

I strained to hear the sweet speech of the players, as a boy carrying the torch of wisdom approached the king.

BOY. Now Sorrow, sir, must bow to Reason's light.
KING. But is not Reason lost in Sorrow's night?
BOY. Yet Grief must bow at length to Reason's stroke.
KING. What shall I gain by taking Reason's yoke?

'What lord is that, Doctor Dee, who sits over to the side of us? Do you know him?'

I paid no attention, though I heard him well enough: I could not take my eyes from the stage, as the actors now turned about in a dance and the king again stepped forward.

My son, whom you see here, seeks my own death
To satisfy apace his own ambition
In killing me to step upon my corse
And snatch that fruit —

I heard no more, for Overbury whispered to me again. 'Do you see that one there in a gown with hanging sleeves? Any eye may see that he is after boys. Is it not true that the play brings out more than the players?'

There had been a wondrous alteration on the scaffold when I looked upon it again, for now the old king, dressed in the garments of the last generation, was lying upon a pallet while viols and trumpets announced the coming of his son.

KING. Who knocks there, like the Devil's porter?

Overbury nudged me at that.

SON. It is I, your dear devoted son and heir.

'A villain, Doctor Dee, I warrant you. I know him by his look.'

KING. Come. No power beneath the moon may stop you.

At which time the son advanced close to him, all dressed in a blue and white garment, and struck his father with a sword to signify his murder; then there must have been something very like a bladder of blood spilt upon the wooden boards, for the liquid ran down over the edge while the viols and trumpets rang out again in more disturbed sort. John Overbury gaped at that, and consented to watch even to the extent of the interlude, when four figures signifying Ingratitude, Death, Guilt and Vengeance did parade with banners before quizzing one another on the meaning of this action.

'Construe that for me, good doctor,' said Overbury, perplexed at their discourse, which was too high for his head.

'It is the glory of the spectacle,' I replied. 'Do you not see how the king's blood represents the mineral spirit of metals, while the sword itself signifies change by fire?'

'Lord knows that was not clear to me. Yet who are these great personages?'

'They have announced their meaning. But the four of them also represent the four stars or the *materia prima* of the philosopher's stone. What more do you wish to understand?'

'Well, sir, it is a riddle indeed which I cannot unriddle.'

'Go to. Where is your mind?'

'I am content with it, Doctor Dee, but if you find it wanting then I am ashamed of it truly.' Yet he was laughing all the while, and at once turned his eyes upon the assembly with 'And how is with you today?' to one and 'What news?' to another. It was certain that he knew many of them well, for there was as great a gathering of villains here as in Clink Street a little way yonder.

> SON. Speak to me, if hounds of hell may speak
> KING. I am your father's ghost, raised up as witness
>   To all your filthiness and perjured guilt.

I looked up to see the prince sitting uneasily upon a chair and cushion, while before him stood his dead father with a white damask cloth over his corpse to signify his return from the grave.

> SON. Stay, infernal fury, and return to fire.
> KING. I will not rest until you are consumed,
>   Whirled by the hurricane —

'In the name of God speak somewhat louder,' John Overbury shouted out towards the players. 'Say that word again. We cannot hear you through the cloth, reverend ghost.'

But I did not join in the general laughter. I was possessed by a strange fear that, if the damask were once removed, then I would see my father's corpse standing above me.

KING. Whirled by the hurricane of punishment.

The player had begun again but, with no little sign of uneasiness at the cries of his auditors, he dropped upon the plain boards the wax candle light which he held: it flamed up against the cloth which covered him, but two servants of the company rushed out bearing a pitcher of water and swiftly doused the fire.

In the confusion (fire being so deadly an enemy to all content in a play-yard) I rose from my chair, still being in the grasp of a panic fear that my own father might suddenly appear before me, and turned my back upon the bright shapes of the players. 'Do not stir,' I said to Overbury. 'Keep your place.'

'The play is not complete, good doctor.'

'I am content with what I have seen. And I will find my own way out amidst this press.'

'No, sir, truly, without lying I am so much at ease in your company that I would not willingly forsake it.' I groaned inwardly at that but suffered him to take me by the sleeve. 'Let us push to get out,' he said and, as we made our way, he called out 'By your leave!' and 'Let us go by, I pray you!' until we came out on to the pathway of Broadwall. Then he stopped and clapped his hands. 'Wait a little,' he said. 'I do not have my silver pen-knife. It must be somewhere within.' So he returned with all speed to the play but, when I followed a few paces behind, I saw him in conversation with the whore or bawd he had called Marion. They came out together a few moments later, and I gazed towards a herring-boat on the river as if they had found me in deep contemplation.

'Well, my master,' he called to me as they approached. 'They say that an ounce of mirth is better than a pound of sorrow. Is that not so?'

'Did you find your knife?'

'It was deep within my pocket. Nothing has been lost, sir, but something has been found.' At that he smiled upon Marion; she was a very fair and plump young woman, her skin as white and clean as the finest ivory, and as I walked behind her towards the river (she with very many looks regarding me over her shoulder), I felt the golden staff of Adam rising within my robe. 'Do you remember,' he continued, dawdling a little until I came up to them, 'how you used to have me whipped when I was late rising in the morning? What was it you used to say to me, reverend doctor, but that the juice of a birch was excellent for a cure to all limbs?' He pinched the arm of the bawd at the word 'birch', and she laughed. 'If you were to apply it again to another worthy object, no doubt you would see another marvellous change.' I knew his meaning well enough. 'Will you come with us a little way,' he added, 'and join us at the inn yonder?' I knew the place: it was a brothel-house or place of disorder for bawds and whores which had more clients than Westminster Hall and more diseases than Newgate. Yet I followed them. Well, Socrates sometimes danced and Scipio played at pebble-stones by the seaside; I can neither crave pardon lest I should confess a fault, nor conceal my meaning lest I be thought a fool. It is said of apothecaries that they love only the smell of urine, and now I was in a similar case: I was like the fly that shuns the rose and lights in shit.

A bundle of railings came from the mouth of some half-drunk scold as we approached the sign of the Lily-White Babe, yet that was nothing out of the ordinary in this quarter. As we came up to the door of the inn itself we were greeted by a slattern with a blear eye, a snotty nose and a blabber lip.

'Mistress Anne,' John Overbury said, bowing to her as he did so. 'We greet you with a very good will.'

'Come hither, lady and gentlemen,' she replied. She had a stinking breath, and her voice was very shrill. 'Will it please you to enter my inn? To enter my Babe? You are most heartily welcome.' She called herself Mistress, yet I knew well the trade of it, and what kind of shop she kept.

'Truly, madam,' Overbury continued with a smile, 'this day has been the coldest there has been this great while. Do you have something here to warm us?'

'Come in, sir, without any more ceremony. I have wine with spices ready mixed.' So we entered, I making way for Marion, who gave the old bawd a curtsey as we crossed the threshold. 'Will it please you to open this door here, gentlemen,' she continued, graciously acknowledging the curtsey, 'and join the company in the inner chamber?' It was a dirty reeking room into which we entered, with men and women idling upon stools and cushions – I know not if Daedalus could have made a labyrinth for such monsters, or Apelles have coloured such misshapes, but in plain sight they all took the form of pimps, strumpets and whores. 'Now, now, children,' said Mistress Anne, sitting herself upon a close-stool covered with cat fur, 'what do you?'

'God give you good morning, mother,' two of the slatterns replied in unison.

'I am come to visit you with my friends, children, and we are very glad to find you all so well employed. Whatever be done, make sure it is well done.' She turned to one of the whores, a pock-marked creature in a soiled red petticoat. 'You have a pretty taste in damask,' said she, stroking her dirty upper bodice.

'I most humbly thank you, mother, and truly it is fair.'

Mistress Anne turned to me, still caressing the bodice. 'The sweetest and most pleasant name that they can give me is to call me mother. Does it not do your heart good to hear it, sir? And to see such faithful children? Would you care to speak to one privately?'

At that John Overbury came between us, and whispered something to her. So now she rose from the close-stool (which I thought she was about to use) and came simpering towards me. 'Wild grapes make pleasant wine,' she said. 'If I should not drink, I should be as dry as a gammon of bacon hung on a chimney. And as for you, sir, is it not the same? I had rather you go without hose than that you should forbear drinking in my poor house. What does it please you to have, sir?'

'Well, mistress,' I replied, looking upon Marion as I spoke, 'it is said that Roscius was always drunk when he dined with Cato.'

'I do not know the gentlemen, sir, but if ever I see them here I will remember you to them.'

At that I laughed out loud. 'Bring me wine mixed with nutmeg. The more spiced the better it will be.'

She returned with a steaming bowl, which I finished instantly. 'Good God,' she said. 'This paper drinks the ink. Go, daughter, and bring the gentleman more.'

'No,' I cried. 'No, no. I shall have the dropsy before the day's end.'

'It is good to drink, sir.' She glanced down at Marion, who was now kneeling beside the fire and holding out a pair of tongs. 'No man can live upon salt butter and Holland cheese.'

'If you say so, mistress, if you say so.'

'Of course I say so. You cannot be too bold here, sir. I pray you command as if you were in your own house, and you shall do me pleasure.' So I drank more, and still more, until my blood beat high in my veins. 'Does it please you,' the old bawd said, 'to have your chamber? Does Jack want his Joan?' At that she nodded towards Marion. 'You shall find sweet meat and sweeter sauce served by her hand than by any other.' She led us into an adjacent chamber, parted by a wainscot door.

'Have you a bolt to this door?' I asked her.

'It is not a necessary thing,' she replied. 'Here are we all thoroughly at ease one with another.'

'But she must be washed,' I went on, rambling in my drunkenness. 'She must be washed before she can partake.' Then, as Marion began to undress herself, I recited the grace before meat. 'All that is and shall be set on this board, be the same sanctified by the Lord's word. He that is king and lord over all, bring us to the table of life eternal. Amen. Fetch me a pitcher and basin, and a cloth, that I may wipe away her filthiness.'

The old bawd hurried off, and Marion made a small motion with her hand as if to plead with me. 'As for me, sir, I have washed. And I have handled nothing since I have washed.'

But I said not a word until Mistress Anne returned with an old cracked ewer and pot, filled with the most brackish water that seemed to have come from some ditch or pond. 'Lie her down upon the floor and wash her face. Lift her hairs and wash.' The old harlot did as she was bid, while the young one seemed to look piteously upon me. 'It is a common shore,' I said, 'that still receives all the town's filth. So wipe her mouth and lips. See, it is like wiping a post. Show me the tongue. Let me see the pallet of her mouth.'

The bawd performed her ministrations with a very bad grace. 'Why do you treat her so?' she asked me. 'She is a fair wench, not a foul one.'

'The causes that move me to this are not now to be expressed,' I told her, 'lest an irrevocable deed be committed.' At that she held her peace. 'What a fair neck,' I continued. 'You are pretty and fat, my little darling. Wash her armpits. Oh, what an arm you have, but your hand-wrist is very small. How do you fare with so thin a wrist? Open your right hand. See, your thumb and little finger are flea-bitten, for the black spots are there yet. Are there any fleas in your chamber? Or do you share your bed with such as harbour them? Pare her nails, Mistress Anne, for fear she scratch herself too much. And I pray you to wipe well the nipple of her dug before she puts it in my mouth, in case there be hair or any other thing. Now lay her down on her belly that I may see her back. Her shoulders are marked, do you see, but the little buttocks are fleshy and have not been bitten.' The stale old woman knew that she had good ware to traffic, so she became more content and merely hungered for her gold. 'Ah, what a woman's thighs are these! Wash the calves of her legs upwards. Now wash the soles of her feet and forget not to make clean her toes, the great toe and all. Now turn her again upon her back.' I knelt down now to make suck of her, but at that moment I spent myself even though I was still dressed. Then I felt such fear and horror that I stood up, trembling, and wiped my hand across my mouth.

'You make too much haste,' Marion said, looking upon me in bewilderment. 'Do you not know that haste makes waste?'

But I had seen, and done, enough. 'Swaddle her again,' I said. 'Put on her dirty petticoat. I must leave now.'

It is easy to fall into a net, but hard to get out again. 'Show us your purse, sir,' the ancient mistress answered urgently. 'We are not so low in the mud that we cannot reach for your money. What will it be, sir?'

I had too great a wish to be gone to enter into any contention with her, so I opened my purse and threw down some shillings for which they both scrabbled in the dust. 'Do you see what a kennel he comes from,' Marion shouted after me, 'that he must treat us all like beasts?'

'You deserve no more,' I replied.

Good Mistress Anne rose from her knees and, looking into my face, spat upon me; I made to strike her with my hand, but then she picked up a chamber-pot and threatened to spill its contents on me. So I let them go and, turning away, walked through the crowd of bawds who were listening keenly in the next room. I said nothing to John Overbury, who was cleaning his teeth with a knife by the threshold, but walked away from this wanton stew, this hot-house, this chamber of whores, followed by the most vile reproaches which a wit used to wicked and filthy thoughts can imagine. So ended the day on which my father died. *Laus Deo*.

FOUR

THE GARDENER FOUND the small bones. He had arrived to clean up the ground in front of the house and, although it was early in the morning, I thought I could smell drink upon his breath. He was wearing the headphones of a Walkman, and seemed to be swaying to some insistent tune. So I watched him as he set to work among the weeds and bushes; he was no more than middle-aged but he seemed very feeble, and immediately I regretted hiring him. The weeds defeated him, and he was bent over one patch of ground with a spade in his hand for several minutes. Then he began to examine the stone path tentatively and cautiously, as if it were about to collapse beneath his feet, before turning his attention to an area of tall grass. He was digging at its roots, without very much success, when suddenly he slipped and fell forward. I could see no other movement, so I hurried outside: he was sprawled inside a small pit which had been dug between some bushes but, more curiously, he had disturbed a ring of bones which had been neatly placed at the bottom of it.

'That's a very unusual thing,' he said, quite unperturbed by his fall. 'To see bones like that.'

My first sensation was that they were the remains of a child, and I looked at him in horror. 'What do you think they could be?'

'A dog. A cat. Some damn thing like that.' He picked up one of the bones and handed it to me; it felt oddly soft and pliable and I was tempted to put it up to my face, when I saw something gleaming by the side of the pit. It was a glass tube, snapped in half, and I recognized it at once: it was the same as the glass I had found in the drawer, with the odd distortion or protuberance at the end.

But it had broken so neatly, as if something had been carefully poured on to the ground.

I went back into the house, and opened the table beneath the window in the ground-floor room; the glass tube was no longer in the drawer. I looked more carefully, letting my hand slide over the dusty wooden interior, when I felt something yield to my touch. Some sheets of paper had been laid here. When I removed them I saw that on the first of them had been written, in crude capitals, DOCTOR DEE'S RECIPE. I stared at the words in surprise: here was the strangest proof of what I had discovered yesterday, and the identity of the one who came before me in this house was now unexpectedly confirmed. But what kind of 'recipe' was this?

So that it may grow without the help of any womb! This is the secret of all secrets, and must remain so until that time of the end when all secrets will be revealed. Let the spagyricus take the seed and place it within a sealed glass, for preference the glass of Antwerp in which all light and heat seem to prosper. Bury it within horse dung for the next forty days, together with four true magnets in the shape of a cross, without forgetting to renew the water within the glass by pouring in the liquid of fresh dew each fourth day; then on the forty-first day it will begin to breathe and move its limbs. It will seem to you like a perfect human shape, but transparent and without any eyes. Now it must imbibe *arcanum sanguinis hominis* for the space of one year, all the while remaining beneath the glass, and at the end of that time it will be a pretty little infant thing. It will be a true homunculus, therefore, and can be taught like any other child; it will grow and prosper with all its intellect and faculties, until its thirtieth year when it will fall asleep and return to its first unformed state. One of the generation of the Inspirati must then cherish it, and place it again within glass, so that this secret and wonderful being may grow once again and walk upon the world. If you speak to it the sacred words it will prophesy about future events most cunningly, but its chief glory is that with proper care and reverence it will be constantly regenerated and so live for ever.

I looked up, and through the window glimpsed the clouds passing across the house. They formed such strange shapes that for a moment I thought I saw my own face among them; but the vision faded, and I looked down again at the papers I held in my hand. How could such things be? Margaret Lucas had told me that Doctor Dee practised black magic, but this was some monstrous fantasy. To create an artificial life within a tube of glass ... I turned to the next sheet of paper, and then saw this.

PASSAGES IN ITS LIFE

It survived the Black Death by taking a compound of tannic acid, which it mixed instinctively. It prophesied the Great Fire, though no one listened. Dogs barked at its coming, and horses were afraid, but nothing else in nature recognized it for what it was. Yet it was loved by cats.

It knew Isaac Newton, and they held many learned conferences in which it explained to him the scientific meaning of the kabbalah. It was present at Newton's death, and was the thing which placed the coins upon his eyes.

It joined the Royal Society, and did several notable experiments upon the functions of the lymph gland.

It created the air pump, and then wrote in its pocket-book: Only our visions give us away.

It was employed in a glassworks, in Holborn, making lenses for the Greenwich Observatory.

It was once attacked by a London mob, which from its pale complexion thought it was a Huguenot.

It was a teacher at St Mary's Infant School in Walthamstow when it was first opened in 1824. Here it made a model of Trevithick's steam locomotive, to the great delight of the children. In the company of young people its natural colour was a light pink, which was ascribed by the other teachers to rapid circulation of the blood.

It has worked in the sewers beneath London.

It looked after Charles Babbage from his infancy, knowing him to hold the key to future prosperity.

It loved to walk among the New Docks at Wapping where there was an iron swing-bridge.

It worked on radar during the Second World War.

It travelled to the moon.

There are times when it leads an ordinary life in the world, without

124

knowing anything of its destiny, but then by accident it causes wonders. It is such a loving subject that it helps others to find their true genius. It remembers nothing about its past or future until it returns home at the end of its thirty years, but it always does return home.

It has a doctrine – it believes in progress and the perfectibility of man. That is why, in the presence of superstitious people, it changes from white to red.

This is its vision of the future. It knows that contemporary science will develop so far that it will return to its origins, purified, and then expound the mysteries of the past. The doctrines of the alchemists and the astrologers, whom the homunculus knew very well, will then be revived within the great vision of quantum theory.

It knew Galen, and says that his beliefs were essentially correct. The doctrine of the humours will therefore be revived. The homunculus further tells us that the theory of the four elements is also accurate in a spiritual sense and will one day be employed by theoretical physicists.

It has one great fear. If the cycle of the ages is not mastered by great scientists, then the end of time (which it prophesies for the year 2365) will be reversed. It knows then that the centuries will roll back and that humankind will return in stages to its beginning. The Victorian and Elizabethan periods will recur, and Rome will rise again before crumbling into the darkness of what we now call pre-history.

I had read enough, but I looked at the paper a little longer; I seemed to know the handwriting, and then at once I realized that it was my father's.

There was a tapping at the door, and I went towards it in alarm. It was the gardener. 'What do you want me to do with those bones?'

'Bury them,' I said. 'Bury them as deep as you can.' He looked so worn and tired from digging in the old garden that I felt sorry for him. 'No. Wait a minute. I'll help you.'

So together we walked over to the pit and covered the circle of bones with dry earth; then I poured more soil upon the spot, and stamped it down with my foot. I had already taken out the two halves of the glass tube, and now I carried them down Cloak Lane and into the churchyard of St James. I would have been happy to linger among the graves, but there were two old men sitting apart on fragments of the stone wall there; it was as if they were waiting for resurrection. I did not want to disturb them and so, on an impulse, I climbed the steps towards the front porch; the great wooden door was unlocked, and I entered the cool darkness of the church. I was still holding the glass, and as soon as I saw the baptismal font by a side altar I knew what I should do. I went over and filled both pieces with holy water; the water seemed warm to my touch, and I placed the halves of the glass tube against the small altar. Then I crept down the aisle, and sat in one of the wooden pews. I do not know if I tried to pray – there was nothing I really wished to pray *for* – but I remember kneeling down and putting my face in my hands. Somehow I wanted to lose myself, and so be at peace. But as I knelt there in the silence I knew there could be no rest for me here: my god dwelt where my love was, and my love was for the past. If I had any deity, it was contained within time itself. That was all I could worship and reverence – that passage of the generations which, as a researcher, I tried to enter. There was nothing for me in this place.

It was midday by the time I returned to Cloak Lane, and the gardener had gone. I hurried along the path, taking care not to look at the mound of freshly dug earth, and opened the door as quickly as I could: I did not want to admit to myself that I was afraid to enter the old house, now that I had found the notes in my father's handwriting. If I once entertained that fear, where might it lead? I might find myself permanently estranged or excluded from what was, after all, my inheritance.

Once again I was surprised by the silence of the house, and I could hear myself breathing as I sat down on the stairs. I was about to climb up to my bedroom, when I heard the low murmur or whisper of water. Was this what John Dee had heard, as the stream of the Fleet flowed down in his garden towards the Thames? Then I realized that the sound was coming from within the house. I could still hear my own breathing as I hurried into the kitchen, but nothing was wrong: I had left the tap running in the sink, and the water was flowing down the drain to the pipes beneath the earth. It was such a clear stream, too. It sparkled in the light of the sun coming through the window, and for a moment I closed my eyes in peace. When I opened them, the water was gone. The current had been stopped. And what was this? I recalled leaving my breakfast cup and plate in the sink, but now I could see them gleaming upon the shelf. I must have cleaned and dried them in some reverie, and it occurred to me that there might have been other occasions when I wandered through this house like a sleepwalker. I went up to my own room and noticed, with some surprise, that the bed had been made; as far as I was aware, I had left it in a state of disarray that morning. After a moment I realized that a small carpet had been laid across the carefully folded sheets. It was then I telephoned Daniel Moore.

He arrived soon after, and listened very quietly as I tried to explain everything that seemed to have happened within the house. For some reason I did not mention the notes about the homunculus, perhaps because it was too ridiculous a fantasy to entertain. But I did mention John Dee, and then for no particular reason started laughing. Daniel got up quickly from his chair, and went over to the window. 'Summer will be coming to an end shortly,' he said, rubbing his hands with satisfaction. 'No more late nights.'

I was about to ask him about his strange knowledge of the house – how he had found the recess under the stairs and how he knew about the sealed window – when the telephone rang. It was my mother and, before I could say anything, she began apologizing for her behaviour two days before. She would have called earlier, she said, but she had been ill ever since. 'I was coming down with something, Matty. I just wasn't myself. I wasn't myself at all.'

'How are your eyes?'

'My eyes?'

'Are you still seeing things?'

'Oh no. Of course not. I'm not seeing anything now.'

'It must have been the house, I suppose.' I was eager to have her opinion on this place. 'Did you like it?'

'How could I like it, Matthew, when I felt so ill?' Her curt manner had re-emerged, but then she apologized again and rang off.

When I came back into the room, Daniel was still looking out of the window and he started to whistle. Then he returned to his chair and leaned over to me, his hands clasped in front of him as if he were praying very earnestly. 'Let's put it this way, Matthew. Aren't we being a little too theatrical? Do you really believe that someone, or something, is living here with you?'

'But what about the dishes, and the carpet on the bed?'

'Perhaps we were doing a little sweeping, or dusting, and left it there by accident.' His hands were still clasped tightly in front of him. 'Haven't we been rather absent-minded recently?'

'Well . . .'

'I'm telling you, Matthew, that nothing out of the ordinary has happened here.' I suppose I was reassured by what he said, although the alternative – that something 'out of the ordinary' had occurred in this house – was too disagreeable to consider. 'Let's stick to what is known rather than what is unknown,' he was saying now. 'Tell me exactly what you found out yesterday.'

'Only that John Dee paid rates here in 1563 and that, according to Margaret Lucas, he was a black magician.'

'Oh, she always has something fanciful to say.'

'You asked me the other day how far I wanted to take this research.' I felt very tired and had the most peculiar sensation of hearing myself speaking from a distance, as if I were somewhere else within the room. 'I want to know everything, Daniel. I won't find any rest until I do. How does that poem go? "And yet can I not hide me in no dark place".'

He looked at me oddly for a moment, as if I had spoken out of turn. 'I suppose it is the right thing to do.'

'It's the only thing to do. It's my responsibility.'

'You make it sound as if you belong to the house.'

'I feel as if I belong to something. Don't you feel it, too?' It occurred to me suddenly that I might hang the carpets on the walls, so that the polished stone of the floor could reflect their colours. 'And don't you think there's a kind of duty involved?

When you come to a place like this? I owe it to the house. I owe it to myself.'

'And to John Dee?'

'Of course. In a sense he's my ancestor now.'

I closed my eyes; I must have been more tired than I knew, because at once I found myself dreaming of the churchyard I had just visited. There was a tramp and a dog walking towards me. But I could only have slept for a moment because now, when I awoke, I could hear Daniel talking as if there had been no interval at all. 'In that case,' he was saying, 'John Dee may be waiting for us somewhere. Where shall we begin?'

★

Once upon a time I was afraid of libraries. Those shelves of books formed a world which had, almost literally, turned its back upon me; the smell of dust and wood, and faded pages, induced in me a sense of melancholy loss. Yet I began to repair my life when I became a researcher and entered the past: then one book led to another book, one document to another document, one theme to another theme, and I was led down a sweet labyrinth of learning in which I could lose myself. It has been said that books talk to one another when no one is present to hear them speak, but I know better than that: they are forever engaged in an act of silent communion which, if we are fortunate, we can overhear. I soon came to recognize the people who also understood this. They were the ones who always relaxed as they walked among the shelves, as if they were being comforted and protected by a thousand invisible presences. They seem to be talking to themselves but, no, they are talking to the books. And so I am a subscriber to the English History Library in Carver's Square, which, of all London libraries, is the most curious and dilapidated; the passages are narrow, the stairs circuitous, and the general atmosphere one of benign decay. The books here are often piled up on the floors, while the shelves can hardly bear the weight of the volumes which have been deposited on them over the years. Yet, somewhere among this ruin, I hoped to find John Dee.

In fact, to my surprise, there were two books devoted to him in an alcove labelled, in old-fashioned Gothic script, 'The History of English Science'. The most recent was *John Dee's Natural Philosophy: Between Science and Religion* by Nicholas Clulee, and as soon as I took it down from the shelf I realized that this was not the history of a black magician; there was a bibliography of thirty-four pages and it was clear, even from my brief examination of the chapters, that this was a serious account of mathematics, of astronomy, and of philosophy. Beside this volume was another, *John Dee: The World of an Elizabethan Magus* by Peter French; and when I took it down, he stared at me. He was depicted on the cover, and in my sudden fright I almost dropped the book. I had not expected to see him so soon, and it took me a moment before I could look at the painting again. The eyes were slightly too large, as if the artist had not known how to capture their brightness, and there was something about his expression that disquieted me. His capacious forehead was framed by a black skull cap; he had a medium-length grey beard, which spilled over his white ruff, and he seemed to be wearing a black gown. And yet what was wrong with his expression? He looked both menacing and confidential, as if he harboured some secret of great importance which he might or might not reveal to me. But his eyes were so wide, and so steady, that I could not help but meet his gaze.

I carried these books back to Cloak Lane, and placed them on the table beneath the window. I suppose that this was for me the strangest part of all – to leave these books about Doctor Dee in the same room where he had once walked. I felt as if I were some magician, trying to conjure him into existence from the grave. And then suddenly it occurred to me that he might have died in this house. I could have opened one of the books to discover the truth of this, but instead I turned and left the room.

I opened the front door and went out into the garden. It was a humid summer evening after another humid day, and I was peculiarly tired and nerveless. I do not think I would have noticed even if the spectre of John Dee had suddenly risen up before me: I felt too much of a ghost myself. I walked slowly over to the side of the garden, where a narrow passage still filled with weeds separated my house from a high public wall. I had never properly examined this narrow space, largely because it was filled with the kind of stray profuse vegetation which might harbour living things. But I walked through it now, and ran my hand across the old wall; it was cold, and some of its crumbling texture adhered to my fingers. I licked it, and it tasted like ancient salt.

It was then I noticed how, near the level of the ground, large black marks were painted across the stone; at least that was how it seemed to me for a moment, but when I knelt down I realized that these stains had deeply impregnated the stone itself. They looked like scorch marks. I turned to the wall of the house, and patches of blackened stone were also visible. Something had burned here. Or the house itself had been touched by fire. And if the original upper storeys of the house had been destroyed, it would explain the eighteenth- and nineteenth-century additions. It could not have happened in the Great Fire, since Clerkenwell was not part of the area of burning London. No, this had occurred at some earlier time.

I looked up at the sky for a moment, shielding my eyes from its brightness, and then without thought I lifted my shirt, pulled down my trousers, squatted upon the ground, and defecated. I was so surprised by what I had done that I rose hastily to my feet and stood there for a minute or so, slowly rocking backwards and forwards. Was it in shit like this that the homunculus had grown? I could have stayed there for ever, looking down at the ground, but I was disturbed by a noise behind me; it sounded like laughter, but then turned into a sigh. Had someone been watching me all this time? I pulled up my trousers and ran back into the house.

★

John Dee was described by Aubrey as 'one of the ornaments of his Age'; Queen Elizabeth called him 'hyr philosopher', and another contemporary said that he was 'the prince of Mathematicians of this age'. Peter French, in his biography, declared him to be 'Elizabethan England's greatest magus'. So much I recognized at once. But then, over the next few days, I began to be surprised by this man who had once inhabited my house; he was an adept in mathematics and astronomy, in geography and navigation, in antiquarian studies and natural philosophy, in astrology and the mechanical sciences, in magic and theology. I consulted other books which chronicled his development: Frances Yates's *Giordano Bruno and the Hermetic Tradition*, *Astronomical Thought in Renaissance England* by F. R. Johnson, and E.G.R. Taylor's *Tudor Geography, 1485–1583*. All these accounts had very little to do with his reputation as a conjuror or a black magician and, as I read various alternative descriptions in other texts, the only familiar image was the face I now knew so well. Every time I entered the ground-floor room, with its thick stone walls and narrow windows, I took up the book and tried to return his steady gaze.

In Frances Yates's history Doctor Dee was described as a 'Renaissance Magus' who continued in England the same hermetic tradition that encompassed Ficino, Pico della Mirandola and Giordano Bruno. But in his study Nicholas Clulee disagreed, suggesting that a large part of Doctor Dee's inheritance came from medieval sources and particularly from the writings and experiments of Roger Bacon. Where Yates tended to see Doctor Dee as the steady exponent of a European philosophy, Clulee described him as a more eclectic and empirical figure. Yet all my books conveyed the same central theme – that he stood upon that ground where the concerns of his age met and could not easily be distinguished. There was another fact which seemed to be of equal significance. John Dee himself had, in one way or another, belonged to every time. He was in part a medievalist, expounding ancient formulae, but he was also an active agent in contemporary natural philosophy; he was an antiquarian, who speculated about the origins of Britain and the presence of ancient cities beneath the earth, but he was also one of those who anticipated a future scientific revolution with his experiments in mechanics; he was an alchemist and astrologer who scrutinized the spiritual world, but he was also a geographer who plotted navigation charts for Elizabethan explorers. He was everywhere at once and, as I walked about his old house, I had the sense that somehow he had conquered time.

Through these books, too, I came to understand the alchemy in which John Dee placed his faith. He believed the world to be imbued with spiritual properties – with 'signatures' and 'correspondences' that reveal its true nature. The seed of the aconite is used to cure optical disorders because it is in the shape of an eyelid; the breed of dog called the Bedlington terrier resembles a lamb and is thus the most nervous of its species. Each material thing is the visible home of a universal power, or congregation of powers, and it was the task of the enlightened philosopher and alchemist to see these true constituents. He understood from the very successful medicine of Paracelsus, for example, how the stars, the plants of the earth and the human body might be fruitfully combined to effect cures. But there was another truth: God is within man, according to John Dee, and he who understands himself understands the universe. The alchemist finds the perfection or pure will within all materials; he knows that salt is desire, mercury is turbulence, sulphur is anguish. When the alchemist finds that will and idea within the material form, then he is able to bend it to his own will. For this was the truth which John Dee maintained all his life – there is nothing in heaven and earth which is not also in man, and he quoted Paracelsus to the effect that 'the human body is vapour materialized by sunshine, mixed with the life of the stars'. When the astrologer sees the sun rise, according to Dee, the sun within his own self rises in joy. This is the true gold of wisdom.

That, at least, was the theory. But in reading accounts of his life (there was even a novel about him by Marjorie Bowen, entitled *I Dwelt In High Places*), it became clear that he was too concerned with secrets and with mysteries – with numerology, cabbalistic tables, and magical technique. He became infatuated with the poetry of power and darkness, which in turn made him susceptible to the demands of envy and ambition. So there were times when he lost sight of that sacred truth he wished to investigate.

I knew now the full story of his life – his intense studies as a young man, his travels to Europe where he had acquired his reputation as an extraordinary scholar, his services to Queen Elizabeth, his scientific and mathematical researches, his creation of the largest library in England, his work as an alchemist and a magician. He believed that he spoke with angels, and as yet I had found no reason to disbelieve him. He was a man obsessed with learning, one who spent his entire life trying to resolve the mysteries of nature and, by various means, to achieve a kind of divine illumination. He knew too much to be impressed by the work of his contemporaries, and understood too much to be unduly affected by their malice when he went beyond the boundaries of established theory. He was energetic, ambitious, determined; and yet, as I said, there was a darker aspect to his love of learning. He seemed to want knowledge, and power, at almost any cost to himself or those around him. Something drove him forward, something harried him into that darkness where he spoke to the angels and plotted the restoration of the spiritual world through the agency of alchemy. Many of his contemporaries believed that the Devil was perched upon his shoulder, but how could I believe that as I sat in the room where he had once worked?

And what books had he written here? Had he composed his mathematical preface to *The Elements of Geometrie of the most auncient Philosopher Euclide of Megara* as he looked from his window at the quietly flowing stream of the Fleet? Had he paced around this room, as I paced now, while preparing his thoughts for *General and rare Memorials pertayning to the Perfect Arte of Navigation*? Had he laboured upon *Monas Hieroglyphica* and *Propaedeumata Aphoristica* in this house? I spoke the titles out loud, but stopped when it began to sound like the chanting of some priest or nun. After a few moments I took up another book, a modern translation of Doctor Dee's *Liber Mysteriorum Sextus et Sanctus*; there was a photograph of the original title-page among the illustrations, and on it were inscribed four signs that sent me racing from the room towards the stairs that led under the ground. I switched on the light for the basement and crossed the floor, cautiously approaching the marks which had been scratched above the sealed door; they were the same as the signs in the book, but some other element was missing from them. In the title-page illustration, 'Sunsfor', 'Zosimos', 'Gohulim' and 'Od' had been written underneath each in turn, but these names were not inscribed upon the door. On this old title-page there was also a picture of a glass bowl, covered with straw, or mud, or some other substance; beneath it I could read the words, 'You will live for ever'. I do not know what happened to me then; I turned and turned under the electric light until I could no longer stand. Then I lay upon the stone floor.

There was a noise in one of the upstairs rooms, and the crash of something falling to the ground. I rolled upon the cold stone, not wishing to leave it yet. But then there was another crash, and unwillingly I rose to my feet: if I hesitated now, I would never be able to remain in this house. When I came to the top of the stairs, by the open door, I heard a sound like rustling coming from somewhere above me; I looked up, but I could see nothing. I crossed the hallway and climbed the stairs to the first landing; the door to my room was open and, as I glanced across my bed, I noticed a white mark upon it like a little globe of smoke. Then something moved across it.

I screamed, and it rose up towards me; I staggered backwards, and would have fallen down the stairs if I had not caught hold of the banister. I thrust out my hands, and they brushed against something very warm. And then there was a fluttering of wings. It was a pigeon. It must have come in through the open window, and was no doubt one of those I had seen clustering around the churchyard of St James. I did not want to touch it: I had a horror of its beating heart beneath my fingers, and of its writhing within my hands. The bird had wheeled back into the room and quietly I followed it, opened my window wider still, and then left it there – beating its wings against the wall – while I closed the door.

There was something amusing about all this. I went back into the room, where the bird was still ineffectually fluttering against the walls and ceilings. There was a book beside my bed – a study of John Dee's alchemical charts – and, with all the violence I could summon with a prayer, I hurled it against the bird. I must have damaged its wing because it slumped down on to the floor and then, with a cry of triumph, I brought my heel down upon its head. I don't know how many times I stamped upon it, but I stopped only when I saw the blood running on to the book which was lying beside the dead bird.

It was then I telephoned Daniel Moore and asked him to visit me that evening: I knew that he was concealing some fact about the house and, in that moment of violence and power, I wanted to discover everything. I was wiping the blood of the dead bird from the cover of Doctor Dee's book when he arrived. 'Sometimes,' I said, 'I'm convinced that there's a madman somewhere in this house.'

'And what makes you say that?'

'Oh, I don't know. Dead animals everywhere. Piles of shit.' He looked at me in surprise for a moment, and I laughed. 'Don't worry. I'm only joking.'

I went into the kitchen, ostensibly to pour him a glass of whisky, but really to devour a plate of biscuits that had been left for me upon the shelf; there were two packets of assorted nuts beside them, and I managed to finish them before coming back into the room.

'If there was someone in the house, Matthew –'

'I know. I would have found him by now.' Then I laughed again. 'Do you want to know why my hands are dirty?'

'I don't think so.'

'I've been doing some digging. Look.' I pointed out the books scattered around the room, and tried to describe precisely what it was I had discovered about John Dee. 'And do you wonder why I'm so confused,' I said, after a long explanation, 'when every book has a different Doctor Dee? Not one is alike. The past is difficult, you see. You think you understand a person or an event, but then you turn a corner and everything is different once again. Just like you. I turned the corner of Charlotte Street and you were different.'

'I wondered when you were going to bring that up again.'

But I brushed his words aside with a movement of my hand. 'It's like this house, too. Nothing ever seems to stay in the same place. And do you know what? This may have been the actual room where Doctor Dee saw his visions. What did I call it just now?'

'The scrying room. Or the chamber of presence. What is the matter, Matthew?'

'Did you hear something then?'

'No.'

'I thought I heard a voice.'

'You'll be seeing him next, glimmering in the corner.'

'Well, I do see him. Look here.' I held up the book, with the portrait of Doctor Dee on its cover. 'Reader,' I said, 'this is the beginning and the end.'

We finished our drinks soon after and then walked slowly to the restaurant by Clerkenwell Green, where we had eaten a week before. I had known nothing then about John Dee, but now my life had changed. It was a warm night, and through the open window I could see the lighted interior of a small printing-works on the opposite side of the Green. Someone was moving back and forth and, in his random gestures against the light, I saw something of the frailty of all living things. A cluster of small flies, or gnats, was hovering near the door of the restaurant; they were circling in the evening air, with the setting sun glinting upon their wings. They might fly over the threshold into this small room, and to them it would seem an almighty palace of wonder. But where was the place to which I might fly, and see the glory around me?

As we sat down at the restaurant table I felt some excitement pass over me, but it was of so rare a kind that it seemed like sickness. I had experienced this sensation once or twice before, and I knew that something was about to happen. Something was about to change. I took the bottle of Frascati which the waiter had brought over to the table, and poured myself a very large glass before handing it to Daniel. There was a constriction in my throat, and some fire within me which I needed to extinguish; if I believed in such things, I might have been embodying the alchemical theory of the dry world aspiring to the moist. Daniel was watching me with uneasy amusement as I poured myself another glass of wine. 'Are we very thirsty?'

137

'Yes. We are. It's not often I sit opposite a beautiful woman.'

He looked at me reproachfully for a moment. 'Do you have to keep on mentioning that business?'

'But I'm very interested in you, Daniel. I become more interested all the time. How did you know that one of the upstairs windows was sealed?'

He put his index finger up to his nose, and sniffed it. 'There are always sealed windows in old houses. Haven't you heard of Pitt's window tax?'

'And by some miracle you also knew that there was a cupboard under the stairs.'

'I guessed.' He was still sniffing his finger. 'Or do you think I have magical powers?'

'Magic had nothing to do with it. You remembered something.' I filled my glass again. 'You know that house very well, don't you?' He shook his head with an uncharacteristically violent motion. 'There's no point in lying to me, Daniel. I think my mother recognized you, too.'

'She doesn't know me at all. I can promise you that.'

'But what else can you promise me?'

'Nothing.' He had lowered his eyes and, when the waiter came over to take our order, he took advantage of the diversion to clear his throat. Then he tightened the knot of his tie with another violent gesture. 'It's very odd,' he said, 'but whenever I come to this area, I always want to get back to Islington again. Is that what they call homesickness? And have you ever wondered who "they" are?'

I was tired of his attempts to divert me. 'Go on, Daniel. It's time.'

He looked at me directly now. 'This is all very difficult.' I noticed that his left hand was trembling, and I watched it with interest as he continued in a low voice. 'You're quite right. I have been to the house before. I knew your father. I went there with him sometimes.'

I had become very still. 'And why was that?'

'There is something I ought to tell you. I've been meaning . . .'

The waiter had brought us a first course of parma ham, and Daniel began to cut it into very small pieces.

'Go on.'

'Your father and I knew each other very well.' He stopped again, and continued cutting the meat without putting any of it into his mouth. 'We met in that club. Where you found me.'

'I don't think I know what you mean.'

'Yes. You do. Your father and I were lovers.' I think I rose to my feet but, at his look of alarm, I must have sat down again. He started talking very quickly, almost incoherently. 'It was about ten years ago. I do prefer older men, you see. And he was very charming. Very gentle.'

The excitement, or sickness, which I had sensed before was now all around me. It was as if I were bathed in some white light which made every movement and every word distinct. I got up again, and walked to the small lavatory at the back of the restaurant. I sat on the bowl of the toilet, and stared at the graffiti on the yellow door in front of me – something about a penis and a tube. I could see them together, Daniel and my father, lying naked in the basement. I could see them kissing one another. I could see my father kneeling against the sealed door, while Daniel knelt in front of him with his mouth open. I could see Daniel's dress and wig being hurled against the wall, while my father smiled that peculiar smile I knew so well. I could see them in The World Turned Upside Down, dancing together in the dim red light. And then I wondered what it would be like to have my father's tongue down my throat. I stood up, and vomited into the bowl.

Curiously enough, when I returned to the table I was smiling. 'Tell me, Daniel. Did he wear women's clothes as well?'

'Oh no.' He seemed almost offended at the suggestion. 'But he liked me to wear them. Around the house.'

I had heard enough. Now I understood the reason he had bought the property in Cloak Lane – it was the perfect cover for his sexual activities. There had never been any reason for him to divorce my mother, because she also had acted as a form of camouflage. But perhaps she had realized this all the time; that was why she remained so angry with him, even after his death. Perhaps she also suspected that my father had left me everything because I was in some way involved – but that was too hard a thought to bear. The whole of my past life had shifted now, and in these few moments had acquired a different shape. It seemed as if I must approach my own history as I approached the history of other centuries. 'Did he ever mention Doctor Dee?' was all I could think of asking him.

'Not as far as I remember.' We had both now assumed our customary manner and tone, as if we were trying somehow to reassure each other that nothing essentially had changed. He ate his food very quickly, stuffing it into his mouth and swallowing it voraciously. 'But he did say that there was something special about the house. He thought that something had once happened there, and he wanted to restore it. Or relive it. I'm not sure what he meant. But that was why –' Once more he hesitated.

'It's a little late to keep any secrets.'

'He believed in something called sexual magic. He believed that you could raise spirits by practising, well, certain things.'

'And did he?'

'Did he?'

'Did he raise the spirits?'

'Of course not.'

So here was another truth with which I had to become reconciled. My father had practised magic in Cloak Lane, in the vain hope of conjuring up the ghosts of the past; that, at least, seemed to be the substance of Daniel's confession to me. He had performed some kind of sexual rite for the sole purpose of finding something which, he believed, still resided within the house. Could it be connected with his speculations about the homunculus? There were dark passages and corners here which I did not want to explore. In any case he should have known something I was now beginning to understand from my knowledge of John Dee: only love can restore life. The rest is illusion, and trickery, and nonsense.

'I never believed any of it,' Daniel was saying now, as some spaghetti was placed in front of us. I stared down at the white threads with something like horror. 'Some historians say that radicalism and occultism were related to each other, but I think it was only an act of despair. It was a way of pretending to have some secret force at your command, of imagining you had a form of power which could destroy the established powers. But occultism is really a refuge for the weak and the desperate. It's radicalism gone sour.'

'But my father was never weak.'

'No. He wasn't weak. Most occultists work in groups – it helps to bolster their confidence. But your father was different. He was quite alone. And he really believed that he had come upon a secret truth. It was as if it were some kind of inheritance.'

There was a meaning in all this which alarmed me. 'Did he ever mention me?'

'All the time.'

'Not when –'

'No. We remained friends, after we ceased to be lovers. He had a great passion for the past, you see. Just like you. He was always interested in what I was doing. Funnily enough, he was the one who led me to the Moravians. He found those meeting-places we visited. Do you remember?'

'Yes. I remember.' My father was coming too close to me, and it filled me with fear. I ordered some more wine, while Daniel tightened the knot of his tie again.

'There's something else I have to tell you, Matthew.'

'Oh God.'

'We didn't meet by accident.' The wine had come, and I started drinking heavily again. 'About two years ago, your father realized that he had contracted cancer. That's when he asked me to watch over you. He said that you were very special.'

'Special?'

'He said that you were unique. And of course you are. He just didn't want you to come to any harm. He told me what libraries you used, and it was easy enough to arrange an encounter. We share the same interests, after all, and London can be a very small city.' He stopped suddenly, trying to observe my reaction; but he could see none. 'I hope you don't think I'm a very dreadful person. We did become friends, after all.'

We had come to the end of our meal, as far as I was concerned, but it was still so early that the restaurant was almost empty. A young man and woman were sitting close together in a corner of the room, and I had already noticed that they were whispering intently. I strained to hear what they were saying, but all I could make out were stray angry words – 'worm', 'bitch', 'cow'.

'I'm sorry,' I said to Daniel. 'I really can't put up with this any longer.' I left the table, and went over to them. They looked at me in alarm. 'Why don't you fucking keep quiet?' I whispered, just as they had whispered. 'Do you hear me? Shut your fucking mouths.' Then I returned to Daniel. 'And that reminds me, my darling. I must get back to the house.'

I left him at once, and as I looked into the window I was pleased to see him bewildered and unhappy. I was no longer aware of any particular sensation as I walked back to Cloak Lane, and instead I began repeating the words of a song I had heard that morning as I sat in the old house. I think it was called 'Fortune, My Foe', but I could not be absolutely sure. I passed the churchyard and then, feeling the need to piss after so much wine, I jumped across the stone wall and urinated on one of the gravestones. Something moved beside it, and after I had zipped up my trousers I stamped on it with my foot. I felt as if I were knocking upon an open door.

THE ABBEY

'I HEAR SOMEONE knocking at my door,' I said to my servant, Philip Fox. 'See who it is.'

He hastened down the stairs, where I heard him talking to my wife's servant.

'Audrey, where are the keys?'

'They hang on the nail behind the door, where they are always to be found.'

'They are not! They are not here!' All the while there was a continual knocking, which was enough to wake the dead; I found myself musing upon my father's old dog, when the sound of Philip's voice roused me. 'Who may be there?'

'A friend, I hope. Open the door, since it rains so hard. I have come for Doctor Dee.' These words terrified me for an instant, and I rose from my chair.

'What is your pleasure? Who shall I say asks for him?'

'Tell him that it is one who was lately apprenticed to a good friend.'

'Come in, sir.' I heard the unlocking and unbolting of the door, and then some more hurried words. 'Sir,' Philip called to me. 'There is a gentleman here who would speak to you.'

'Cause him to come up. No, wait. I will come down.' I wanted no stranger to see me at my work and, further, I much doubted who it was that enquired for me. I put on my gown and, with some trembling, went downstairs to greet him. Yet it was nothing but a spruce sprightly fellow, and I swallowed my fears as I approached him. 'You are welcome,' I said. 'How do you?'

'Well, sir, by God's grace.'

'And how might I call you?'

'Kelley, sir. Edward Kelley. For seven years I was apprenticed to Ferdinand Griffen, who often spoke of you.'

'I knew him well. I have not seen him these last twenty years, but there were many times he did me the turn of a good friend. How does he do?'

'He is dead, sir, of a cancer in the breast.'

'I am sorry to hear of it. Yet he must have been a pretty aged man.'

'True, sir, very true. But before he died, he begged me to make acquaintance with you.'

This Kelley was wearing a jerkin of well-padded leather and a short cloak in the Spanish fashion; now, as he was giving me this great courtesy, I could see the rain soaking into his apparel. 'Come dry yourself in my chamber,' I said to him. 'You are wet through. Philip, go fetch some more wood and make a good fire. Bring up a bushel of coals, too, so that Mr Kelley may thoroughly warm himself.' I invited him to climb the stairs and, as I followed him, I could smell strong drink upon his breath; he was a young man, no more than twenty-two or twenty-three years, of small stature and with a red beard cut like his cloak in the Spanish fashion. He had a great mane of red hair which, as I pressed close upon his heels, I could see to be oiled and perfumed. Here was a gallant gentleman indeed, yet for the sake of Ferdinand Griffen I was civil enough to him. 'Sit down beside the fire,' I said as I entered my chamber, 'and tell me of my old master in art.'

'He reverenced you, sir, as one of the order of Inspirati.'

'No, no, it is nothing. Nothing at all.' I did not want him to come too close to my pursuits. 'If it had not been for his faithful and diligent care, I would never have reached the first step in skill or power. There was never an untrue action, nor an imperfection, in any of his practices.'

'Yes, sir. Truly he was a great magician.'

'I did not say that,' I added hastily. 'Mr Griffen was a philosopher when I shared his lodgings and worked with him.'

'But many philosophers are certainly great magicians. Is that not so, Doctor Dee?'

I saw now that he was no mere roaring boy, and I suspected that he might be some agent sent to inform against me. 'I suppose that there may be some secret philosophy,' I continued, 'but, for me, it is a thing not in the air.'

'And a secret knowledge of nature?'

'Well, that may be, that may be.' Now I thought to test him, as Philip came up with the coals. 'But tell me, what was his work in these last days?'

He looked at me strangely. 'We had travelled to Glastonbury, sir, about a month ago.'

'Truly? Why so?'

'Oh . . .' He seemed unwilling to speak. 'There is a time when such things can be spoken of, but —'

This made me prick up my ears (as they say), but I resolved to keep my own counsel and await the occasion: I knew well enough that Glastonbury was the most ancient seat of learning in the entire kingdom, where, it is said, the giants who originally inhabited this realm had placed their secrets. 'You have come suddenly upon me,' I continued, smiling, 'but perhaps you will stay for a scholar's collation? It is plain food, but I hope you will take it in good part.'

'With all my heart, Doctor Dee. What do they say? Talk after meat is best?'

'Yes. That is what they say.'

And so we went down, where Philip was already preparing the board. My wife meantime was busy about the basins and towels, but gave acknowledgement to Mr Kelley's bow and answered his questions boldly enough. Yet it was all tittle-tattle, and soon I had endured enough of it. 'Rinse the glass, mistress,' I said to her, 'that I may taste the wine.' It was a Flemish grape, and somewhat sharp on the tongue; but I love bitter fruit, and supped it up willingly. 'How do you like this wine?' I asked our guest.

'I like it very well.'

My wife laughed at this, and I turned upon her. 'Why do you laugh, mistress?'

'Why? The face of our guest was plain to see when he tasted it.

You are not a subtle fellow, Mr Kelley. You cannot deceive us that you like our wine.'

'No, madam, no. You imagine evil where there is only goodness.' He spoke in a railing sort, which seemed to please her. 'The wine delights me. It has a northern taste.' Philip and Audrey had now covered the table, and Kelley burst out with, 'Oh, sir, it is too much. There is as much meat as at a wedding.' I suspected then that he was no spy, or agent, but indeed what he claimed to be.

We took our places, and after I had spoken the grace we fell to the dishes.

'I pray you,' Mrs Dee said, 'I pray you, husband, cut a little of that powder-beef, the sight of which makes Mr Kelley long to eat of it. Is that not true, sir?'

'Certainly, madam, it is true.'

'Or will you eat of this veal, sir? Or this leg of mutton?' Then she continued with the railing which he had begun. 'Yet I believe you are so fine that you cannot eat such gross meats. Is that not so?'

'I can eat anything if it be from your table.'

'Philip,' I said, 'give me your knife. This one is not sharp, and cuts nothing.' I was in an ill humour, since I cannot abide too much talk at dinner. 'The crust of this pie is too much baked,' I continued, looking at my wife opposite to me.

'No, no, it is well enough done,' she replied. 'But it is a great pity that the sauce is so run out. It is the fault of the baker: I wish that he had it in his own stomach.'

'Wife, have we nothing else?'

'Yes, husband. Perhaps Mr Kelley will try our shell-fish while he waits for the meat to be cut. Or will you try these smelts and eels? There is good Parmesan beside them, Mr Kelley, grated with sage and sugar in the London fashion.'

'In these cold days,' he replied, 'no food can be too hot, and the physicians say that there is nothing hotter than shell-fish. So I will eat them with a good grace, if it please you to serve them to me.'

I like to set a full table before strangers, even though I myself eat quickly and without any savour. For what is the lot of man but

146

to hunger after that which he does not have, and distaste that which is set before him? The appetite is great, the practice meagre. 'Do not speak to me of physicians,' I said. 'They know nothing. Less than nothing. There are some fools who cannot have a fart awry but they must have their purgation pills or, if there is the least spot upon the face, then they must have a pill to curb hot blood. But not I. I do not wait at the door for the apothecary with his lozenges and antidotes.'

'Truly, Doctor Dee, you are wise in that.'

'What is there that an apothecary would have me know? That melancholy may be cured with sovereign hellebore, or choler with the rhubarb? Well, I will tell him this in turn, that the stone incurius takes away illusion from the eyes. These men traffic in nothing but flesh and blood, and other filthy merchandise.'

'Take the white of this boiled capon, Mr Kelley,' my wife broke in. 'Some beyond the sea marvel how Englishmen can eat their capons without oranges, but we should marvel more how they can eat their oranges without capons. Is that not true, husband?'

But I paid no heed to her, being still intent upon my own matter. 'And you must know, Mr Kelley, that I have learned how to minister to my own ills. Do you remember, wife, when sorrow came to my kidneys?' She seemed distracted, and said nothing at all. 'It was a great fit of the stone as I felt it, and all day, Mr Kelley, I could do but three or four drops of water. But I drank a draught of white wine and salet oil and, after that, I ate crab's eyes in powder with the bone in the carp's head. Then at about four of the clock I ate toasted cake buttered, with sugar and nutmeg upon it, but I also drank two great draughts of ale with it. And then do you know the effect? I voided within an hour all my water, together with a stone as big as an Alexander seed. So what would these physicians have me learn from them, when I know all?'

My wife looked at me, as I thought, with pity. 'Why, husband, I believe that you must have eaten that mutton, you speak so gross.'

'No, no,' said Kelley. 'It is a necessary lesson for those of us who are still haunted by apothecaries and chirurgeons.'

Then the two of them began prattling away on other matters

while I sat silent, and regretted all that I had said. I would rather eat alone and fall upon my food like a dog: to watch others eat, and laugh, and say anything, is to observe how far removed we are from the spheres and stars. It is a terrible thing to be reminded of the flesh. 'I pray you see, mistress,' I said when I could endure no longer, 'that our guest has his towel. There are too few for us to clean ourselves.'

At that Edward Kelley made shift to rise, but my wife entreated me with a look. 'Let us not rise yet,' she said. 'Is it not good to sit a while after dinner? I wonder, Doctor Dee, if our guest knows the proverb:

> After dinner sit a while,
>
> After supper walk a mile?'

'I suppose,' I replied, 'that you have reason there.'

'Truly,' said Kelley, 'I am content to do anything that pleases you.'

At that she clapped her hands. 'John, shall we have a song?'

He took up her theme. 'Yes, sir, a song is always a cause of content. It is a long day that has no grace note.'

What could I do but assent? 'The books of music are in my chest,' I said. 'Philip, take the keys from out of my closet. You will find them in a little till at the left hand.'

So our part-books were brought to the table, and within a few minutes they had taken their tune. I let them sing, though it was no more than the old ditty 'Remember Me As I Do Breathe', and I only joined in with the chorus:

> 'Deliver me out of this time,
>
> Of rash mutability;
>
> Set forth my song in rhyme
>
> Of sacred permanency.'

After we had ended, I took Edward Kelley to my private chamber for more discourse. First I asked him why he had come to visit me. 'You have not lived obscurely, sir,' he answered, 'and for many years have acquired a good name and fame.'

'I am glad of it. But I am a modest astrologien —'

'No, sir, truly more than that.'

'Well, of course I must know the mechanics of astronomy as well as the rules of astrology –'

'And you have written of such things, in books that will endure as long as our language itself. But further than that, surely?'

'Further than that, I cannot say.'

'My late master –'

'If you mean Ferdinand Griffen, then he is our late master.'

'He spoke often of the trinity.'

'And what trinity is that?'

'The book, the scroll and the powder. And then he mentioned once the calls, or the entrance into the knowledge of the mystical tables.' I said nothing. 'And he taught me the principles of putrefaction, solution and sublimation.' Kelley got up from his chair and, going to my chamber window to look out at the marvellous storm of rain, he recited this to me: 'The art is within yourself, for you are the art. You are a part of that which you seek, for what is without is also within.'

'Go further, if you may.'

'Bring forth the water by which nothing can be made wet, then bathe the sun and the moon within it. When this is completed, breathe upon them and you will see two flowers spring forth, and out of these flowers one tree.'

'And what is your interpretation of this, Edward Kelley?'

'Nature pleases nature, sir. Nature conquers nature. Nature produces nature. This is the image of resurrection.'

I was much surprised by this, since he had uttered certain obscure words. 'Did you learn this by piece-meal?' I asked him then.

'No, sir.'

'So you speak it from art?'

'And from reason, which, as Mr Griffen taught me many times, is always the ground of art.' He turned around from the window, and looked me in the face. 'But as for the image of resurrection, what is your knowledge of it?'

The secret of the homunculus was not to be vouchsafed to him, no, nor to any man. 'It is a branch of nature's life. It is appointed for a time and a purpose, but I can tell you no more.'

'Nothing at all?'

'Some things are reserved for the ministry of seeing and hearing. To blab out secrets, sir, without leave or well-liking, is to do no good. No good at all.'

At that he burst into laughter. 'I was merely putting you to the test, sir, to see how close you kept your counsel.' This was sauciness indeed, and I was about to turn upon him in anger when he sat down again beside me on a joint-stool and said, very earnestly, 'For I have something of great moment to tell you.' Then he put his hand across his face, and I saw moisture like a dew upon his fingers.

'Are you sick?' I asked him.

'Yes, and of an evil sickness.'

I started back in my chair, fearful of any contagion. 'What has invaded you?'

'Lacking of money.'

He laughed again, but not so loud as I. 'Oh, take heed of that, Mr Kelley. Lacking of money is a pain which there is nothing like. I know it well.'

'That is why I have come to see you, Doctor Dee.' I was mightily interested, yet I endeavoured to give no sign. 'There was a time,' he said, looking into the fire, 'and that time not many hundred years past, when miracles were the only discourse and delight of men. That is truly why I have come, sir. To tell you of a miracle.'

'And what miracle may that be?'

'There was a gentleman who died no more than two months ago, whose name and dwelling-place I could deliver –'

'Come now. Be not so coy.'

'Did you know of a certain Bernard Ripley?'

'His name and reputation were known to me. He was a very grave and learned antiquary.' I put my gown around me, to ward off the dampness. 'I have his chronicles in my library here, in which he has demonstrated that the isles of Albion and Ireland should be called Brutanicae and not Britanicae, after their noble discoverer and conqueror Brutus. It was Ripley, also, who in his chronology of this island proved that Arthur, the descendant of Brutus, was the first true king of Britain. I did not know that he was dead.'

'He died raving.'

'But how could that be? He was a man of good parts, and there is no work of his which is not very orderly and laboriously gathered together.'

'I believe, sir, that he dreamed too much of old times past. He could not rest until he had discovered all, and that was why he journeyed to Glastonbury.'

'If it were a sign of frenzy to journey there, then we must all be out of our wits. Its ruined abbey is the treasury of many famous and rare carcasses which, if they are secretly preserved (as many say), will bring glory once more to our nation. Edgar is buried there, and likewise Arthur in sorrowful and reverend state lies somewhere beneath the ruins.'

'And if they could be made to speak again? What then?'

'Then the secret of time might stand revealed.' I was looking into the fire, together with Kelley. 'Why do you question me thus?'

'This same Bernard Ripley, when he knew that he was dying, sent to Ferdinand Griffen and begged him to travel to Glastonbury where he would disclose to him a great matter. My master was always of a curious and froward disposition, as you know, and without more ado we were on our way to Ripley's lodgings in that town. He was staying in an old inn or hostel, not far from the ruined abbey itself, and there in the last stages of his disease he told us the history of his actions.'

'Which were?'

'That in his desire and thirst for knowledge he had consulted a conjuror in Salisbury. That the said conjuror often repeated to him that he could restore the dead to life and cause them to speak —'

'It is a diabolical pursuit, this questioning of the dead for the knowledge of future accidents.'

'Not of the future, Doctor Dee.'

151

'What, then?'

'Of the past.' He looked steadily at me now. 'I do not justify the ways of the conjuror or of Bernard Ripley but, believe me, Mr Griffen and I were only secondary actors in this horrid business.'

'And what was then the substance of this discourse? What was this great philosophical secret which Ripley imparted to you?'

'The Salisbury conjuror told him that, in questioning of the dead under the moon, he had learned of very ancient scrolls of written paper preserved somewhere within the ruins of the abbey; that in these papers were certain notes and peculiar marks relating to this island in ancient time, with various arithmetical rules and descriptions concerning the original city of London.'

'Oh, Mr Kelley, this is the mere idle tittle-tattle of some bankrupt magician more concerned with cozening a fee than in expounding a truth. Did he inform Mr Ripley how the dead spoke?'

'He said nothing of the black arts employed, as far as we can tell. Only that, when they began to speak, a strange meteor in the form of a cloud crossed over the sky: he said that this cloud was forked for a while and, though all the sky was clear about with fair starshine, it lasted as long as the dead did speak.'

'Prattle of a loose tongue, and no more. Did he calculate its degree of height, or how it lay over our zenith? I never listen to an astrologer who is not also a mathematician. I wonder that Mr Ripley swallowed such stuff.'

'Yet here is the strangest thing, Doctor Dee. These old papers, or parchments, were found by Bernard Ripley just in the place declared to him.'

I grew more attentive at that, yet I believe I kept a grave countenance. 'In what place was this?' I asked, all the time revolving in my mind the possibility of dead men acquainting the living with news.

'Near the foundations of the abbey, on the west side, was found a great stone hollowed after the fashion of the head of a man. Therein, when it was opened, were found such parchments as I have mentioned, together with a stone as clear as crystal.'

'This was a round stone?'

'In the shape of a tennis ball, yet not so big. And, as Bernard Ripley said, you might see in it most excellent secrets. He said also that it was some token from the lost and ancient city of London.'

'But who might believe all this without sure evidence?'

'Oh, sir, there was evidence enough. For indeed I saw.'

'*You* saw?'

'I was granted possession of the stone for a moment: I looked within it, and had sight *in crystallo* offered to me. Yes, I saw.'

'What did you see?'

'A cloud of brightness parted, and I glimpsed some ruinated place where all former trade and traffic were decayed. The light of the air above this place seemed somewhat dark, like evening or twilight.'

'Was there anything else you took notice of?'

'Nothing within the stone itself. I saw certain English words written upon the parchments discovered beside it, but I had no leisure to read them thoroughly. My master knew of them and, with constraints and difficulties, managed to pry them out. He mentioned such names as Sunsfor, Zosimos, Gohulim and Od.'

'Why,' I replied, in a sudden heat, 'I know those names. I know them very well, for they are contained in books which lie even in this chamber.' I sprang up from my chair and went over to the little table where I kept by me Humphrey Lhuyd his *Breviary of Britain*, and *Historiae Britannicae Defensio* by the very worthy John Price. These were only lately printed, yet already I had their matter by heart. 'The names are there in Lhuyd,' I said, on coming back to my chair with that book, 'as comprising the names of certain Druids who founded the city of London or, rather, built around the temples and houses of our ancient originals and giants. Did Ferdinand Griffen have an opportunity to study these parchments? Were they given to him for a time?'

'They were given to him for eternity, Doctor Dee.'

'How so?'

'Bernard Ripley, even as he lay dying, had called him to Glastonbury because he knew him to be a very excellent and faithful scholar. If he had sinned in employing the arts of a magician (he said), then he wished to confess his fault and be shrived by bequeathing these ancient and wonderful remains into the care of one who would publish them for the benefit of the living. So with many gracious and heartfelt words he left them with Ferdinand Griffen, even hours before his hard death.' Kelley rubbed his eyes, as if there were still a sight which he wished to blot out. 'Then, as I have told you, my very good and reverend master took a chill from the air of Glastonbury and died soon after. So it was that the stone and the papers were left in my sole care.'

'A thing almost incredible!' I had not meant to speak out loud, but the words burst forth.

'At first it seemed that I must burn the papers.'

'Oh no.'

'I was so troubled in my mind that it would not be quiet, how or where to place these treasures.'

'Do you have them with you now?' I was close to trembling, but I kept myself within bound.

'No, sir. I purchased for myself a coffer and then carried it back to London at full speed: a good friend of mine, a jeweller near Cheapside, was very willing to preserve it while I looked for advice. He does not know what is contained in the coffer, but on my pressing instructions has hidden it beneath the floor-boards of a little parlour that he has. And now, Doctor Dee, have I come to beseech you to help me in this matter and entreat you to give me your good advice in the disposition of these papers and of the crystal stone.'

'What an excellent workman would he be,' I replied, 'that could cast the whole map of our city into a new mould! No doubt, Mr Kelley, you have been used to good cities?'

'I have seen many, sir.'

'As I have. But this ancient, long-buried and long-forgotten London was a wonderful great city, according to the testimony of former times, where many say that the holiest temple of this country stood. Then truly was Britain the incomparable island of the whole world.' I paused for a moment, to catch my breath. 'Yet there lives no man that knows the entire truth of the British originals.'

Edward Kelley looked brightly upon me after I had spoken. 'Then, sir, with these antique papers we may open such a window that the light shall for the first time be seen. Two thousand years have passed, but now all may be revealed.'

I was in a fever to have these papers in my hands, yet I kept myself somewhat reserved. Was not Simonides ever slow to utter and swift to conceal, being more sorrowful that he had spoken than that he had held his peace? There is that within me, also, which shrinks from any show as the worm shrinks from the fire. 'Somewhat is known,' I said, 'which may aid us, for this famous city of London derives itself from a divine original. As Geoffrey of Monmouth reports, Brutus was descended from the demi-god Aeneas, the son of Venus, daughter of Jupiter, about the year of the world 2855. Now this Brutus built a city near the river which we call the Thames, which city he then named Tronouant or Trenouant. King Lud afterwards, in the years before Christ's nativity, viz. 1108, did not only repair it but also added fair buildings, towers and walls, and called it Lud's Town after his own name. The strong gates which he erected in the west part of the city he likewise, for his own honour, called Ludgate.'

'If that is what I saw in the stone, then it will be a treasure indeed.'

'Not so fast, Mr Kelley, not so fast. There is another history, fully confirmed in many ancient chronicles and genealogies, that speaks of a yet earlier foundation in those misty days of the world when Albion conquered the Samotheans, who were the earliest inhabitants of Britain. We call them giants, in respect of the vast earth tombs or mounds that have been found by Mr Leland, Mr Stow, and in recent days by Mr Camden.'

'I know of them, from the discourse of Ferdinand Griffen in the evening.'

'But it is a difficult matter to learn the origins of these first Britons. In those days, covered now by the fog and darkness of past time, the island of Britain was no island at all but part of the ancient kingdom of Atlantis, which, when it sank beneath the waves, left this western part to be our kingdom.'

'And so this lost city of London –'

'We are too far to hit the mark as yet. It may be from the age of Brutus, or of Lud, or from that more distant time of Atlantis. We know only from ancient memorials that this buried city contained triumphal arches, high pillars or columns, pyramids, obelisks, and a thousand fair buildings adorned with innumerable lights.'

'But that was what I saw! In that crystal I was given the vision of old arches, decayed walls, parts of temples, theatres with confused heaps of broken columns – oh, lord, everything lying as under ground and altogether resembling the ruins of some great city.'

'You have seen a wonderful thing, Mr Kelley. If it be a true vision, it is something that has been hidden from the sight of men for many thousands of years. All that ever we were left is the London Stone, which is a visible portion of the lost city. Do you know it? It is on the south side of Canwicke Street, near St Swithin's, and speaks to me always of our common past. And you must have heard of this doctrine during the course of your labours with Mr Griffen – sometimes the earth trembles as if it were sick, the waters pour forth weeping, the air withers and the fire consumes, yet still the stone survives. And do you know that sentence of the learned master, Hermes Mercurius Trismegistus, that God is a standing pillar? Why do you think it is that I mark my works with my own London seal of Hermes?' I stopped short then, for fear that I had said too much.

'So tell me, Doctor Dee, what do you think of this case I have put to you?'

'I can tell from your dutiful looks, and from the proofs you have offered me in the telling, that this is no coarse home-spun tale fit only to serve as winter talk by the fireside.'

'I gladly assent to that.'

'No, sir, the names of the ancient inhabitants you mentioned, and all the details surrounding your discovery of the ancient scrolls –'

'And the crystal stone.'

'Yes, and the stone. All these evidences lead me to believe that this is a business no man could open his mouth against. Of course I must now see the papers with my own eyes to accept the verity of them –'

'Which you shall do soon enough. At once, if you so please.'

'But I shall not fight against my shadow of doubt. Give me your hand, Mr Kelley. This enterprise is so great that, as to this time, it never was to my knowledge achieved – to find the very portion or circuit of ground where our ancient city lay, and by the apt study of that place to discover its contents, why, it is a marvel indeed. It is hard in these our dreary days to win due credit for the exercise of any art, but in this venture I believe that great glory will be found.'

'So shall we work together in this, Doctor Dee? Is that your conclusion?'

'Well,' I replied, 'since you might have no other employment but licking dishes, I will set you to work myself.' He laughed at this, and seemed much relieved. 'But I must warn you,' I added, to master his mood, 'that those who have in past days used me ill have suffered a foul crack in return.'

'Be merry, sir, for in me there shall want no thing to make you merry.'

'And deserving honour of our great discovery.'

'And rich.'

I said nothing to that but, taking him gravely by the hand again, we plighted our faith to each other. Now I itched to be gone for the parchments yet it was a wonderful dark sky letting forth showers of rain, and so we agreed to depart for Cheapside on the following morning. Mr Kelley had been lodged by the waterside, in a mean tenement next to Baynards Castle, but I informed him that he could find nothing better, either for love or money, than a room in my own house. He readily agreed and, departing at once even in the middle of the storm, returned that evening with a porter bearing all his gear. He wished for no supper, but in good fellowship came to sit within my chamber before bed.

'Tell me,' I asked as we sat before the fireside, 'what else did Ferdinand Griffen teach you?'

'It is too late an hour to embark upon mysteries –'

'Of course.'

'– with which you will already be acquainted. But let me see, he told me how to make a stone burn without fire, and, yes, I recall now, he showed me how to make a candle that will not go out until the whole substance is wasted. He taught me how to make hens lay eggs all the winter through –'

'He was a great scholar to bother with such trifles.'

'– and how to make an hollow ring to dance by itself. Then he showed me how to make an apple move upon a table. Likewise he taught me how to make a man see fearful sights in his sleep.'

'Oh, I know that piece of foolery. You take the blood of a lapwing and with it anoint the pulses of the forehead before going to rest. Is that not so?'

'Yes. It is so, Doctor Dee. I see that none of these arts escapes you.'

'They are a diversion for those like Mr Griffen and myself. They are mere gimcrackery, and truly there is nothing to be said for them. Do you know how we are supposed to make a chamber appear filled with snakes and adders? We kill a snake, put the same into a pan with wax and thoroughly boil the two together; then of that wax we make a candle and after, when it is lighted, it will appear as though a thousand snakes were creeping in the chamber. Mere toys for boys, sir. Toys for boys.'

'But is there not some truth in it? Surely it is based upon those same principles of harmony and association that you notably expounded in your *Facsiculus Chemicus*?'

'Oh, you know that work, do you? It was privately printed.'

'Ferdinand Griffen showed me his copy. And did you not say in another place, which I have not in memory, that out of the smallest comminglings spring the greatest wonders?'

'It is true,' I replied, 'that even the smallest clouds carry water.'

'And slender threads sew sure stitches.'

He was flyting me, and so I replied in kind with all good humour at his impertinence. 'Little hairs have their shadows.'

'Blunt stones whet knives.'

'From hard rocks flow soft springs.'

'The whole world is drawn on a map.'

'Homer's *Iliad* is found in a nutshell.'

'And the queen's picture on a penny.'

'Enough, sir,' I said. 'Enough. One day I will show you something greater than magician's baubles. Did Ferdinand Griffen ever expound to you the manner of drawing aromatic oils? Perhaps I may even relate to you the great secret of the elixir of salt.'

'These are secrets which I would hope to be worthy of, sir. I will relish them well, but only after I have given you good reason to trust me and welcome me in your laboratory.'

'That is well said, Edward Kelley. But do we not share a great secret already? Tomorrow we must rise early and find our way to Cheapside. Then, once the ancient papers have been restored to us, we can begin our search for the long-buried city of London.'

'Sir,' he said, rising from his chair, 'you have made acquaintance with me and offered me great courtesy. For which I thank you.'

'And so good night. Philip will light your way to your bed-chamber.'

After he had departed, I climbed up the back stairs towards my laboratory, which was always locked and bolted from prying eyes; it is a rambling, winding stairway, looking out upon my Clerkenwell winter garden, and when I put my eye against the narrow casement I thought I saw some dark form or shape running through the rain. Then it seemed to enter the very fabric of the house and, within a few moments, I heard something scurrying behind me up the stairs. In horror I put my gown around my knees in case this thing tried to clamber upon me, even as I heard it make another turning: then, when it came into sight, I saw that it was my cat. It was running in curious fashion, and then dropped some other thing at my feet. I moved it, but it was quite dead: it was a pigeon, and one which had only a single wing naturally. How had it grown so sleek and so fat without any chance to fly? So I took it with me into my laboratory, and laid it aside for further study, before taking down the carefully turned glass vessel in which I hoped to grow my little man.

'God send you good rest,' I said to my wife before retiring to my chamber.

'Are you not weary, sir,' she replied, 'having trotted out so many words with Mr Kelley? I have not known so long a discourse before, unless it be in St Paul's.'

'It is true, Mrs Dee. I am weary. Will you call Philip to me? Ah, there you are, you knave, skulking behind the door like my neighbour's dog in the rhyme. Philip, come in and make ready the candlesticks with the wax candles: I have a long day before me, and cannot endure the smell of tallow. Where are the snuffers? Where is the warming-pan? And see that the chamber-pot is under the bed. Is the close-stool basin clean? I pray you, Philip, put clean water within it.' All these preparations were made as I requested, and yet still, as I lay upon my bed, I could not sleep: I dwelt so much on the substance of Edward Kelley's discoveries, and on the likely events of the morrow, that I kept myself from sleeping as the crane does when she keeps a stone in her foot.

★

'Are you up, sir?' The voice of Philip woke me from some flight into the upper air, when I dreamed I was leaving the dross of my mortality.

'Yes, Philip, yes. What is the time?' I groaned at my return to my mortal state.

'It is not late, sir. It is still dark, and the merchants had not yet opened their shops when I passed them.'

'Command Audrey to prepare a dozen new-laid eggs rolled in the embers. We have a guest with us.'

'I know, sir. He was drinking wine and singing to himself half the night.'

'Go to, Philip. Say no more and help me to rise.' I cleaned myself and dressed pretty quickly, but when I came into the hall Mr Kelley was already warming himself by the fire while my wife helped Audrey to prepare the table. I wished them all good morrow, and he asked me how I did. 'Well, God be praised. And you also?'

'Well, thanks be to God, seeing that I could not sleep all the night.'

'You could not? Well, neither could I. I slept no more than the compass of an hour, before being startled out of my trance by my servant.'

'I know. The minutes fell thicker than acorns around me, and I spent my time in taking out my watch and setting its wheels.'

'But now we may have a fit restorative. Where is the ale, wife, to help us in our quest today?'

'It is by your hand, sir, waiting for you.'

We made a quick meal, not wishing to lose even a minute before embarking on our journey, and Edward Kelley was about to call for his mare even as we ate. But I prevented him. 'I fear for our horses in the streets around Cheapside,' I told him. 'It is a place notorious for thieves, and if we were so much as to turn our backs upon them, they would be spirited away as if by city demons. No, sir, we must walk.'

'Will that not lose us time?'

'Time is never lost, for we make our own as we venture forward. If we go by way of Charterhouse and Smithfield, we will be within the city faster than you know.'

So we took our course, well wrapped up against the cold, and pretty soon had passed through Aldersgate and down St Martin's into Cheapside. 'Where shall we find your friend?' I asked him. 'There are so many jewellers in London that we might be in the glittering cave of Rebus. Where does he keep?'

'I know his sign when I see it. It is of the moon, and a hare jumping over it. He is somewhere over the other side of Eleanor Cross.'

We made our way, but not without being called for and hindered by the merchants who were already at their stalls and who set up such a bawling and shouting that you would imagine yourself in hell.

'Sirs, what would you gladly buy?' cries one. 'I will sell you as good and cheap as any man within London.'

'Sirs, will it please you to enter into this shop,' calls another, 'and see if I have anything which serves your turn?'

One came up to me so close that I could smell his stinking

breath. 'Come in, come in. I have very fair and good cloth here, sirs. The best of the town.'

'We have no use for cloth,' I replied.

'But of what colour do you lack?' He brought out a roll which he put in front of me even as we tried to pass. 'It shall cost you only a crown a yard, sir. If I charged you less, I should lose in it.'

'It is all one to me whether you sink or swim.' Edward Kelley laughed at my words. 'Now let us be on our way.'

'You are too hard, sir. Truly you are.'

We had come up by the corner of Bread Street, and I looked around for the jeweller's sign which Mr Kelley had mentioned. 'What is the name of your friend? Perhaps we may ask for him.'

'His name is Porcliffe, but I know his place by sight.'

'Oh,' said the pert little merchant who was still following us. 'Do not venture near Porcliffe. Go to the next shop on the other side of the street, and he will let you have whatever you wish cheap for my sake.'

Then Edward Kelley saw the sign, half-concealed behind the ladder of a workman and a wagon piled high with straw. 'I know it now,' he said. 'I have been here only once before, but I know it well.' So he hastened forward while I stepped briskly behind him, hearing the taunts of the merchant as we crossed over Cheapside. 'Let you go,' he called out. 'I wish you God-speed. Truly you are like calves which, when they have run their bellyful about the fair, will be glad to come back again.'

Edward Kelley laughed again, and let out a 'Moo! Moo!' into the air.

We had come up now to the quarter of mercers and goldsmiths, and there under the sign of the moon and the hare saw three shallow steps leading down into an artificially lighted room. 'Madam,' a very ancient old man in a damask coat was saying as we entered upon this fresh scene, 'madam, what will it please you to have?' He had laid out certain stones upon a velvet cloth. 'Mistress, I will show you the fairest stones in London. If you do not like them, you may leave them. You bestow nothing but the looking on, and the pain shall be mine to show you.'

She was another ancient old party, in a blue farthingale as big as a church bell; she wore a French hood, but I could see that her lips were so lavishly red and her cheeks so sugar-candied and cherry-blushed that she might have been a painted shape upon a wall. Mr Porcliffe glanced at us, yet he was for the moment intent upon other prey. 'Precious stones, my lady, have many great properties, but I can tell you the virtue of these just as the lapidary describes them. Have you heard of such ancient naturalists as Isidore, Dioscorides and Albertus Magnus?'

'No indeed, but if they be as grave and as learned as their names, then by my faith I adore them.'

'You have a great heart, mistress. So may I tell you plainly that Isidore named the diamond as the stone of love? Do you see it here, twinkling in the light of my candle? It is esteemed the chiefest of stones, which, by the hidden virtue that nature has given it, draws good affections towards those who carry it. Do you care for good affections, mistress?'

She simpered a little at that. 'Truly I cannot say.'

'I would not give this diamond to any faint-hearted woman, no, not at any price. Only to one who can withstand the wearing of it.'

'But I will not give you a pin above three pounds.'

'Not so fast, mistress, not so fast. I have others here to show you. Do you see the emerald here? It has the power to resist enchantment —' At that he looked upon me and smiled. 'I will be with you shortly, sirs,' he said, before once more addressing the ancient crone. 'This emerald also quenches lasciviousness.'

'Oh, sir!'

'Increases riches and beautifies the speech. Now as to this agatha here before you, it stirs up storms —'

'In the heart?'

'Wherever you may tread, mistress.' She simpered again. 'It also gives the interpretation of dreams, and makes the person to be agreeable. But you have no need of that. Would you have the sapphire instead, which is a royal stone and was called by the ancient heathens the Apolline Stone? It chases away melancholy, and is very profitable to the sight.'

'My sight,' she said, 'is as good as ever it was. But as for melancholy, well, there are those who sometimes find themselves in a drooping humour. Now that my husband is dead . . .' She fetched a sigh from somewhere within her farthingale. 'Show me again that one you call the stone of love. Is it true that it comes from the entrails of the swallow?'

'Enough,' I murmured. 'Let her try the topaz, which is good for lunatics.'

The jeweller, making no sign that he had heard me, now took up the diamond and put it in the palm of her right hand. 'And on what finger is it to be placed, mistress? In our old books it is said that the thumb is the emblem of Venus, but we always have given the forefinger to love.' Then he put the jewel on his counter once more. 'How much will it please you, mistress?' he asked, more earnestly. 'How much will you give to me so that I may have your custom?'

'I will give you forty shillings.' She no longer trifled with him. 'If you will take my money, make short, for I have other business than to tarry here.'

'Truly I would be sorry to deny you if I could give it at that price, but in truth I cannot.'

'I will give you forty-five, and not one half-penny more.'

'So. Done. It is done. The stone of love finds its proper bearer. I do but my duty.' A very few minutes later she was gone from the shop, and the jeweller turned to me. 'I see,' he said, 'that you know the virtues infused in stones.'

'I know of them, sir. With visitors such as her you should wear calcidonie upon your person, since it has power against devils.'

He laughed at that, and then bowed towards Mr Kelley. 'Ned,' he said, 'Ned. I know for what you have come. Will you please walk into the inner shop? Look for the step there, it is mouldy.' We walked into a small chamber, where he left us; then, quickly enough, he came back to us bearing the oaken coffer of which I had heard. Mr Kelley took a key which had been hanging around his neck, and with trembling fingers unlocked the lid: I stood close behind him as he opened it, and saw there various papers together with a small globe of clear glass. 'Do you wish to go to an upper room,' he asked us, 'to view them the better? There may be others coming into my shop.' With that he led us up into a parlour and, once he had left us, I closed the door.

Edward Kelley put the coffer upon a small table and, taking out the several contents, I observed that there were seven pieces of parchment – the smallest of them being in length about eight inches and in width five inches. 'We may be sure,' I told him, 'that this was once a roll of papers, with the one here which is of the smallest size rolled inmost and sealed separately because it contained the most important matter. The six others were rolled over it one after another, like so many covers but each with its own separate writing.' Upon the smallest sheet I observed lines and markings which seemed to be of an arithmetical sort: there was no time to read any of this matter, but there was enough to fire my curiosity. 'Here,' I told Mr Kelley, 'is a jewel more precious by far than any in the room below us. Do you know, from Isaiah, '*the heavens shall be rolled together as a scroll*'? Well, this is a prophecy of another sort.'

'So you see something which may be of use to us? As for me, I cannot puzzle out the secret.'

I had been examining the smallest piece of parchment, and was bowed in contemplation over it for some minutes after he had spoken. 'There is no secret here,' I said at last. 'Not to the light of understanding. Do you see these marks like the figures of algebra, these squares and rounds? Someone has laboured diligently to set out buildings upon a portion or circuit of ground. This is geo-metria, which, according to the very etymology of the word, signifies land-measuring.' I looked upon it a little longer. 'Let us concur that this is the ancient city of London. Well, then, do you see here the serpentine line? Without doubt it is that river we call the Thames. And do you see how it bends somewhat at this place?' I put my finger upon a portion. 'There is no other spot like it, but the one just by the Wapping stairs where the river curves around into the Shadwell fields.' I paused, and carefully placed the sheet back in the coffer. 'So if this is a faithful image fetched up from the old world, then we must look to the east for our lost city.'

'There is nothing in that quarter but low and rambling tenements.'

'Yes, Mr Kelley. Is, not was. You have seen what is visible in the upper air, but there are always things under the ground.'

'Were those the sights I viewed?' In my hot haste to be gone to the ancient places, I had almost forgot the stone. But now he took it from the coffer with much reverence. 'When I looked *in crystallo*, I saw the foundations of old things. And corridors between place and place, as it were for secret passageways.'

'I recall everything you said, Mr Kelley.' All the while I was gazing upon the stone, which was as clear as day but with a curious lightness about it as if it were hollow within and contained nothing but bright air. 'There is a saying of any rare and precious thing,' I continued, 'that it is older than anything Merlin ever wrought. And truly if the glass has lain here for all these centuries past and has not lost its brightness, then it is more ancient and more wonderful than anything Merlin devised. You have seen, whereas as yet I have not; therefore you must become my berrylisticus.'

'I would be honoured, sir, if I knew of what you spoke.'

'You must be the scryer, the watcher in the stone, the observer of marvels. And now we must carry it with us everywhere, well wrapped in leather against the frost of this season, for it is known that in crystals, as in mirrors or the surfaces of water, it is possible to see most excellently and certainly the emblems of the past world. Come. Shall we go back to Clerkenwell for our horses, and make way while the sun stays in the sky?'

And so we returned to my rambling house where, with great care and discretion, I made a full copy of the parchment map before entrusting those ancient papers to the safe-keeping of my locked laboratory. I placed the crystal stone within a very commodious leather satchel and, now that our horses had been made ready, we returned by Cheapside into Leadenhall before passing out of the city at Aldgate. We came up to St Botolph's and then crossed over Goodman's Fields towards the Thames: I knew a track there just before the river bank which led eastwards into the hamlet of Wapping, and so we rode that way. 'If this great original city is to be found,' I called to Mr Kelley, who rode a little behind me where the track was but narrow, 'it will become the foundation for all our hopes. We will discover marvels which are not registered in chronicles or annals.' We had come up now by some mean and straggling tenements and, consulting the marks upon the map I had copied, I passed further on. 'If we could look back clearly into those old times, in the very first years of the world when our ancestors walked upon this ground, then might many great secrets be revealed.'

'What secrets are those, sir?' He had rode up now beside me, where the path had grown more broad.

'There are some who say that Arthur is not dead but sleeps – I cannot recall the authorities now – and yet what greater awakening would there be if the entire mystical city of London were to emerge from the night of forgotten things? Here we must turn north a little –' We had now come some way from the waterside, amidst a jumble of wooden buildings with nothing around us save mean and dismal sheds or outhouses. It was still day, yet the sun was so low in the sky that I could look at it without winking. 'This is the area of the ground that conforms to the markings,' I told him. 'Look and see if you can find any notable or odd signs of pits, or passages, or suchlike. We might have had the use of a gauging rod, if we had prepared ourselves the better.'

'But you know other arts, Doctor Dee.'

'There are those who practise *ars sintrilla* with vessels of wine, water and oil in which the beams of the sun or the rays of the moon and stars may be reflected. Yet we have something more certain than divination by candlelight or by the smoke glare of the sun: we have the crystal stone, do we not?' I took it from my leather satchel, and handed it to him with care. 'You are the scryer. See if there is anything within which will inform us if we are on the right path.'

'I thought you said we had found the proper place.'

'Yet it is good to ask it. Do.'

So he took the crystal stone from my hands and held it up to his face, as if it were a chalice to be blessed, when suddenly I noticed

167

how the long rays of the sun entered the stone and were refracted out of their proper path.

'Here!' I cried out. 'Do you see it here? Do not move yourself, but keep the stone high. There is a line of light coming from out of the crystal and pointing that way.' I rode ahead eagerly, and found that the beam of light had led me to a straight and narrow track so overgrown with briars and brambles that there was almost no passage left. Yet I thrust forward, Edward Kelley now following, and found that we were being led towards a portion of old ground where there was no sign of life or cultivation. 'I think I know this place,' I said after a moment of contemplation. 'It is called the Field of Folly, where nothing can be made to grow or prosper. It is said by the common people to be the abode of spirits, which is the reason why we see no tenements or buildings.'

'I did not tell you this before, but when I first looked into the crystal at Glastonbury I saw something very like.'

I dismounted, and began to walk quickly towards a mound of earth a little way ahead. 'Do you see the stone there?' I cried out. 'That vast bulk there upon the side of the mound? It is like a piece of old causeway that in times past might have been some street or by-lane.' Oh, what was here in time past but the most wonderful city on the face of the earthly globe, a mystical city universal, containing the race before the Flood! Wherefore did I know that the city was once here? Because in my mind's eye I could clearly see it, with its fair buildings and gardens, its stone passageways and temples, now rising all around me on the cold Wapping marsh. I had read of it in the old chronicles, this city of giants, but now with the power of the place around me I conjured it in my imagination – all compact, and shining more than the rays of the sun.

Edward Kelley came running up behind me, but he was so far out of breath that he was not able to speak. So for a minute I let him bluster and blow, as I surveyed the marshland.

'The sun is going down,' he said at last. 'I am afraid we will not ride back by daylight.'

'Are you weary?'

'Not so much weary as afraid, since this is no place to be left by night. Let us make haste, Doctor Dee, I pray you, for they will soon close the gates.'

'Well, I have seen enough for this one day.' The gates of London may close upon me, but the gates of this ancient city will ever be open for those who have eyes to see, yes, even now as I look upon the drained marsh and hold my face against the chill wind.

He went on before me, in his yellow doublet and blue cloak, and I saw him walk nimbly across the dark earth like one whose feet were scorched. 'We will return,' I said to him, when we came up to our horses. 'There is work for us here. Buried now beneath us are the ancient seeds of London, but they have not lost their force. And if it were possible to raise this lost city above the ground, what then?'

'Then there would be riches.'

'Yes, riches. But also glory and everlasting renown. So you are still with me, Mr Kelley?'

'Yes, sir, I am with you.'

I will be with you always. Did he speak those words, or were they brought to me in the wind from some other place? I looked back upon the marsh, and thought I saw there a figure all white and naked with its hands crossed upon its breast.

FIVE

A FIGURE, ALL in white, was standing outside the churchyard. When I pissed on the grave and stamped on the ground beside it, I had been watched by a woman; she was wearing a white leather coat, and when I walked over to her, I could see that she was quite young. There was a violet light around her, and for a moment I believed that it was emanating from her like some shadow of the soul; then I realized that it was coming from a place behind her. There was a confused noise of music, beating somewhere beneath the surface of the pavement: it was a night-club, on the other side of the Green, much larger and louder than the one I had passed in Charlotte Street. Its presence here was somehow appropriate; it was as if it had always belonged in this particular spot, even before it existed. But how could I have neglected to notice it? Was I so concerned with the history of this place that I could not see what was, literally, before my eyes? It had been fear that held me back, that blinded me. And now I was afraid no longer. I walked away from the churchyard, and approached the woman who had been watching me. She did not move, but looked at me curiously and cautiously as I came up to her. 'Don't be frightened of me,' I said.

'I'm not frightened of anyone.'

'What are you doing here?'

'What do you think?' I remembered the three women of Turnmill Street, who had been taken away in a police van. 'And what are you doing? Dancing on your mother's grave?'

'Something like that. Where are you going now?'

'Nowhere. Just looking for some action.' She had a pretty but slightly unformed face, as if her true character were still waiting to emerge; her eyes were brown, her nose briefly sculpted, her lips very full and, for a moment in the half-light, she looked a little like a mannequin. 'Where are you going, then?'

Ever since I left the restaurant I had been filled with a strong sense of sexual desire; something about the relationship between Daniel Moore and my father must have excited me, I suppose, and I could hardly restrain my eagerness. 'Oh, I'm hanging around.'

'Chilling out?'

'Yes, that's it. I'm chilling out. What's your name?'

'Mary.'

'And where do you live, Mary?'

She tossed back her head. 'Over the river.'

'Over the river is half-way home.'

'What?'

'I was just saying that it's a nice place to have a home.'

She had a peculiar laugh; it was like a sudden expulsion of breath. 'Not when you're on an estate it's not. Where do you live, then?'

'Around the corner.'

'Is that so?' We started walking together past the church, and surreptitiously I cupped my hand across my mouth to smell my breath; the wine had washed down the last traces of vomit. She kept her hands deep in the pockets of her white leather coat, and did not look at me at all; she stared down at the pavement, and seemed to be going in the right direction without any guidance. We arrived at the entrance to Cloak Lane, and she glanced around for a moment. 'I've got a confession to make,' she said. I stared at her, but gave no reply. 'I'm a bit short of money, you see. I'm out of work for the moment.'

I had expected this. 'That's fine, Mary. I'll give you something. Don't worry.' In fact it did not displease me at all; it excited me even more, and I put my arm round her as we walked towards the old house.

'Is this yours?'

She sounded very interested, even eager; it may have been my own guilty imagination, but I did not want her to know that I lived alone in this house.

'No,' I replied. 'I live with someone. I live with my dad.'

'I thought I saw someone.'

'You couldn't have seen him.' I put my hand on her shoulder. 'He's out. He won't be back for a while.'

'Where is he, then?'

'He's at the bingo.'

'Don't talk to me about the bingo. My mum loves it.'

She did not resist as I pulled her closer to me and, kissing her on the neck, almost dragged her up the path. As soon as I opened the door, I knew what I wanted to do. 'Let's go down to the basement, Mary. No one will see us there.'

'Suits me. But I need my money first.'

'You'll get your money.' I wanted to hit her across the face, just as my father might have done, but instead I went upstairs and took some five-pound notes from an envelope I kept in my bedroom. I picked up a bottle of whisky, too, and then came down to her: I knew that I could not do what I really wanted until I was quite drunk. I led her down into the basement without putting on the light, but a few rays from the lamp in the hall penetrated the gloom and seemed to cluster around the outline of the sealed door. I took her across to it and, propping her against the wall, began to take off my clothes. Then I undressed her, and poured whisky over her breasts before licking it off greedily.

'Mind my tits,' she said. 'Don't leave any marks.' But she gave a little yell of delight as I bit deeply into her.

This must have been the corner where Daniel and my father performed their own rituals and, as I grew rougher with Mary, I knew that it had been used for the same purpose in much earlier times; it was a strong house of sex, and we were its latest inhabitants. I do not know how long we remained in that basement, but while we stayed there I felt I was not in the world at all: there was no reality beyond this pleasure given and this pleasure received. There were no ordinary laws of behaviour, no responsibilities, no beliefs, no cause and no effect; I understood, too, that with such fury and excitement anything could be conjured into existence. Mary lay on the floor, bruised, dirty, stinking of the whisky I had poured over her. 'When my father made me,' I said, 'he made me strong.'

I think I was spitting at her. 'Not in my eyes,' she said. 'Be careful of my eyes.'

Then I thought I heard another voice whispering to me. 'Why did you call me?' I left her and, wiping my mouth with my hand, climbed the stairs. I managed to find my own bathroom, and washed myself as quickly as I could before putting on some clothes. When I returned to the basement, she was gone. I was now so drunk that I could hardly remember what had happened, and I staggered out of the house in search of someone else – some other woman, or girl, to continue the ritual I had begun. Everything had changed, and the houses towered above me as if I were lying down on the road. I found myself in various places without knowing how I had reached them, and I held conversations with people who seemed to disappear without warning. I was inside a pub, or night-club, leaning against a video game which spun and danced before my eyes. Then I found myself crouched in a urinal with the piss running down my legs. There was an old man there. He leaned across me, and put part of me in his mouth. I lay back, and laughed. Enough. It was complete. This was the night when I discovered the truth about my father.

★

I was lying in my own bed the following morning. I do not know how I had reached it, and could remember nothing of the previous night except moments preserved in the ambergris of shock or surprise; yet I felt curiously peaceful, as if I had rested for a long time. Then, as I turned to sleep again, I knew that there was someone lying on the bed beside me. There was a figure there, breathing softly in the light. I thought for a moment that it was Mary, somehow still inside the house, but it was my father. He was smiling at me. I groaned deeply, and he was gone. When I woke up I was lying, fully clothed, upon the stairs. The door was open and somehow, in my drunkenness, I had found my way back to the old house. But now the place disgusted me, and I could hardly bring myself to climb the stairs to my room.

I knew then that it was time to visit my mother; it was time to explain to her what I had discovered from Daniel, although I suspected that she had always been aware of her husband's clandestine life. But how was it that I had never noticed her distress, or ever thought of comforting her? The prospect of taking her in my arms disturbed me, even now, more than I cared to admit.

There are times, after heavy drinking, when all customary perceptions are destroyed and the world seems very clear. That was why I could now see my mother so simply. I suppose that I had never really looked after her, because I had never looked *at* her properly. I had never tried to understand her life, and so she had remained for me the same cut-out, throw-away character to whom I responded in the same casual way. I had never recognized the pain within her life, or cared to understand the nature of the long marriage which had formed her; but, more importantly, I had never bothered to love her. No doubt that was why, over the years, she had become so brisk and distant with me. It was a way of defending herself against my indifference.

I told Daniel that I recalled nothing about my earliest childhood but, as you must have gathered by now, that was not entirely true. I once read an article about an Italian who had emigrated to America when he was very young, but who, for the last few years, had painted nothing but the streets and houses of the village from which he had originally come. That in itself is easy to explain; what was surprising was the fact that, according to the photographic evidence, his paintings were accurate in every detail. After an interval of some thirty or forty years, he perfectly remembered the shape of every house and the contours of every lane. In the same way, when I look back upon my own childhood, I can still see very clearly the streets and houses that surrounded me then. I observe the small white villas of Wulfstan Street, the row of red-brick council houses in Erconwald Street, the scout hall at the top of Melitus Street, and the small park beside Braybrooke Avenue. But in my imagination there is never anyone there. Even when I remember my own house as it seemed when I was a child, there is no one anywhere within it. As far as I can remember, there are no people at all. No. There is one thing. Once my mother had taken me on her knee, when I was still quite young, and had started crying: I had walked out of the room without saying a word.

That memory came back to me when I returned to Ealing on the following day. It was a bright and agreeable morning and, as I turned into Melville Avenue, I stepped lightly over the pavement; it was the old children's game – step on a crack, break your mother's back. She was 'working' in the garden, Geoffrey told me when he answered the door. He seemed surprised to see me, and carried on talking nervously as we walked towards the kitchen door. I could see her through the window, bent over some late-flowering shrubs, and realized once more how frail she had become; we looked at each other, and for a few moments neither of us had any expression at all. Then she smiled and, wiping her hands on a piece of tissue, came over to me. 'This is a privilege,' she said. 'Kiss please.' For once I did not feel distaste as I put my lips to her cheek.

'I was hoping to see you in Clerkenwell again.'

'It's a long way, Matthew. And the garden needs me at this time of year. Before the autumn comes.' I looked around at the lawn, the shrubs and the crazy paving: it was all as I remembered it from my childhood, although in those days it had seemed to make up an entire world in which I could conceal myself. 'Besides,' she was saying, 'it's that house of yours.'

'What's wrong with the house, mother?'

At that moment she found something of great interest at the side of the lawn and bent down to retrieve it; it was a piece of broken glass, and she buried it carefully under the soil. 'Let's go inside,' she said. 'I'll make you something nice.'

'You can be very aggravating. You always seem to know more than you say.'

'That's one of my charms, isn't it?'

She tried to be coquettish for a moment, but she did not succeed. Something was troubling her; I suspected, even then, that she knew why I had come. We went into the house and, while

175

Geoffrey made coffee, she busied herself with the preparation of one of the thick cheese sandwiches I had been given as a boy. 'Get that down you.' She sounded almost vindictive. 'You used to love a good sandwich.' I had always detested them, as far as I could recall, but dutifully I began to eat it.

'Oh, that reminds me,' she said. 'I found something in the cupboard.' She was still very uneasy with me, and now seemed pleased to leave the room while Geoffrey stared after her. But she returned almost at once with a large brown envelope. 'I didn't want to keep them.' She hesitated, as if she had said quite the wrong thing. 'I didn't want to throw them away. I think you ought to have them.' I opened the envelope, and there fell upon the table some five or six photographs. In all of them I was alone with my father. In one of them he was holding me up in his arms (I must have been five or six at the time) while in another we were sitting together on a low wall. Some of them seemed quite recent – one, in particular, showed us mounting some stone steps – but curiously enough I had no recollection of their ever being taken.

'He was a handsome man,' I said.

She opened her eyes very wide for a moment. 'Do put them away, Matthew. You can look at them later.'

She had not been able to disguise the distaste in her voice. Geoffrey quietly left the room, muttering something about the car, and we sat together in silence for a while.

'It will be your birthday soon,' she said, running her finger round the rim of her cup. 'My birthday boy.'

'I know about him, mother.'

She put her hand up to her face. 'What do you know?' She sounded angry.

'I know what kind of man he was.'

'And what kind of man was that?'

'I think you probably know, mother.'

I thought she was stifling a yawn, but then I realized that it was a cry or perhaps a groan. 'And all this time I thought you had forgotten.'

'Forgotten?'

'You were so small at the time.' I felt some great upheaval within me, as if I had been turned upside down, and I was a child again. And then, all at once, we were both crying. 'You do know, don't you?' she said. She came over to me, and put her arm around me. 'But I protected you. Your mother was good for something, even then. I stopped him. I only caught him with you once, but I threatened to take him to the police.' I was looking at myself with infinite patience and curiosity: I looked at myself as I walked through the streets of London, I watched myself as I toiled among my books, I listened to myself as I discussed my childhood with Daniel. I had not known myself at all. 'I never left you alone with him after that,' she was saying. 'I defended you.' I was staring very intently at the table – I noticed the grain of the wood, I noticed the knots and stains, and I looked so hard into the heart of that wood that I seemed to be spiralling down within it. I had become part of its vortex. 'He swore that he never harmed you, Matthew. He said that he never touched you. But after that I always hated him.' And then, as I lay at peace with the wood, I realized a truth which, for some reason, had eluded me before – the material world was the home of eternity. One secret had led to another secret, and slowly I was pulling back the veil. 'God help me, there was a time when I thought that you and he –'

'Your own son?'

I listened to her silence for a while, and then I looked up at her. I do not believe I was crying now. 'You're not my son, Matthew. He found you. He adopted you. He said that you were very special. Unique. I had to go along with it, because I knew that I could never give him any children.' Now I recognized the source of her rage and bitterness, even on those occasions when they had been directed against me. My father had slowly destroyed her, just as surely as if he had fed her poison. And what had he wanted from me? What had Daniel called it? Sexual magic? I knew now why I had forgotten my childhood, and so forgotten myself. I knew why there were no people in my memories. I had been lost from the beginning. It was only with unbearable exhaustion that I could look upon that period of my life which I thought to have forgotten, but which in fact had formed me.

For the rest of the morning we talked through everything, and I explained to her what I had discovered about his life in Cloak Lane. She was not in the least surprised by it, and had suspected for a long time that he owned what she called a 'lair'. Even as we talked we became known to each other; it was as if we were strangers who by degrees grew acquainted. It was the oddest feeling: once we saw him clearly, we saw ourselves. 'It was so difficult, Matthew. He was always there, you see. You were his child somehow, never mine. People talk about love, but –' That was the secret, after all. I had grown up in a world without love – a world of magic, of money, of possession – and so I had none for myself or for others. That was why I had seen ghosts rather than real people. That was why I was haunted by voices from the past and not from my own time. That was why I had dreamed of being imprisoned in glass, cold and apart. The myth of the homunculus was just another aspect of my father's loveless existence – such an image of sterility and false innocence could have come from no other source. Now everything had to be changed.

I rose from the table, and embraced her. 'At least we have some cause to be grateful,' I said. 'We survived, didn't we?'

'I suppose so.'

At that moment Geoffrey came back into the kitchen. 'Have I missed anything interesting?'

'No, darling,' she said. 'We were just reminiscing.'

'That's all right then.' I realized now why my mother had chosen such an apparently average man: he represented the ordinary course of life which she had been denied all those years. Yet what was so ordinary about it, when at last it afforded her happiness? When we start looking for eternity, we find it everywhere. I stood by the kitchen window and, as I looked out towards the lawn, he came over to me as if he needed to comfort me. 'Gardens need work,' he said. 'Come and see your mother's sunflowers.' I looked around for her but she had left the room, and so I followed him down the crazy paving towards the beds of flowers. He suspected that something had happened, I knew that, but he could no more have broached the subject than he could have stripped naked in front of the neighbours. 'You had a talk then, did you?'

'Yes. We did.'

'That's good.' We walked slowly down the path, admiring each shrub and plant in turn, until we came to the sunflowers, which were growing beside a rubbish heap near the back of the garden. 'It's amazing how they grow out of all this muck and dirt,' he said.

'I don't think they do. Not wholly.' He looked at me in surprise, but said nothing. 'Why do you think they are called sunflowers?'

'Because they always face towards the sun.'

'No. They are the sun.'

'I can't follow you there.'

'You mean you don't follow the son?' I muttered this under my breath, and he had not heard me.

'I know what would interest you, Matthew. You know that I'm working on the new London extension?' He had told me on many occasions how he was acting as a surveyor for the development of an eastern 'corridor' into the city. 'The other day we were plotting the course of the old river Soken, just to make sure there was no danger of subsidence. It runs from Waltham Forest down through Bethnal Green and Shadwell. Do you know where I mean?' I nodded, although I was hardly listening; I was looking up at the window of my mother's bedroom. 'We were inspecting some old sewers which ran into it, when we came across something.' Now he did have my attention, and we sat down together on a wooden bench at the side of the lawn. 'We found some narrow tunnels, somewhere between Wapping and Shadwell. Of course I assumed they were built at the same time as the sewers, but then I realized that they weren't in alignment with them at all. Not at all. So we decided to walk down one of them – it was wet, and slippery, and smelly, but we're used to that. And then we came across the strangest thing.' My mother waved from her window, and I waved back. 'We came out into an open space, and there were some old stones there. One looked like a fragment of a pillar, and one like a paving stone. You know, it was worn smooth. And then there was a piece of archway, just lying on the ground. What do you think of that?' I thought only one thing: a buried city had been discovered. Something from the past had been restored.

At that moment my mother's cairn terrier came dashing out of the house to greet us with its strident bark. I had never really paid much attention to the dog before, but now I was able to see its brightness and fierceness. It was a creature of the fire world, in this garden of water and earth. But was there some place where the elements might be reconciled – where ghosts and real people, lost cities and present ones, my past and present lives, my mother and myself, could be reunited in love? Geoffrey picked up the little dog, and excitedly it licked his face. 'It's time for me to go,' I said. He was about to rise and leave the garden with me, but I put my hand upon his shoulder. 'No. Stay with the dog. I'll just find mother.'

She was waiting for me in the kitchen and, for the first time, we shook hands. It was the strangest gesture, and yet somehow it was appropriate. Then I kissed her on the cheek. 'I'll be back,' I said.

I left the house, and was walking down Wulfstan Street when the first wave of feeling hit me. Something had risen within me, and dashed me against the brick wall of a front garden. I knew that I was struggling on the surface of some emotion more voluminous and powerful than anything I myself possessed. It filled me, and then after a few moments it was gone. I was still leaning against the wall, and now I put my hand up to my face. After a while I turned the corner into Braybrooke Avenue and started walking towards Ealing Broadway. This was the place of my childhood, which I had once despised and rejected, but now I felt oddly contented and even joyful. I saw a girl helping an old man across the road, and I could hear someone singing in the distance. It was then, I suppose, that I began to pity my father.

THE CHAMBER OF DEMONSTRATION

'Have you purified yourself, Mr Kelley? You know well that whosoever attempts this and is not pure shall bring upon himself the judgement.'

'I have abstained from coitus for one day and one night. I have refrained from gluttony. I have washed all, and I have cut my nails.'

'Go forward then, and enter. This place is holy.' And so we proceeded into our secret study, our scrying room or chamber of demonstration, bearing with us the crystal, which with all due reverence I placed upon the silken cloth. 'Sit down at the table of practice,' I said, 'and hold yourself in readiness for anything that might be seen or heard.'

'No harder task is there, Doctor Dee. This work consumes me.'

'Well, you are whole yet.' I stood beside him in my customary place, since it has not been given to me to have visions *in crystallo*. 'Is there anything that you see as yet?'

'Nothing. Nothing appears in the stone, not even the golden curtain.'

'The stone is its natural diaphanite?'

'It is so.'

'Then we must wait faithfully, knowing ourselves to be entrusted with a great power. We have learned much and will learn yet more.'

'I see the golden curtain now,' Kelley whispered after a little time. 'It hangs very still within the stone. No, it moves. It seems to be far backwards, and the stone is clear between the curtain and the forepart. Under the curtain I see the legs of men up to the knees. Now all remains still.'

'Possess your soul in patience, Mr Kelley, for these things are wonderful.'

So once more we began our course. Each action takes a day, yet since there is much care and trembling anxiety in this pursuit we enter the chamber of demonstration once upon a week only. There is much matter to be interpreted also, and I am compelled to pore over my books for the meanings of all we see: these truths are not to be snatched up greedily, as a dog takes a bear by the ears in Paris Garden.

It is a full twelve months since Edward Kelley entered my service, on that day when we first travelled to the drained marsh of Wapping in search of the ancient city of London. Yet the mists of time were not to be so easily dispersed: we journeyed back several times to the same ground, but found nothing further beyond the mound and the piece of old stone. On a winter's evening when all was quiet (much to Edward Kelley's misliking), I even went so far as to set up a table upon the mound and to place there the vessels of oil, wine and water: it is reported by Agricola in his *De re metallica* that the candle's ray, when reflected by some polished metal upon the surface of these liquids, will reveal the shape of forgotten things. But there was nothing within the beam to aid us, and all remained concealed. We might have dug deeper into the ground itself, but only at the risk of our plans being discovered. 'I feel myself to have been born out of my time,' I said to Edward Kelley as we rode back that night from the Wapping marsh. 'It is as if I had been given sight of a wooden globe, when I long to behold the entire sky.' Indeed I was then close to despairing, when suddenly I found the arrow which might hit our target by another way. 'But then again,' I said to him, 'why should you not see for me?'

'Which is to say?'

'We must turn our eyes back to the stone. You know well how the parabolic speculum, or burning mirror, will employ the rays of the sun. Why should our holy crystal, our principal stone, not magnify and objectify the world of spirits which surrounds us? Where could we find better guides into the buried city?'

'Certainly,' he replied, 'there is a mystery within it, for already I have obtained sight of wonderful things. But I am not sure –'

'This is no time for a faint heart, Edward. If indeed it does contain mysteries, then surely they must be preserved and guarded. I will furnish a little room beyond my laboratory, which will be closed and locked to all comers – no, not even my wife will dare enter. And there, in this reserved chamber, we will consult the stone with many very constant and diligent enquiries. It is the only course now open to us.'

And so it was that the scrying room was perfected, which work I began on the very next day. Upon the ground I inscribed the magical circles, characters and invocations made known to me by Cornelius Agrippa in his *De mysteria mysteriorum*. Then with the aid of the *Mutus Liber* I made a crystalline table which was round like a cartwheel and painted upon it certain characters and names in yellow and blue; its sides were also adorned with signs, written in red, and placed beneath each foot was the waxen seal of Hermes Trismegistus. A great seal was placed upon the centre of the table, bearing the impress of holy names; this and the table were then covered in red silk, with the crystal stone set upon them. Nor were our careful preparations in vain since, *laus Deo*, it has proved a true angelical stone which opens up at Edward Kelley's sight; very many objects, or species of objects, have been gathered through this glass, which I have no doubt were conveyed to us by God and his messengers.

The first visitation came upon us within a week of our laborious preparation and beginning. 'There is a curtain,' said Kelley, who was bowed over the crystal, 'and now it is being lifted up as if by a hand.' I was all on fire with curiosity and amazement, and earnestly entreated him to tell everything exactly as it happened. 'Now I see a young boy. He brings a little book out of his pocket. He looks upon a picture in the book.'

'Do you see what picture it is?'

'No. He turns the leaves of the book. There seems to be someone calling him, whom I cannot hear. His own garments cast a light around the stone. Now he seems to put the air over him, and so to enter into a cloud of invisibility. Now he is gone.'

The second visitation came on the following week. 'The curtain moves,' he said. 'I have something here, but I cannot come upon it yet. Yes, it is a man walking upon a white road. He is a tall and aged creature, without a hat upon his head.'

'Can this be real?'

'I see into the stone with my external eye, Doctor Dee, not with my imagination. And look, now, he walks close to the house here. He has come up to the old well.'

'As close as that?'

'He approaches the house. He makes as if to knock upon the door. But now he stops and laughs.' Kelley then moved back with a sudden jolt. 'He throws dust out of the stone towards my eyes.'

'Look back into the stone,' I entreated him. 'He is so near to us.'

'Now he has plucked the curtain, as if he had pulled it round the stone, and I can see no more.'

He fell back into his chair, trembling, and I might have joined him in his fever fit: what spirit, or demon, was about to beat upon my door? And then I recalled my father. 'Did this aged man have a grey beard, forked?' I asked Kelley, who was now leaning upon the table of practice and looking upon the stone like one in a dream.

'He had no beard. He was dressed in strange fashion.' Then his back arched, and he sat upright. 'But now I see another who is all in flame. Yes, he is divided into a great many pieces of fire. Now he is become like a great wheel of fire, like a wagon wheel, which turns within the stone. Now it is gone. Now all that show has vanished away.' He was sweating mightily, and passed his hand across his face. 'I can do no more today. These things are not granted to mortal men, except at great cost.'

'Why talk of cost,' I said, trying to revive his spirits, 'when there is a richer prize than all to be gained? There is treasure here within the stone.'

'You do not mean the secret of gold?' He seemed suddenly in a sweat again. 'I thought you knew of that.'

'No, not gold, but greater riches by far. If these spirits are sent by God, as I am firmly persuaded that they are, then they may assist us in our search for the contents of time itself.'

'But the secret of gold is known to you? You need no other assistance in that matter?'

'I know many secrets and mysteries, Mr Kelley, about which I shall speak at some later date. But now we are approaching a greater mystery, so I beg you keep to your employment. If you wish for gold or jewels or any precious thing, fix your gaze within the holy crystal.'

Two weeks following this discourse, there was a change about the table of practice. I had entered a little after Edward Kelley, being delayed by some high words with my servant for leaving my close-stool uncleansed, and found him sitting back in the chair as one amazed. 'Do you hear any noise?' he asked me.

'Where?'

'Where but in the stone? There are sounds in the stone. Can you hear them?'

I took a step back in fright, but then there came upon me a great curiosity; I approached the crystal and a very few seconds after I heard it creaking or crackling, although no hand touched it and no mortal or worldly thing seemed to move it. 'I hear something,' I whispered to him, 'like the sound of a bunch of keys, as if they had been quickly and strongly shaken.'

'You wished to hear voices, sir, but these are mere sounds.'

'Who knows what might follow? This may be the first note of an entire air.'

And so it proved in the weeks following, when Edward Kelley huddled over the stone and, through his scrying, I found myself able to talk to spirits. The first who came to us was a little girl no more than seven or eight years: he saw her clearly, sitting upon a rock in a desert place, and he questioned her as to who she might be. I could see and hear nothing, but he told all.

'I am the first but one of my mother's children,' she said to him. 'I have little baby children at home.'

'Ask her where that is, Mr Kelley.'

And she replied thus, after he had put the question to her. 'I dare not tell you where I dwell. I shall be beaten.' But then she put out both arms to him, saying, 'I pray you let me play with you a little, and I will tell you who I am.'

185

'Is she an angel,' I asked him, 'or some lesser spirit come to entertain us?' But at that she vanished away.

I knelt down and began to pray, while he put out the candles one by one. 'If you are interceding with the author of these beings,' he said to me as he snuffed the last of them, 'be sure that you are not deceived.'

The chamber of practice was now quite dark, since I kept a tapestry before the window and made sure that the doors were all perfectly locked. 'And what deception may that be?'

'The Devil takes strange shapes, Doctor Dee, and before we trust these spirits within the stone we must question them further.'

In the following week we were at a loss, with nothing appearing *in crystallo*, and we were about to quit the chamber when I heard a very great noise about the stone, as though men were beating down mud walls. Pretty soon it became a thumping and a clattering which seemed to shake the whole house. We stopped our devotions, and looked at one another in fright; then the noise ceased, and all was still.

Another week passed before we entered the chamber of presence, and immediately upon sitting down before the table of practice Edward Kelley saw a movement in the stone. 'I see two men,' he said, 'conversing with one another.'

'Can you hear their words?'

'One says that he saw the other in Harlot Street or Charlotte Street.'

'There is no such street.'

'The other groans. Now both are vanished away.'

This was marvellous indeed, but a yet greater marvel was to follow when we returned to the chamber the next week. 'It thunders in the stone,' Kelley said to me as he approached the table of practice. 'And there is something like a confused light in which I see a figure.'

'Is it one we know of?'

'It is a man,' he said. 'He has a black satin doublet, slashed.'

'What manner of creature is it? Has he been waiting for us all week long?'

Kelley repeated my questions and seemed to be listening intently to a reply. 'He that speaks to us is to be asked no such matters,' he said.

'Can he tell us his name?'

'He says that his name is Zalpor, one of the Elohim. Now I see him clearly. He has a ruff about his neck. It is a long one, edged with black or blue.'

'It will be black. Speak to him, lest he should disappear.'

'Be patient, for he approaches. Now he laughs, ha, ha, ha! a great laugh. Now he says, Dee, Dee, I know a privy enemy of yours.'

This made my heart to jump. 'Who?'

'Mankind.'

'Oh,' I replied, 'he has hit the mark with his jest!' Then I added, more quietly, 'So be it. He says only what is true.'

'Dee, Dee, such has God's mercy been in suffering wicked men to prevail against you that they have made a scorn of you in this your native country.'

I thought then of certain men who had stood against me – Oastler, Rushton, Dundas and the rest – and all my rage entered the chamber of presence. 'Yes,' I replied, 'I give losers leave to talk while they prosper. But the fattest goose comes soonest to the spit, and I will draw their fortunes to their last date.'

Kelley motioned me to be silent. 'He speaks again,' he whispered. 'But I cannot make out the words. Oh. Now I do. I hear all. He says you must rejoice to think how these silly flies play with the fire that will burn them. Now he shakes. Oh God. Now he seems to turn his head about his shoulders.' Kelley continued to watch the stone, and spoke these words to me as one under direction. 'Dee, Dee, have an ear to my foretelling. Run that run can.'

He departed from the stone after that, and Edward Kelley was sorely troubled in his mind by this apparition – for, as he said, how are we to know from what sphere he comes or whether he be an angel or something else? 'I am contented to see and to make true report of what he will show,' he said to me, 'but my heart stands against him.'

I had recovered myself pretty well, and told him there was

nothing at all to fear and much to gain. 'There is a world of learning through which these spirits may guide us,' I continued. 'If they be good or evil, and I would willingly swear now that they are good, they bring us news from elsewhere. Remember that you and I may only inhabit the region under the moon, and have the thick air assigned to us a prison. Should we stop our ears to these voices from another sphere, or close our eyes to such wondrous apparitions? What else can we do but aspire to knowledge of the higher regions? I have consumed my whole life and labour in the pursuit of a great truth, quite apart from the common practices of mankind, and there is nothing in the world that now can change my course. I know that you wish to win money by distillation and alchemical conclusion –'

'No sir . . .'

I put up my hand. 'So you do. And so do I. But I see a light more refulgent than any gold, and it is one that leads me forward even to the very edge of this crystal stone. So no more talk of devils. We must go on.'

He agreed to this after much discontent, but my resolution was well rewarded during the next action in the chamber.

'There is a noise around the stone,' he told me on that day, 'a great noise of many voices. Now the sound is of pillars falling.'

'Does anything appear to you?'

'Here is a young man coming, and he is smiling upon me. He stands as though he were behind a desk, and preached or taught.'

'What else do you see?'

'He wears a strange robe, without wide sleeves. He has no hose or breeches but some kind of cloth around his legs. Now I see another man without a doublet, in his shirt, and with the same cloth upon his legs. They have some little discourse or conference together.'

'Can you hear what they say?'

'They speak softly, like the murmuring of the wind, but now I think I hear somewhat. They are named Matthew and Daniel.'

'Holy names.'

'Now they talk of you with much laughter.'

'Of me?' At that I was mightily afraid, but yet more curious than all.

'Now they have gone. Now another comes forward. He is a man having a velvet gown, all furred with white, and he makes motions as if to address you. I will speak it as I hear it.' Then Kelley proceeded with the following discourse.

'John Dee, John Dee, have you been turned off the ladder of life?'

'Yes, I have,' I replied, with much trembling. 'Many times, and wrongfully so.'

'And has the highway to preferment therefore been barred to you?'

'Indeed it has.'

'Well, John Dee, there is little friendship in your world. But take heart: no other passion prevails among your enemies except that of fear. Do you know one Richard Poynter, known as well-arrayed Richard?'

'Yes, an arrant knave, a thief, and a cozener.'

'He lives yet to spread false reports about you, but his time is likely to be short.'

'Ah, your will is sweet.'

'Not my will but your own. John Dee, John Dee, be familiar with all but trust none. I know the height of your ambition and your unrest, but it is given to you to encompass all your ends. Remember that no moss may stick to the stone of Sisyphus, no, nor grass hang upon the heels of Mercury: so aspire further than you think you may reach, seek the knowledge of the whole world, and mint gold both material and spiritual. I tell you this, John Dee, you shall have time and days to live that, when you die, you shall depart this world with fame and memory to the end. And remember this: your little man will lead you far beyond the glass in which he dwells. Now farewell.' And at that Edward Kelley fainted away. I was amazed to hear him speak of my homunculus, which even then was no more than my dream and my hope, with no certain substance; but I had forgotten that from their sphere they can see all, even the secrets lodged within my own breast.

The gates of eternity had opened wide and, in the weeks following upon this last visitation, various mysteries and shows were performed in the chamber of presence. There came a time when it seemed to Kelley that the spirits left the stone and flew about the room, and he was sorely vexed by their mischief. There were sounds about his head – nothing appearing to the eye – and a mighty weight or invisible burden came upon his right shoulder as he sat in the green chair by the holy table. It seemed to him that something was writing upon him, but I saw no words. Then on the same day in the next week, Friday being always our day of scrying, in the afternoon as he sat by me he felt on his head some strange moving. After this a spiritual creature seemed to him to be heavy again on his right shoulder, and it was very warm where it lighted upon him.

But there were more wonders still: pretty soon after that, while I stood by the table, there appeared to Kelley a round globe of white smoke over my head. Then there came about his own face little things of smoke, round and about as big as a pin's head, and he had great trouble in putting them from him. 'These spirits have power indeed,' I said after, as we sat in my study considering these latest actions. 'They have become visible in the world, not only in the stone, and they are able to affect us by their material agency. So why should they not, like the bees, furnish both wax and honey?'

'How so?'

'I wish to know all and yet, too, I wish to perform all. Only then will I reach the topmost rung of my ambition. Shall I tell you more about the ancient city that we seek?'

'I am always ready for learning, as you have cause to know.'

'I have by me narratives of ancient times, more than three thousand years before our present age, when there was such power upon the earth that all men were like gods. This was the race before the Flood, who – if I am not in error – founded the mystical city of London. Buried within those ruins, somewhere under the earth, may be tokens and emblems of that sacred generation whose authority was such that they were termed giants – not giants of physical but of spiritual power. And who knows what strength might not be ours if we found their relics and memorials, just like this crystal stone dug up at Glastonbury? Could we not move the spheres, and reach out to touch the fixed stars?'

'You have schemed farther than ever I thought, Doctor Dee. Why did you not tell me of these matters before?'

'I would have mentioned them then, if you could have understood me.' He was about to say more, and I brushed his words aside. 'But it is not enough to scheme and plan. It is for us to act upon such knowledge as we now possess. It was prettily devised of Aesop that the fly sat upon the axle-tree of the chariot wheel and said, what a dust do I raise. We must not be like the fly. We must turn the wheel with our own strength.'

'I do not see your meaning.'

'We must raise up our spirits in the stone, as we have done, but now we must question them clearly about these matters. We must ask them to guide our steps to the very treasures of the ancient city. We must approach them with prayer and trembling, so that one day they may lead us under the ground to find our forefathers. If they are our navigators, then we will need no other compass.' He seemed to recoil at my words, and began pacing up and down the study before breaking into a great storm of doubting and misliking of the spirits.

'They can be our instructors,' I replied.

'I do not trust them.'

'But you cannot condemn them out of hand, without having heard what they may say.'

'I have heard them already, have I not? Who knows if they will lead us to some place of night and terror?'

'Be more cheerful, Edward. They are our arrows. Do you consider we should not try to hit the mark with their aid?' I paused for a moment. 'It will make you rich.'

'I do not care for gold, sir, if it comes from devils.'

'Very well. *I* will make you rich. Depend upon me, and not upon these spiritual creatures.'

'Truly?'

'Truly. I will preserve you from their words and actions if you so desire it. Only do as you have done and act for me as their translator. I will expect no more. I will not set your house on fire to roast my own eggs.' This soothed him a little and, after more debate, he promised to question them at the time of our next action.

So it was with a trembling spirit that I approached the table of practice on that day. 'The noise is marvellous great coming through the stone,' he said, 'as if a thousand water-mills were going together.'

'Do you see anything?'

'I see two things, or spirits, I do not know what to call them now. There is a tall fellow on a horse; he has a cut beard and wears a sky-coloured cloak. I cannot see what road he follows, yet it is familiar: yes, he rides down Charing Cross. There is another man on horseback, a lean-visaged man with a short cloak and a gilt rapier.'

'Ask them where they are going. Perhaps they have the news that we seek.'

He repeated my question, and then listened intently with his ear close to the stone. 'They are going in no certain direction,' he replied. 'But now they are coming closer to me. The tall man holds a little stick with his fingers crooked and on his left hand he has the scar of a cut. The lean-visaged man has on a pair of boots, which come straight on his legs and very close. He lifts his stick and points to you from the stone.'

At this I was very much afraid, and felt myself turn pale as a cloth. 'Are they willing to do my bidding?'

'I believe so.'

'Then tell them to ride to the ancient city. Tell them to guide us to all that buried glory.'

'They hear you, and they begin to laugh. Now a young woman comes forward, covered all with a white robe; she takes the horses and leads them away from Charing Cross towards the city.'

'Perhaps she has heard my plea, and directs us the proper way.' I was eagerly on the chase now. 'What more do you see?'

'They are riding furiously, while the young woman still goes on ahead with her arms spread abroad and her feet not touching the ground by a yard in height. They seem to be passing through those fields behind St Botolph and just beyond Aldgate.'

'They are making their way to the site of the old city.'

'They come to a halt beside the drained land –'

'We have stood there ourselves many times.'

'Now they point to the foundation of an old building, as it were of a church or temple.'

'Has it something to do with the stone which we found lying there?'

He took no notice of me, but continued staring *in crystallo*. 'But now all is changed. All is bright. They are in the middle of a city, where the houses are of stone and very stately.'

'Is it possible? Is it the ancient city itself, as if seen in a vision?'

'It is not like the sight vouchsafed to me in Glastonbury, but I will ask them.' Then he listened again at the stone. 'Its name they will not tell me, or do not know.'

'What else do they say?'

'The lean-visaged man approaches and calls for you.'

'Tell him I am here to do whatever he commands.'

'He hears you and says thus. Dee, John Dee, I am here to instruct and inform you according to the doctrines delivered, which are contained in thirteen dwellings or callings. There are four natural keys to open five gates of the city (for one gate is never to be opened), and by their means will the secret of this place be righteously and wisely granted to you.' These were dark words, and I could not as yet puzzle out their meaning. Mr Kelley was gazing eagerly into the stone, and now continued. 'He approaches a broad open part of the city, like our Smith Field. There is a great stone in the middle of it, of about eighty inches square in mortal reckoning, and there is a fire in that stone. Now he takes out a casket, opens it, and there is within a waxen image of a pale colour like candle wax. Now his companion with the cut beard holds something like a glass vessel over the image, yet I still can see that it is marvellously scratched. Or perhaps it has been very rudely made with dents and knobs in the legs of it. I cannot tell. Now they pour blood out of a basin upon the fire, which springs ever higher in the middle of the stone, and now they cast the waxen image upon it where it seems to grow.'

I knew well enough the story here, since the spirits were acting in dumb show the very birth of the homunculus. 'What more now?' I asked him eagerly.

'Now all that spectacle is vanished away.' Kelley rubbed his eyes, before bending once more over the stone. 'The two spirits are looking out over the drained land where lately we walked. Both are sighing, and one points with his stick to the ground. Oh God, now he grows big and swells up within the stone. Now I see only his mouth, which gapes at me. Oh Jesus, protect me from this sight!'

At that he fell back from the table of practice, and had *tremorem cordis* for a while. But I was very glad and well pleased – not only to have had intercourse with the spirits through which they obeyed my commands, but also to have been strengthened and confirmed in my siting of the city. 'Make an end for today,' I told him. 'Give over. We have seen enough, and now we must make ourselves ready for tomorrow's action.'

'Tomorrow? Why change the order of our proceedings now?'

'We must warm our hands, Mr Kelley, while the fire is still high.'

'I had thought to rest myself, sir, for these things are terrible to behold. Yet now, so soon again . . .'

'We cannot rest now. We must march on.'

Soon after that he left me, pleading once more the great fatigue of the scrying, and I walked into my study for the better contemplation of all that had occurred. I will confess here that my mind was still troubled, so I took down and opened *Of Wicked Spirits* by the learned Abbot Fludd, in which he counselled against the calling-up of any apparitions whatsoever they might be. I did not follow him in this, however. If these spirits have knowledge greater than our own and if, as the commentators agree, all knowledge is virtue – why, then, where is the fault in acquiring virtue? The breath of the lion engenders the dove as well as the serpent, but for fear of serpents, are we to have no doves? I was meditating upon this when I heard my wife's foot upon my study stairs, and I counterfeited the reading of my book as she entered.

'I have given Mr Kelley's boots to be cleaned,' she said, without wishing me good day or any such thing.

'It is well done,' I replied without looking up from my book. Thereupon she sat down in the chair by my table and, softly humming to herself, took up in her hand one of the other volumes I had left there. 'Do not lose my place, mistress.'

'Do not worry about that. These pages are so stiff I can hardly turn them.' It was my copy of *Maleficia Maleficiorum*. 'It makes my head ache merely to look upon these words,' she continued. 'What is that, husband?'

I saw her looking upon a symbol of the star demon, much used by certain good scholars of Prague and Hamburg. 'It is part of the kabbalah. Take care that it does not burn you.'

'I have seen Mr Kelley examine your books eagerly enough, and he was never scalded.'

'Edward Kelley here?'

'He is often among your papers when you are away from the house. I wonder he has not told you.'

'Well, he needs no permission to use my library.'

'If it be so, it is good. For I have often heard him murmuring words into the air, as if he were trying to learn them by rote.' This caused me a little disquietness of mind; in spite of my calm words to my wife, there were papers here that I wished no one to see without my leave or well-liking – no, not even my wife herself, for who knows what may be blabbed out without doing any good by it? I knew well enough that I had left here certain notes on the preparation of new life, which were for no eyes but my own. But what were these words that Kelley had by heart?

'Why do you frown,' she asked me now, 'is there something amiss?'

'Nothing. Nothing at all.' I looked steadily at her. 'Have you any more that you would say to me?'

'No.'

'But you seem in disturbed sort.'

At that she got up from her chair, and began walking up and down as she spoke. 'Mr Kelley has stayed with us in this house for many months, and yet we know no more of him than any citizen passing in the street. He slips in and out of his chamber as if he were not willing to be seen, and looks with such scorn upon Philip and Audrey that you would think they had crawled out of some kennel.'

'These words are very large, mistress, but I think there is nothing within them.'

'Nothing? Is it nothing that he has the key to your private chambers, and goes among your books and papers when you are away from home? That he takes volumes from your study and pores over them with the light of a candle?'

'He is a scholar, Mrs Dee, and has a great thirst for knowledge.'

She laughed at that. 'A thirst for everything, sir. I have seen him drink so much wine that he must have a quagmire in his belly.'

'He has an elevated mind, and it is said that those who see furthest drink most.'

'And what does he see, sir?'

'I cannot speak of these things today.' I was angry with her, and was unwilling to let her go without a bite in her arse. 'I tell you this, mistress. I would sooner bequeath all my papers to the privy, leaf by leaf, than have them examined by a fool or a thief. But Edward Kelley is not of that mould. He is *semper fidelis*, and I demand that you afford him as much trust and reverence as I do.'

'If that is your wish, then so be it.' She rose, curtsied and was about to leave the chamber. 'Far be it from me,' she added, in a low voice, 'to mention that a plaster may be small amends for a broken head.' I did not understand her words, but before I could question her further she turned like a little whirlwind and was gone.

In the following week, although he and I came each day into the scrying room, all about the stone was quiet; on having conference together, we agreed that the sudden change in our practice had perturbed or angered the spirits. So we agreed, further, that no more was to be done for the space of seven days.

In the meantime Mrs Dee had taken my words to her heart, and conversed in all civility with Edward Kelley when they sat together at the table. In the gallery, too, she bestowed kind and amiable words upon him. 'Tell me, sir,' she asked one afternoon when we all sat together, 'do you prefer to work by means of memory or inspiration?'

'That is a nice question,' Edward Kelley replied. 'Suffice it to say that memory without inspiration is barren indeed, while inspiration without memory is like the horse that gallops without a rider. Does that answer you?'

'Very well, sir. It is what I would expect from a scholar such as you are, who knows in which direction he must ride.'

This was merry talk indeed, and yet two days later she came suddenly into my study. She seemed to be in a marvellous great fury and rage, and held up her hand as if she were willing to strike someone. 'My bracelet and rings have gone,' she said. 'All of them clean gone.' She was in such a great rush of words that I asked her to calm herself. 'I was looking for my bodkin,' she continued, 'because the eyelet holes of your hose were broken, and so I went into my closet where I keep my boxes of stuff. And it was gone.'

'What was gone?'

'The wooden casket where I keep my rings. Good God, what a short memory you have! Did you not buy it for me last year, in Poor Jewry? The very intricate carved box, with the figure of the mermaid upon it? Well, it is gone! Conveyed away, with my rings and bracelet!'

'You mean that you cannot find it. Where did you set it yesterday?'

'I did not have it yesterday. It sits where it always sits, and I mean that it is stolen.'

'But who would do such a thing? Philip? Audrey? We have no other strangers in the house.'

'Philip and Audrey are no more strangers to you than I am. You have forgotten your Mr Kelley –'

'Katherine!'

'Did he not tell you of his friendship with that jeweller in

Cheapside? And I have heard him discourse on the virtuous properties of natural stones.' I thought then, as she talked, that he spoke only what he had learned from me. 'How do we know that he has not secretly bereaved me of my goods, and carried them into the city?'

'Katherine. Mrs Dee. There is no more honest man living than Mr Kelley. Has he not worked by me, and assisted me, these last twelve months?'

'You are as blind as a mole when you are buried within your books. Have you not seen, by diverse actions and express words, that he is a hollow friend to you? All his dreams are of gold, all his hopes are for advancement and the Devil take the hindmost. I cannot abide him. No, I abhor him. And here, in my own house, I am misliked by you because I favour him no better.'

Her words were spoken in great pangs and disquietness of mind, and I tried to soothe her. 'It is not so, wife. It is not so. Has the loss of your rings meant that you have lost your wits as well?'

'I tell you this, Doctor Dee.' She went over to my window, and looked out on to the garden. 'Audrey has observed him by the path there, muttering to someone over by the wicket-gate. She swears to me that she has heard slanders against you and all your work.'

I was amazed at that, but even in my first alarm I could not believe any such abominable misusing me behind my back: it was the knavery of Audrey, I knew well, and I was about to bring her up in order to examine her when Kelley himself came indiscreetly upon us. I thought that my study door had been shut, and I greatly feared his rash opinion of such words as he might have overheard. My wife stepped back, and put her hand to her mouth. 'The woman Audrey,' he said, 'is a brazen-faced liar. Bring her here, and see if she is ashamed to affirm so apparent a falsehood before my very face!'

My wife's words were of more smarting efficacy than she could have known and, being heard by him, had that steel and metal in them which pierced and stung him to the quick. 'What is the cause,' he said to my wife now, 'what is the cause that you will not be better acquainted with my feelings for you and for your husband?'

'I know your feelings very well,' she replied. 'Like the ravening crocodile, you have pity for no man other than yourself.' Whereupon he declared that she did fable, and she was so moved that she called him 'hypocrite' and 'conniver'. I told her then to remove all spitefulness, and tried quietly to pacify them, but it was all to no avail. 'Well, I have forewarned you,' she said, turning to me with the fire still in her eyes. 'I have done the part of a wife. It had been better for you not to have changed an old friend for a new.' Then with an angry look she walked away, and shut the door of the study upon us.

I arose and went after her, and took her by the shoulders to keep her from the stairs. 'My opinion of you, mistress, is clean changed. How could you spin such fantasies and wild words?'

She said nothing for a moment, but looked steadily at me. 'You speak of spinning, but I know of one who spins lies better than any man. And remember this, sir. There is no wool so white but the dyer can make it black. I have no more to say.'

'Then go to your duties. And call Audrey to me.'

I went back to my study, and with all levity I tried to entertain Edward Kelley. 'There never was such a shrew as my wife,' I said. 'But words are mere words, and she means no harm.'

'I forgive her. She has been tricked by her brain-sick maid into false witness against me.'

After a few minutes up came that slattern, shaking like an aspen leaf. 'Why is it,' I asked her, 'that you have spread false reports and malicious slanders against Mr Kelley, who has done you no harm in the world?' The water stood in her eyes, and she was not able to answer one word until she had well wept. 'When did you enter the year of your service?' Still she stood, weeping, and said nothing. 'Was it not on Michaelmas Day? You have from me three pounds a year in wages, and a gown cloth of russet. Is this how you repay me? What do I get by this expense but mischief?'

'I meant nothing by it, sir. Only –'

'Nothing? Do you call it nothing to condemn my guest as a thief and a malicious backbiter?'

'I heard him in the garden, sir.'

'Yes, and where were you? Close under a hedge, playing at jack-in-the-box? Or was it something worse? Well, you are discharged. Do not come near my house again.'

At that Kelley stepped forward, smiling upon her now. 'Do not be so harsh, Doctor Dee, I entreat you. I see from her tears that she is in a state of contrition. Can we not play the priest and shrive her?'

'Do you hear, Audrey? What do you say to that?'

'I would humbly thank you, sir, if I were forgiven.'

'No. Do not thank me. Go down on your knees now and bless this gentleman for preserving you.' She did so, with a few broken words, and then left us weeping as hard as if she had been burned through the ear. 'You were kind,' I said, 'to one who was less than kin.'

'I do not blame her wholly.' He went after her, and firmly closed the door to my chamber. 'There is something else. There is something in this house which is more busy than any bee that I know.'

'How is that?'

'What melancholy conceit is it that pesters their brains, so that your wife is turned against me and her servant sees nothing but phantasms? Who whispered those abominable words to that errant strumpet, Audrey, and who devised those most unhonest and devilish dealings against the property of your wife?'

'How did you know about the property?'

'Audrey told me of the theft.' And then he went on, more quickly than before. 'Do you not understand that these spirits we have raised within the chamber of practice, and have seen within the holy crystal stone, have not returned to their habitation (wherever that might be) but have entered the walls, the floors, the very frame of this house? Upon what black shore of mischief have we sailed, to take on such passengers?'

I was amazed at this. 'Surely you put a false construction upon words which signify no more than a fart? Do the spirits haunt my privy?'

I could not help but smile, despite the cause of my ill-humour, but this provoked him all the more. All at once he damned and condemned anything that had been heard or seen in the chamber of presence. 'Our teachers are deluders,' he said, 'and are not good or sufficient instructors.'

I told him that he did err in so saying, and that there lay before us a world of knowledge and of power. 'What does it profit us now to turn our backs upon that golden city, the first of Albion, when lying under the ground are treasures beyond dreaming? We must recover that which has been lost to our country for many thousands of years. It is too late for us to consider what we should have done, in addressing these spirits or apparitions, and it rests only for us to determine what we must do. It would be the worse for me if I lose my labour in this, Mr Kelley, and I mean to make my chance and prove my destiny.'

'Do you call it destiny? It is the maddest destiny that ever I heard, but if you wish it, then so let it be. I make only one condition for going forward with you.'

'Which would be?'

'That you no longer conceal from me any mysteries of your craft, even to the highest, and that you share with me all secrets contained in your studies or in your alchemical practice.'

I could see which way the wind blew. 'You wish to approach the philosopher's stone? You wish for gold?'

'Yes, in fit time.'

'Or is it more? Is there other knowledge you wish for?'

'All in time.'

'Well then, so be it. I can deny you nothing.'

He put out his hand. 'I shall not forsake you, not now or ever.'

'You are one with me?'

'One with you, Doctor Dee.'

It was the week following this, our latest compact, that my wife fell ill of a fever. At first she had nothing more than some wambling in her stomach, but when she tried to break her fast with sugar sops, she vomited them up speedily enough; a hot sweat then came upon her, so I put a poultice of eggs and honey, blended with the nuts of a pine tree, upon her breast. Yet I knew very well that this sickness was her fantasy, a fond foolishness brought on by the loss of her rings and by our hard words together. So I went to work as eagerly as before, and was in a great study at my desk while she kept to her bed. 'How does my wife?' I said, entering her chamber two nights after she was first despatched there.

'Well, sir, I feel some grievous pangs and pains.' She was still in a sweat, and moved her head from side to side.

'It is the rheum,' I replied. 'Be patient, and take the mineral physic I have prepared for you. It is no dangerous sickness.' Then I went out of her closet with a light heart, and spoke with Kelley about the next day's scrying.

It was arduous work indeed, with the action of that day, and on the following night I sat in my chamber and studied the responses which had come out of the stone. It was my practice to note down everything as it occurred, so that I had a full record of each week's proceedings, and I was bent over my papers half the night long. Thus:

Spirit.	4723 is called the mystical root in the highest ascendant of transmutation.
Dee.	These phrases are dark.
Spirit.	It is the square of the philosopher's work.
Dee.	You said it was the root.
Spirit.	So it is a root square, the square thereof is 22306729. And the words are, by interpretation, *Ignis vera mater.*
Dee.	What does this signify?
Spirit.	Enough. It is at an end.

I was puzzling out the meaning of this within my chamber, when I heard a strange noise of knocking; and then there was a voice, ten times repeated, somewhat like the shriek of a man in pain but softer and more long-drawn. I was strangely troubled at that – and yet more so, yes, close to fainting away, when I thought I saw a spiritual creature standing upright in the corner, with its hands stretched out towards me. Very quickly it stepped across my chamber until it came to a halt, its back to me, in the corner opposite. Then it turned its face to me with the same long call of pain: it was my father, dead more than a year since, as fully drawn and delineated from the sole of the foot to the crown of the head as if he were a painted image.

'In the name of Jesus, who are you?' I cried. It did not answer me. 'I know that the Devil may appear in the shape of a father or mother, for the very reason that some will sooner listen to it in that familiar guise. Is that what you are? Speak.'

Then it showed me the palm of its hand and there were words written upon it, as if it were the leaf of a book: it was so far from me that I could not read it but then, *mirabile dictu*, the spirit seemed to be very much nearer to me than his hand. 'You cannot give me the slip,' it said. 'All your cunning will fail you now. Your ship is almost built.'

'What ship may that be?'

'The ship of sorrow, of which you are the sad captain.'

'Are you my father?'

'Do you see any other? I was nothing to you in life, but I shall be something now.' I was too much amazed and astonished to speak more, for I perceived that I could see clean through him to the other side of my closet where a candle stood twinkling upon an oaken chest. 'Do you not see my bowels within me?' the spirit asked. 'They are the bowels of pity. Yet you would have sooner watched them fall out before me with poison than you would have helped me.'

'If you think, Devil or father, or whatever you may be, to hear a repentant man speak and tell a large tale of his penitent woes – then you are deceived.'

'Is this your answer? If I begin with you, I will make you leave smiling for ever.' He seemed to look down into himself, and plucked a little plume of smoke from his stomach. 'I see you are so crazed with schemes and so laden with disgraces that you are consumed to the very bones. Now I see you standing in a great bay window with a halter about your neck.'

'I care not a fig for your prophecies.'

'Not prophecies, but things of present moment.' I turned to depart, but it seemed as if the thing took me by the throat even though I could feel no touch of his hand upon me. 'I do not mean to let you escape so, for now I will let fall my style a little to talk in reason with you that have none. I have words for you laid in *aqua fortis*: you will be what you are, you are what you will be.'

'Does the Devil himself speak in riddles?'

'Do not vex me, Doctor Dee. For I have come to open to you the secret knowledge of the earth.' At that I started as if from a dream, and he gave out a laugh which was no more than a cry of pain. 'I see your heart leaping up and down like a kite in the wind.'

He had read me right. 'Truly,' I replied, 'I have laboured for that knowledge all the days of my life.'

'I will make you a gift of it. For hear this: sorrow is at hand in all the earth. Listen to what is spoken to you. God send you good rest. I will return.'

I do not know how he departed, whether he flew through the air or out of my casement, or whether he went downward through the floor of my chamber; but there came a thing like a wind that plucked him away so that he was quite vanished out of my sight. But I was glad to be rid of him and sank into my chair, until there came a voice again. It was as if I heard my father fetching a deep sigh from his breast, when he had been lying within the hospital where I saw him last, and speaking in his own old voice. 'Not to have loved is a fearful thing. Now, good doctor, look upon this. Look upon the world without love.'

THE CITY

Now look upon this. Look upon the world without love. I awoke and found myself in as black a night as I had ever known; but I was not in my chamber. I was walking abroad, with the help of a lantern and candle, and now stood beneath the wall of the city. The stone rose before me like the face of that idol discovered in the Devonshire mines, yet as I raised my lantern I saw all the wrinkles, cracks, crevices and flaws that lay within the ancient stones. It seemed that the whole edifice was made of nothing but light and rotten stuff, and how could the city be protected if that were so? Then one of the stones moved before me: I stepped back with an oath when I perceived that it was a spider (a most rare one in bigness and length of feet) which shifted and was just as suddenly gone.

I passed in through the More Gate even as there came the sound of a horn, and one blown with such force that the echo redoubled again in the dark London air. I knew these streets so well that without any light I could have made my way but, when I put up my lantern by All Allowes in the Wall, I saw many citizens walking slowly through the lane there in long gowns and velvet coats. Each one held a wax candle lighted in his hands, and sighed continually as if his bowels might break. They seemed to be pacing the dungeon of the night, a night which was a nurse of cares, a mother of despair, and a daughter of hell itself. Why did they walk and moan continually, down Wormwood Street and Broad Street? It was as if they had been hatched in the womb of sorrows and now, being brought forth into such fogs and filthy mists, had become no more than spectres or works of darkness which could not be seen in the daytime. And therewithall the stench was so strong that I might have been in the city dog-house on the other side of the fields.

I was struck into a sudden dump and, as I stood on the corner of Bartholomew Street, I saw my old master, Ferdinand Griffen, walking before me. 'I thought you were dead,' I said. 'But now I see that you are in life.' He made no answer to me but advanced with a slow pace towards a low wooden house which had seven or eight flaring torches upon its roof; I knew it to be a strong house of sorrow. I followed him and, when I came up to the door, I saw a man in a purple gown sitting before the window: the house was very like my own laboratory, with all manner of glass vessels hanging there, and I saw in many of them the small creatures which I had thought to grow. I looked closer still, and observed that these things were without breath or spirit; so this experiment was ended. The man all in purple had a wart upon his cheek, and there stood by him two girls in green petticoats. One of them was a little fair girl, who now ran along a gallery until he called her back to him; he made a sign to her, smiting one hand on another and drawing it under his throat as though he threatened the girl unless she kept a secret. But I knew the secret well enough. I knew the rites of *amor sexus* which, God help me, had in darkness and concealment been practised within my own house: it was in my younger days, when the spirits were willing and the eyes of the demon glowed in the corner. Now my old master, Ferdinand Griffen, appeared again before the window, and spoke to me. 'See here,' he said, 'I have news. I have the new map of London, just lately delineated. Does it please you, good doctor?' He held it towards me, and I saw that all was truly pictured on it, with the latest dwellings by the Finsbury Fields clearly marked and even the lanes of Southwark inscribed; but as I stared upon the whole design of this city straddling the river, it seemed to me like the image of a man mounting a woman and coupling with her in a rape.

So great was my fear, and so great my anger against him, that I put out my palms to ward him off. 'I have no true acquaintance with you,' I replied. 'No, nor with any man, dead or alive. I feel myself to be alone.'

I turned back down Bartholomew Lane into Lothbury, where a great concourse of people was hurrying with silent feet. With much sighing I made my way through them until I came to the newly erected hospital on the corner of Colman Street: I stopped, amazed, when I saw one leaning from the door, all besmeared with men's filth and with a visage most ugly and fearful which, imbrued with congealed blood and eaten away like a raw ulcer, made him too ghastly to behold. 'Why stand you astonished at my deformity,' he said to me, 'when there is no living man but who is thus inwardly disfigured? You think this to be a hospital? Well, Doctor Dee, the entire world is a hospital where we must remain cloistered and immured, so barricaded with graves that we cannot step out of doors without coming upon the dead and the dying. Do you see this damp mist which now rolls over the city like smoke from a cannon? It is the contagion of the earth, thick rolling clouds of churchyard matter which environ us.' I was utterly undone, and when I looked into myself I saw only a place of horror, stench and darkness. Truly this is a world of corruption, where all fade equally.

It was somewhat lighter now, about an hour after the rising of the sun, when I left him and walked down Old Jewry towards the clock; there were men standing all along the way, with pikes in their hands, and they were looking directly towards the water-cans in Poultry – upon which stood a man who declared with a loud voice some matter of importance. I could not hear his words, but bent my steps until I came within a few yards of him. He was not speaking out words but numbers, as a merchant might reckon his bill behind a counter; he spoke of nothing but sums of money, and repeated them so often, and with so many grimaces and cries, that he must have been clean out of his mind. Yet now I stood quietly and listened. 'Fifteen shillings,' he called. 'And now some pennies more. Will you give me five pounds? No? An angel here.'

It offered me strange comfort to hear the money told, so I smiled and nodded to him. 'One thousand pounds of gold,' I said.

He stepped down from the water-cans and whispered to me. 'If you think this is good, we may make a turn in the Exchange. It is not far from here, and I must purchase a silk rope to hang by.'

'But the Exchange is not yet completely built.'

'In this city it is built. Come.' He saw me trembling, and laughed aloud. 'Is it so cold? Button your doublet – are you not ashamed to be so untrussed? It is always cold here.' He walked on before me quickly until we came to a very stately building, constructed of squared stone; there was an open space within, neatly paved, where men in black robes were walking up and down with sad and heavy countenances, conferring now and then by two or three together. 'You might think we were in Bethlehem Hospital,' he said to me, smiling, 'and these men most lamentably troubled by hypochondriac melancholy. But it is not so. These are men of business, merchants, brokers, creditors, retailers. They are the foundation of our city, which will grow larger and still larger upon fraud and usury and bribery and extortion and other such tricks. It is the true city universal, expanding like the black clouds which bring rain. Does this please you, good Doctor Dee?' There was now such jostling of one another that it would have grieved any man living to be in the throng amongst them. Nothing could be heard but noise, and nothing of that noise be understood, except that it was not the sound of men. These seemed to be the very emblems of hell, not Bedlam, in which there are only darkness and separation. And was this what my city had become? Was this life a continuance of death, or was this a death in continuance of life?

I went up and down London crying, like a lantern-and-candle man, when suddenly I came upon a concourse of citizens standing as in a half-moon; there, in the midst of them, was an excellent pageant hung with cloth of gold. One of the players came forward, dressed as a musician and carrying his lute, who began to speak to the citizens: 'All the pleasures of this life are but as children's dreams. All the glories of the world are artificial fireworks that keep a blazing for a time, but then die in stinking smokes. All the labours of men are like the toiling of the winds which strive to raise up heaps of dust that, in the end, are not worthy of the gathering.' They laughed at every jest and clapped when his speech was ended; still smiling upon them, he took up his lute. His was new music, instinct with woe, yet the notes seemed not to rise up into the sky but to be trapped within the streets and courts – viz. the music filled Bridge Row, Walbrook, St Mary Botolph and Canwicke Street. And even as he played, I grew weary of myself and all my strivings. What had I laboured for but fame and pre-eminence, though these were but shows and gewgaws giving no pleasure even in the tasting? Had I tried to conquer time and nature only to find myself impaled upon them? And if I had found the philosopher's stone, or spanned the secrets of the stars, what benefit to me if I went to my death unconfessed? Yes, no doubt I was already dead, and this was the place to which I had come. This was the city of darkness. For now a woman came from behind the pageant, went about the musician, and tied his sweet mouth with pack-thread.

Then all went off in procession, and the streets were new gravelled with stone from Abchurch Lane to Lombard Street. The buildings were hung with cloth of arras, with carpets and with silks, while Birchin Lane was arrayed in cloth of gold and cloth of silver, as well as velvet of all colours. First in procession came the children, all in blue and green, with the arms of London embroidered on their sleeves. Then came all the crafts of the city walking in their livery both red and yellow, with their banners and streamers carried before them: they were met at the corner of St Nicholas Lane by the bachelors in crimson damask hoods, with drums and flutes and trumpets blowing, and sixty gentlemen following in blue gowns and red capes according to custom. Then came the pensioners in white gowns, then aldermen in scarlet with their serjeants-at-arms richly habited in yellow and gold, then knights in blue and purple, and then after, lords: each had the colour of his rank and station in life, just as each of the spheres has its own proper note and motion.

But what was this following on the end of the procession? There came fifty clerks and priests in their black gowns, chanting the Miserere, and behind them the poor men with white staffs in their hands. I saw then that the street by Finch Lane, close to St Anthony, was hung in black. 'How comes this to pass?' I asked one near me. 'Here is such gear as I never saw!'

'Did you not hear the news? Today is the day of death. There was one who poisoned the wife of a citizen, and has not long since been boiled in lead, but now we celebrate the execution of a very skilful and cunning man who helped to build this city. Here he comes now in the cart: that thing upon his shoulders is soon to be set upon the gate, while the rest of his corpse is burned in a pit near Wapping Stairs. I pray Jesus have mercy on his soul.'

'But what was his crime, that so much vengeance is to be wreaked upon him?'

'He kept too many secrets.'

The cart of the condemned man had been driven up into Finch Lane, and had come to a halt beside a great scaffold covered with canvas. Yet, Jesus, what was this and how could this be? I saw my own self being taken out of the foul cart, quite naked except for a white gown very like a shroud. Above my head, as I was brought down and bound with a strong rope, was a banner with these words written upon it: 'What is below is like that which is above, and what is above is like that which is below.' I tried to cry out but suddenly a marvellous hoarseness, and in a manner speechlessness, took me. Now was I utterly undone. No constable had followed me with hue and cry, no bailiff had pursued me with a writ out of the King's Bench, and yet here I was being taken to my death like a pig to the spit. Then only one thought possessed me – that by some means I must prefer my suit to the queen, attending for eternity (if need be) until I came to her presence.

So, fixing upon this resolution, I walked quickly down Bow Lane and Garlic Hill into Thames Street; I hurried all the more when I seemed to catch sight of some figure following me and crossed the way in order to shun him, until I came down by Watergate and the new stairs there. I stood now on the lower part of the steps, just where the water of the Thames lapped at my feet, and called for a wherry-man. One stood off, seeming to bargain with me, but I soon put an end to any such hurly-burly. 'Master waterman, there is none so simple in London but does not know your fares. I know what is due between this place and Whitehall, so here is the penny.'

'Any eye may see,' he replied, laughing, 'that you are hard like the adamant.'

'You may quote me a dictionary of abuses, but it will not alter me.'

'Well, well,' he said, rowing up close to the stairs, 'I will take you, sir.'

I heard him murmur beneath his breath that he would like to see me stuffed with hot steel, and I was about to answer his frowardness with a 'beware what you say', when I saw that around his neck was tied a black scarf; of what purpose it signified I knew not, so I sat back in the dirty craft and said nothing.

We had just shot the bridge, at the still of the ebb, when I heard someone salute me and bid me God-speed. I turned my head and looked back, but on seeing who it was I suddenly started and was greatly afraid: it was the figure of myself, with a halter round my neck, waving from a wherry close behind. I gave out a piteous shriek, and my waterman burst into such loud and vehement laughter that, for the time, he was not able to deliver a word.

'From the shrillness of the noise,' he said at last, 'it seemed to be some woman's voice. But take heart, Doctor Dee, the waves will not overwhelm us. There is some other bed waiting for you at the last.' I did not understand what he meant by that, or how he knew my name, but I was not able with patience to endure his laughter; and so, in the grasp of fear and anger equally mixed, I told him to make speed to Whitehall and escape from the thing that followed us. 'Oh, make me not go too fast,' he said, laughing still, 'you will be my wrack and undoing. But truly, sir, I am not disposed to prolong the time in idleness.' He had a huge worm-eaten nose like a cluster of grapes hanging downwards, and now he put one finger against it. 'I have my own purpose and destination, Doctor Dee. Why do you think it is that I wear this black scarf?'

'Ply me no more with such vague words, but speak out truly. How is it that you know my name?' I looked behind me fearfully again, but the figure or double of myself was nowhere to be seen.

'Well, good doctor, I will give you the whole discourse of my adventure. I am Charon, and I am carrying you to hell!'

At that moment we had come up to Whitehall stairs, where all the barges were decked with streamers and banners. Throwing my coin upon the bottom of the boat, I jumped out and made haste to climb the bank away from this feverish madman. I heard him calling after me as I made my way, crying, 'You leap as quickly as if your guts were being taken out by the hangman! God-speed, good doctor! God-speed!' Then he laughed again. 'But remember this. It will come in the night by water.'

I turned, but all was in a mist, so disordered in my mind had I become. Then I found myself suddenly close within the wall of the Whitehall palace. There was a great door before me, unlocked; I went in that way, crossing past a very fair landing at the foot of some stairs, and came out into a room of good state and largeness where I saw a multitude of men with budgets of writing under their arms. I took them to be serjeants and benchers, counsellors and lawyers, and indeed there some of them were nailing up mandates upon certain images of wood. One lawyer, wearing a damask cassock edged with fox fur, came up to me without seeming to move – like the point in the dial which, though it go, none can see it going. 'You should know,' he said, 'that there are as many causes decided here as there are clients that complain and counsellors that plead; I have grown hoarse, good doctor, in the service of demurs and *audita-queraela*, writs of error and of *ne exeat regnum*, writs of rebellion and writs of outlawry. The suits are infinite and the judgements not to be numbered.' He seemed to smile then, but put his cassock up to his face. 'But I tell you this,' he continued. 'I am not so busily engaged that I will not make a very faithful and inviolable promise of great importance. Come, come, give me your hand and let us be friends. I know that it is not your custom to look back to every dog that barks, but there are some here who wish you ill. Should you hire me now, I may preserve you for a year or so yet. Will you have a plea or an action? Are you criminal or civil, good doctor? I can give you either verdict or demur, while you may give me confession or default. Come, what will it be? I have not all day to stand and gossip. If any sin have been committed, either in process or form, matter or judgement, then you must speak aloud.' I was about to reply to him, when he took up his sword and struck me with it upon my breast. 'That's for you,' he said. 'Pay me when you are able.'

Then all at once everyone in that place stood around me as if I were before a privy court. 'You are already dead,' said one pale clerk, 'though it is from the general sickness of the world.'

'What have I done,' I cried, 'that I should be treated in this way? What rape or deceit, what perjury or fraud or subtlety have I committed? What fault is mine that I should be hanged?'

I fled from them and came out into a gallery all paved, and from there to some other room of pillars. Here was whispering enough to fill St Paul's nave, and so dark that you would think it sunk under ground and become a place of shadows. But I roused myself from fear and, on looking round, I perceived that I was in an inner court among a wilderness of halls, parlours, libraries, chambers and galleries. Here were privy lodgings and privy chambers, and among them were gathered all those who wait upon the queen's majesty – the chamberlains, the wardrobers, the falconers, the housekeepers, the lackeys, the scullions and the special men.

Suddenly there was a noise of guns and trumpets, and in the torch-light I caught sight of the guards in doublet and hose all bejewelled with diamonds. 'She is here,' said one close to me, in great fear. 'She has been brought through the hall into the chamber of presence.' Banners of black and white were raised around, and the high men of state all at once hurried away into their own privy chambers. Yet it was a stroke of fortune for some, since I remembered now for what I had come: to give reverence to the queen, and ask her pardon for any fault committed.

I had no manner of knowledge concerning her chamber of presence, yet I was guided by a continual brightness of candle, fire and torch-light that came from a room at the end of a well-embellished gallery. On entering it I saw that it was some privy lodging, or room of dressing and preparing, all hung with cloth of gold showing the deaths of those martyred for the old faith. There was a further room beyond which shone as sunbeam gold, and I saw within a throne studded with very large diamonds, rubies, sapphires and the like that glittered among the other jewels as cold and as hard as ice before it melts. Her majesty was nowhere to be seen but I moved forward and, knowing that whosoever speaks to Elizabeth must kneel, I sank down upon a cushion embroidered with gold thread where, in secrecy and silence, I made great reverence and obedience to the empty throne.

'*Vivat regina*,' I cried as if I were in a delirium.

And then a low woman's voice answered me from the opposite corner of the room. '*Gratias ago. Gratias ago.*'

I stood at once and, turning about, saw the queen before me. She was very nobly apparelled in a gown of purple satin, embroidered with gold and very richly set with such stones as amethyst, opal and lapis lazuli; upon her breast was a chrysoberyl in the figure of a hanged man, and upon her head was a whole bird of paradise spangled with gold and with a bush of violet feathers. I could not look upon her face yet, though I knew her bright eyes to be upon me; but then, when I did so, I shrank back with horror and amaze. There was a great spider upon her face, its legs extending over her whole visage as if it were sucking the breath from her mouth. 'Come forward,' said she, her voice muffled by the body of the beast. I made my three curtsies, and then she offered me her hand to kiss. 'You mislike my little pet?' Whereupon she took the thing from her face and hurled it from her, laughing merrily all the while.

'Great majesty,' I said, 'I have a very strange device of sorrow that weighs me down. May I discourse to you all the circumstance of my care?'

She smiled upon me. 'Nothing can be with better will said by you than it shall be graciously accepted by me.' And so then I told her to what a low ebb I had come, alone and friendless, without reputation or gain. 'So,' she replied, 'you wish for fame and gold, and for all the renown which should be the product of your great labours.'

'It is no less than I deserve, gracious lady, and no more than I desire. I have neither recounted nor foretold anything to your majesty but that which I have found true by my sorrowful experience; and because my case is very lamentable, therefore I do humbly crave on my own behalf that you will be a suitor to the hangman and save me from his rope.'

'And then after?'

'That you will give your gracious consent that I may be restored to my previous estate and worthiness.'

She turned about and seemed to be busying herself over some action, when there came a noisome stench from the same corner of the chamber. 'We will enter a disputation,' she said. 'I shall be the Asker and you the Replyer, in the old style, and our voices shall echo in the House of Bones.' I did not understand her, but bowed and approached closer to the presence. Then, when she moved a little, there was a minute of dreadfulness. There before her lay a naked corpse with a white cloth over its head; the breast had been cut open and I could see within the flesh and fat, the sinews and muscles, the membranes and fibres, all revealed. The queen stood with her hands sunk into the body up to her wrists. 'I am in great anxiety for the well-doing of things,' she said. 'Come by me now. We require you not to fail.' I could say, or do, nothing. 'Here,' she said again, 'I will set wide open the closet door of nature's secrets. For what is my realm but that of nature? See the power which I possess over all the parts and notable devices in the body of man. This is my true kingdom.'

With that she seemed to be lifting up a bone from the body laid open. 'Do you see, John Dee, how the bones are, of all the parts of the body, most hard and dry and of earthy substance? It is within my power to have them broken or crushed upon a wheel, just as I put my feet upon the dust of the earth and regard it not. Now do you see the marvellous workmanship here, as intricate as the jewels set upon my gown, where nature has constructed the framework of the body with cartilages and swathed them every one in ligaments and bonds? Come closer still, and join the game.' Whereupon her majesty laughed well, and asked me if this was not a lively pastime? In the same merry mood she quizzed me now. 'What do you call that?' she said, pointing to a lump of fibrous flesh.

'I cannot tell.'

'It is a muscle. You see how it is covered with flesh, that the body might be large?' At that she put her hand upon my arm, leaving the blood and slime upon my sleeve, and I bowed in reverence. 'It has nerves along it, likewise, so that it might join in with that motive virtue which springs from the brain. It is like the state itself, of which all the parts must move in unison and be nourished by the blood of its sovereign head.' Now she turned back and put her steaming hands into the corpse once more. 'And why do you suppose it is called a muscle, John Dee? It is after the likeness which it shows to a mouse. Do you see here with its small head, its broad belly and its tail long and narrow?'

'It is also like a fish, your majesty.'

'Then we shall call them our little fishes swimming in the body. But what shall we call the corpse itself? What name shall we give it?' Then she took off the cloth which covered the face of the object and, to my unutterable horror and anxiety, I saw my own visage as if I were already in old age. 'It was a fishy one,' she said, 'that has come straight from the Devil. Do you like my lesson in anatomy, John Dee? For here may you see, in my use of power, the whole history of man laid out before you. One Faith, one Prince, one Sun, one Phoenix, one Heart, one Way.'

I looked again upon my own dead face, as white as a cloud, and was close to fainting away. 'I marvel,' the queen continued, 'that you are so disturbed in this point. But I am not here now to chide, only to show you the manner of my power and the ways of our city where we rule. Do you not think these muscles and tendons become you very well?' At which she leapt, and frisked, and clapped her hands. 'I have done well today,' she cried, 'because I have had good matter. Now it is time for meat.' Then, with her hands still reeking of my gore, she put on a pair of gloves, perfumed and garnished with embroidery. 'My good doctor,' she said, 'I have wished you well, and my favour is now so locked up for you that you shall partake of this banquet with me.'

The trumpeters came into the passage and, with solemn blast, declared her majesty to sit and eat. There entered then a multitude of the guard, every man having in his hand a torch staff for the lighting of this chamber, and some serving-men who strewed the floor with rushes to soak up the spilled blood. 'Do you know the old saying,' the queen asked me. 'They flee from me that sometime did me seek, with naked foot stalking in my chamber?' She laughed again, while the serving-men spread the table with cups and bowls of gold, goblets and jugs of crystal garnished with silver, and other trenchers and basins and ewers all glittering in the torch-light. Yet what was being placed in them now but portions of my own body, more horrible by far than toads or shrieking mandrakes? 'Do you see,' she said, 'how the ends of the muscles are in tendons, or what we commonly call cords? And here is the tongue, for your delight.'

I could not speak, or look, or do anything. Her mouth then opened wide as if to engulf me, and I ran shrieking from the chamber of presence. I hastened into the courtyard and, following the nearest way, came out by the gate opposite the Whitehall stairs. I thought now of nothing else but flight from this place of stench and horror, this second Hades; yet I was afraid to meet my Charon on the river once more, and so I footed it up the nearby lane until I came out by Scotland Yard and Charing Cross. From there it was an hour's march to Clerkenwell, and all the way I felt myself to be pursued by something as dark as the place from which I had just come. It seemed to dog my steps like some bound creature or indentured agent, yet when I looked back fearfully I could see nothing – nothing, that is, except my own shadow which grew larger and larger as I made my way homeward.

I knocked upon the door of my house most urgently, but there was no answer. Then I looked about me, and saw that my ancient house was now in quite another guise with great tenements of stone and brick all around it. What was this place, which was my own and not my own? The door opened to me, and when I walked within I saw nothing that I knew. Here was my chamber of presence, but it was empty and clean swept. And what was it doing here, lowered upon the earth when it should have been two storeys high? I descended some stairs into an area beneath the ground: here was my laboratory, but then I started back when I saw a man and a woman lying quite naked upon the floor. He turned and cried to me, 'Why did you call me?'

I was struck dumb by this, and climbed again into my old scrying room from which I looked out upon my garden: there was nothing there now except some trees leafless, and others torn up by the roots, in a confused landscape of broken stone. This was indeed an image of my condition and, deeply plunged in misery and bewilderment as I was, I put my hand up to my face. Into what labyrinth had I now brought myself? All those whom I knew were dead long since and, for the first time, water came into my eyes; then, in the glistening of my tears, I thought I saw a shape strangely moving before me, not perfectly seen but as if it were viewed through a cypress.

At that moment there came a very strange knocking and rapping within this room, and after a little while my father appeared in the corner by the great perspective glass. He was naked yet tied with bonds, of a smoky or ashy colour spiralling about his breast, and his feet seemed not to touch the ground by the height of some inches. His face was of one long dead, and I stood up in great fear. 'The cankers are ripe,' he said, 'and the biting worm seeks to grow into the lily.'

His speech was quick, round and steady; but I did not understand the purport of it. 'What is this meaning, father, or spirit, or angel?'

'I thought you had known nothing else.' Then he spread the air, or opened it before him; and there in miniature, like a little wooden globe, I saw myself wandering once more through the dark city. 'This was a vision of the world without love, John Dee, but one you yourself have fashioned. You hoped to create life, but instead you have made images of death. Think of this, and repent in time. Now farewell.'

My father walked towards me, sighing. I stepped back and tried to open the outermost door to flee from him, but he was there before me. He was within my very bones and sinews, like a mist, and then he was gone.

SIX

I DECIDED TO go through my father's papers very carefully and very patiently; I had only glanced at them after his death, but now I wanted to understand everything. I knew now that he was not my 'real' father; he was even closer to me than that, and had formed me in ways I could only begin to imagine. If I discovered more about his life, I might discover something of my own. There were documents relating to the old house, for example, which I had stuffed into a carrier-bag at the time of the funeral and later stored in one of the empty bedrooms here; now I took them down with me into the kitchen, and spread them across the table. Certain invoices for the 'Cloak Lane House' had been neatly tied with a blue ribbon, and I looked through them quickly. There was nothing of any significance amongst them, except for the fact that my father had bought the house from Mr Abraham Crowley on 27 September 1963 – that date aroused fresh speculation in my mind, since it was the one we had always celebrated as my birthday.

There were also some papers relating to my father's other properties, as well as a brown envelope which I had not noticed before. He had written something across it in block capitals – THE DOCUMENTS IN THE CASE – and, when I removed these 'documents', I saw that my father had numbered them in his usual precise manner. They contained passages in several different hands, scrawled across various types of paper, and the first of them was in an irregular, angular script which seemed to be of the seventeenth century. I could barely make out the words, and I held it up to the light streaming through the kitchen window.

We, the believers in the revelation of the true God and the rebirth of the

Spirit among men, do exhort and beseech the citizens of London to watch for the fire and the pestilence which have been foretold. But let all fear and trembling be banished from among you, since you are all gods and on the last day will be restored to the sight of one another in your divine raiment. There will be neither rich nor poor, neither man nor woman, but all will be burned up in delight.

It was signed 'The London Meeters of Clerkenwell' and dated August 1662. This was interesting enough, but on the next page and in a different hand there was a longer document:

We never trusted in the Romish superstition that there be such phantasms as *guardian angels* but since we have been sequestered in this house, through illness and want, we have come upon a strangeness which has quite bewildered us and led us out of the path of our old certainties. My poor brother lay sick upon a summer evening, just by the window which looks out upon the river and the fields; there were only two of us left in the world and he had become my constant companion no less than my constant care. 'Look,' he said. 'Look upon that wall there. Do you see the face of a man appearing?' I told him that, since this house was built above two hundred years ago, it was merely the dampness of old stone. He seemed satisfied with that and, lying back upon his pallet, said nothing more that evening; but his pulse was pretty high, and I feared a return of the brain fever. I stayed beside him all that night, therefore, with a bowl of sweet cordial to bathe his face. Then, in the hour before dawn, something shifted and moved about him; I thought it a shadow of the waning night and the flickering candle, but as it took shape I knew it to be some spiritual creature: it had the very form and feature of my brother, but much lighter in colour, and it rose from him as a mist rises from falling spray. It left him and straightened itself, whereupon I could see that it was one or two feet higher than his human frame; it was in outline all over silver, and seemed to clean itself now with its hands as if it had risen from meat. Then it smiled at me and bowed low, before turning and pointing at my brother. It was my own brother gazing at himself, and for a moment I felt some brightness enfold me. Then it closed its eyes and lay down again within the sleeping form. My brother awoke at that moment, and I knew his fever had broken: there was no more sweat now, and his pulse was beating steady like a drum. Indeed my heart was so full that I poured out to him the news of this strange visitation, and we knelt together in prayer. How was it that we two humble men, living in this crumbling tenement of Clerkenwell, should be so touched by God's grace?

Previously we had been of the little congregation of God's Brotherhood, which met in a room above the sign of the Compass in Cripplegate. In their company we had been instructed in certain true doctrines, viz. that all men and women partake equally of the divine fire, that the city wherein we dwell is no more than visible corruption, that when the gate of everlasting is opened there will be a general raising up. Then the powers and kingdoms of this world will be utterly undone, while the citizens of the spirit will be arrayed in glory. These doctrines, to which we readily assented in the little room above Cripplegate, now gave me and my brother a further certainty and assurance: we had seen the citizen of the spirit in all its brightness, and we understood that even those as poor and as weak as ourselves might be blessed. Praise be to God! Written this day, January 12, 1762, in the Cloak House of Clerkenwell.

Someone else had written, in the margin, 'The Same Faith Being Continued'. I turned the page, and found attached to it a cutting from the *Graphic* magazine of 5 October 1869. The first thing I noticed was the engraving which had been dropped into a column of text: it was a representation of the old house, very much as I knew it now, except that in the artist's imagination it had become a great deal larger. There was another illustration beneath it, which showed a group of people sitting round a table; one of them had his arms raised, in surprise or horror. The headline to the article had been set in mock-Gothic type – 'The Medium Astonished: Stephen Cosway in Clerkenwell' – but the rest was plain enough:

It is a rare circumstance indeed when a spiritualist medium professes to be alarmed by his own conduct, but that seems to have been the case when the renowned healer, Mr Stephen Cosway, visited a very old and very shabby dwelling in the parish of Clerkenwell. He had been drawn there by a request from the London Working Men's Union, which eight months ago took over the tenancy of the building. If it seems singular

that such a rational and progressive society should call upon the services
of a man who professedly speaks to ghosts and spirits, then we must
count it just another of the paradoxes of this paradoxically modern age.
The officials of the Working Men's Union had, for a number of months,
noticed the intermittent occurrence of an 'atmosphere' in the ground-
floor rooms of the house. They were perfectly aware of the researches of
the late Mr Faraday into fields of 'magneto-electricity', and at first were
inclined to believe that this was some strange but intelligible activity of
the physical world. But then two of these worthy gentlemen happened
upon phantoms: they were standing together in the basement of the
house, when they distinctly saw what they described as 'a young woman
and a young man without clothes', who promptly disappeared. It was
after this event that Mr Cosway was called. The rest of the affair can now
be narrated in his own words, since last week he was thoughtful enough
to send us a report of his actions. The reader can believe or disbelieve as
he wishes. 'As soon as I came into the Clerkenwell house,' he begins, 'I
knew that there was some power, benign or menacing, which resided
there. But I could not have foreseen the dreadful consequences of . . .'

I turned the page but there was only a book review on the other
side; the rest of Stephen Cosway's account was missing, but
someone had written a comment in the margin. 'No more of this.
Cosway's vision dimmed by his own fraudulence and trickery.'
There was one other piece of evidence among these documents
which my father had preserved. It was on lined paper, and looked
as if it had been torn out of some old-fashioned ledger or account
book. The handwriting was very neat, and kept exactly to the red
margins drawn down the side of each page.

I confess to one obsession, or fear. It always visits me when I am inside
the house at my writing-desk, and rarely follows me beyond these walls.
It calls at about ten or eleven in the morning, and stays with me for an
hour or so; during this period I perspire freely, and walk throughout the
house without being able to settle anywhere or concentrate upon any one
task. But why should I be haunted by an anxiety so ridiculous, so
laughable, that I can smile at myself later for entertaining it? Nevertheless
it always comes back – this fear that whatever I happen to be writing

comes from some other source, that I am stealing someone else's plot or words, that I am relying upon the themes or images of other novelists. That is why there are occasions when I leave the house and travel to the London Library in St James's Square. The shelves of English fiction there are both my terror and my consolation: I search for evidence to convict me, but I find nothing. And yet, even in that moment of relief, I am still haunted by the fear that somewhere among these volumes will be discovered the same novel I myself am writing.

My obsession is most extreme when I have finished a book, and am waiting impatiently for its publication. In those months the essential fear is recapitulated in a variety of forms – that I have used dialogue from the work of another novelist, that a plot comes from a book I have read and forgotten, that I have simply written down the words of someone else. And this is the strangest anxiety of all – what if that other person were actually within me all the time? This was my state of mind yesterday, just after I had sent my typescript to my publishers in Fetter Lane. I had written the entire novel in this house; in fact I do not believe I could have written it anywhere else. It reeked of the place, and I had even gone to the trouble of setting the story – about the copper-beaters' strike of 1740 – within this area. The scenes of suffering and of poverty, of riot and of death, had actually taken place among the alleys and streets of Upper Lambeth; but I had moved them to Clerkenwell, and set them among the ruined tenements which once stood beside the church of St James. This is what is called artistic licence, I believe, although true artists are never free.

And then, yesterday, it happened at last. I was in the basement of the old house, choosing the wine for my solitary dinner that evening, when I was overtaken by the old fear. My book had been written before. I was convinced of it. I did not understand the process involved (I presumed there was a name for such phenomena) but I knew that, somehow, I had copied another novel word for word. Even the title was the same. I cannot describe the horror which this realization provoked in me; it was as if my entire identity had been taken from me, as you would take a net out of water, and I was left with nothing of my own.

I left the house at once and took the tram to High Holborn; from there I walked to the library in St James's Square. I happened to see Tom Eliot by the issue desk, and I had enough civility left to greet him before I hurried up the stairs to the shelves of fiction. Then I began what I knew to be a fatal search – fatal in the sense that if I found the book and confirmed my fears, then my life as a writer would be at an end. I would no longer be able to trust any of my words, or believe anything which I fondly thought I had imagined. It would always come from some other source. And then I found it. There was a book here with the title I had only recently chosen. It had been published two years ago – 'London, 1922' was on the spine – and as soon as I opened it, I saw the same words as I had manufactured on my typewriter. This was the novel I had just written. 'I am nothing,' I said out loud. 'Nothing can come of nothing.' I came back to this house, which unaccountably I consider the cause of all my woe, and I chose to sit here at my desk. But am I, even now, writing what others have written down before me? And if this is so, what am I to do?

The manuscript stopped here, on the last line of a second sheet of paper. I turned the page and, in sudden alarm, recognized once more my father's familiar hand. He had written in large letters across an otherwise empty sheet, 'He Is Raised a Spiritual Body'. I put all the papers back into their carrier, and quietly returned them to the empty room.

I have always been able to sleep in this house – a deep, dark sleep from which I awake with the taste of night in my mouth like a sour fruit. But that evening, after I had examined the documents, I was too restless even to close my eyes. The light from a street-lamp at the bottom of Cloak Lane flickered upon the walls and ceiling; it cast strange shadows around me and I seemed to see a drawn sword, a horse with a rider, and a kind of cloth billowing down from the sky. Then I tried to amuse myself by pronouncing words backwards, but some of the sounds unaccountably scared me. It must have been just before dawn that I crept down to the hallway, and pulled out the box of toys beneath the stairs. What were they doing in this place? I had never spent any of my childhood here – my mother had defended me from that – but they appeared to have been manufactured only twenty or thirty years ago. But then the reason for their presence in this house became clear to me; my father had played with them, even as he conjured up his visions of sexual magic. I sat upon the floor and, with great seriousness, began pulling to pieces the spinning top and the folding man.

★

On the same morning, somehow refreshed despite my loss of sleep, I read John Dee's last will and testament. It ought to have been deposited in the Chancery records with other ancient wills, but according to the bibliographies it had been placed in the Manuscript Department of the British Library. This suggested to me that no will had been lodged at the time of his death; he had either died unknown, or in some distant place from which nothing could be recovered. It was also possible that the original had been lost, and that at some later date a copy had been found among his papers. There were many of these, and among the documents of Doctor Dee listed in the catalogue of manuscripts I could see treatises on navigation and on mathematics, accounts of the horoscope of Queen Elizabeth and of the cure for migraine, maps and charts, tables and genealogies. But I had come for his testament.

It was bound in a green leather volume, together with another of Doctor Dee's manuscripts. The title of this other document intrigued me, 'Strange News From the Angels', but I could make out very little of its meaning. I noticed at once how the faded brown ink seemed to be racing to the margins of the page and even now, in this quiet room within the British Museum, there was a kind of anxiety or panic evident in the very formation of the words. Some phrases were underlined two or three times, and certain sentences had been enclosed in hastily drawn squares and circles. The main text seemed to be in the form of questions and answers, while in the margins there were numerous scribblings, jottings and diagrams. Then I noticed the word WAPPING in large capitals, while beside it an angel or some other feathered creature seemed to be flying towards the edge of the page. It meant nothing to me then, except in the sudden recognition of so familiar a name; it was also the last page of 'Strange News', and I turned it eagerly in order to read John Dee's will.

It seemed to have also been written in extreme haste: the letters were scratched and unformed, while various small stains on the page testified to the ink which had been carelessly dropped from the quill. There were other curious features. It was dated 1588, some twenty years before the supposed time of Doctor Dee's death, and the fiduciary testament was very brief indeed. He left sums of money to two servants, 'one Audrey Godwin' and 'one Philip Fox', and then bequeathed everything else he possessed 'to those who come after'. In the next paragraph he mentioned the house in Cloak Lane – 'my old rambling tenement in Clerkenwell' – but his bequest was very peculiar indeed; he simply left it to 'the one who has need of it'. It was not surprising that this will had never found its way into the Chancery records. But then there was a more baffling entry still; there was the mention of a stone, which 'has been left there for those who may find it'. Under this was a sentence composed in more ornamental style. 'Follow my footsteps beyond the grave.' Was it possible that he had been buried somewhere beneath the house, with a stone laid upon his grave as a memorial? I turned the page, and was delighted to find a map or plan crudely drawn in the centre of the will: it depicted a river and some houses, as far as I could tell, but nothing else was recognizable. There remained only one paragraph, above his huge signature, which I could barely decipher. 'I, who made him, will live within him for ever. He, who owes his life to me, will return to me.' No doubt it was some final prayer, and I closed the book upon his testament.

I returned it to the assistant, who took it eagerly enough. 'Did you get what you wanted?' He had a cast in his left eye, so it was hard to tell whether he was looking at me or at someone behind me.

'I think so.'

'Did you read the angelic signs?' I was surprised by his interest, partly, I suppose, because I had come to consider Doctor Dee the object of my own private quest. 'I suppose you know that his sacred crystal is in the museum?' I shook my head; he had two or three white scars upon his neck, and I resisted the impulse to stare at them. 'Oh yes. In the Tudor Gallery upstairs.' He laid the bound volume gently upon his desk, and stroked it with his hand for a moment. 'How do you think he saw what the angels were doing?'

It did not take me long to find Doctor Dee's sacred stone. I climbed the stairs from the main hall of the British Museum into the remains of Early Britain. The bowls, and knives, and beads were preserved within glass cases in which I could see my own face reflected; I peered for a moment at the stone carving of a small human figure, and then turned away. I passed through Roman Britain and the Medieval Period quickly; various religious objects were bathed in subdued light so that they seemed to float within their cases, and I was reminded of the water within the holy well of Clerkenwell. Did it glow like these reliquaries, in the unnatural stillness of past time?

The Tudor Gallery was ahead of me now, and the narrow passageway towards it was shrouded in the same indirect light; it was almost as if I were entering a tomb. Various objects were displayed in a cabinet within the passage itself – a richly embroidered glove, a magnifying glass, some roughly cut coins. But I noticed the globe at once. It was not as large as I had imagined, no bigger than a tennis ball; how could the angels have entered so small a room, and displayed there the spiritual universe to Doctor Dee? The light seemed to wash the air around it rather than enter the glass itself, and I was able to read the small card beneath it without any difficulty: 'This is the crystal with which John Dee (1527–1608) performed his "scrying" or magical interpretations.'

There was beside it a cloth, with blue, red and yellow images painted on its surface; in my imagination I watched myself drape it round my own shoulders, sighing and lifting up my eyes towards the ceiling of the basement room. I heard someone cough behind me, but I still gazed into the crystal globe. I saw only the planes and contours of the light as they shimmered around the glass; everything within it seemed blurred and indistinct, as if I were looking at a candle through tears.

'Do you see how it does shine?'

The voice came from behind me, but I did not look away from the stone. 'Yes,' I said. 'I see it very well.'

'Like a most precious jewel.'

'No, not so hard.' I turned around then, but there was no one near me. Who could have spoken in so low a tone? I thought I glimpsed a figure moving away, through a crowd of Japanese tourists, but it was no more than a sense of change and displacement. I looked back into the crystal, and now I could see nothing at all.

I took the bus from Great Russell Street to the Clerkenwell Road. Summer was now coming to an end and, as I walked from the Green to Cloak Lane, I sensed in the colder air the sour exhilaration of autumn. There was someone crying in the garden, and it sounded like a child. As soon as I opened the gate, I saw that there was a small boy sitting upon the ground; his head was bowed, and he wept as his little fists clenched the weeds around him. 'Who left you here?' I asked him. 'Has anybody hurt you?'

'My name is Matthew.'

'Like mine. I am called by the same name. What has happened to you?'

'I am a very little boy.' He was still weeping, but now he managed to draw breath between his sobs.

'Where do you live, Matthew?'

'I live in my house. If I tell you where it is, my father will beat me.' And at that, he looked up at me and yawned. I cannot tell you the horror I suffered, for I was looking at my own face as a child. It was the face I had seen in the photographs with my father. But then the small boy leapt to his feet, and ran out of the garden.

Once again I felt that peculiar sensation of sickness, or emptiness, which seemed to be following me everywhere. I stood for a few moments, fighting for breath; then I hurried into the house and shut the door behind me with a loud crash. I think I was trembling, but everything else was still. This angered me very much, and I remember calling out to someone whom I believed to be waiting for me within the house. Naturally there was no reply, but it was with something like fury that I opened the door to the basement and rushed down the stone steps; as soon as I had turned on the light I saw the markings upon the old wall, but for some reason I was more concerned with the rectangular outline below it. I crossed the stone floor and knocked upon the sealed door.

Then something opened the wall and came in. At least that was how it seemed at the time, but when I drew breath I did not seem able to place the figure anywhere in particular; it was almost as if it had become a feeling within me. Then I believed that I could hear voices.

'I thought that there were only spirits in the stone, but now you seem to see people in life.'

'It is God's will, sir.'

'Oh is it? Is it God's will, or your own?'

'You know my case, and can well consider how all things stand justly between us. Stop a moment. Do you see something here? Something in the shape of a man?'

'I see nothing. Nothing at all.'

'I tell you, Doctor Dee, that the stone has opened up the gate to hell. This room, this house, is terribly haunted.'

'Tell me,' I said out loud. 'Tell me your opinion of ghost stories.'

'Do you hear anything?'

'I hear only the wind.'

'There is a theory that they reflect sexual unease, but what do you think? And if ghosts are a sign of frustration, what about all the other elements – the locked door, the disordered bed, the weeping child? How do they fit in? Do you have anything to do with my father?' I realized then that there was no voice here except my own; but instead of being relieved by the silence and emptiness, I felt strangely disconcerted. I had wanted to hear the voices, if only to reassure myself that not everything is lost. But how could the dead speak?

THE CLOSET

OH JESUS, WHAT was this dream? I was within my chamber once again, and seemed to be poring over my papers, yet I was so extremely terrified by my vision of the dark city that I was close to screeching out in fear. It was an hour before dawn, and I could smell my stinking breath within my hand: what a night had I passed, to disturb me so! I remembered myself in the wherry pursued by my own image, and in the presence of the queen with her hands inside my corpse, but surely these were mere phantasms and bugbears of sleep? Yet I felt something changed within me also. I had seen the world without love, and knew well enough why it was my father who had granted that vision to me: my love for gold had been greater by far than any love for him, and at his death I had felt only dislike and fear. Now see to what a pass I might come, if there were a world created in my own image!

Who could save me from that darkness? There was only one, yet I had grown so accustomed to her presence and to her love that I had scarcely thought it worth the reckoning; yet it was my wife who might save me. No, there was a better and firmer way: I must save my own self by finding again the affection and well-liking I harboured for her. I must refresh myself at that spring of love which runs through everyone; but I must take my own path to that spring, that origin. So I had become like the statue Praxiteles made – if one stood directly before it, it seemed to laugh; if on the left side, to sleep: if on the other side, to weep. I had been turned to my right side, weeping, and had seen the world from another vantage.

Some music seemed then to come secretly and strangely out of the ground but, when I crept from my door into the passage, at once I knew it to be the virginals within my wife's parlour. I came down the stairs on tip-a-toe and listened for a while outside her chamber; then I took aside the tapestry that hung before the door and, seeing her back towards me, I entered and stood a pretty space. She played excellent well of the melody 'Passing Strange', but she left off immediately when she heard my breathing. She turned round and, to my great dismay, I saw how meagre was the flesh about her face. It was as if the person I knew had stepped away, and left another in her place; yet was this not occasion for the new beginning of love?

'I thought you were sick,' I said, trying to cheer myself as well as her.

'I am. But I played to shun melancholy.'

'Why are you so melancholy, wife?'

'Why? Do you need to ask?' I said nothing. 'I have this night been troubled with a colic and a cramp, sir, and I have a megrim sore.'

I felt her pulse, and marked her looks. 'Truly you are sick,' I told her, 'but you are not in hard case. Come now to your closet and lie you down. I will make you a broth to master your belly, and to provoke urine. All will be well, Mrs Dee, all will be well. And you must have flowers in your room. Dried roses comfort the brain, and recover the spirits against any flux of the belly.'

'Mr Kelley has administered to me already.'

'Kelley? What did he do?'

'He gave me a cordial mixed with wheatmeal and the seeds of melon. He called it a fomentation, and lord! it was bitter enough. I was all unready, and in my night stuff, but he asked me to drink.'

'Come,' I said. 'No more words now. I will prescribe a straight diet, and then you must sleep.'

I led her to her closet, and had Audrey strew the floor with sweet herbs and with nosegays finely intermingled with fragrant flowers, which were meant to cheer and delight her in her sickness. I prepared a subtle soup of cabbage sodden with hen's flesh, of which she tasted only a little. Then I prepared a decoction of violet, which, when placed on the feet and forehead, provokes sleep in even the sharpest sickness. And so she remained for two days, faring no better but seeming to decline: I scarcely knew what to do or to say, but sought out the company of Edward Kelley, who each morning walked in the gallery beside her chamber.

'How does she do?' he asked me on the day following these events.

'Very bad.' I had quite forgotten, until now, his own preparation. 'What was it that you gave her?'

'Only some wine and nutmeg.'

'She said that it was bitter.'

'No, no,' he replied. 'That was only her deluded fancy, which can go astray, like a sick man's dream. You know how the sense of taste may change with a fever fit.'

On the next day he again asked me how she was, and seemed much disturbed when I told him she was no better. On that same day, about an hour after twelve, Audrey came running to my chamber with the complaint that Kelley had sent her from the side of her mistress upon some errand but that she, peering through the keyhole, had seen him give Mistress Dee something. I went down at once and, going into the chamber, saw him weeping and praying beside my wife's bed.

'What you do here, sir?' I asked him. 'It is not fit. It is not wise.'

He turned from his prayers, and looked at me through his tears. 'Perhaps you expected a wiser man,' he said, 'but what do you seek from one who has always loved your wife in brotherly kind?'

'Audrey saw you give her a cordial or some such.'

'No. I bent over to smell her breath. She needs some vinegar or garden mint upon her gums.'

My wife, lying on the bed, suddenly woke from her slumber and looked very earnestly at me; so I desired Kelley to be gone and, after he departed, I stood beside her. 'He has used you very grossly,' she said in so low a voice that I could scarcely make out the words.

'And how is that?'

'I feel it. I know it.' She paused a little for breath. 'Yet he is no friend of mine, neither. I believe he puts something between my lips as I sleep.'

All this was spoken in great pangs and disquietness of mind, but now she put her hands to her throat and began to sing 'The Digger's Song' before turning her notes to 'Follow Thy Fair Sun, Unhappy Shadow'. 'I have a hundred more ballads,' she said earnestly to me. 'They are wrapped in parchment and bound with a whipcord.'

'You must rest now, my wife. You may sing when you are well, but not now. Not now.'

'I have heard, Doctor Dee, that two pigeons may be caught with one bean and two woodcocks with one spring. Can two fools be caught by one villain?'

I knew of what she spoke, but I could think of nothing to the purpose. 'It is late. Lay down your head and rest.'

'You are in the right. Let us hear no more of these grave matters. But, husband, think of this. Perhaps, with the loss of all, we can be in peace at last. Who rests so much as those who have been beggared? Who can sing so merry a note as those that cannot change a groat?' Then she fell into a delirium, and for that day and a night she was lost in a fever that broke only with the breaking of the day. She awoke very pale, and feeble to the last degree. 'I do not well remember what I have done or said,' she whispered to me.

'You have slept, and in sleep you have refreshed yourself. That is all.'

'No, sir. I am not refreshed. I feel something else coming upon me. The longest summer's day, as you know, has its evening.'

'Hush. Do not talk so.'

'But, husband, they say that strawberry leaves, dying, yield a most excellent cordial smell.'

'You are rather like the basil, which the more it is crushed the sooner it springs up again. Or like the poppy, which the more it is trodden with the feet the more it flourishes. Take heart.'

There were some gulls crying above the house, and for that moment she seemed to believe that she lay by the margin of the sea. 'It is too late for hope,' she said. 'I am content to wait here.'

I left her in doleful sort, not knowing how to cure her or care for her in this extremity. Yet neither the daily shaking of her continual fever, with a double tertian, nor her vehement headache without intermission, could put the remembrance of Kelley out of my own troubled mind. He knew well enough that I had no time for scrying in my present pain, but why had he been at her side on several occasions? I could only believe her when she affirmed that he had given her some liquor to drink, but could that have been poison to stop her uttering more words about his misdoings? No, it could not be; yet I was in a wretched state, and could devise no remedy.

He came to me one evening as I sat in my chamber, while I was still marvellously out of quiet, and stood silently before me. 'I know you to be a rare physician,' he said, 'who understands more than any apothecary or herbalist. Can you not speed her cure with some mineral physic?'

'Such as you gave her, Mr Kelley?'

'I? I gave her nothing but my prayers and my tears.'

'So be it.'

I looked hard upon him, and he turned his face away. 'I know that you have had neither leisure nor opportunity to enter the chamber of practice in these last sad days,' he said. 'But is this not the time for scrying?'

'To what purpose do you run?'

'If we cannot work with the dry or viscous portions of the earth, why not leave off from our glasses and retorts in order to consult the spirits within the stone? I have railed against them, I know, but in this extremity I will try anything to –'

'To ward off her present dying?' I had not thought to say the word, and I felt my heart sink within me.

'It is believed that a vehement wish may be more powerful than any material cure –'

'I hope it may be so.'

'So if a strong imagination can work better than unassisted nature, why should we not consult within the stone and see what our angels instruct us to perform?'

I assented to this in sheer weariness of mind, whereupon Kelley prepared himself for the chamber of practice. I could not sleep all that night, for fear of what news the morning might bring: could it have been some spirit, escaped from the stone, who had wrought this mischief upon my wife? Then truly I would bear the blame. On the morning I quietly followed Kelley into the secret place of demonstration and, as was still our custom, I knelt beside him while he bent over the sacred glass and looked *in crystallo*. 'Now all is in a cloud,' he said. 'And now all is clear again. There appears one on the very top of the frame of the show-stone, and seems to go along a great path very speedily. It is Mistress Dee.'

'My wife?'

'Now I hear a great voice of thumbling and rumbling in the stone, and your wife runs out of her chamber and seems to leap over the gallery-rail and to lie as dead.' I stood up and shut all the outermost doors, in case any should hear him. 'Now you come out of your own closet,' he continued, 'and kneel, and knock your hands upon the floor. The servants take up your wife, but her head wags this way and that. She is dead. The right side of her face and body is fixed and cannot move. She is bare-legged, and has a white petticoat upon her. They hold her up. Now they carry her out of the gate. You seem to run in the fields before them. You run through waters. And now all disappears.' These were strange terms in which to utter a strange tale, and I wondered how he could so lightly prophesy my wife's death. I put my hand up to my eyes, and I thought I could see him smiling. 'Be of good cheer,' he said. 'I will be with you always.'

'Sir?'

'All of us must die, and it is better to take comfort now than cry hereafter. Do you not know that after death there is peace?'

'No, not peace but glory. If she were to die, which I cannot conceive, she would be reunited with the divine fire that is within the godhead. But how can this ease my own lot?'

'I shall be here to aid you, good doctor. We shall be like student bachelors again, in the pursuit of true knowledge.'

He was glad to have my wife out of his road – this I saw, as clearly as if *in crystallo* – so that he might bind me more tightly to him. I had some inkling now of his nimble tricks and shifts. 'I thought that there were only spirits in the stone, but now you seem to see people in life.'

'It is God's will, sir.'

'Oh is it? Is it God's will, or your own?'

At that he grew suddenly enraged. 'You know my case,' he said, 'and can well consider how all things stand justly between us. Stop a moment. Do you see something here? Something in the shape of a man?'

'I see nothing. Nothing at all.'

'I tell you, Doctor Dee, that the stone has opened up the gate to hell. This room, this house, is terribly haunted.' He paused for a moment, and seemed to listen to something speaking. 'Do you hear anything?'

'I hear only the wind. But enough of this now, Kelley.' I was like the bear tied to the post, while the lion roams around. 'You say that there is justice between us, but how does it stand between you and my wife?'

Still he was distracted by this ghost, or spirit, of his own devising; but then suddenly he breathed more easily. 'It is gone,' he whispered.

'I was speaking of my wife.'

He looked directly upon me now. 'I do not complain of envy or bitterness,' he said, 'since she lies so low. If it be that she is dying –'

'You suspect so. Or do you know so?'

'I have seen it in the stone.' At that I burst out laughing, and his anger grew higher. 'From this day, sir, I will meddle no more with you, or your wife, or your household. I am not so base-minded that fear of any living creature should make me do that which is not just. I am not of so foul a lineage, or carry so vile a mind!' He turned around and seemed about to pick up the stone, as if to hurl it or carry it off. 'Do you question these spirits? Well, no more than I. No more than I. These actions, these appearings and shows and voices, have troubled me from the beginning. Have I not only doubted and misliked them, but also on diverse and sundry times have sought to be separated from them?' He was stumbling on his words in his rage, yet I listened to him carefully enough. 'Their doctrines and exercises have the savour of hell about them. Have I not boldly inveighed against them, yes, even in your presence, urging them to depart or render better reason for their unknown and incredible speeches?' He was still in a hot torrent of words, and would not be stopped. 'But now you accuse me and condemn me for inventing all these things. It is not just, sir. It is not right.'

He hastened past me, and for a minute I stood bowed before the stone: I saw nothing there but plain glass, as empty as it had been during all these days and actions. I could hear him pacing up and down upon the rushes in my private study, and then suddenly he returned. 'I repent my high words,' he said, 'when I know under what burden you are travelling. Why do we look back in sorrow at that which has gone, when we should address our endeavours to posterity? For surely, though your wife is sick, we should continue our work?' He took me by the hand and, though I was unwilling, he raised it and kissed my ring of Solomon. 'You think to wade deep in suspicion and mistrust,' said he, 'where the ford is truly but shallow.'

'Well,' I replied, 'I am not one of those who, having wet his foot, does not care how deeply he wades. I will meet you upon dry ground.'

'Bravely said, good doctor. We will walk together still.' All this time I was greatly suspicious of him, though without proof of any kind: I, who was so deeply learned in antiquity, and in dark visions had been granted the wisdom of former times, was now in a present maze where I could not see the issue. I, who had dreamed of creating new life, could not even save that of my own wife. I said no more but went down again to her.

She lay upon her bed in a sweat, scarcely seeing anything before her, while Audrey sat with a handkerchief cloth and a stone basin containing clean and wholesome water of roses to cool her. I told her that it was my best and only happiness to see her in safety and in health, which I was sure would long continue after her illness had vanished quite away, when she took my hand and spoke softly to me. 'Doctor Dee, Doctor Dee, I am not well and look for no present remedy.' I urged her to take some broth but I could not persuade her to eat anything. So I sat by her side, contemplating what a wretched state I should inherit if she departed from this life; as the turtle, having lost his mate, wanders alone, joying in nothing but solitariness, so would I roam. But then I bitterly dispraised myself for my errant fantasies, when the real anguish was that which she now suffered at leaving the world. How great a sorrow is it to know that your light is dying?

I watched her as she slept, and Audrey, wiping the cloth across her forehead, whispered to me. 'She cries a little, sir, when she thinks that no one watches. And, lord, it would make a heart break to see her smile at me when I come back to her chamber.'

'This is sorrow enough, Audrey. No more.'

'But, sir, I must say more. There is poison in her blood. Whether it comes from his potions or from his art, I do not know.' I knew of whom she spoke, and bent my ear to listen very unwillingly. 'He has used so many menacing speeches to her, and sat beside her all in a rage, that the very air would blast her.'

'How do you know of these things?'

'Fearing for her life, sir, I listened by the door.'

'But words are like wind, Audrey, no sooner spoken than gone. We have nothing to charge against him.'

She looked at me steadily now. 'I know, sir, in what privy place he keeps his papers and his letters. Perhaps there is something within them that may be brought to your knowledge, face to face.'

'By what means did you discover this?'

'I mistrust him so much that I have watched him, and observed him to conceal stuff very secretly.'

I listened for a moment to my wife's labours in breathing, and saw upon her face the image of her coming death. 'And where may that stuff be found?'

'In his chamber. There is a small box there which he brought with him on that fatal day he entered this house —'

'No more now. I hear him.'

Kelley was crossing the hall, and, when I came out of my wife's chamber he greeted me. 'I am away to Southwark on my mare,' he said. 'There is an old companion there who wishes to talk with me.'

He was still greatly in doubt of my heavy displeasure, as I knew, but I did in all lenity respond to him. 'Are you coming back again soon?'

'Not till the end of the day.'

He left the house with speed, going out by the Turnmill. 'So, so,' I said to Audrey. 'We have separation before solution.'

'Sir?'

'Nothing, Audrey. Nothing at all. Is my wife in so profound a sleep that we may leave her for a minute?' She nodded. 'Well, come then quickly. Let us go to his closet.'

'We climbed the stairs in hot haste, and entered his chamber. Audrey crossed the floor and, reaching to the far side of the chimneypiece there, put up her hand within a brick. 'I have it here somewhere yet,' she said, 'but I cannot come at it. Ah, here.' She took out a curious small carved box, fit to hold jewels or coins or some such. 'There is a lock,' she said, 'but no key.'

'Did you not know, after all these years, that I am skilled in the mechanic arts? Go back down to the parlour, and bring me a little silver tooth-pick.'

She did this speedily, and pretty soon I had opened the box and found within several small papers, with lines and scribblements going athwart the lines. I could read them easily enough, and they were worth the reading in diverse respects – for there, in a careful hand, Kelley had written, 'He made projection of the red stone upon the like quantity of mercury, the five and twentieth day of April following. By this magistery, he hopes to obtain the elixir of virtue'. Then he had added, at some later time, 'He will tell me how that which is corrupt and imperfect may be brought and turned from imperfection to perfection'. And then again, on another paper, there were some broken words which I could easily distinguish: 'The human body can be formed by dew, starlight, and the sublimation of *amor sexus*. If that is refined and enclosed within the glass, then the precious seed will breathe.' It broke off then, but I knew the sum of it: he had found some secret of the homunculus among my concealed papers. By guileful and hypocritical dealings he had approached the foundation of all my work, and was close to stealing away from me that secret which is a hundred thousand times finer, more pure and more exalted than the most fine alchemy: to create a being which lives and grows. And yet there was something else, for beneath these papers there was a letter hastily written: 'He is almost in our power. With his wife dead, he will be ours. Here I make an end. John Overbury.'

Overbury. Oh God defend me. My old servant, whom I had met by chance (or so I thought) by the Paris Garden, was here in concert with this other wretch in preparing my fate. And now at last I understood the full measure of Edward Kelley his knavery: I could not yet say that they were in league for the destruction of my wife, but there was some evil in their design directed against me and her.

Now within three hours of this discovery Kelley came up my study stairs, unbooted. When I saw him I was very angry inwardly, but I continued writing my records; he went into his own chamber after greeting me, then came out again. Just as he was going down the stairs once more, I left my closet and saluted him. 'Did you see any play in the Garden,' I asked him, 'or was there some other kind of game?'

'Garden? I was in no garden, sir, and had no game. I met a very reverend and ancient friend, as I told you, in the neighbourhood of Southwark. He is not known to you, sir, but he sends his greetings to one who, as he said, is so skilled in all the sciences.'

'I thank him.' Then I continued in graver style. 'I am a man in the middle years, Mr Kelley, and apt to be full of doubts. But I believe that you have done me some ill turns.'

'Do you any ill? I would sooner hop up the stairs to the top of St Paul's, or ride through Venice on horseback. I could never do you ill.'

Yet I thought his colour changed as he spoke. 'Audrey says that you have been discoursing in high words with my wife, even as she lay in her sickness.'

'High words with one so troubled as she?' He burst out in

anger. 'That stall, that trug, has once more put some suspicious construction on my words. She is like the camel that will not drink until it has troubled the water with its feet – she can never staunch her thirst until she has raised a disturbance against me. I know that I am only your servant –'

'More, much more, than a servant.'

'But I am in every way hindered and crossed by those who profess to care for you and for your wife.'

'It is a fine speech, Mr Kelley. But I have encountered other fine words. Did you not say that, with my wife dead, I would be within your power?'

'I assure you that I have never spoken such words at all.'

'Oh no, I cry you pardon. It was John Overbury who said so.' At which point I took out from the pocket of my gown the letter, and he started back in amazement. 'I have many times been informed,' I continued, 'that you had a dislike for me and my family. But my informers never had proof of any such thing. Now in clear sight I know that you have dealt doubtfully and dishonestly with me.'

'Sir.' He put his hands through his perfumed beard. 'I know myself to be without fault or colour of fault. This letter was sent to me by the wretch Overbury, without my knowledge or agreement.'

'So why then did you keep it secret in your chamber? No, Edward Kelley, there have here been most dishonest, hypocritical and devilish devices employed against me!'

He burst into tears now, and for a moment hid his head. 'You know that you have always found me friendly and well disposed to you, good doctor. Even to the very intercourse with the spirits, when I would as soon have burned all the books in the world to save my immortal soul!'

'I fear now that you have invented these spirits, or wonders, or devils, so that you might more fully deceive me and draw me into your spread net.' I thrust out my arms, so that my gown billowed around me.

He eyed me coolly enough. 'I will be quiet, sir, and arm myself against even this wrong with patience. I shall remain to do that good I can, however I am misused, for I will never forget my duty or stain my honesty.' He stopped, seeing my face so stern against him. 'It is my fate, I know it. I shall count myself as lower than I am, rather than crave benefit by anyone. You have done your worst, sir, and I remain humble beneath your stroke.'

I saw now that the villain sought to excuse himself with untruth after untruth, so that now he laboured upon a whole mountain of lies and deceits. I waved the letter before his face, and tore it in three pieces. 'I shake you off, Edward Kelley, and I renounce you. I have spent my gold to buy false hope and false friends, so I pray you trouble me no more.'

'What is that you say I have done, so that I am treated thus?'

'I say you have wickedly lied and deluded me. I speak now of the spirits you so cunningly created in my chamber, but there are things you have done against my wife which as yet I know nothing of. I mean to discover the truth. Of that you may be sure.'

'You are impudent, sir, and over-bold. How dare you vex me, and tax me with such faults?'

'You have wrought your own wreck. What more is there to say?' Then once more I commanded the knave to get out of my service, and never after come within my doors.

'You have used me very dishonestly, Doctor Dee. If I owe you no service, then perhaps there is some greater power in the land who will be glad to hear of your conjurations and devilry. Who would not wish to know about the little man you so deviously desire to create?'

I laughed aloud at his idle threat, explaining in brief words that no one would believe any such thing; then I told him that he must leave before this night. Thereupon he grew into such a rage that he said he would not pass one foot beyond the door unless I paid him a sum of fifty angels for all his labour. I refused, and at that he put up his hand to strike me. So I called aloud to the servants, 'Come here now, there is violence offered to me.' And then he left me, cursing.

I sat down upon my stool, shaking like a leaf in a hurricane, and did not know for a few moments who I was or what I had said.

But then Audrey knocked upon my closet door. 'She has grown worse and worse,' she said. 'Just at twilight she began to sicken again and grow very ill, and she cannot be brought to eat or drink anything. Can you come to her now, sir?'

I went to my wife, any thought of Kelley having gone from me, and knew at once that there could now be no hope of recovery. All her body was withered and consumed, wasted down to the bones; she was more like a ghost than a living creature and, in my pity for her, I fetched a deep sigh as I approached her bed. 'You see me exceeding lean,' she said smiling, 'but do not be angry with me.'

'How could I be angry with you, Katherine? You have daily decreased your rest and feeding, and that has disturbed me. But no more than that.'

'There is no need to be disturbed. I feel such a lightness around me that I need neither sleep nor eat. I feel sometimes that I am rising into the air, and that the case is altered with me.'

'Shall I fetch Audrey to play some tune or ditty for you on the virginals? It lies idle behind the tapestry there.'

'No, no. Music will make me weep now. I hear within it the rise and fall of all created things.'

'But it makes true harmony also. There is an incorruptible heaven, ornate with signs and stars and planets, to which you belong. You will come to it in time, as a bee alights upon a flower.'

'Is that why I seem to be returning to the beginning? And am become a child again?'

'The stars enter our bodies with their subtle influences and, according to our state, we are imbued with their light. But rest now. You are full of thoughts, and thoughts may prevent you from becoming whole again.'

'No. I have plucked up my spirits, now that you are near me, and I am quite merry. Quite merry. Should I not be happy as I move towards the grave? There is nothing more to fear.'

'Do not talk so.'

'But why should I not talk of happiness, when these may be my last words to you upon the earth?' At that I turned away, so that

243

she would not see me weeping; when I turned back, her eyes were closed. 'I see you now by faith and imagination,' she said. 'And where there is no faith, there is no life.' I knelt praying by her bedside for that next hour, hearing every breath as though it were her last and knowing that the precious warmth within her would soon ascend towards its origin above the stars. She stirred then, and when I gazed upon her, her eyelids opened and something was looking fondly upon me. 'We will meet again, John, and till then farewell.' And with one more sigh she died. How I took it, I mean not to tell it.

I called aloud to Audrey, who was standing by the doorway all bathed in tears. 'Prepare her hair,' I said. 'I cannot stay longer by her side. I will remember her as she was, and imagine how she will be.'

I left her chamber and went out into the hall. There was some fine linen cloth of her own stitching in a heap there where Audrey had left it; it had the savour of gillyflower upon it, and I put it up to my mouth and nose as if I were about to deny myself breath and end my own life. Then I heard the steps of Kelley coming down the stairs behind me.

'Now,' he said, 'now that I know the depth of your ingratitude, I willingly shake you off and renounce you.' He had as yet no knowledge of the death, and I would rather have been torn apart by dogs than reveal it to him. 'But I tell you this, Dee. You concluded wisely. There never were spirits except of my own making, and there was no token of a lost city found in Glastonbury. These were shows and devices arranged by John Overbury, who knew your mind well and understood the best way to reach your heart – if heart it is. I thrust myself into your service with the sole design of winning your confidence, so that in the fullness of time you would reveal to me the secret of the philosopher's stone. When I learned of the homunculus, I saw that there was much more to be gained than gold. Yet now I doubt that you know even that.' So he and Overbury had sought for gold, and then wished to take from me a greater secret. Well, well, none of this concerned me now. 'I leave at first light,' he continued. 'Your lost city is quite gone, and my own self with it.' I said nothing but, with my back still turned to him, I held my wife's linen cloth against my face.

The rest of that day, and that night, I spent in my scrying chamber. I could not sleep, but I sat with my head bowed towards the ground in memory of my dear wife – for what else was there for me to do but decline towards that earth in which her own corpse would lie? It was four of the clock in the morning, and in the very depth of the silence, when I heard a faint whispering or calling about the stone. After a very few moments there appeared a woman far off, though it were only in the corner of the room, so clear and so transparent that I could see a man child within her. She advanced towards me then, her arms outstretched, and I perceived that this child inside her womb was my own self.

'Mother,' I cried. 'No, not mother, but wife. You are my wife standing before me in spirit! How could you bear me within your womb?'

'John Dee, I am sent of God.'

'Oh to see you again so soon! I thought I should never look upon your face in this life, nor hear your voice again on this sad earth.'

'I have come to teach you to look inwardly, John Dee, and to see what belongs to the hearts of men. Then shall you have a new gown put on you, and it shall be of a different colour.'

'What gown? What colour? I am lost in a maze.'

'I will forsake descant and give you plain song:

> To you I say, how learned soever you be,
> Go burn your books, and come to learn of me.

How plain is that?'

'May I ask you something? Does love always begin with grief, and end with death? Is it always a pleasure full of pain, and a joy replenished with misery? What good can there be that ends with such sorrow?'

'You ask me that even now?'

'Yes, even now I do not know what love may be.'

'That is why, with all your scholarship, you have found only hatred and ambition in this world. You have read in vain and done nothing but lose time. Now understand something which will be more profitable to you by far: this world is your own self, John Dee.'

'So how is it to be changed?'

'When you are quite changed. Once you saw the world without love. Now look upon this, and see the world with love.'

As soon as she had said this, the spiritual creature, my own wife, seemed to sink through the floor and was gone away in a fire. At that my whole chamber began to burn, but it did me no injury. Then it vanished away.

THE GARDEN

Now see the world with love. I was standing within my garden, which lies aslope down to the Holborn river, yet it was all quite changed. The air was sometimes infested with vapours from the ditches and the puddles that lie thereabouts, but that evil had suddenly been banished away and all around me was sweet and salutary; vanished, too, were such beasts and flies that commonly annoy my garden. Everything seemed refreshed with some new waking and, in the midst of this array, I saw a fair rose tree that climbed up a hollow oak. Its flowers were white and red, while its leaves shone like fine gold, and at the foot of this oak boiled a fountain of most white water. 'I know of this,' I said aloud. 'This is the philosopher's garden, which is normally closed with such locks and bars that no one may enter.'

And indeed here were the diverse flowers and blossoms that signified the stages of the great work: the rose, which is the flower of the sun; the mulberry, which signifies the mystery of change; and the myrtle, which is a true token of immortality. These were the flowers of the chemical theatre, together with the never-failing fountain in which our labours are refreshed. Here also were the plants and herbs which according to their natures are drawn to the power of the planets, whose beams of light quicken, comfort, preserve and maintain the tender seeds of the world. That is why all things must be sown and gathered according to the places of the heaven above or under the earth. Let the coriander and the dill be sown when the moon increases, and let them be gathered in the waning of the moon. The leaves of all herbs are best from the twenty-third day of March to the twenty-third day of June, when their strength and virtues are increased by the rays of the celestial bodies. Yet truly this is the affair of apothecaries, who employ their pains to extract some rare quintessence: there is a greater secret by far to be found in the Philosopher's Garden, for in the gathering of the dew you may find the spirit of new life. Take it up in the month of May, with a clean white linen cloth spread upon the grass, and distil it within a glass alembic —

'Enough, John Dee. Enough. I read your thoughts aright.' There was a little willow tree near my right hand, just by the new stairs I had laid to the river; but now, oh so suddenly changed and cleaved in two, as my own wife stepped forth from it. She was dressed in white silk, bordered with jewels the size of beans, and over it wore a mantle of blue cloth shot through with silver threads. She was of such exeeding brightness that my eyes dazzled, and I put my hands up to my face. No, it was not my wife. It was my own mother, whom I had not seen for all these years. No. It was not her but someone other, and she it was whom I had seen in all my dreams since childhood, but, waking, could never find. Yes, it was she. 'Enough,' she said again. 'You have walked in the garden of alchemy. Now open the wicket-gate yonder, and find that which will be more pleasant and virtuous for you. Climb the hill of forsaking, and make an end to this knowledge born out of fear and ambition. I have no more to say.'

At that she vanished away. This little gate was upon my left hand, away from the main garden, and with good heart I obeyed her command; I opened the gate and entered upon a field on very level ground, covered with pretty grass even to the brinks of the horizon. It was bright with the sunlight but I could not see the hill of which she spoke; then it was suddenly before me and I began to climb, knowing that I would move upon more certain ground. Very soon I came to the top of this hill and, after I had panted a little for breath, I looked forward over large gardens laid out in elaborate pattern. Here were terraces of fine grass, sweet trees and flowers, alleys of green, delectable shadowed walls of hedges, and a garden with very many fresh bowers, arbours, seats and walls that with great art, cost and diligence had been appointed. Even from the summit of the hill I could smell such sweet fragrancy of odours breathing from the plants and herbs, and could hear such natural melodious music and tunes of birds, and could see such colour and variety among the flowers, that I was moved to speak out. 'God Almighty first planted a garden to be a dwelling place and now I have seen, oh Lord, the beauty of Thy house.'

I came down from the hill and entered upon a fair green, which had on either side a covert alley made with hedges of burrs and thorns; like the hedgehog who lodges in the thorns because he himself is full of prickles, so among the hedges sprang many sturdy plants such as cloves, mace, lignum aloe, mastic and bole armeniac, which heal the infirm body. This was an emblem of those times when it is better to gather herbs for the stomach than sweet flowers for the senses. For the world can heal as well as injure; and though by basil the scorpion is engendered, by means of the same herb it can be utterly destroyed. And was it now that I scented the savour of rue, which makes all serpents and other venomous beasts fly from the garden? Indeed this was an innocent and harmless region, where the various simples may teach men to be humble and wise. It was a merry lesson to drive me from melancholy, and with a quiet mind I walked across the finely shorn grass towards the garden itself.

And what was arrayed before me but a ground all tapestried with rare and choice flowers? Here were fair roses, graceful violets, fragrant primroses, lily flowers, carnations and sweet johns; here, too, were yellow daffodils, chequered pansies and ground honey-suckle both white and red. I would have needed some curious herbal to know all the names and operations of the flowers and plants before me, but they seemed to be of seasons intermingled: the true lovers' primrose and gentle gillyflower of the spring were mixed here with the lavender and sweet marjoram of winter, while the yellow crocus of January bloomed beside the columbine of June, the white violet of April with the poppy of September. Here was profusion indeed, with so many sweet odours suddenly coming forth that it was as if all the herbs and flowers had been well dried and kept in a dark place before the door was opened before me.

Then suddenly came the scent of wallflowers, and in that

moment I was returned to my childish days when I played at span counters close under the barn wall within our fields at east Acton. And here is my mother in her white petticoat, holding out her arms lovingly towards me. I pray you speak still to me, mother, though I am no longer so little, for I have need of your voice and comfort in these my latter years. How once you held me fast and kissed me, so that there would be no more fear! Then there was nothing before me, and nothing behind me, only a present love. Oh mother, there can be no night or mistiness where you are, for in my memory you are one whose beams wrapped up the darkness as whirlwinds take up dust. So the scent of the wallflowers lingered around me, as I stood entranced within the garden.

I walked on a little after, until I came into a natural enclosure set about with slender elms, where there were also set little trees and plants to bear up vines. Here were marigolds, thyme, isope and rosemary, and suchlike flowers for the city (or so I thought), when suddenly I savoured the sweetness of the gillyflowers which smell like cloves. Where had I known that scent before? It was in a small bag, fast knit up, which my wife always had around her neck; then I saw her clearly as she once was, in our first days, wearing her blue damask gown while waiting for me at the door of our lodgings in Postern Street. Oh, how I long for that moment once again, which I surely should have enjoyed without the customary burden of my fears! It was a sacred minute which then I had not seen or understood, and now all hope of knowing it was gone for ever. Just as gold may lie unnoticed upon the rough earth until it is picked up by some child, so the gold of the world has been glimpsed and gathered by other men than me. I sought to understand the world, but I never saw it truly; I looked for knowledge, but in my fear I never looked around me. I had sought for certainty in dreams of the past, and in visions of the future, yet I had never known that moment of true presence when my wife waved and smiled upon me as I approached her. Oh to see her again as once she was, and to hear her voice . . .

And then she came out from among the trees, and stood before me as she had done in life. At first I was amazed and fearful, in case my lamentation had conjured up some treacherous spirit. 'Fear nothing,' she said, reading my inward thoughts. 'My coming is not to do you any manner of harm, but to request a matter at your hands which you cannot deny me.'

'What could I deny you, in life or in death?'

'I wish you to cure yourself. Wounds cannot be cured without searching, so come with me now upon our quest. I have offered my soul to God as pawn,' she continued, 'to come here and discharge you of all your fears. I will be as good and as faithful a wife as ever I was, while we have this little time together. Shall we walk abroad and take the fresh air?'

So I walked towards her, and saluted her with weeping. Yet she shook her head, as if to tell me that there could be no more tears. I dried my eyes then, and spoke to her gently. 'Where have I come, wife? I do not know this place, except that it may be some alchemical garden which I have seen among the emblems of my books.'

'This is no garden of alchemy. This is the garden of the true world, where among many flowers we shall see the sweet rose and the sharp nettle, the pleasant lily and the pricking thorn, the high vine and the low hedge. It is by heart that you must learn its lessons, for what good is knowledge if you do not live according to the same?'

'Like the seed which lies deep hid in the ground of nature, until it is refreshed and quickened by the spiritual sun, so shall I grow and flower under your instruction.' Then I began to declare that neither any man living, nor any book I had yet read, was able to teach me those truths which I desired and longed for.

She laughed at this. 'Others with a proud sniff might disdain the counsel of a wife.'

'But not one who makes intercession and prayer to the giver of wisdom, so that at last I might find the light.'

'Let us go then into the winds of this world. The south wind harbours corrupt and evil vapours, yet it blows itself out in this garden. The north wind purges colic, the west wind induces melancholy, but the east wind is temperate, brisk and fragrant. See which way it comes upon you here as we walk.'

So we went into the garden where we saw once more a great variety of flowers, with the merry daisy, the loyal lavender and the gentle lily among them. 'I wish that God would grant me the key to this place,' I said. 'I would like it better than the fairest chamber.'

'But you have the key. Did you not know, or did your hieroglyphical writers never tell you, that the figures of plants and flowers express the mind? See how the rose and canker can be in one bud. And do you see here the rose with all its thorns, showing us that there is no sweetness without bitterness and no pleasure without sorrow? And now look at those vines, growing up among the elms beyond that bank.'

'What news will this disclose to me?'

'Some such news as partly you know. As the gardener weds his elms to vines, even so does the true philosopher wed earth to heaven – that is, he weds lower things to the endowments and powers of higher things. Shall we go over and pluck the violets among them? Or shall we pluck the damask roses? What shall it be? Do you prefer the fairest flower before the sweetest, or the sweetness before beauty? In picking one or the other, you will show your true desire.'

'But are they not both equally to be prized? They are both ever renewed, and yet never the same. All other things wither, die and waste away; but there is a spirit within these flowers – the spirit of beauty, the spirit of colour, call it what you will – that burns with a quenchless flame, like a blazing beacon, or like a sparkling torch, that can abide what you have called the winds of the world.'

'I see now, John Dee, that you are beginning to understand what is written here. Come now. Will you walk further with me under the oaken wood leaves, or in the orchard under the vine bower? Or, if you are weary of walking, shall we rest under the arbours? Do you like it so?'

'Yes,' I said. 'If I am weary, I will soon be refreshed in such a place as this. May we enter this grove, where the grass is still wet with the dew?'

'Some say that these are the tears of the world. But listen. Hear how the small birds chatter their sweet tunes. And just as there must be order to create divine harmony, so there is order here. Do you know that the thrush never sings in the company of the nightingale, for fear of discordance? So what bird would you wish most to hear – the nightingale, the linnet, the finch, the thrush, the lark or the sparrow?'

'I do not love the sparrow, since he has no pleasant tune.'

'Yet he is called the bird of Venus for his amorous friskings.'

'So can all the creatures of nature be seen as emblems of mankind?'

'Not of mankind alone, but of the spiritual powers and virtues which animate the whole frame of the heavens.'

'Then I wish I did not have to leave this place. I am like the grasshopper, who, being sprung of the grass, would rather die than depart from it.'

'Then would I in turn be like the turtle, because of her conjugal loyal chastity without her mate.'

At that I sighed, and would have cried again. 'But my wife, my dear wife, are you a vision or a living thing still upon the earth? Surely you come in spirit, because, alas, I saw you perish before me.'

She said nothing to that but, laughing, took my hand. 'Let us rest ourselves by the side of the silver stream.' So we made our way out of the arbour and came to a little brook that seemed to spring from a natural wildness of trees and thickets. There were willows and osiers close to it, for they love to be set in watery and moist places, and the stream issued into a lake as delightful as it was artificial. 'Is it not marvellous cool here?' she said, looking down into the running water. 'What a sweet noise this stream makes among the pebble stones.'

'But do you see the small wind which makes the water prettily to move over the lake? One wave folds itself into another, while one overturns another upon the bank. It enchants me almost to sleep.'

'No. This is no place for sleeping. Do you not know of the cypress which, the more it is watered, the more it withers?'

'I am not like the cypress but the almond tree, which bears most fruit when it is old.'

'And so, John Dee?'

'So love has the greatest faith when it grows in age.'

'Indeed you find something to your purpose in this enchanted garden. Shall I take your lesson another step forward, by discoursing upon the oak which you see in the wildness?'

'I could listen to you for eternity.'

She laughed again. 'Well, do you see this oak from whose body so many arms spread, and out of whose arms so many fingers come? This in emblem resembles your strength and happiness: strength in the honour you receive, and happiness in the truth which has been revealed to you. Your heart must be of oak, than which nothing is surer and nothing sounder. All must be woven in one root, also, so that nothing is more constant or more natural. It is the tree of Our Lord, whose root is so deeply fastened that fear and hatred, though they undermine the windings, cannot find the centre; and its top is so highly reared that envy and ambition, though they shoot high, cannot reach it. So it is that under the arms of this tree you will find both shade and shelter from the heat of this base world.'

'This is a lesson indeed to me, to shake off fear and envy. I thank you, wife, for you also are like a tree.'

'What tree is that?'

'The tree on which the phoenix came to rest. For as there is but one phoenix in the world, so is there but one tree in which she builds.'

At that point she took my hand and led me beyond the stream and the wood, towards a secluded part of the garden where there stood a maze. There were four fruits placed in each of its corners, and its trimmed hedges were set with winter savory and thyme. 'Now,' she said, 'now we may join the dance.'

'What dance may that be?'

She replied nothing to me then but led me through so many alleys and turnings that I grew quite distracted. 'Do not be dismayed,' she said. 'All will be revealed to you. For the world itself is very like a maze.'

Then at last, after various twistings and turnings, we came into an open space where men and women were set for dancing; each one chose his mate, as the custom is, and then I watched as they fell in succession to the galliard, the coranto and the pavane. 'Do not think,' my wife told me, 'that this is some senseless or wavering light inconstant multitude that will dance after any man's pipe. These are the humane beings who have taken the true path of life, for what shape or pattern can it better form than that of the dance?' And as I watched, I saw such feats of agility in tumblings and castings, such leaps and skips, such somersaults and flights, that I laughed out loud: there were so many windings and gyrings and circumflections that I felt as if a ton weight had also been lifted from my own shoulders. I had read of those spirits who dance in rounds upon pleasant lawns and green meadows, with noise of music and minstrelsy, and who vanish away when anyone comes near them; but these were beings of a different sort, who traced the proper movement of the world to the sound of viols, violins, flutes, recorders, lutes, citterns, sackbuts and virginals.

'Do you remember the old song that your mother used to sing to you?' My wife had murmured softly to me, even as I stood amazed.

'Yes,' I replied. 'I remember it well.

> 'From slumber soft I fell asleep,
> From sleep to dream,
> From dream to deep delight.'

Now she took my hand and led me down another alley of the maze, until we came out into a bright light. 'Look,' she said, 'at these paths of delight and merriment.' Here suddenly were very strange kinds of fire, which mounted high in the air upward and seemed to burn unquenchable. 'For every one who dies, and who is born, there is a light that cannot be snuffed out. As by small sparks or kindled coals a great fire is made, so does this earth glow within the firmament. That is why this place is brighter by far than any sun, if you have the eyes to witness it.'

Then to my amazement I saw that we were part of a vast concourse, some standing around, some in a ring, some above, some below, and that the maze itself was a pattern of people in perfect order and symmetry. Now their eyes were bent upon a spectacle I could not make out, but again and again they expressed their joy with great delight. 'What is it that they see?' I asked her.

'They see the world with love.'

'I pray you, where is it?'

'It is everywhere.'

'Yet I labour to find it, and do not see it.'

'You need not employ labour in this place but, rather, faith and prayer. You do not require the study of a long time, but humbleness of spirit and cleanness of heart. In finding nothing, you will gain all things.'

'So fast has this understanding now taken root in my heart,' I replied, 'that the more it is digged the deeper it grows, the oftener it is cut the less it will bleed, the more it is laden the better it will bear.'

'These are sober and right earnest words, John Dee. But be merry now. Once you saw the world without love, now join in the world with love.' And with that she took my hand, guiding me in a pavane. 'Do you see now that you are a star man?' she said, when we had completed the patterns of the dance. 'You are all grace and not envy, all lightness and not triumph.'

'I have sought for such a being always.'

'He is within you, where he has always been, but he cannot be found by experiment or speculation. He proceeds from virtue and has so noble a nature, by the divine infusion of goodness, that where he takes root he rises beautifully and brings forth an everlasting fruit.'

'I see that you test my old faith in my art and science.'

'Your faith must now be placed in love and not in wisdom, in surrendering and not in power.'

'Say more, and help me.'

'Love is a sweet essence that burns before God, but it is so secret a mystery that few can describe it or tell by what inward affections it is conveyed to the heart. Few know that content and gladness, when the powers of man and woman leap in the bowels of the body for joy at the instant of recognition. I am your true wife, so embrace me now and I will be joined with you in essence. Love is the light of the world.'

'Yet still I must walk by my own light, wife. These are visions given to me by spirits, and I must find my own vision before I may be redeemed. There is a great city which I believe to be my proper home, for is it not true that each man must spend eternity in the house he has built for himself?'

'It is true,' she replied, 'that the imagination is immortal, and that thereby we each create our own eternity.'

'So be patient with me, wife. When I have understood my own vision, then will I find my salvation.'

'Take care, John Dee, that you choose justly.'

I was about to tell her that I would abjure the path of worldly knowledge and seek that original spirit which dwelt within me, when she arranged the brightness around her like a cloak and vanished away.

SEVEN

So who in this world can make the dead speak? Who can see them in vision? That would be a form of magic – to bring the dead to life again, if only in the pages of a book. Or within my own mind, as I lay in bed that night and considered the events of the day; the discovery of the documents which my father had preserved, the reading of John Dee's will, the child in the garden, the voices by the sealed door, all seemed now to be part of the same process. I could hear the bells of St James marking the hour and, as I cradled my head in my arms, I had one of those waking visions which sometimes precede sleep. I was on an enormous plain, and I could see a wide stream of lava slowly moving across it from some unknown source of power; parts of this lava spread more rapidly than the rest, so that there seemed to be many different surfaces, while smaller streams had branched off to the side and had already begun to harden into familiar shapes. Whirlpools of fire rose from the main current and, at the edge where I now stood, there was a glow of dying time that sent out such warmth that immediately I fell asleep.

My father received a letter the following morning. I was so surprised to see his name on the envelope that for a moment I had the strangest fear that he had written it himself. Of course that was absurd: it had been sent to him by Elizabeth Skelton, of whom I had never heard, and she thanked him for 'allowing us to see Doctor Dee's house'; she apologized for her delay in writing, and then went on to enquire how 'your researches in Wapping are going'.

I let the letter fall gently to the floor. Here was more evidence of my father's interest in Doctor Dee, although even now I could not adequately fathom it. What secret sympathy did he feel for him? Why had he transcribed the formula for the homunculus? I picked up the letter again, and noticed the passage about his 'researches' in Wapping; that had been the place written down in Doctor Dee's manuscript, and I recalled then how he had drawn an angel flying towards the margin of the page. But what could my father have been doing in east London?

There was a telephone number at the top of the letter, and I rang it at once. I forgot to introduce myself to Elizabeth Skelton when she answered, but began talking loudly and rapidly. 'You wrote to my father, but he's dead now.' There was a silence. 'You wrote to him about John Dee.' I expected the customary regrets – I had grown used to them around the time of his funeral – but she did seem genuinely upset. For a moment she sounded as if she were about to cry, so I became very curt with her. 'Can you come tomorrow morning?' I asked her before putting down the telephone. 'There is a good deal I have to ask you.' Then I telephoned my mother. I wanted to show her all my father's papers, so that we might begin to exorcize the past; she listened to me in silence and then, a little reluctantly, agreed to visit Clerkenwell the following day.

Elizabeth Skelton arrived the next morning; she was a plump, almost fat, woman who did not carry herself well. Was she one of those sad people who, according to Daniel Moore, were naturally attracted to occultism as a way of escaping the world? 'The house seems quite changed,' she said as she came into the hall.

'You must be mistaken. It's just the same.'

'Are you really his son?' The question horrified me, and I simply stared at her. 'I'm sorry. I didn't mean anything by it. It's just that your father never discussed any family. We all assumed he was a bachelor.'

I took her into the ground-floor room, but she seemed to know it very well already. 'And who are we?'

'Oh, just the Society.' She sat down, without being asked to do so, on the faded blue sofa. 'The John Dee Society. There are quite a few of us, scattered about the place. Surely you knew that your father was a member for years and years?'

'Of course I did.' I decided to find another subject. 'Why did you think the house seemed changed?'

'Oh, I don't know. When your father lived here, it seemed uninhabited somehow. But now it doesn't feel like that at all. It feels like the house is full.'

I fought back my rising panic. 'I wanted to ask you something, Miss Skelton.'

'Elizabeth.'

'What was my father doing at Wapping?'

'It was quite a new piece of research.' She answered very eagerly, and with some dismay I realized that John Dee might remain a living presence for others beside myself. 'He had found out – I don't know how, precisely – that Doctor Dee had been undertaking some kind of investigation to the east of the old Tudor city. Then he came across the name of Wapping among his papers –'

'Yes. I saw it, too.'

'– and discovered that John Dee had bought some land there. I think your father was just about to track it down.'

'What exactly did he expect to find?'

'We were never quite sure, but we thought that it might be some kind of excavation. Your father said that he was going to buy it back. I don't know how far he got before . . .'

'That's easily solved,' I said. 'Wait here.'

I went up to the empty bedroom, and took from the carrier-bag those papers which dealt with the details of my father's various properties. There was an office building in Barnstaple, a block of flats in Ilfracombe, an area of commercial land outside Cardiff, a house in Clerkenwell, and there, finally listed on a separate sheet, was a small lock-up garage in Pass Over Street, Wapping, E.1.

I came downstairs again. 'I'm sorry,' I said. 'There was nothing there.'

'I didn't really think there would be.' She was still smiling. 'It was just a theory, after all.'

'And theories can do no harm.'

'That's true.' She looked around the room with an expression of enormous satisfaction, as if she belonged here. 'Can I tell you anything else?'

'I don't think so, Elizabeth. Oh, there is just one thing. Did John Dee ever practise sexual magic?'

'What?'

'Did he raise spirits by means of sex?'

'Of course not. He was a Christian.'

'But don't you sense it here? Don't you smell it, Elizabeth?'

I had turned to the window, but I could hear her getting up hurriedly from the sofa. 'I should really go now,' she was saying. I made no reply, but traced one of the secret signs in the dust of the wooden table. 'You really must excuse me.' Then I heard her leave the house.

I was still standing by the window when my mother arrived. 'You left the front door open, Matthew. You never know what might creep in.'

I was looking out at the traffic flowing down the Farringdon Road; it seemed to me then that it would go on for ever, in the various forms of various centuries, following the direction of the old Fleet River. 'In ancient days,' I replied, 'a door was left open when someone was about to die. Then the spirit could pass through into the air.' I turned around to face her. 'But before we can open the door, Mrs Palmer, we must find the key! Where is the key?'

I rushed upstairs and looked through my father's papers once more, but I found nothing. Then I remembered the box in which he had kept various cuff-links and tie-pins; I had put it in one of my bedroom drawers, and when I opened it I found what I was looking for. There, wrapped in tissue paper, was a ring of four bright keys. I took them down to her in triumph. 'We'll take them with us,' I said.

'With us?'

'On our pilgrimage. To Wapping.'

In the taxi I tried to explain to her the significance of the place, according to Doctor Dee's manuscript, and the possibility that her husband had found some form of excavation there. She listened to me patiently enough, but without much apparent interest; it was clear to me that she wanted to know nothing else about his life. It was only when I disparagingly mentioned the possibility of 'treasure' that she became intrigued, and eagerly stopped the taxi when she saw Pass Over Street coming up on our left hand. It was beside a familiar patch of London wilderness, separating it from a council estate of high-rise tenements. The waste ground was encircled by rusty iron fencing, and I could see the tower of a church rising somewhere beyond it; of the lock-up garage itself, which my father owned, there was still no sign.

Then she knelt down, and peered through a hole in the cor-rugated iron fence. 'There's something in the far corner of the field,' she said. 'It might be a garage.' But there was no way of entering the area from this spot, and so we were forced to follow the circumference in search of a gate or door. I was explaining to her how strange it was that someone four centuries dead was still controlling our movements, when I noticed a gap that had been literally carved out of the fence. As I bent down and hurried through to the other side, I did not care to consider who or what had created this makeshift opening. And there, in one corner of the waste ground, was a small square building. I shielded my eyes to look more closely at it, when I saw something glinting beside it; it flashed across my face, and in that momentary brightness I thought I heard the sound of horses' hooves.

My mother was walking ahead of me towards the building, her previous frailty quite gone. She seemed very determined as she strode among the rubble and the weeds, and for the first time I wondered whether my father had ever mentioned John Dee to her. It still seemed peculiar that this alchemist and philosopher should exert any influence at all; but perhaps there is a kind of intelligence or vision which never really dies. Suddenly the ground felt strange beneath my feet, as if I were not quite centred upon it – as if I were walking above a vast cave or hollow space.

'Do you have the key?' She was shouting to me, as she stood beside the locked front of the garage.

'Wait a moment. I'm coming.' There were discarded cans and

bottles around me, and it looked as if this entire area had become the dustbin of the neighbourhood: cardboard boxes, pieces of old newspaper, rusted metal, twisted plastic, had been left among the nettles and the pale bindweed as if they too might grow and flourish beneath the sky. So I walked carefully, looking around me as I went forward, and at first I did not notice the tramp standing at the side of the field. He was holding up some glass or metal object which glinted in the sun, and he was waving it at me; at that moment I struck my shoe against a stone, and with a cry I bent down towards my foot. When I stood up again, the tramp had gone.

'Did you see that man?' I asked her, as she waited impatiently beside the closed garage.

'What man? Do try that lock, Matthew. I can't wait to see what's inside.'

It was really quite easy: one of the keys I had brought with me fitted the two padlocks and, without waiting for me to assist her, she rolled up the door of the garage. I hesitated for a moment, wary both of the darkness and of the sodden damp smell which came from the interior of this enclosed space. It must have been locked since my father's death – and I believe I was afraid, too, that I would see him walking towards me out of the darkness. My mother had no such inhibitions. 'I really don't think there's anything here at all,' she said, stepping into the shadows. 'Oh no. I beg your pardon. There is something.'

I followed her and saw, in one corner, a large piece of stone. Its outline was distinctly marked against the dark brick of the garage, and in fact it seemed to emit a vague glow; it was only when I walked over to it that I noticed the patches of moss and lichen which spread across its surface. It was as if the stone had been sprinkled with a green powder of age and time. 'You know,' she said, 'I could swear that these are steps.'

I realized at once that she was right: the large piece of stone had been roughly carved into three steps – although, on the concrete floor of this modern garage, they were certainly not leading anywhere in particular. 'I'm going to climb them,' I said. There was no need for me to speak, but I felt as if I ought to be addressing someone. 'Watch me in case I disappear.' She seemed perplexed by this, and so I carried on talking. 'Do you know that song, "I'll climb a stairway to the stars"?'

'Perhaps they're leading down and not up.'

I already had my foot on the first step. 'As you can see,' I said, 'up and down are the same here.' I mounted them easily enough, and naturally I felt nothing at all. But I put out my arms as I stood there, on top of the stone, and my mother laughed out loud; the sound rang around this small space, and it seemed for a moment as if someone were laughing beside her. My sudden movement had left me dizzy, and as I climbed back down the steps I had so strong a sensation of vertigo that I might have been descending miles into the earth. I believe I would have fainted if she had not taken my arm and helped me outside. I waited there, while she continued what she called her 'investigation' of the interior. I did not expect her to find anything; it was clear that my father's search of this area had come to an unexpected end before he could discover any object of value. There was a glass tube or bottle on the ground, among the other debris; I was about to kick it away when a powerful scent of violets hovered about me, and I put my hand up to my mouth. This perfume reminded me of the scent Daniel Moore had worn, as he climbed the steps from the club in Charlotte Street.

'Nothing at all.' My mother came out of the garage, wiping her hands fastidiously upon a white handkerchief. 'I was hoping for a bit of history.'

'There is no such thing as history,' I said. 'History only exists in the present.' And there was the tramp again, waving at me now from the centre of the waste land. 'Like those steps. We see them now. So are they part of the past or of the present? Or of both?' He was shouting something at me; at least, his mouth was opening and closing, although I could not make out any words. My mother was looking in the same direction, but she was pretending to ignore him; this was obviously the most appropriate response, and so I started talking more loudly than before. 'I don't believe in the past any more,' I said. 'It's a fantasy.'

Then a dog barked somewhere, and the tramp disappeared: perhaps he had decided to hide, although I had the impression that the dog had been beside him. I locked my father's garage and, as we made our way back to the road, I felt that same strange emptiness beneath my feet. No, it was not emptiness. It was some kind of shifting force, as if a hurricane were blowing within the earth. We walked south to the river, and then my mother complained that she felt very tired. 'I'm done in,' she said. 'Your father has done me in again.' So I hailed a taxi, and asked the driver to take her to Ealing. I could have joined her, I suppose, but I was suddenly filled with such energy that I decided to walk back to Clerkenwell.

It was a misty evening, or at least everything seemed to be wreathed in mist; it was as if a rainstorm covered the city and, as I walked beside the bank of the Thames, the objects of the world became dark, and intense, and slow-moving. After a while I came up into Newgate, just by Greyfriars Passage; I knew the area well, because there was a genealogical research library in a nearby square, but I found myself turning down an unexpected and unfamiliar lane. That is the nature of the city, after all: in any neighbourhood you can come across a street, or a close, that seems to have been perpetually hidden away. It would have been easy to miss this particular turning, also, since it was no more than an alley with dark shops and houses along one side.

Then the ground shifted once more; it seemed looser and more uneven but, before I could look down, I realized that my right foot and leg had gone quite numb. It was as if one side of my body had suddenly been plunged into an abyss. But the numbness lasted only a moment and, after that, everything seemed very agreeable: the old houses with their fronts arching over the lane, the curiously carved doors, the wooden barrels piled at the corner, all of these things delighted me. There was a man in a dark overcoat standing beneath a porch, and I smiled at him as I passed by. 'Hello, my little man,' he whispered, and then he knelt down before me. I was surprised by this, of course, but I said nothing; I carried on walking until I came out by Newgate Close, and the roar of the traffic brought me to my senses.

I soon returned to Clerkenwell, and I believe that I was humming some tune as I entered the old house. Could it have been 'Fortune My Foe'? But as soon as I walked into the ground-floor room, I knew that something was wrong. Someone had been here before me. The sofa had been moved sideways, the drawer of my cabinet was open, and a book had been left beneath the window. I ran out into the hallway and was about to leave the house, in flight from any possible intruder, when I was stopped by the smell of burning. There was something on fire within the house – something on fire above me – and I could hear the crackling of the flames even as I ran up the stairs. I hurried from room to room but there was nothing at all – no smoke, no flames, no intruder. I walked down slowly, wondering at my own foolishness, when I heard voices coming from the ground floor. There were two of them, raised in fear or pain, and the sound was like a roaring in my ears.

'And what of Kelley? Is he aflame?'

'He has gone, sir. Gone with your alembic and your writings.'

'Well, let him run while he can. A greater one follows close on his heels.'

I crept down the remaining stairs and, as soon as I touched the floor of the hallway, the voices stopped. There was no one in the room.

It was then I telephoned Daniel Moore, and he arrived soon after. 'Something has happened again. Is it your fault?' This was what I called out to him, even before he had reached the door, and I hurried him into the ground-floor room as if he were being followed; when I told him about the fire, and about the voices, he looked steadily at me and made no attempt to interrupt. In fact he seemed to be smiling.

'I thought you didn't believe in ghosts,' he said at last.

'I believe in this house.'

'Could it be that someone was following you?'

Then I described to him the dark alley I had found on my way home, and the words of the man in the shadow of the porch. 'He called me his little man, and then I left him.'

'Homunculus,' he said. 'The word of the alchemist. It is the name of the creature formed by the magician, and grown within glass before it reaches its maturity.'

'But what has that to do with me?'

'That's what you are, isn't it? A homunculus? That's what your father told me.' And, at that, Daniel vanished away.

There was no help for it but to part. John Dee was waiting for me downstairs, and without another word I turned and went towards the basement door. I followed him down the steps, taking care not to touch him or to come too close. He went over to the sealed door, and ran his finger across the marks inscribed above its lintel.

★

'This is interesting,' my mother was saying. 'What are these?' I was standing in front of the garage in the waste ground, trying to regain my composure; it was all happening again. When I turned, I could see her peering curiously at some marks painted on the brick wall. 'I don't know,' I replied. 'I've got a boat to catch.'

There was a vast sheet of water ahead of me; the evening sun made a path across it and, following this line of light, John Dee came towards me in a small craft. 'It is time,' he said. 'Time to cross to the other side.'

I was still looking at the signs with my mother but, when I turned around, the tramp was calling to me again from the middle of the waste ground. I could see now that he was holding up the glass tube. I walked towards him, not daring to look into the glass itself. 'Do you bing Romewards?' he asked me. 'For my part, I am hurrying home.'

I looked around at the glittering streets, the high bright walls of jewels, and the gleaming towers. 'Who ever thought that the city could be so beautiful?'

'And in this city, Matthew, the beggars are kings.'

★

'But what do they mean?' My mother was perplexed by the signs, and had climbed up the steps in order to see them more clearly.

'I don't know. Abandon hope when you enter here. Something like that.' I helped her down the steps, and I was no longer alarmed by her soft weight against me. 'I have to go back now,' I told her. 'There is someone waiting for me. Can you find your own way home?'

We locked the garage, and I took a taxi to Clerkenwell. There was an unformed creature perched upon the gate when I returned, and for a few moments we looked at each other: the human regarded the homunculus, reflecting upon its long life and upon its vision of the world, and the homunculus regarded the human.

'I have been expecting you,' I said, 'although I know you are a figment and a sick man's dream. You are the fantasy of those who believe in the reality of time and the power of the material world: while I clung to those illusions, you haunted me. You were my father's creature, and so you were an image of my fears. But there is a higher life by far, quite beyond the passage of time. So now I leave you. There never was a homunculus.' Then it opened its mouth and screamed. I walked down the path, and went inside the house where he was expecting me.

THE VISION

I WAS WALKING within my garden when the brightness of my
wife's vision left me, and I looked down upon my own garments
somewhat muddied by the earth. It was late in the evening and, as
I guessed, about an hour after the setting of the sun when a light suddenly leapt out behind me and cast my flickering shadow on the path
that leads down to the stream. I turned, hearing shouts and screams
coming from within my house, and saw a flame leaping out of my
upper chamber and continuing terribly even to the roof. Now Philip
came running into the garden and calling me. 'Sir,' he said, feverish
in his fear, 'Mr Kelley has caused a fire within your chamber.'

I had been so much wrapped in thought at my latest visitation
that I could wonder at nothing now. I ran forward, seeing the
flame grow higher, and called out to Audrey who was even then
taking out a tapestry. 'How can this be?'

'He was at work within your secret room, sir, when the lamp
was all overthrown. Seeing that there was some spirit of wine too
near, and his glass not being stayed with books about it as yours is
wont to be – I saw all this because I watched him, sir, knowing the
hard words between you – then the same glass flitting to one side,
sir, the spirit was spilled out and burnt all that was on the table
where it stood. Good linen, and written books, and then, oh sir,
the flame overthrew everything.'

In the haste of her muddled words I caught the drift of her
report: that Edward Kelley, before he left my service for ever, was
engaged in some untrue action with my alembics and retorts. I led
her out into the garden, where Philip stood trembling. 'And what
of Kelley now?' I asked her.

'He has gone, sir. He ran from the flame, but not before he took away some of your writings.'

'And the glass vessel,' Philip said. 'He took that glass upon which I have seen you at work.'

So here was the truth of it: Edward Kelley had taken from me the secret studies upon the homunculus, and now the topmost part of my house was about to fall down in ruins. 'This fellow has overthrown my work,' I said to Philip, 'even while his baggage was in a readiness. Everything is in flame, and I feel I have the terrible Polonian disease that covers the eyes with a red mist. For look now what has happened to our poor dwelling!' I could see the light coming from the west window of my study, and I knew then that I was destitute of all my former comfort. It was at an end – the show stone, the holy table, the candlesticks, the sacred cloth, all burnt within the chamber of presence. And then what of my books? Had I laboured in the collecting of my library so diligently, only to see it gone? Yet I remembered then the words of my wife in my vision, that although I might begin in nature, I must end in eternity. Elsewhere there was no abiding city. And at that my heart was eased of its great weight.

'I abjure these arts,' I said to Audrey.

'Sir?'

'My homunculus, my search for new life, was a delusion.'

She looked at me in blank ignorance, so I walked away from her a little and spoke to the earth and the sky. 'The spirits of my father and my wife have shown me that there is only one true immortality. There is no way to conquer time and live eternally except through vision. The vision, not the body, transcends this life.' I had seen this world often, but not by faith and imagination, and there was a new journey to be entered into.

Then Philip came running up to me. 'The servants are all gathered about, sir,' he said, 'and no more harm can come to anyone living.' The tears stood in his eyes, and with a linen cloth I wiped them. 'Smokiness,' he said. 'Only smokiness.' Then he held out a heavy, well-made volume towards me. 'I saved the book,' he said. 'It was in your wife's chamber.'

I knew at once that it was the Bible which she carried with her everywhere during her sickness. And this, of all my books, to be saved! 'Now, Philip,' I said to him, 'perform this last great service for me.'

'No, sir, not the last –'

'Open the book where you will, and place your finger where it wishes to go.'

He dared not disobey me in my extremity and, with the light of the flames around him, he balanced the book upon his knee and opened it out upon a page.

'I have taught you to read,' I continued. 'Now tell me what you have marked with your finger.'

He wiped his mouth on his dirty sleeve and then, with much stumbling and hesitation, vouchsafed this to me. 'When I shall bring thee down with them that descend into the pit, with the people of old time, and shall set thee in the low parts of the earth, in places desolate of old, with them that go down to the pit, that thou be not inhabited.'

The noise of the fire had died down somewhat, but the parish watch had come with their engines and barrels of water. Philip closed the book, and amid all the cries and shouts he spoke loudly to me. 'Ezekiel,' he said. 'The words of the prophet.'

I took the Bible from him, turned my back upon the clamour, and walked down to the stream. I placed the book within the running water and, at that moment, I knew that I must depart from this house in order to find a more enduring home.

The flames that consumed my study and library were now all but extinguished; leaving instructions with Philip for the care of the other servants, I walked out past the throng to my stable by Turnmill Lane. I took my horse and rode through Finsbury Fields and past the gun foundry near St Botolph's, but here my horse became so ill from smokiness in the lungs that I sent it back to Clerkenwell by means of a messenger. Then I continued southwards to the river on foot.

Reader, nothing is set down by a fanciful hand. I viewed everything here related in broad seeing, but if my poor pen should be caused anywhere to stumble, you will consider in recompense all the unseen and unknown ways through which it has toiled and laboured.

The rain was continually falling when I came to the Wapping marshes, and there was nothing there except the decayed bulk of stone and the mound lying desolate and waste. Edward Kelley had informed me that it was all his trick and delusion, yet I knew well enough that something was buried beneath this earth; I had felt its material presence and influence, although, in the company of that villain, I had seen nothing plain. 'But here I stay,' I said aloud, 'until all is revealed to me. Here will I make an end to the world, and bid good night.'

I stood there for an eternity, until I had changed and become someone other. Something was breaking within me, and I believe that I wept. No, the sound was not my own. It was the general weeping of the world, and through this veil of mist I saw the bulk of stone rise up and become part of a great archway. I went towards it and yet, as I tried to approach, I knew that I was moving downwards. I was walking down ancient steps even while I was going forward. They were of old stone, covered with moss, and there was something in their green and broken state which was of inexpressible comfort to me. It was as if I were treading backward into the past – yet it was not my past, but that of others. These steps bore the signs of an age I had never known, and as I descended I could hear myself saying in an ancient tongue *Oculatus abis*. You depart, seeing.

I found myself in a city with walks fairly paved, and with cellars underneath; here were pyramids and temples, bridges and squares, great towering walls and gates, statues of pure gold and pillars of transparent glass. It seemed to come from some new heaven or new earth, and to be a holy city where time never was. There came down now towards me a figure I knew, and his dog followed after him; he was no longer clothed in foul filthy garments but shone in brightness like the sun. 'You have come lightmans, in the breathing of Judah,' he said, and then he laughed. 'But no more canting speech now. I am no longer solitary walking, but exist in all things.'

'The buildings of Thebes were raised by music,' I replied. 'What power is it that keeps these great works erect?'

'Do you not know the secret? The spirit never dies, and this city is formed within the spiritual body of man.'

'Does each of us possess such a body?'

'Yes, but we are part of each other and of every living thing.' He bent down then to pat his dog. 'There is no more death, neither sorrow, nor crying. Neither shall there be any more pain, for the former things are passed away.'

There was a light, as of a setting and a rising sun, so that the whole city seemed to burn and to tremble in the middle air. I knew of the fire that exists in all things, and now the city seemed to glow with the heat of that flame which dwells in eternity. I walked through Clerkenwell towards Purse Alley, and was met at the corner of Turnagain Lane by my father and my wife, who took me by the hand and greeted me. Then there came another up to me. 'I am Dan Berry,' he said, 'who was looking for his family. Now it is done. I am the beginning and the end.' As I made my way down Holborn Hill, there came one towards me, smiling. 'I looked for the origin of all my words in the books of others, but no longer. I make all things new. Now my words are true and faithful.'

Never had I known my city so beautiful and, as I walked, I saw everything for the first and for the last time. As it will be in the beginning, and as it was in the end. Those whom I thought lost were saved, and those I thought to be of the past were still within the living.

'Yes. I'll tell you a very curious thing. About a year ago I was walking by the Thames. Do you know, near Southwark? When suddenly I thought I saw a bridge of houses. A shimmering bridge, lying across the river.'

'London Bridge is falling down, falling down, falling down.'

'No, seriously. It was like a bridge of light. It only lasted for a moment, and then it was gone. But there was, for that moment, a bridge connecting two shores.'

'It could have been anything, Matthew.'

I turned the corner, and observed them walking towards me;

their faces were so like those I had known that I put my hands up and saluted them. This was the true elixir of life which I had sought in gross material ways: this was the elixir that heals all ills because it exists before their beginning and after their end, that preserves life for ever, that allows me to talk with spirits.

'Listen to me now,' I said. 'That bridge of which you speak was once no more than a stone causeway in the third century after Christ. In my time it was the haunt of needle-makers, but then the houses were cleared. In that same place so many new bridges have been erected I cannot tell you all . . .'

'And there was something else, too. Are you listening, Daniel? When I saw the bridge shimmering above the water, I thought I saw people crossing it along a line of light. They rose and fell together, just as if they were walking across waves. But I don't expect you to believe any of this.'

They entered a great house, which was built very narrow in the front towards the street; I followed them, to tell them more, but where I had expected timber and plaster I saw only shining glass. A child stood on the threshold before me, saying, 'I trust so to open this door, John Dee, that the light shall be seen for the space of a whole thousand years. What is now opened, no man can shut.' But then the house vanished from my sight. 'Do you see how I calculated right?' The child stood there again. 'For, lo, the thousand years have gone.' Then I heard the sound of many bells ringing – church bells, plague bells, the bells of tradesmen, and the bells used to ward off spirits.

And then there came to me my mother who, being with child, cried out as if in the labours of birth. 'You have been born again, John Dee, and will grow up in a city called London.'

'But I know London –'

'This city you cannot know. Another will take your place there, and although you live again within him, he will not recognize you except by repute. Yet it may be that he will find you, even as he tries to find himself.'

And that at least is true – to the extent that I do not understand how much of this history is known, and how much is my own invention. And what is the past, after all? Is it that which is created in the formal act of writing, or does it have some substantial reality? Am I discovering it, or inventing it? Or could it be that I am discovering it within myself, so that it bears both the authenticity of surviving evidence and the immediacy of present intuition? *The House of Doctor Dee* itself leads me to that conclusion: no doubt you expected it to be written by the author whose name appears on the cover and the title-page, but in fact many of the words and phrases are taken from John Dee himself. If they are not his words, they belong to his contemporaries. Just as he took a number of mechanical parts and out of them constructed a beetle that could fly, so I have taken a number of obscure texts and have fashioned a novel from their rearrangement. But is Doctor Dee now no more than a projection of my own attitudes and obsessions, or is he an historical figure whom I have tried genuinely to recreate?

Oh, Dee, Dee, come out from that passage where I glimpsed you then for a moment, wandering through the eternal city of your own time and mine. He being told of my standing without, at his coming forth he did not or would not speak to me: no doubt through some grief conceived at having been used to furnish a story. Yet still I imagined that I had not deserved his great displeasure, and we walked through the city together disputing the issue. He blamed me for my manifold untrue reports, whereupon I observed that I had brought him back into the life and memory of humankind. 'So you may cheat the world,' he said. 'But I know well that you have not painted and delineated me correctly, except in a worm-eaten fashion to suit the worms within your wits. Your ditty is but lame. I am not your little man. I am not your homunculus. And so, I tell you, make an end of your old songs and bid good night to this history.'

'Must I say good night before I see my invention live?'

'Why not write of your own time? Why do you fly from it? Is it because you fly from your own self?'

I heard the sound of this argument, which was followed by much laughter. And as I walked through the city, I saw so many houses and streets fading before me that I seemed to be forever treading upon shadows. There were citizens standing in doorways, and when their doors opened they were flooded in light; and then there were the outlines of men and women moving towards water, since there had once been a sea here; and there were people walking past hills that billowed like smoke, past ridges of red clay and coral, past stone that would be fashioned for the streets and houses where I still walked and thought of Doctor Dee. It was believed by him that light descended into matter, and that in the very constitution of the material world would be discovered the great mysteries of the spirit hitherto covered by cloud and darkness. Then, as I shone my light in the dark streets of London, it struck against the great roof of fog that enclosed me: it was as if all the heaven, and earth, and sea, and the fountains of water, and dust of the streets, were mingled and wreathed together. Here also were walking beside me the forgotten inhabitants of London, the light upon their faces for the first time – the Moravians of Arrow Lane, the Ranters, the followers of Jakob Boehme. And who else was with me? Mary, in her white leather coat; Nathaniel Cadman; Margaret Lucas; Ferdinand Griffen; Matthew Palmer; Edward Kelley; Daniel Moore; Katherine Dee; and so many others, all of them still living within the city.

I had begun in nature, where like an orphan I had looked for signs of a divine home among the dark materials of the world, but now I had found my end in eternity. This was no lost city under ground. The veil had been torn aside, and though the blazing stars had gone for ever, the light of the imagination filled every corner and every quarter, every street and every house, of this place from which I had come and to which I had returned. The imagination is the spiritual body, and exists eternally. It is done.

'Anyway, that's the whole story. After that he disappeared.'

'How could he disappear?'

'There was a fire in the house here. But Doctor Dee was never found.'

'How do you know so much?'

'Oh, I know nothing really. The past is difficult, you see. You think you understand a person or an event, but then you turn a corner and everything is different once again. It's like this house. Nothing ever seems to stay in the same place. And do you know what? This may have been the actual room where Doctor Dee saw his visions. What did I call it just now?'

'The scrying room. Or the chamber of presence. What is the matter, Matthew?'

'Did you hear something then?'

'No.'

'I thought I heard a voice.'

'You'll be seeing him next, glimmering in the corner.'

'Well, I do see him. Look here.'

John Dee heard all these things, and rejoiced. And, yes, I see him now. I put out my arms in welcome, and he sings softly to me.

'London Bridge is falling down,
Falling down, falling down . . .'

Oh you, who tried to find the light within all things, help me to create another bridge across two shores. And so join with me, in celebration. Come closer, come towards me so that we may become one. Then will London be redeemed, now and for ever, and all those with whom we dwell – living or dead – will become the mystical city universal.